# BRANWEN OSHEA

# The Calling

*Finding Humanity, Book 1.0*

Sigma Orionis Publishing

*Library of Congress Control Number: 2020920691*

*Publisher's Cataloging-in-Publication Data*

*provided by Five Rainbows Cataloging Services*

*Names: OShea, Branwen, 1969- author.*

*Title: The calling / Branwen OShea.*

*Description: Hamden, CT : Sigma Orionis Publishing, 2020. | Series: Finding humanity, bk. 1. | Summary: In a future ice age, humans emerge from their subterranean haven to learn they're no longer the dominant species.*

*Identifiers: LCCN 2020920691 (print) | ISBN 978-1-73591-599-9 (paperback)*

*Subjects: LCSH: Young adult fiction. | CYAC: Quests (Expeditions)—Fiction. | Glacial epoch—Fiction. | Extraterrestrial beings—Fiction. | Civilization, Subterranean—Fiction. | Future, The—Fiction. | BISAC: YOUNG ADULT FICTION / Science Fiction / Apocalyptic & Post-Apocalyptic. | YOUNG ADULT FICTION / Dystopian. | YOUNG ADULT FICTION / Action & Adventure / General.*

*Classification: LCC PZ7.1.O84 Cal 2020 (print) | LCC PZ7.1.O84 (ebook) | DDC [Fic]—dc23.*

*First edition*

*ISBN: 978-1-7359159-9-9*

*Cover art by Rai Fiondella*
*Illustration by Rai Fiondella*

*This book was professionally typeset on Reedsy.*
*Find out more at reedsy.com*

*To Rana, for opening the door.*
*To Bleu, for sharing his shame regarding good intentions and the road to hell.*
*To Ayanna, for her wit and fire.*
*To Atsushi, for insisting I tell his story his way.*
*To Savas, for challenging my concepts of good and evil.*
*To Kahali, for teaching that even the greatest darkness contains humor.*
*To Kalakanya, for always being there.*
*Nur & Samina, this is for you, for inspiring me to see humanity's potential and for tolerating my frequent excursions into Rana's world.*

Vocat (It Calls)

Like prisoners in time,
humanity has waited
for its freedom from its
imprisoning shell.

The Call from beyond this world,
heard by few who knew
that one day It would be answered.

The Stars, the Callers,
waited patiently for their visitors.

The time has come to leave.

-FROM THE JOURNAL OF AYANNA REINIER

# Contents

# THE CALLING

Finding Humanity Book 1.0

## Branwen OShea

# Chapter 1

*Northern Haven: Bleu Reinier*

Taking advantage of his friends' rowdy laughter around the cafeteria table, Bleu leaned toward his kid sister and whispered, "I should go alone."

"And have all the fun without me?" Ayanna shook her head as she doused her porridge in more syrup than any human should consume in a week, let alone a single breakfast. "No way. You're stuck with me."

"Like I've been for the last fifteen years?" he teased. *Shast, she'll never back down.* He never should have mentioned his little escapades to her.

"Aw, my birth was the best thing that's happened in your small life."

"You're right," he agreed. It was well worth making fun of himself for the resulting shocked look on her face. He laughed as she swatted him in annoyance.

Okay, he'd just have to make sure today went exactly as planned.

On schedule, the cafeteria filled with its peak number of sleepy-eyed diners. With everyone at Northern Haven scarfing down their breakfasts, the forbidden hallways would be much easier to access. Bleu's leg jittered as he sat on the metal bench beside Ayanna, forcing down his scrambled protein, toast, and massive vitamin D capsule. Someday, he'd see the real sun and not need monster vitamins to survive.

As he choked down the pill, he snickered at Ayanna's imitation of the councilors debating last night. Her flair for impersonation had their friends snorting juice through their noses. She reeled in admirers, while he avoided them.

Checking the time on his comm for the umpteenth time, he leaned over and whispered into her ear, "Now."

Ayanna lowered her fork and with a mischievous glint turned toward Bleu's best friend, Stamf. "Hey, I think I'm going to cut out of breakfast early. My big, brave brother is afraid to check the graduate application statuses on his own."

*Why can't she stick to the script?* Bleu rolled his eyes as the entire bench of amused diners turned toward them.

"Really?" Stamf grinned. He waggled his fork, waiting for Bleu's comeback.

"Ayanna, you're full of it." Bleu threw his toast at her. "You probably have a date before class."

"No guy can wait for this face." She stood and waved her hand around her face with exaggerated drama.

Stamf chuckled.

"Don't encourage her, Stamf. I have to live with her." Bleu stood and narrowed his eyes at the next table, where two teenage boys ogled his little sister. They looked away. Height had its advantages. "But I do need to check the decisions."

Stamf grimaced and lowered his voice. "You're both leaving? There goes my excuse not to sit with whichever councilor wants to harass me today."

"Ah, that's the price you pay for being the prime minister's nephew; they all want to claim you as their apprentice." Ayanna mock bowed to Stamf and carried her plate between the rows of brightly covered tables to the kitchen window.

Bleu caught up to Ayanna as the dining hall doors hissed shut behind them. "I hate doing that to him. He wouldn't tell on us." Poor Stamf would sit alone for ten seconds before one of the politically savvy adults sidled up to him.

Ayanna shrugged, continuing down the hall. "Nope, he wouldn't. He'd say it was too risky."

"It *is* risky." Bleu stopped. "Wanna go back? I know you wanted to see the plants, but you don't have to come."

2

"I'm not backing out." She tossed a look of mock worry over her shoulder. "Are you scared, big bro-bro?"

Bleu snorted. "Only of you getting us in trouble as usual."

She grinned and tugged him forward by his tunic sleeve. "I'm your sister, that's my job."

The Agricultural Levels were off limits, but the council never really expected anyone to try to sneak in. To everyone else living underground, Nature was the enemy, the monster that had turned against them and frozen the planet. But not to Bleu; he had been sneaking into the Ag floors for years, called by the surviving remnants of the natural world. Hopefully, if his graduate application was approved, he'd start legally working with the living soil, heady grains, and fruit trees this week.

Until then, the trick to his secret visits was timing—get in and out before the scientists arrived. Well, that and using the elevator door code he'd borrowed from his dad's files.

A few sprinted hallways and a quick tapping in of the code at the elevator later, the car thudded to a stop. They'd arrived. As the door slid open, the luscious scents of moist earth, oxygenated air, and whatever magic the plants exuded rushed to greet him, filling his lungs with vitality.

Bleu craved this illegal nature time. The need to smell and touch something from the natural world had been building all week. He was weird like that. Besides, it wasn't as if he and Ayanna would hurt the invaluable grains.

He climbed up and perched on a silent harvester, looking over the cavernous agriculture floor. Keeping lookout, he sucked in the earthy, sweet scent, so different from the sterile, dry air they normally breathed.

Below, Ayanna caressed the plant crowns with her palms. The heavy-laden grain stems rippled in the circulated air under the steel ceiling. The plants were ready for harvest despite the real season on the Surface being late winter. Everything down here was artificial.

Tearing his gaze away from the verdant leaves, he checked the time on his communication device. *Never get enough time here.*

"Ayanna!" His harsh whisper echoed in the cavernous room. "Time to go. This morning is the harvesting—"

"Yeah, relax, I won't get you fired before you start," Ayanna said, face upturned toward the artificial sunlight. Her dark eyes closed as if in silent reverie, but her lips quirked upward in a teasing half-grin. Long, black hair spiraled loosely down her back and twisted around the golden-brown stems as if anchoring her in place.

Bleu understood her delay. Other than the holographic gaming rooms, this was the closest they ever got to experiencing what it must have been like before the Descent, when their ancestors had entered this subterranean world. This grain was real, with roots buried in rich soil and stalks reaching toward synthetic sunshine.

He again inhaled the heady scent, but today it brought none of its usual relief. It was as if his nature retreat produced only so much vitality, and Ayanna had sucked it all up for herself. He remained a husk, yearning for fresh, wild scents blown by non-mechanical air currents. But these Ag floors were the closest to nature he could get without facing the wintry wrath on Earth's Surface.

No, that wasn't quite true. Another place existed that might satisfy his longing. It was trickier than coming here, but the idea of returning home without relief nauseated him.

He sprang down from the harvester and swept his footprints away with his shoe. Even though he was the only one he knew of in Northern Haven with any interest or knowledge of tracking, his little sister was with him today. *No risks.*

He strode toward Ayanna and brushed her arm to get her headed toward the exit.

"Classes aren't starting yet," she responded, not even opening her eyes.

"Wanna go somewhere even better?" He grinned as her eyelids sprang open. "If we hurry, I could show you the door. We'll only be able to stay a minute—"

"*The* door? The one to the Surface? You've been there?" Her face aglow, she studied him with new admiration.

"I've been known to visit it." He laughed, realizing the last thing he'd

4

want the authorities aware of was the fact that he periodically snuck to the Surface door. "Well, fortunately, *not* known to."

"Whoa," she exclaimed, clearly impressed. Then, sweeping her turquoise scarf over her shoulder, she bounded toward the elevators. "Let's do it."

"Slow down." He grasped her shoulder, but she shrugged away and pressed the elevator call button.

A nebulous warning formed in his gut. Did he really want to show her his secret method for passing security? He'd spent his life rescuing her from herself and her affinity for trouble.

"Maybe you shouldn't come. I'm the one obsessed with the Surface," he said, trying to backtrack.

"And I'm obsessed with trouble." She grinned and zipped ahead of him as the elevator door opened. Two steps inside the elevator, she pitched sideways, catching herself against the wall with her hand.

"Yanna!" Bleu rushed to her side. "What happened?" He glanced back over the gray floor, seeing nothing that could have tripped her.

She shrugged and gave him a shaky grin. "I'm fine. Just got light-headed for a moment."

He frowned. "You sure? You ate breakfast, right?"

"Of course. Everything except the piece of toast you threw at me."

"But that was special delivery," he teased.

Ayanna rolled her eyes.

"You sure you're okay?"

"Yes, Mr. Cautious."

*She seems okay now...* His stomach tightened as he considered the odds of convincing her to go home.

No. Now that she knew he'd seen the door, he'd better either show her the proper way, or he'd get blamed when she got caught there on her own later. He checked his comm again. One hour to rise over thirty levels, make it across the residential area, pass the research laboratories, enter the forbidden zone, and return. *Piece of cake.*

****

The elevator thudded to a stop. As they exited it, Bleu glanced sideways at his sister. Despite her fifteen years, the top of her dark head barely cleared his bicep. His gut churned again. While he needed these little retreats to help quench his longing for nature, she accompanied him for the adrenalin rush. Perhaps she needed the high like he needed fresh air.

"Come on," he said.

They scurried through the residential tunnels until the walls changed from murals to plain yellow. Bleu held up his hand, and they both stopped. Regular citizens never passed beyond this point unless their work required it.

He scanned the dim research and administrative hallways for movement. The orange emergency lighting that kept Northern Haven's subterranean darkness at bay during its artificial nights cast everything in murky shadow. No light came from under the double doorways of the research labs that lined these halls. Nothing moved.

Bleu checked his comm. Morning Lights wouldn't kick in until seven, when the earliest researchers would arrive, which left forty-five minutes to reach the door and return.

"I checked Dad's schedule. No one's doing maintenance today, and they haven't started training for the second expedition yet," he said.

"So, what are you waiting for?" Ayanna grinned up at him, a light sheen of sweat covering her face.

Odd. It hadn't been that a strenuous trip.

Bleu shrugged it off. "Keep up and do exactly what I do."

He slipped down the hall with her close behind. Pressed to the wall to avoid activating the automatic lights, they remained undetected—a trick he'd figured out years ago.

The founders had never expected a resident to leave, and the Undescended—those unfortunate humans left on the Surface to die—had never invaded. As long as he and Ayanna activated no lights, they'd set off no alarms. Then they could pass undetected to the Surface elevator doors. Once there, those massive doors were all that separated him from the world beyond. Just seeing them cooled the burning inside, granting him another few weeks of peace.

Sidling to the end of the hall, he turned a corner and stiffened. Men's voices drifted from behind one of the closed doors.

"We should go," he whispered over his shoulder.

"No, they'll finish and leave. No one ever goes near the Surface door unless it's announced weeks in advance," Ayanna countered.

He turned and studied her, unsure if she had been born fearless or masked her fear with such nonchalance. She met his scowl with a roguish grin.

*Definitely born fearless.* Motioning for her to crouch, he crawled beneath the window.

As they hunched under the glass, the prime minister's voice rang loud and clear. "Commander Savas, we appreciate you bringing this proposal to the council, but the matter of the Sickness requires much debate."

*Sickness?*

"Yes," the commander replied, "but as the Council's Strategist, it's my job to propose alternative policies. Once the teens are diagnosed, they become a drain on our limited resources. Since they never recover, perhaps we should cut our losses and provide them a peaceful end to their torturous existence."

Bleu shuddered at the man's callousness toward life. Tucked behind the man's charm and intelligence lurked something Bleu could never quite trust.

Why the secret early morning Council meeting? And why wasn't his mother—the lead medical researcher for the Sickness—invited?

Beside him, Ayanna motioned strangling the commander or perhaps the whole council. His thoughts exactly.

Bleu paused, torn between eavesdropping for his mother and his selfish need to visit the door. How would he ever explain to his mother about overhearing the Council if he stayed? No, if he remained to listen, his mother would be furious at his sneaking around and endangering himself and Ayanna.

That decided it—the door. He scuttled past the meeting room and around the next corner, Ayanna's soft footsteps matching his own. After four more turns, the mysterious sealed doors appeared at the end of the hall.

Smiling, he inhaled deeply. This is what he lived for, what quickened his spirit and made his heart thrum with joy. Someday, he'd get past those doors. The massive, engraved metal portal summoned him down the orange-lit corridor, but he dared go no farther. This hallway had too many alarms even for him.

The doors before them guarded an elevator that rose to the ultimate treasure—the wildness of Earth's ancient Surface. Its call promised another world, one that was untamed and deadly. Only Commander Savas had returned alive from last year's doomed First Expedition. The ice age had devoured the Surface and spit out the bones of any humans who braved it.

Regardless of the dangers, Bleu would still go. Not alone, though. That was suicide.

He leaned forward and sucked in a deep breath. The air was different here, colder and sharper. He grinned at Ayanna as they both sank to the floor in a recessed doorway that faced the huge, armored doors.

This alcove, his secret retreat, had inspired years of researching survival skills, tracking, and zoology. It made living in this underground maze tolerable. Plus, the beautifully engraved doors at the end of the hall validated that others had also valued the world beyond. Once upon a time, others had also appreciated this solitary escape route.

"I want to volunteer for the next expedition," he blurted out.

"Everyone dies up there. Stick with the agriculturist position." Ayanna sat back and clasped her hands together in her lap.

Not the response he'd expected. And since when did she sit so stiff and proper?

"Are you actually admitting you'd be worried about me?" He grinned. Her stiffness at showing affection was endearing. She wasn't exactly the warm and fuzzy type.

Her face twitched. "I think you should be more grateful for what we have down here."

Bleu put his hand over his mouth to stifle his snort of laughter. "Seriously? What's wrong with you?"

She gave him an odd look that seemed to stare right through him. Her face became a blank canvas, all the colors of her usual sass missing. "Lions practice gratitude for every sunrise."

*What the shast does that mean?* As he looked her over, his frown deepened. "You all right? Your hands...are they shaking?"

Sweat glistened on Ayanna's brow as she stared at her tremulous hands. "We'll all die down here."

"No. We've survived here for centuries, and Mom's team will find the cure. We'll be fine." *I hope.*

He had outwardly adopted his mother's optimism last year when he had realized Ayanna's greatest fear was developing the Sickness and hurting her family. But deep inside, he feared that Northern Haven was becoming humanity's tomb. With more and more teens developing the Sickness each generation, soon there'd be too few people left for an adequate gene pool or to keep the ventilation and food supply running.

He put his hand on hers, and her fingers stiffened. "Ayanna?"

She shrugged away and jerked onto her feet. The tremor spread into her shoulders.

Something wasn't right. "Are you cold? Maybe we should get going."

Men's voices echoed from somewhere down the maze of halls as the meeting broke up. Ayanna snapped her gaze toward the voices and teetered at her own sudden movement. Turning, she sprinted toward the Surface door as if her life depended on reaching it.

Bleu winced as automatic lights triggered, flashing around them.

"Ayanna! What are you doing?" He raced forward and pulled her against the wall, but it was already too late as the siren's wail pierced his eardrums.

Struggling to get free, Ayanna smashed her head backward into his nose. Pain radiated through his skull as his head smacked against the metallic wall, and she almost pulled free from him.

"*Shast*, Ayanna! What's wrong?" A cold sweat trickled down his back. The thought sprang loose in his mind—*the Sickness*—but he shoved it aside.

Ayanna would be fine.

Fortunately, he was quick and towered over her slight, fifteen-year-old frame. He pinned her against his chest as gently as possible, ignoring the throbbing pain in his shins where she'd slammed her pointy shoes into him. She kicked and pummeled him, her scream bouncing off the walls.

"Ayanna, we can't be found here," he said, trying to calm her down.

His heart hammered against his chest. If this was the Sickness, she'd be taken to the Unit and locked up until her death. Even if it wasn't the Sickness, with her shakiness, erratic behavior, and violence toward him, it sure looked like it. Those symptoms were more than enough reason for her to be taken.

Being found at the door was nothing compared to losing her.

# Chapter 2

*orthern Haven: Bleu Reinier*

Northern Haven: Bleu Reinier As Bleu held Ayanna to him, the hallway seemed to close in, trapping them. If they were on the Surface, he'd be free to run in any direction and hide her. In this labyrinthine hell, he only had one chance: make it back down the hall and choose the corridor without guards.

Ayanna stopped striking him and wilted. Sporadic twitches jerked through her limbs, and low moans rolled from her throat. Bleu glanced down, his body tensed in preparation for another attack, but she remained limp. He scooped her up in his arms.

"Stay with me, Ayanna."

No response.

Her normally lighter skin was pallid and clammy against his own darker brown tone. Cradling her against his chest, he raced down the still empty corridor, fumbling with each side door he passed. Every entrance required an access code he didn't possess. He'd need a miracle to get her back to their module unseen.

Distant men's voices yelled in confusion. The alarm hadn't gone off in ages. Probably never. Footsteps were fast approaching.

*Think, think!*

Bleu couldn't go back the same way. At the end of the hall, he turned right this time and ran around the corner just as armed men entered the hallway he had exited. Footsteps raced toward the Surface door, not the direction of their retreat.

*Please don't let this be a dead end.* Frantic, Bleu continued to test every side door until the hall ended in a double doorway. He shoved his shoulder against it, but it remained immovable. *Locked. Of course.* He turned in circles, Ayanna in his arms.

"Where's the button?"

As if Ayanna could answer.

No button or handles. He kicked at it as the voices grew closer, but it held firm. He backed against the wall as his mind fumbled for a story to tell the men. Nothing came. "We are so screwed…"

In frustration, he thumped his head against the wall and noticed a red light protruding from the ceiling, the pale beam angled toward the door. *An old locking sensor?* He laid Ayanna on the cold floor and jumped, his fingers straining to reach the light. *Almost…*

He thrust his hand into his pocket and pulled out his ID badge. Holding it, he leapt and jabbed the hard edge at the light. The bulb broke, and the door hissed open as he shook glass from his hair.

"Down here!" Commander Savas' voice echoed closer this time.

Bleu grabbed Ayanna and ran through the door. It swung shut behind him.

"Who is that? Stop!" A bullet hit the double doors. *Guns?* The only working guns belonged to the Expedition Team.

Bleu's heart jumped into his throat as he careened around the next corner. Somehow, he ran faster, taking every turn of the ancient corridor in an attempt to lose their hunters. With each step, Ayanna's head lolled against his shoulder.

He had never explored this part of Northern Haven. The dusty walls, like the walls of all residential sections, displayed murals of Northern Haven ancestors in ancient Surface activities. Normally, their expressions and poses amused him, but as he raced past, their weathered faces mocked him. *You left us to die on the Surface. Now it's your turn.*

He sped on. At least these residential sections contained more in-terconnecting halls and no dead ends in case of a fire. Only the ever-present orange emergency lights guided him. No security existed in this abandoned area, a remnant of Northern Haven's more populous past.

As he panted down endless corridors with Ayanna clutched to his chest, the voices of their pursuers fell behind. Finally, he found an ajar door marked Module Res1555 and burst through it, billowing up clouds of dust in the abandoned module. He coughed and flinched as the door clanged shut behind them.

Racing behind a large broken bed, he lowered Ayanna to the grimy floor and collapsed beside her. Dust swirled around them as he struggled to silence his coughs, his lungs burning from their mad dash and the stale air.

Bleu's sweaty hand worked his communicator out of his deep pocket. He whispered, "Dr. Cassandra Reinier."

A moment later, his mom answered. "Bleu, what's going on?" Her harried work voice had never sounded so sweet.

\* \* \*

Their mother arrived fifteen minutes later, having found them by the module's number he'd given her. Though, knowing her, she could have sensed her way to them by instinct alone. She was wildly intuitive about the two of them, a trait highly undervalued by trouble-making Ayanna and the scientifically minded community of Northern Haven.

As soon as her tall figure appeared at the end of the hall, alone, his shoulders sagged with relief. Clicking off his comm, he braced himself for the angry lecture that had to be brewing in her since he'd contacted her.

A tempest of emotions surged across his mother's face as she rolled the large, metal crate used to transport her medical equipment from one ward of the Sickness Unit to another. Perched on top, her medical bag wobbled with the wheels' motion.

At Ayanna's moan, she hastened to her daughter's side, but her fury was reserved for him. "What the hell were you thinking, bringing her to the door?"

"It's been safe every other time," he replied, wincing at his pathetic excuse.

"Oh, Bleu. How many times have you risked this?" Her dark eyes shone with disappointment. "Never mind. Keep watch."

She bent over Ayanna, examined her, and drew up a syringe of something. As the needle pierced Ayanna's arm, Bleu winced as if it had been his own.

"That should keep her quiet for a few minutes. Any sign of the guards?"

He shook his head, unable to tear his gaze from Ayanna's crumpled body. Images of his friends dying from the Sickness tumbled through his mind like a jigsaw puzzle of death.

"Did you run into any?" he asked.

"No. They're all near the door, making sure no one blasts it open. Commander Savas contacted me on my work comm, saying he'd seen someone running around like a maniac." She scowled so fiercely that Bleu's innards withered like a dying plant. "He thought one of my Sickness patients had escaped. Do you realize what a needless nightmare you've created?"

"Sorry," he mumbled.

"We have to hurry." She motioned to the crate. "Gently. She should just fit." His mother glanced over her shoulder toward the still silent hallway.

Bleu awkwardly lowered Ayanna through the top of the crate into the hollow portion. It was a tight fit, even for her petite frame. He lowered the top, tension flooding his body as the hinge squeaked. Holding his breath, he waited, but the hall remained silent. Had their pursuers had given up?

His mother removed her jacket and arranged it over the grated top to appear like it had been casually flung there. Bleu, sweating from his run, tossed his outer black tunic there for good measure.

His mom's brows furrowed as she walked around the crate and examined it from every angle. "It'll have to do. If we meet anyone, let me do the talking. People don't question doctors."

They hurried briskly down the hall. Bleu fell behind his mother, swirling the dust with his steps to cover their tracks. Men's shouts echoed down distant halls, and she sped up. As they turned a corner, her rolling crate nearly collided with a tall man. His mother yelped in surprise as she struggled to control the cart.

"Stop!" Commander Savas pointed a gun at them, then narrowed his gaze. "Dr. Reinier? Did a patient escape?" He lowered the gun.

Bleu's mom gave an amused snort. "Of course not. What kind of a Unit do you think I run?" She flashed him a fake smile, the type she saved for politicians and others opposed to financing her life-saving work.

Commander Savas seemed to buy it.

She continued. "From your description, I thought maybe another teen was ill. I brought Bleu with me, and my supplies, you know, just in case." As if she and Bleu alone could safely contain a fully psychotic, violent person without any of them getting injured.

Savas, a bit disheveled from the morning's unusual excitement, raked his fingers through his dark-blond hair and holstered his gun. "That was not particularly safe, Dr. Reinier." He looked Bleu up and down as if measuring him against the spotted intruder.

*Shast*, if the commander remembered the intruder wearing black and spotted his black tunic on the cart, they were screwed. Was his white undertunic different enough to avoid suspicion? Despite the iciness of Savas' gaze, sweat trickled down Bleu's back.

Bleu met the commander's steely blue gaze full on. Anything to avoid him looking at the cart. He willed Ayanna to remain silent.

"Perhaps not, but I always put my patients first." His mom flashed another smile befitting a Council member seeking votes.

"You okay, Bleu? You seem a bit...overheated?" Savas raised an eyebrow as sweat dripped down Bleu's brow.

Bleu swatted it away. "It's just the excitement. You should see when Stamf and I hunt at the Gaming Arena."

At the mention of Stamf, Commander Savas' face lost all its rough edges and warmed. "Right. You two hang out a lot, don't you?"

"We're the number one team." Bleu hated braggers, but he'd be anything to impress this jerk and get Ayanna home safely. *Don't move, Ayanna. Stay quiet.*

"We haven't found anyone, and I need to get back to my patients. Good luck!" His mom shoved the cart into motion and motioned with her chin for Bleu to follow.

15

The back of Bleu's neck prickled from the commander's gaze until they rounded the corner.

"Too close," his mother muttered.

"I'm sorry," he said, casting his gaze to the floor.

They passed no one else until they reached the inhabited area. There, the halls buzzed with Northern Haveners gossiping about the alarms. Every glance and question from the hopeful newsmongers made Bleu stiffen and fear Ayanna would make a noise.

However, his mother gave them such boring answers that their neighbors stopped interrupting them. After all, a doctor and her son moving equipment couldn't compare to the thrilling threat of a loose patient or an attack by the Undescended.

When their module door finally slid shut behind them, Bleu blew out a huge sigh of relief and helped his mom sequester Ayanna in her sleep quarters. The small space contained only a bed, a chair, and a small closet. Stacks of drawings and art discs covered the floor, and Bleu hastily piled them onto the chair so his mother could work without tripping. He hovered near Ayanna's bed, unwilling to leave her side.

Ayanna stared at the wall, her eyes glazed and her body slack. She was unresponsive to everything they tried.

Their mother again held a glass to Ayanna's lips, and her elbow bumped his leg. "Bleu, give me some space."

"She's too out of it to drink. Can't you let her rest?" He twisted his body to get out of his mother's way, scooted around the side of the bed, and enclosed Ayanna's damp hand in his.

Her limbs convulsed and her eyes opened wider, but she didn't acknowledge him. Bleu tensed, waiting for the next dreaded outburst. Would the next screech be the one that alerted the neighbors and brought the council guards?

"Bleu, I'm the doctor. Less stimulus." She turned and rested her hand on his shoulder. "Let go of her hand. Trust me and leave the room."

Ayanna's glance twitched toward him, her eyes wild. His instincts screamed for him to stay put, but Mom was the doctor. He slowly unwound

Ayanna's tremoring hand from his own and stood.

"Noooo!"

Ayanna's sudden shriek caused Bleu to stumble backward into the chair. Her artwork and research discs tumbled back onto the floor. He scooped them up a second time, heart pounding as he glanced at the thin wall to their neighbor's module. Her single scream still jangled his nerves, and now she fought with the sheets, thrashing and growling.

"Leave, Bleu." His mother's voice quavered. She drew up a syringe of what he guessed was a stronger sedative. She had engaged her full Dr. Reinier mode, professional despite her patient's chaos.

"She screamed when I let go of her hand. She thinks I'm deserting her." Bleu hesitated in the doorway.

"Bleu." His mom sighed. "I need you to prevent anyone from entering our module." She flicked her hand toward the door. "Go."

"Fine," Bleu grumbled.

He took one last visual check of Ayanna's breathing before slowly backing out of her room. Striding through their living room toward the module's front door, he searched for familiar objects, anything that might pass as an excuse for his sister's shouts. Turning up nothing, he wilted onto the floor, his back against the front door, legs splayed in front. If the council guards appeared, he needed a good explanation for Ayanna's screaming.

Would they believe she'd been injured? Feverish? His mind whirled in an exhausting tornado of fears.

The latest sedative apparently worked, because the module fell still except for the scrape of the chair against the floor in Ayanna's room. His mom must be resting as well.

Bleu leaned his head back against the door. On the opposite wall hung a video frame, displaying a recording. In it, a younger Ayanna and he played with their gaming equipment. Tiny, tough-faced Ayanna posed to shoot as her adult-sized equipment belt slipped to her feet. As he attempted to keep her from tripping forward on the belt, they both ended up toppling into a laughing pile. The video replayed again and again.

Back then, it had been easy to keep Ayanna safe. Now, the carefree recording taunted him. The Sickness stole everything from families, and his appeared to be its next victim. He squeezed his eyes shut and groaned.

This was his fault. He was older and had always been the responsible one. If only he hadn't taken her with him to the Surface doors, then maybe none of this would've happened.

*Just let her be okay...*

Exhausted, Bleu wilted against the cool metal of his module's entrance and his head bobbed toward his chest as darkness took him.

\* \* \*

Bleu found himself floating in deep space surrounded by stars. From both above and below, they twinkled their cold light. Dizziness washed over him at the strangeness of such open space, and he yearned for the safety of the enclosed tunnels of home, or at least some solid ground to stand on.

*This must be a dream.* He sucked in a breath of cold air, and its iciness spread throughout his chest. Electricity charged his limbs with a new sense of vitality. *Doesn't feel like a dream.* He remained motionless for fear of tumbling into the heavens below him.

As he strained his eyes in the darkness, the forms of two women appeared in the distance. One woman stood over a kneeling one. An unseen force pulled him toward them. He floated, the space between them decreasing. One woman glowed with brilliant platinum light. Like a protective angel's, her arms wrapped around a dark-skinned woman who knelt beside her.

Bleu drifted until he was only a few meters away. There was something familiar about the kneeling woman—her long, black hair; burnished brown skin; the proud way she held her chin even though tears streamed down her face.

"Mom?"

Both women turned to face him.

"I knew that one day he would come." The upright young woman, sparkling like the moon against the starry background, smiled at him in recognition and nodded approvingly to his mother.

Open-mouthed, he stared. The luminescent woman was stunning. Her jade eyes lit with a warm smile that enveloped him. The stars around them began swimming in circles as if time had sped up. Lightheadedness wafted over him.

"I don't know how to save her. I just...I just can't see any way out of this," his mother managed in between sobs.

"He knows what to do." The angelic woman nodded toward him.

*Me? I don't even know where I am, let alone what would help Ayanna.*

As if she had heard him, the glowing woman stepped closer and extended her slender hand. Out of nowhere, a mirror appeared in her open palm. His mind grappled for some sense of normalcy like a desperate fish flopping around on land. Nothing had existed in her pearly hand a moment before. His knees turned to rubber, and he wobbled, disorientated by the vastness of space below him.

She reached out and steadied him.

*Great. I meet a beautiful woman from outside and I can't even stand?*

Smiling as if amused, she held the gilded mirror closer to his face. Bleu squinted as his blushing reflection faded from the mirror's surface and an image appeared. He saw himself standing on snow-covered ground with a blue sky above him. A wide grin spread across his face and expansiveness filled his chest.

A real sky. He'd give anything to stand there, free beneath the spacious heavens. The luminous woman withdrew her hand, and the mirror blinked out of existence.

"That which you seek is on the Surface," she said.

"But...how will I find it?" he asked, at a loss.

In response, she again extended her hand toward Bleu. A dagger constructed of a cream-colored substance was balanced on her palm. Carved ebony symbols spiraled up the handle.

"I fear you may need this." Her smile faded. "Keep it with you. Always."

He reached for it, but his body didn't move normally in this strange star place. Before his fingers could grip it, the dagger disappeared, the stars

19

tilted, and he fell...

Bleu's head bobbed back up, and he again sat in his family's small module. *What the hell was that?* He quickly scanned their module, but all was quiet. Adrenaline coursed through his body. He never awoke from sleep this alert.

Across the room, the video frame continued to cycle through his and Ayanna's tumultuous gaming pose. No sounds came from Ayanna's room. He blinked and sucked in a breath. *What if I have the Sickness?*

No, it wasn't possible—hallucinations weren't a symptom. So, either he was the first, or...His stomach fell.

Or he'd finally inherited his mom's curse. Was that why she had also been there? Her visions hadn't started until she was married and pregnant with him.

*No.* He squeezed his eyes shut and clenched his fists. He would not inherit that curse. *I'm fine. And Ayanna will be okay too.*

He stood to stretch, and something heavy fell to his feet. He leaned over, gasped, and then stumbled back against the door. At his feet lay the sheathed, cream-colored dagger.

He blinked, yet the image remained. *It can't be real.* Bending over, Bleu brushed his trembling fingers along the carved handle. Cold and hard.

Real.

Nothing like this had ever happened to his mother. His vision had bled into reality.

# Chapter 3

*Northern Haven: Bleu Reinier*

Bleu held his breath as he unsheathed the impossibly real dagger and examined the bone-colored blade's glinting edge.

*Keep it with you,* the woman had said in his vision.

Today, all before lunch, he'd been shot at, handed a lethal dagger, and had an unwanted vision like his mom. Not to mention Ayanna appeared to have the Sickness. *What a day from hell...*

He sheathed the blade and dropped it into his deep pocket where it thumped against his comm. As he practiced sitting without letting the dagger's bulk show, Ayanna shrieked again. He winced at its power, his heart sinking, whispering the truth he'd been squashing. This is how the Sickness had started with his schoolmates. He drew in a jagged breath.

His heart sped as Ayanna's scream climbed in pitch. Their neighbors, Neviah Thanh and her father, lived on the other side of that thin wall. Neviah worked from home, but no one had yet notified the guards. Was she out running an errand or notifying the guards at this very moment?

His need to know grew intolerable, and he stood, checking that his new weapon was safely concealed. He could go knock and be back with more information in minutes.

Behind him, the sleep chamber door hissed opened.

"Ayanna?" He spun, seeing it was only his mom backing out and closing the door behind her. He thrust his fingers through his coarse hair in frustration.

His mother's deep brown eyes shone full of sadness; her lips pressed together tightly. Her glance skimmed past Bleu's face to the door. "No one passed by outside?"

"No, and I haven't heard any noises over there." Bleu jerked his thumb toward the right wall. He waited, his heart thumping out the seconds until his mom gave his sister the fatal diagnosis.

"I had to sedate her a third time." His mom slowly released a long breath as if her whole body was deflating. "As a doctor, I should know more. I just— I just can't see any way out of this."

*I just can't see any way out of this.* A direct quote from his vision. *Or hallucination. Am I losing it?* The image of the spinning stars returned, and Bleu teetered in place. He shook his head, trying to clear the fog. "Is it...?"

His mother collapsed onto the living room couch, her head in her hands. "Yes."

Bleu put his hand against the wall to steady himself. Hearing it from his mother was too much. "No." He shook his head. "It can't be. No one in our family has it."

Tears ran down her face. "There's no other reason for this episode. I— I don't know what to do."

In his mind, Bleu saw the beautiful woman from his vision. *He knows.*

*He* was an eighteen-year-old graduate, old enough to know that the Surface alone wouldn't cure Ayanna. Yet that calling, that sense that something up there could help her, rose from his gut.

"Is she okay?" he asked. He flinched at his ridiculous question; inside, he was a child again, desperate for her reassurance that everything would be all right. "I mean, it's over this time, right?"

"For now." Her glance skirted the door to the corridor. "We can't let anyone know. Any of them. If we hide her illness, maybe she will have..." Her voice caught in her throat. "A few more months of normalcy. Sometimes, the second episode doesn't happen for weeks..." She pressed her face into her hands.

They sat together in silent desperation. The Sickness. It had been unknown to doctors prior to humanity's descent into Northern Haven. Most scientists suspected it to be a genetic weakness due to the limited gene pool. Living isolated for generations underground will do that sort of thing.

"Mom, we overheard Commander Savas talking to the Council. Not the details, but you know what he's like. Things are going to get worse for those with the Sickness."

She stared at Ayanna's door. "I know."

Bleu couldn't imagine worse. He'd lost friends to the Sickness—observed its attacks on the unlucky, and every generation was more susceptible than the previous one. The images were ingrained into his mind—friends in severe panic, screaming, and becoming violent in short, unpredictable episodes that escalated until they spent hours wildly thrashing against the walls. The outcome was always the same— drugged, bedridden, and dead.

*What if I'm next?*

He smashed his fist against the tabletop. "There has to be a cure."

His mother didn't bat an eyelash. She had spent her life acting on that belief. In a few more generations, there wouldn't be enough healthy adults left to keep the Northern Haven running. Humanity would perish, buried in a tomb of its own making, with no humans left alive on the Surface to mourn them.

His stomach churned. If he could just figure out how to live up there, then maybe Ayanna would heal. No Sickness had existed prior to their descent to Northern Haven. Or if he joined the expedition team and found the other three Havens, one of them might already possess a cure.

Bleu grimaced and squared his jaw. "They're asking for volunteers for the next Surface team. I want to go."

His mom raised her dark eyes to his, and some of their old sparkle resurfaced. She remained silent, waiting.

"It's dangerous, I know, but I could be up there—"

"In nature," she finished. The corners of her mouth curved up slightly. "Your dream."

He nodded. His mother and sister were the only ones to whom he could admit his secret desire to stand in a forest, hear birds, smell moist earth, and experience the sun on his skin. Or, more likely, the frigid winds.

"Stamf and I were thinking of signing up together." He held his breath, hoping for agreement. Stamf, his best friend, would go regardless of Bleu's decision.

His mother smiled, a weary expression on her dark face. "You and Stamf on the Surface…"

"You're okay with that, right?" His heart pounded as he awaited her reply.

"We both know you're going up there someday. But with Ayanna's illness…" She sniffed. "You should probably spend as much time with her as possible."

No, he would not sit back and watch his little sister slowly lose her mind. No way. "You've always believed the unnatural conditions underground contribute to the Sickness. If I go up there, maybe I'll find something to help."

She gave a sad laugh. "Bleu, even if you did find something, you can't drag someone in her condition into an ice age. If I thought that would work, I'd do it myself."

*That which you seek is on the Surface.* A chill ran down his spine. Ayanna didn't have that long. Who should he believe—the reason of his mom or the angel in his dream?

Footsteps and men's voices drifted through the front door. Alarmed, they both froze, gazes meeting.

"Is it…" His mother's face took on a ferocious quality. She glanced over her shoulder toward Ayanna's room and then strode toward the corridor door ready for battle. Boisterous laughter filtered through the door, and she paused mid-step.

"It's just Stamf and Dad," Bleu said. He sagged with relief and wearily rose to greet his best friend. The raucous noise reached its peak as the door opened, and Stamf and Bleu's father, Tadwell, tumbled through the door, still jesting with each other.

Bleu noticed for the hundredth time how much Tadwell's paler face and brown eyes looked nothing like his own darker features and hazel eyes. Tadwell was his father, the one who had married his mother and raised him, but like most people, his father differed from his paternus, or genetic father. Bleu didn't know the identity of his paternus and really didn't care. What mattered was that he possessed a good genetic rating.

Strike that. *Had* a good genetic rating. Ayanna's illness, once discovered, would change everything.

Stamf and Tadwell fell silent as they noticed Bleu and his mother watching them.

Tadwell shook his head. "Ah, it's a mess out there. The Council has ordered everyone to stay in the residential area. Apparently, something set off the Surface door alarms. Can you imagine? We were just discussing what kind of fool would try to have a picnic on the Surface."

"Hmm." Bleu struggled to force a smile as he swallowed the rising bile in his throat.

"That's...odd." Bleu's mother succeeded in sounding only casually interested. "Do they have any theories?"

"No. Maybe dust in the sensors?" Tadwell looked from Bleu to his mother and furrowed his brow.

Bleu had to get Stamf out of their module now. His father obviously sensed something, and Stamf was sharp. And what if Ayanna started screaming again? His friend would be torn between helping Bleu and his loyalties to his uncle, the Prime Minister.

Bleu forced a smile and slapped Stamf's muscled shoulder. "Let's go, Stamf. The Gaming Arena is well within the residential area. I'm afraid it's time to kick your butt again." He shoved Stamf into the corridor and waved to his father before the door hissed shut.

They stood, surrounded by the ever-present painted murals of ancestors; the tall black man Ayanna had dubbed "Renoir" studied him with soulful eyes as if saddened by his sister's current condition. Renoir was surrounded by "Frida," "Picasso," and "Bada Shanren." Ayanna loved ancient painters and had nicknamed the unknown ancestors after them.

Stamf grinned, eyebrows raised over light-brown eyes that perfectly matched his expensive tunic. While shorter than Bleu, he had a more muscular build and wasn't usually shoved around by others.

"Butt kicked? You, my friend, paused the game, because you had no ammo left. How are you going to kill the lions? With stones?" He gave a good-natured snort. "Face it, I won. The lions did, too. They get you for dinner."

Bleu chuckled, the day's tension draining from his body. "Yes, I'm a rare delicacy." He smirked at Stamf as he clomped noisily down the hall. "But you only win because it's a game. Real animals would hear you coming kilometers away." Bleu flourished his arm toward Stamf. "Behold, Stamf the Loud Foot—Holographic Hunter Extraordinaire."

"I beat you every time." Stamf swaggered down the hall.

Bleu snorted. "Thanh's holographic program ignores your noisy feet, lack of tracking abilities, and disregard for animal behavior. Put us both on the Surface in a *real* safari, and let's see who eats well."

"Time's past for that, my friend. It's just you, me, and the computer. Now, maybe if we were both up there…" Stamf's voice softened conspiratorially. "Did you ask?" He brushed his fingers through his shock of sand-colored hair and raised his eyebrows in expectation.

Maybe he could blame his request to join the Surface Expedition for the tension? "Yes. Didn't you see how stressed out my mother was when you arrived? I had just told her our plan."

"Ugh." Stamf shook his head. "Well, she is your mom, and the First Expedition didn't exactly go well…"

"No, but we've learned from their experience. We could be the heroes who find the other Havens," Bleu said, getting excited again.

"We'll be *exotic heroes* to the girls there…" Stamf laughed, wiggling his eyebrows knowingly.

Bleu rolled his eyes. Stamf was obsessed with women. As obsessed as they were with him.

Stamf chuckled as he strolled down the hall, pretending to greet and kiss the hands of imaginary admirers at the other Havens. "Yes, dear, I'll see you tonight. And you, my lady, tomorrow night."

Bleu laughed. "Do you even care about any of them?" Stamf was a great friend, but a horrible boyfriend.

Stamf shrugged. "Only in the moment. I guess that makes me terrible…" He grinned, clearly not ashamed. "Though I've been told I'm actually quite good."

Bleu snorted and shook his head. Stamf always got a kick out of making him blush.

Stamf clapped him across his back. "Let's see if the Gaming Arena will make the games more challenging for us exotic heroes."

"Or more realistic for us geeks who actually study nature," Bleu countered.

It was Stamf's turn to roll his eyes. "You can't study nature in this steel cage." He sped ahead. "Hurry up, my geeky friend. The lions want their dinner."

The corridor turned again, and the Gaming Arena came into view; Bleu's stomach tightened. How could he go on acting normal when his world had collapsed? Meanwhile, Stamf, clueless to Bleu's new burden, rambled on about the other Havens. The Gaming Arena door slid open as they approached.

"Welcome, Stamf Herrick." The entrance's facial recognition for the top player only had to recognize Stamf—he always held the position.

Other than this greeting, entering the Gaming Arena was always a new experience. The entrance room mimicked the Surface scenery of the game currently being played in the first and largest of the four gaming rooms. The old African continent was in vogue, largely due to Stamf's success as the number one player. His gaming choices attracted a lot of interest. Fortunately for their friendship, Bleu was not the jealous type.

Today, the walls glowed with moving scenes of an ancient African savanna. They found Neviah's father, the mastermind programmer of Bleu's nemesis lions, to the left of the entrance in his workspace. He was surrounded by computers and talking quietly with a young woman.

Bleu's heart skipped a beat. In the shifting light, it looked like Neviah, his neighbor. Had she been here during Ayanna's episode, or was she here telling her father what she had heard?

"Hello, Mr. Thanh." Bleu fell into his usual formality with the withdrawn game controller as he and Stamf approached the desk.

Mr. Thanh grunted, his eyes never leaving the multitude of screens.

Neviah glanced up through her dark hair and shot Bleu a shy smile.

"Hey, Neviah." He returned her grin. "Is your father training you to run the games?" *How long has she been here?*

"Neviah has no interest in games," Mr. Thanh stated, his judgement clear. "Have you ever seen her in here playing?" She was well known for her technological savvy, not her recreational pastimes.

"No," Bleu said, "but she could always surprise us." That earned another grin from her. Maybe everything was okay?

"Neviah came to report something interesting." Mr. Thanh regarded them both with suspicion.

Bleu stiffened. "Something interesting? Are you still monitoring for messages from the other Havens?" *Anything, as long as it's not Ayanna.*

Neviah's large eyes sparkled with excitement as she tucked her dark hair behind her ear. "Yes! I found something in the old drone footage from eight years ago."

"That's great!" He slumped against the counter in relief. "Why re-examine old footage, though?"

"The drone was destroyed. A lot of them end up that way—probably from the cold or winds, though they're built to withstand the weather." She threw up her hands in a gesture of bewilderment and smacked Bleu. "Oh, sorry." She grinned and patted where she had hit him, her hand lingering slightly on his arm.

"I'm fine. You should see how Ayanna hits me." He was joking, of course, but it broke the tension.

She laughed. "Anyways, my new program cleaned up its final static-filled footage."

"Really? That sounds like some program." Bleu had pegged her as a genius in their classes years ago, but this was impressive, even for her.

"Nothing, really." She shrugged and pointed to the screen that held her father's rapt attention. Bleu and Stamf circled the desk and crowded behind Neviah and her father.

Mr. Thanh held up his hand. "Wait, boys. I think the Council should see this first. Not gamers."

"Oh, Dad." Neviah placed her hand on her father's shoulder. "What can it hurt? I've seen it."

"My uncle…" Stamf cleared his throat in an authoritarian manner that made Bleu bite his lip to keep from smirking. "My uncle, the Prime Minister, shows me all kinds of stuff. He keeps me *very informed*." Stamf flashed his winsome smile.

Mr. Thanh narrowed his eyes at Stamf, who somehow held his perfect, confident grin. Bleu knew he was inconsequential at moments like these.

"Fine, just keep it quiet. Neviah gets the credit." He looked about, making sure no one else could view the screen.

"Of course," Stamf replied. They all leaned in as Mr. Thanh restarted the video.

At first, the screen showed only the white and gray of a snowy mountainside framed by blue sky. The grainy video panned over dark, jagged, protruding boulders. When two of the dark areas moved, the drone's video feed rushed toward them and caused Bleu's stomach to lurch.

He leaned over Neviah for a closer look. Two shaggy creatures slowly climbed the face of the mountain. They maneuvered like the apes or upright bears he had seen in the ancient zoology videos he secreted from the library. The drone stopped its approach as the creatures spun to face it.

"What are they?" Bleu nearly knocked over Neviah as he pushed his face closer to the screen.

The video wobbled, and the creatures let out a howl. Bright light flashed from one of them and the video screen went black.

"What the *shast* was that?" Stamf had jumped back at the weapon fire.

"Told you." Neviah grinned. "What do *you* think it was?"

"Not possible?" Stamf scowled and reached over Neviah's shoulder, hit the replay, and watched again.

Bleu mentally searched through the nature files he had studied of ancient

Surface wildlife for anything close to a match. He crossed everything off the list and then pondered the yellow flash. "That light seemed like a weapon. What animal has weapons?"

"This…"—Mr. Thanh tapped the screen—"is why I would never go up there. That was no normal animal. That's not from Earth."

# Chapter 4

Northern Haven: Atsushi Collins

Atsushi Collins was a genetic freak. Even worse, all his classmates—no, make that everyone in Northern Haven—knew his freakishness. All anyone cared about anymore was one's genetic rating, and his was off the charts excellent. That should be good, but everyone treated him like a breakable glass beaker containing a rare cure, set safely away on a high shelf and ignored until needed.

The overprotective Council had assigned him parents who obsessed over this. To them, he was a statistic, a genome, not a son. With humanity's numbers dwindling, the gene pool had gotten dangerously narrow. As the last surviving frozen embryo from the Surface, his anachronistic healthy and varied genes might hold resistance to the Sickness. That alone made him Super Unique Boy.

But wait—there was more. In a multiracial populace that had interbred for centuries, his biological parents, rest their souls, were both supposedly of pure Japanese descent. Atsushi had taken enough science classes to know that race didn't show like that in genes, but it still made him the last of his kind. Whatever that meant.

He was Japanese, but had no idea what that meant, and very limited resources with which to uncover the truth. If only his parents had been allowed to leave him a letter. All they'd given him was his first name, so he treated it like a letter:

*Dear Atsushi,*

*We named you Atsushi. It was important to us, but we can't tell you why.*

*Love,*

*Atsushi's parents*

Everyone else in Northern Haven had been randomly assigned a first name and country at birth to study, based nothing on their genetics or looks or family. It was just an outdated way to keep some sort of connection with the past cultures. It made his own name, purposely picked centuries ago by his Japanese parents, extra special.

He'd researched everything on his name in the database left by Northern Haven's founding organization SHAST. Apparently, the Subterranean Human Advancement of Science and Technology had assigned only two phrases to his name's meaning—compassionate warrior or warm.

Perhaps his parents liked the idea of their son being warm in the ruinous ice age, or had named him *compassionate warrior* because they were a military family or they had studied martial arts. Or did they want him to grow up to be a *compassionate, warm* man? Or study the art of being a warrior? His name held many possibilities and left even more unsaid.

All he knew for sure was that he was the last surviving frozen embryo conceived before the Descent and born eons after his Japanese parents perished on the icy Surface. He shivered at the chilling thought as he sat cross-legged in his cramped sleeping quarters, school and library computer discs lying helter-skelter around him amidst last night's leftover snacks.

As he scanned the titles, Educator Girak's past warning stung him. "Atsushi, all the records in the library, even the one recorded year of the internet, have been curated and edited by SHAST. You can't trust what it says about being Japanese. It's probably all stereotypes. The answer, if it still exists, is in you. Don't let them define you."

Educator Girak meant well enough, but what else did he have to go on? Himself? That seemed laughable.

Because of his name's meaning, the records he had taken out this month featured ancient Japanese warriors and martial arts. Every time he tried to meditate like the records said to do, he'd end up frustrated and his hands would curl into fists. He was so lost and misplaced by cryogenics that Ayanna would never be interested in him. No girl would. *I was born an anachronism, a freak from another time...*

*Focus. Follow the breath...*

The Japanese people weren't extinct. Well, not really. They, like all the other nationalities, supposedly had equal genetic representation in the various United Peoples' Havens. But their way of life, language, and look was gone, preserved only in the records. They were in the same position as every other racial or ethnic group.

*I've just outlived them all by being frozen...I'm the last one.* It was a huge responsibility for his fifteen years.

*Breathe. Follow the breath.* Instead, an image of his brother's smirking face loomed in his mind's eye. Liam always teased Atsushi, saying he wasn't really family, only a freezer-burned, outdated leftover from a dead world.

"Argh! I'll never master mind training." The infuriating video from the Records Room was wrong about learning meditation first. Sword fighting was much more practical for handling his classmates.

Atsushi glanced at the clock, and his stomach fell. School started in ten minutes.

He tore off his pajamas and pulled a tunic over his shoulders. Pants tied, he slammed his feet into his shoes and tried to shake his irritation. He should be happy. He was about to spend the day in Educator Girak's classroom.

The only person who didn't treat him like a museum specimen was the educator, probably because he'd also been born to two frozen embryo survivors. His ruddy, freckled skin, red hair, and reddish-brown beard made him stand out almost as much as Atsushi. It gave Atsushi and Educator Girak a special bond. The genetic freak bond.

Slapping the panel to open his module's front door, Atsushi swung his bag over his shoulder and rushed out the door. If he was lucky, he could finagle a seat next to Ayanna.

Maneuvering around the corridor corners with ease, he hi-fived his favorite mural characters on the corridor walls as if they were real friends. "Sorry, guys, can't stop and chat. Late as usual."

He wouldn't get in trouble—the only advantage to being genetically prized. The council, who ensured humanity's genetic viability, spared no pains ensuring his wellbeing. If only Ayanna paid him as much attention.

He swung through the classroom doorway and stopped short. Ayanna stood a meter from him. *She's back.*

As she swung into her chair, her long, spiraled curls cascaded through the air, gracefully rounding her shoulder and landing like a black fountain on her slender hips. Atsushi stood, mesmerized.

"Nice of you to join us, Atsushi." Educator Girak chuckled and his beard twitched with amusement. "Grab a seat."

Atsushi dove into the nearest chair, conveniently next to Ayanna. *Yes!* He hid behind his bag, grinning as he dug out his computer. She sat so close that her fruity scent filled his head. He stole a glance while she sketched a line portrait on her screen. It was an odd alien-like creature's face.

"Nice," he whispered.

Without looking at him, her lips curled upward. She deleted the drawing and dated her notes for today's lesson.

Why was she sitting near the door instead of in the back with her friends? Atsushi looked over his shoulder at her usual seat, and James, Councilor Bergstrom's son, sneered at him.

Educator Girak cleared his throat. "Today, we're starting with a video of Descension Day, the day our fortunate ancestors were escorted by SHAST's soldiers to the secret locations of the four havens, ours being Northern Haven. The Subterranean Human Advancement of Science and Technology project decided which humans from all nations had the best genes and skills. Imagine the responsibility of making that decision." Girak surveyed his class, his blue eyes blazing with animation.

Atsushi grinned back. Somehow, his educator's passion was always contagious.

"Now, we face a similar difficult decision—the council's proposed referendum. The referendum will remove basic controls over one's genetic material and has been proposed in reaction to the continuing increase in the Sickness." His face tightened. "In light of these parallels, I thought we should reexamine the original issue."

A three-dimensional holograph popped up a few feet from Ayanna's pointed shoes. In it, a huge, unruly crowd pushed its way toward the guarded Descenders.

"I found this clip in the records room," Educator Girak noted, walking toward the back of the room. "As you see, the camera is not with the descending team, meaning it was smuggled down here before the locking."

The class sat transfixed as a redheaded woman spoke directly to the recording device. "Rhetta Jones here, reporting for"—she glanced at the military shoving people to her left—"for humanity. Humanity has wagered its survival completely on the human genome and science. None of us here will live long enough to see the outcome, but our concerns must be recorded for future generations."

"Rhetta, hurry! Throw it to him now." A woman yanked on Rhetta's arm that held the recording device, causing a ripple in her image. "The Descenders are passing now!"

"We must ask ourselves," Rhetta continued, her voice wavering, "is it purely genetics that makes us human? Our greatest inventors, philosophers, our founding fathers—was it their genes that made them who they were? We say, no, there is more to surviving than our DNA. Never forget the power of the human spirit to overcome obstacles! This is not the en—"

At this point, the impatient woman appeared to grab the recorder as she yelled to a passing Descender. The holograph sputtered out.

The class was silent. Atsushi shifted in his seat. A voiceless guilt gripped his surviving human body.

"So, class," Educator Girak boomed, bounding to the front of the room. "What do you think? Will it be genes that save us? Or our human spirit?"

Atsushi willed another student to break the riveting silence. He should have been born up there...died up there. Luck had made him a time traveler.

*Rap. Rap. Rap.*

Insistent blows on the classroom door broke the collective daze. Someone outside flung it open, and Prime Minister Pridbor burst into the classroom, flanked by a council guard.

Despite being shorter than Girak, the prime minister managed to peer down at them all. His lizard-like watery eyes, bulbous nose that sniffed out dissention, and fake smile unnerved Atsushi. Instead of being humbled by his looks, Pridbor's bearing resembled that of a medieval lord inspecting his serfs. An exquisitely embroidered tunic and matching pants completed his imperious look.

His gaze locked on Educator Girak.

*Not good.*

"Where's the recording, Girak?" Pridbor growled, his eyes darting to the power button on the holograph display.

"Welcome, prime minister." Educator Girak beamed. "You mean the recording from Descension Day? I thought it'd be a good introduction to your referendum. Surely you want our youngest citizens well informed?"

"Educator Girak, I need to speak to you outside. Now." His narrow eyes scanned the students as if his stare could decontaminate them from the holographic exposure.

The prime minister's cold gaze passed over Atsushi, sending a shiver down his spine.

Girak, a terse expression on his face, strode out of the silent room. Pridbor nodded a thin smile to the students, spun on his heels, and exited. The guard followed, pulling the door shut behind himself.

Atsushi's gaze naturally jumped to Ayanna. Her hands were trembling. Odd. She'd never struck him as the nervous type.

"I'm sure he's not in that much trouble. It's just a recording," he reassured her.

Ayanna smiled weakly and rushed out of the room by another door.

He started to rise to follow her, and then sank back into his seat. Prime Minister Pridbor and Girak would notice if two of them left. He'd only get them both in trouble.

His heart sank as he stared at the door that had swallowed her up. What had upset her? Sighing, he pushed himself deeper into his seat.

Behind him, the abandoned class had erupted into whispers and muffled

36

laughter. He resisted turning around. Connecting with his peers only brought trouble. *Only I would miss an educator when he's pulled out of the classroom.*

Atsushi leaned forward, straining to hear what was happening in the corridor.

Prime Minister Pridbor's voice rose like that of an angry father lecturing a wayward son. "You need to stop using your special status to get away with stuff like this. This behavior is less than I would expect of an educator. That holograph recording was off limits, and don't pretend you weren't aware of that. This behavior can impact your wife's access..."

Educator Girak's voice, still calm, was too low for Atsushi to hear. He imagined Girak standing in the hall as a Japanese sensei, calmly smiling at the furious prime minister.

"Hey, Att. Can you hear?" James Bergstrom, usually uninterested in everything at school, was suddenly full of energy and creeping chair by chair up behind Atsushi. They both tilted toward the heated discussion on the other side of the door.

The door burst open, and Atsushi and James sprang into their seats.

Educator Girak smiled broadly at them both. "Yes, James, you *will* hear today's lesson better from the front row. Good thinking."

James squirmed lower in his seat, a distinct crimson spreading over his neck and ears.

"I apologize for the disruption. Prime Minister Pridbor felt that SHAST Project holograph may be too distressing for your young minds."

Atsushi detected a forced calm in the educator's delivery. *Had something else happened between the two men?*

Girak's gaze fell on the empty seat next to Atsushi. "Where did Ayanna go?" He addressed the leader of Ayanna's girl pack in the back of the room. "Sera?"

"I'm not sure, Educator Girak. She seemed upset or maybe ill." Sera's eyes flickered with uncertainty.

"All right, then." Girak made himself a quick note. "Let's try to get back on schedule."

As the discussion of genetics versus the human spirit whirled around him, Atsushi worried about why Ayanna had left. She had been so close. He inhaled deeply, warmed by the brief memory.

"Atsushi?"

Startled, he suddenly sensed it wasn't the first time Educator Girak had called his name.

"Hmm?" Atsushi mumbled.

"Your thoughts on the referendum?"

"Oh. Uhm..." Atsushi fumbled to erase *Ayanna* from his screen. "Well, it's not that big a deal for guys. But for women, it's more complicated, and they're more upset about it."

"And you're okay if you have no direct say over what happens to your potential children"—Educator Girak stroked his beard—"because you're a young man?"

Atsushi shrugged, hoping to shake his educator's attention.

Educator Girak narrowed his eyes and paused as if considering his words carefully. Something in his thoughtful gaze set off alarms in Atsushi. "It would appear that my male-identifying students have no concerns with this Referendum." He waited as the guys all shrugged. "Interesting." He zoomed in on Atsushi and worry creased his brow. "You, too?"

Atsushi wanted to stand up and shout, "Why am I different?" But Girak must be extremely concerned and desperate about this referendum to spotlight him, because they shared the frozen embryo situation, and Girak wouldn't normally call attention to that in public. Certainly not in front of Atsushi's peers. Even so, it ate him up inside to be made the center of attention.

Girak continued, "Your unique genes, which may theoretically be in, let's say, high demand"—chuckles erupted here from classmates James and his sidekicks—"don't affect your belief?"

Atsushi's jaw dropped. How dare he, of all people, bring this up in front of the class? *Breathe. Be the nonchalant warrior.*

He narrowed his eyes and glared at Girak. "The Sickness is the real issue. I don't think the Referendum changes anything. We have mothers and fathers that raise us, and matras and paternuses that are our genetic parents. What difference will this make?" His words were laced with anger. Still, the effect they had on his educator unsettled him.

Disappointment and hurt flashed across his teacher's face, then disappeared into a controlled grimace. "The difference is control, class." Educator Girak's gaze stayed locked on Atsushi for a moment, and then swept the entire class. "Now, we can be requested to donate our eggs or sperm so we can be a matra or paternus. Note the word 'requested.' The referendum takes away that choice. If it passes, you could be required to donate eggs or sperm. Women could be required to carry other couples' fetuses. You could be required to undergo laboratory procedures that are unpleasant, especially for women.

He turned toward Atsushi's side of the room. "The benefits? James, what are the benefits?"

"We live. Don't get all inbred, weak, and die from the Sickness. Nobody wants that. It's a simple choice if you want humanity to survive." James harrumphed, as if anyone who disagreed was out of his mind.

"Is it?" Educator Girak turned about, looking for several seconds into each student's face. "Think about it, class. This will change all our lives one way or the other."

The ending bell rang.

As Atsushi got up, James raced to the back of the room and tapped Sera on the back. "Wanna go to the Gaming Room with us?" James gestured to several other boys, avoiding Atsushi's gaze. "Stamf and Bleu have a new game setting today. Totally new. It should be more exciting than this was, for sure."

They hurried out, jostling him with their bags as they passed. Uninvited again. Not that Educator Girak had pointed him out as a fellow genetic freak or anything. Sighing, head down, he trudged through the doorway.

"Atsushi," Educator Girak said.

*Great. Hasn't he made things bad enough?* Atsushi looked away and slid past him in the doorway, ready to bolt.

"Atsushi. Wait, please."

Something in Educator Girak's voice made him stop, but as his teacher's footsteps slowly approached, he refused to turn around.

Atsushi's whole body tightened. He wouldn't allow this man he had trusted to shame him again.

Girak stopped and sighed. "Hear me out. Please?" That sadness again permeated his words.

For some unknown and completely illogical reason, the sadness tore at Atsushi's gut. Girak cared. He could feel Girak's concern, something no one ever showed him, and it infuriated him. He stood stiffly, braced against whatever kind words were about to confront his fury.

"Look, I didn't mean to embarrass you. I just wanted you and the others to realize how serious this referendum is." Girak walked around him until they were face-to-face. "And for some of us"—he stared straight into his eyes—"like you and me, it will make a bigger difference."

Atsushi narrowed his eyes, then stepped backward. "Maybe. Maybe not." He understood his point and knew his educator's concern was genuine. Still, his emotions roiled inside.

"I'm sorry I've upset you. Will I see you at the Spring Reigns Festival tomorrow?"

He shrugged. "I guess." He studied the gray floor, anywhere being preferable to meeting Girak's concerned gaze. Not knowing what else to say, Atsushi turned and hurried down the corridor toward his family's module.

Gaining distance didn't help. He stood outside his door, raw and exposed. Shamed in front of his peers, yet also, strangely...his chest filled with warmth. Was this what it felt like to have a father that cared enough to challenge you? Wonderful and horrible at the same time?

He entered and slumped in the chair farthest from the sleeping quarters. Anything to avoid the argument emanating from his parents' room. This was the noisiest discussion recently, and that said a lot, given the grandness of their usual debates. Words like "referendum" and "my body" tossed about like daggers. The same debate that raged all over the Haven.

Atsushi glanced at the wall's digital sky image. The peaceful, blue sky with puffy clouds lazing across it contradicted the mood permeating his living room. Maybe he should reprogram it to turn stormy when they yelled?

Just then the corridor door opened, and his younger brother, Liam, strolled in. He brushed his stylish bronze hair from his shifty eyes and pulled out his music ear buds. Now hearing the yelling, Liam paused, raised his eyebrows, and smirked at his brother. "Let me guess, the referendum?"

Atsushi nodded.

"Mom's for limits, Dad's not?" His brother asked as he plopped his whole body onto the sofa in one smooth move.

Currently, they were the same height, though Liam was more solidly built. Everyone always forgot Atsushi was older. Actually, way older, if he figured how many centuries his embryo had been in a deep freeze.

Atsushi's head continued its nod. It was best not to engage his brother in conversation. He tensed, waiting for the attack.

"They can have all of my sperm," Liam shrugged. "What do I need it for?" He crossed his arms behind his head, his entire body reposed.

"Nobody wants *yours*." Atsushi muttered to himself and then chuckled, his chest and shoulders shaking while the rest of his slim body remained at rest.

Liam glared at him and leaned forward, itching for a fight.

*Shast. He overheard me.*

"Well, watch out, big brother. As the genetically sound Freezer Baby, they'll want you at the clinic every week." Liam's smile shifted into a ruthless sneer.

Atsushi's eyes narrowed and then lowered to the brown floor. He hated it when they called him that.

He rose and stormed out of their module, stomping toward the records room to lose himself in the records of ancient Japan. It was his safe place when lonely, and he ended up there nearly every day.

If he was lucky, he'd find Neviah there. Their paths had crossed last week when she had been searching old drone records. Before that, he'd seen her around, though they'd never had reason to talk.

That day, he'd nicknamed her The Hair-Pusher, because like clockwork, every thirty seconds she brushed her hair out of her face only to have it immediately fall back. Her pointless activity amused him until The Hair-Pusher noticed she was being observed. Her hand froze, temporarily tangled in her hair, and they both laughed.

The hair tangle had broken the ice, and they had talked awhile. It was nice to discuss his research with someone other than the computerized voice of the records room.

Today, as the records room door hissed shut behind him, Atsushi scanned the cavernous room. *Yes.* Neviah was here, in the far corner. He wove around research stations and slid into the computer booth nearest hers.

"Hey!" She gave him a quick grin. "What's today's research project?"

He shrugged and tapped his fingers nervously on the desk. Would she judge him as obsessed for again looking up Japanese culture? He decided to risk it. "I'm looking for anything about Japan that I haven't already read."

"I bet you've read lots, but have you accessed the videos?" she asked. "Not the ones listed under Japan, but the ones the Japanese people themselves recorded?"

His jaw dropped. "Those exist?"

She grinned. "If you know how to search...creatively." She held her index finger to her lips, signifying to keep secret what she was about to do, and then she began typing. Moments later, she accessed old, flat videos and photographs of Japanese tea ceremonies and the Japanese theater with its amazing clothing.

Atsushi's eyes widened in delight. "Are these curated by SHAST as well?"

"Everything here is. Only, some stuff is more hidden. Can you imagine having outfits that detailed and complex? I mean, with our limited resources, we can hardly manage a few basic changes of clothing." She frowned down at her plain tunic and pants. "Life was so much easier and stylish up there."

"You mean in Japan?" he asked, not sure what she meant.

"No, anywhere on the Surface."

"Oh. I guess." He shrugged. "They had wars, though." He considered the tea ceremony playing on the screen before him. "This is cool, but I'm not sure they did this every time they had tea. I mean, it's not practical, is it? Do you really think every Japanese person drank their tea like this?"

Neviah pointed to the translated title at the bottom of the screen, *Japanese Tea Ceremony: How the Japanese Drank Their Tea.* "It says it is, but I see your point."

"You do?" Elation filled him. He'd never had anyone to talk to about these things except Educator Girak, and he was different.

She nodded.

He hadn't found the answer to what it meant to be Japanese, yet he'd found someone else to understand his question. Not personally, like himself. Still, it was a start.

*A new start*, he mused.

Tomorrow's Spring Reigns Festival was all about a new start for humanity, ever hopeful that the ice age would someday yield to Spring. Usually he hated the crowd and endless superficial conversations with his parents' friends, but maybe this was his year.

Maybe this year it wouldn't be so bad.

# Chapter 5

Northern Haven: Atsushi Collins

The next day, Atsushi awoke earlier than the morning lights. The MLs were installed in every room and mimicked a twenty-four-hour day with a gradual sunrise, a fourteen-hour bright cycle, and a decrease leading to an eight-hour night. The early morning was his quiet time, unburdened by Liam's cruel remarks or the snickering of his classmates.

He quietly padded out of his sleeping room, careful not to awaken anyone, and typed a quick, "I'll be back," on their message board. Just in case. He hated to worry his mom. If something happened to him, she really would get in trouble with the council. Slipping on his shoes, he exited their small living module, wincing as the door hissed shut.

Atsushi slunk through the dark corridors toward the Gaming Arena. Neviah had invited him to help her and her father, Lee, set up the festival. An unusual treat. His heart hadn't been this happy since the day Ayanna had told Liam to shut up. That had been superb.

The Spring Reigns Festival was originally held the first Spring Equinox after their ancestors had descended below Surface. It celebrated the ancient spring season that had occurred before the Great Change; its warmth, its gift of renewal of life, its promise that the Earth was still hospitable to humanity. The Festival was a celebration of hope that warmth would again heat the Surface. It was a big deal.

He turned to enter the Gaming Arena and then paused, listening for movement beyond the door. What if it was locked? How would she know he was here? He hesitantly pushed his slender hand against the sensor. Nothing happened.

Neviah couldn't have been fooling him all along, could she? Would he get in trouble for being found in the darkened halls before the MLs came on? He rocked uneasily from foot to foot as he glanced up and down the black corridors.

*Woosh.*

Atsushi jumped back as the door opened. Neviah stood with electronic cords wrapped around her shoulder, both hands full of tools.

"Think I forgot?" She grinned and motioned him inside with her elbow, the only part not engaged in holding tools.

"Maybe," he admitted. He extended his arms to relieve her of her load. "Need a hand?"

"No. Get those," she said, pointing her chin to a pile of small boxes on her left, "and follow me."

"What are these?" He picked up the boxes and fell in step behind her.

"An added surprise this year." She winked mischievously over her shoulder and continued onward.

Dumping her armload on the closest table of the main entrance room, she announced, "I'm going to show you how to detach the walls that usually divide the gaming rooms. Then, we'll have a huge open space that will fit everyone."

Neviah grabbed two tools, handed one to Atsushi, and then led him to the front corner. He squatted next to her to observe.

"See this pin?" She motioned toward a large metal shaft locked through several circular hooks. "Use that"—she pointed to the tool she had given him—"and hook it here, and then pull up." She jerked the pin upward, releasing it. "See, easy, right? Then simply fold the wall back like this."

She deftly pushed it back like an ancient accordion. It folded neatly into the rear wall. Neviah glanced about the room as if looking for spies and then grinned impishly. "Okay, Att, here's the fun part."

"What?" Atsushi was confused by her sudden change from serious worker to fellow conspirator.

45

"A hideout. You know, for when you want to stay at the Festival, but you need a break from others. Right?" Neviah tucked her hair behind her ear.

"You haven't been an adult for long, have you?" He teased, putting down his tools and wiring on the makeshift table of boxes.

"No." She laughed.

"Okay, how does this hideout work?" He searched the wall for a hole.

"Well, as long as most of the wall's folded in, it's programmed to disappear and won't show in the holograph." She pulled out a small section of the folding divider wall and then stood in the large fold and grinned triumphantly. "See? As long as I leave this little bit out, during the festival this little space"—she extended her arms dramatically—"has complete privacy. You're invisible in here."

"Cool!" He couldn't stop grinning at her thoughtful antics. Was this what it was like to have a good friend?

"I always program a few flowering spring trees in front of the fold. Then nobody sees you disappear, right?" Neviah proudly waved her arms toward the future trees, flashed him a grin, and knelt to grasp her tool bag. "I put in a cherry tree for you."

"Why?" *Oh no.*

She continued her work without looking up. "I did some research. Wasn't that tree really important in Japan?"

"I guess? I mean, thanks, but..." He looked down, unsure how to acknowledge her effort and also explain his jumbled reaction. "I mean, that's not all there is to being Japanese."

She stopped bumbling around and turned toward him, her face pinched. "I messed up? I'm sorry, I thought you'd like it."

He tensed. "I do! I mean, I'm sure I will. I've never seen one." Frowning, he searched for the right words. "It's just kinda stereotypical and like that tea ceremony we found. I mean, every tree in Japan couldn't have been a cherry tree, right?"

She laughed. "No." Then, tucking her bangs behind her ear, she grew serious. "Should I remove it? I can reprogram it."

"No, it'll be pretty. And I appreciate you thinking of me." Yet even more he valued how he'd been able to explain his reaction to her, and she'd accepted it.

Grinning ear-to-ear, he examined the faux wall. "This hiding space… You create it every year?" Who knew he wasn't the only one who wanted to avoid crowds?

Neviah nodded. "Yeah, but this year it's all yours. I want to see my father's reaction to the surprise."

"Which is…?" he leaned forward in anticipation.

"A surprise." Neviah winked, handing a tool to him as she stood to retrieve a large padded bag from a nearby table.

"Come on…" He waited expectantly.

She giggled. "I'm horrid at keeping secrets. Can *you* keep secrets?"

He grinned and nodded. "That's what friends are for."

"All righty then. Look—"

As she swung the large padded case off her shoulder, he jumped back. "Whoa!"

"Sorry." She chuckled as she lowered it more carefully to the floor. "Do you know what fireworks are?" She swept her long bangs out of her eyes.

Shaking his head, he eyed the bag dubiously. A fire in Northern Haven was a thing of nightmares.

"It's not real fire," she reassured him.

As she explained what would happen in the holographic fireworks, her face brightened at his speedy grasp of the technology. Soon, she was explaining the controls and how to program it. His ear-to-ear grin was so great that by the time she'd finished her explanation, his face muscles ached.

From her pocket she produced a rare piece of choco, broke it in two, and handed him half with a grin. "This is my thank you for all your help."

"Thanks!" The cafeteria handed out a bag of choco candy to each person once a year. He hadn't seen any in months.

She nodded. "Okay, enough fun. We better get to work. Remove the walls, and when you're done, let me know." She hugged her holographic contraption to her chest and moved past, pushing the other tools she needed with her feet.

Neviah kept him busy for over two hours, but the sweet, creamy choco had enough caffeine to keep him moving. As soon as the MLs came on, he thanked her and hurried home, erased his note, and pretended to just rise.

He reveled in his perfect plan for the day. Families always arrived together for the Spring Reigns Festival, but this year he could avoid spending the day with Liam and his obligated-to-raise-the-genetic-freak parents. And Ayanna would be there.

Sliding on his best green tunic and black pants, he ran his fingers through his coarse hair, wondering for the thousandth time whether Ayanna preferred it longer or the standard thumb-length imposed by the council to conserve bathing water. He couldn't really keep his that length, or it would poke out in every direction, and he didn't like it cropped. So far, he'd gotten away with his illegally long length, but he tied it back in a short ponytail so as not to flaunt it.

Now he needed an Ayanna Engagement Plan, or he'd panic as usual and waste this opportunity. He could offer to get her a glass of punch, or maybe ask her to dance? No, that was too risky, because he had no idea how to dance. Maybe he could show her Neviah's hideout?

"Atsushi? Hurry up." His mother sounded tense. She always got performance anxiety before social events.

"Coming," he called back.

Rushing into the living room, he ignored Liam's smirk at his curated appearance and trailed his stiffly dressed parents out the door. Liam, music plugs in place, walked ahead, assuming his family would follow. Atsushi's eyes narrowed at the swaggered pretense of the triangle of people preceding him.

Yet when they rounded the last corridor, Atsushi was astounded by the holographic grandeur he had helped create. The door to the Gaming Arena opened, revealing a beautiful meadow, strange bird calls, and bubbling streams of the Surface. Chimes hung in the flowering cherry tree, and newly leafed willows fluttered gently in the warm breeze. Bright green grass carpeted the ground. Insects chirped and songbirds fluttered about. To the left, butterflies graced a small flower garden, and two small Magnolia trees stood guard at his secret cave. The overall effect was breathtaking.

Atsushi scanned the gregarious crowd for *her* until his ears caught her laughter past the food tables. She and her friends clustered around the butterflies, attempting to safely catch the fluttering insects though they were holographic. Ayanna giggled as one flew through her outstretched hand. The back of her blue dress tunic fluttered loosely as if she had her own pair of wings. Below her smiling lips something sparkled. His gaze fell to a blue-and-silver pendant nestled in the slight curve between her breasts. He sighed. Hopefully, the greeting of his parents' friends would end soon.

An hour later, Atsushi's parents finally slowed their promenade around the massive room, secure that they had courted all the other important families. They found another suitably important couple and delved into a discussion of the latest genetic tests. Liam made an excuse and sauntered off toward his lackeys.

*Now or never.* Approaching the food tables, Atsushi found the fruit tarts Ayanna loved. He'd learned her preference at last year's festival because, despite his crush, he had lacked a plan and had only noticed all the stuff she enjoyed, filing it away for later use. He was not going to wait another year. Selecting the best two, he placed them on a plate, took a deep breath, and turned, ready.

*I can do this*, he reassured himself, twisting through the crowd and mentally practicing the lines he'd formulated while getting dressed. Completely entranced by his internal rehearsal, he missed the foot subtly stuck in his path. As he crashed to the ground, the tarts smashed in front of him, giving his face a berry-covered landing strip.

Crouching on the fake grass, a smoldering fury filled him. He knew full well whose brotherly foot had caused his downfall.

Using the sleeve of his new tunic to quickly wipe off the purplish, sticky fruit, he arose, fists clenched. Concerned adults extended hands, asking if he was okay. Liam, of course, was gone. Ayanna's friends giggled, while she stared, her hand over her mouth.

Face burning, he turned and rushed between the two magnolias. After checking for observers, he stumbled into his sanctuary and sank onto the low, wobbly stool Neviah had left for him. If the revelry hadn't been so loud, people would have overheard his suppressed sobs drifting eerily from the flowering magnolias.

He sat, staring at the tree trunks through the speeches, the feasting, and now, the dancing. All his careful planning had again been ruined by Liam and his friends. The holographic band piped and thrummed, and in the distance, jovial people danced and careened in circles. Was Ayanna dancing with someone? His fingers brushed against his stained, sticky tunic, and he sighed. Even if she was bored to tears, she wouldn't want to dance with a mess like him.

Hushed laughter made him look up as two people, one of them Ayanna, approached his trees. Was she sneaking off with another guy? Body tensed, Atsushi silently thanked Neviah for the hideout as he strained for a better look.

He sank in relief. It was Ayanna, but the guy she walked with was her brother, Bleu. Bleu was three years older than her, and, like his sister, commanded a powerful charm. His milky-brown skin accentuated his hazel eyes, which rolled at something Ayanna had just said. Atsushi wished he had been blessed by such racial blending.

Ayanna was now very close. Unlike her brother, she had her mother's ebony eyes. Eyes that always made Atsushi's stomach flip like a blind fish at the hatchery. He shrank back on his stool as Bleu pulled Ayanna behind the flowering trees. They were so close, Atsushi could simply extend his arm and brush Ayanna's back. He leaned in, entranced by her fruity smell, and then straightened. What if they heard his breath?

"Shhh. Stop laughing, Yanna."

"But why are you being mysterious?" Her head cocked to the side, a dark eyebrow raised in playful judgment.

When met with only silence, she sighed and plopped down on the ground, cross-legged. She reached up and pulled Bleu down next to her. As he sat, there was a strange clank.

Atsushi narrowed his gaze at Bleu's clothing.

"What was that?" Ayanna tilted her head.

Bleu's face froze a moment and then recovered. "Just something in my pocket."

"Duh." Ayanna playfully punched her brother's upper arm. "What are you hiding?"

Bleu smiled and shook his head as if admitting his guilt. "I've been trying to find a chance without mom or dad around to tell you. I'm still trying to figure this"—Bleu tapped his pocket—"out, and it relates to what I need to tell you. It's..." He threw a checking glance over his shoulder and then turned back to Ayanna. "It's a...dagger." His eyes twitched as he said the last word.

"A dagger?" Ayanna threw up her hands in disgust. "Okay, Bleu, what's going on?"

*A weapon?* Atsushi gasped and then froze as Bleu jerked his gaze in his direction.

Atsushi's heart skipped a beat. Ayanna's back was only an arm's reach away, and Bleu faced him at eye level. Could Bleu see him? Their eyes met, yet no recognition shone in Bleu's eyes. Atsushi's heart thudded off endless seconds.

Bleu, apparently convinced that the magnolias were the only thing there, turned his attention back to Ayanna. "I have a plan. Just between us, okay?" Bleu's eyes searched Ayanna's face.

"Okay," she assured him, but her shoulders tensed under her silky, blue tunic.

Bleu again checked behind him. "I want to get us out of here."

"Huh? Leave the Festival?" Ayanna's voice wavered.

"No, you know, go up there." Bleu pointed with his index finger toward the ceiling. "On the Surface."

"What? Are you kidding?" Ayanna erupted in playful laughter and then reassessed her brother. "Look, just because we're celebrating spring doesn't mean we can go up there. It's an ice world."

"Ayanna, look at us." Bleu motioned beyond the trees to the dancing inhabitants of Northern Haven. "This isn't right. We live under fake lighting, eat mostly fake food supplemented with laboratory-created vitamins, and are corralled by walls. This meadow is beautiful, but it's a lie." Bleu ended his tirade and studied his sister's reactions.

So did Atsushi. He wished he could see Ayanna's face.

Bleu had lost it. *Live on the Surface? Don't fall for this, Ayanna, please. It's suicide.* Atsushi's head spun. He had believed Bleu was a cool guy. Protective of Ayanna, yet nice. And sane.

Ayanna sat very still.

Atsushi's heart raced. *Why isn't she laughing at her brother's ridiculous idea?*

She looked up at Bleu and nodded. "But how would we survive up there?"

*What is she thinking?*

"I've submitted my name for the second expedition. Mom's not thrilled, but I have to go up there to learn more. I had a vision...like Mom." His voice fell as he rubbed his face like he was trying to block Ayanna from seeing it.

She recoiled. "A vision? Not you, too..."

*What are they talking about? What have they seen?*

Bleu jerked his head up. "Forget the vision. I'm supposed to go, Ayanna." Bleu's words sped up, his eyes luminous. "Humans survived the last Ice Age. I've researched survival in the records room. I just..." Bleu shrugged his shoulders and closed his eyes.

Atsushi tried to imagine Bleu the gamer holed up in the records room, researching the Surface like Atsushi researched ancient Japan. It didn't seem possible.

"I belong on the Surface," he said at last. Bleu opened his eyes and grasped her forearm. "We *both* do. The cure's up there. But I won't leave you..."

*Cure? Is he helping his mom with her research?* Atsushi's eyebrows furrowed, and he willed Ayanna to tell her brother he had lost his mind.

"Whatever you do, we do together." She raised her fist, and he fist bumped her.

*What?* A wave of lightheadedness flooded Atsushi.

"But Bleu, one does not simply walk onto the Surface and live there. We'll need a plan…and shelter and supplies. And Mom and Dad."

"Working on it, sis." Bleu smiled.

Atsushi reeled backward in shock. His arms made pin wheeling motions as he tried to regain his balance on the stool. He toppled sideways against the bent wall. He froze, his heart racing and the hairs standing up on his neck. Had they heard? He slowly unwound his body and raised his head.

To his horror, Ayanna and Bleu were both staring at him.

# Chapter 6

*orthern Haven: Atsushi Collins*

Northern Haven: Atsushi Collins

Panicked at his sudden exposure, Atsushi found himself grinning like a fool at the stunned Ayanna and Bleu.

He clambered to his feet. By the time he righted the stool, Bleu's shock had given way to fury. Behind them, the holographic band played a dizzy tune while everyone whirled in circles, drunk on either alcohol or the music.

"Sorry," Atsushi tried. "I didn't mean to overhear you. It just…happened." He shot Ayanna a pleading look. "Technically, I was here minding my own business and got trapped by you two."

"How long have you been here?" Bleu growled. His tone—low, quiet, and controlled—froze Atsushi in place. All the times Liam had cornered him flashed through his mind.

"Well?" Bleu demanded.

Atsushi glanced at Ayanna, hoping she wasn't mad at him, too, but her narrowed, calculating gaze made him step backward. *Oh, Shast.* He wanted nothing more than to dive back into Neviah's hidden spot and disappear.

"I…I was …avoiding the crowd. I had no idea you two would come over here."

"Did you hear everything we said?" Bleu fumed as he cast a glance around them as if making sure no one else was listening.

No one was.

Anger radiated off Bleu, and Atsushi's gaze fell to the bulging dagger in Bleu's pocket.

It took another retreating step for Atsushi to remember Bleu wasn't Liam. He stood his ground and met Bleu's gaze. "Yes, I'm sorry. I heard everything, and I promise I'll keep your secret."

"Why exactly would you do that?" Ayanna challenged, cocking her head and grinning that grin that undid him. A breeze riffled across the meadow, making the layers of her silky dress shimmer.

"Because..." He wasn't about to tell her he'd do pretty much anything for her—at least, not with Bleu glowering at him. "Because I shouldn't have overheard it, so I'll pretend I didn't. Friends help each other avoid trouble, right?" He ignored Bleu and shot her a hopeful smile.

As her lips curled downward, his heart sank. But her frown was directed at his chest. Atsushi followed her gaze to the ridiculous berry streak down the center of his dress tunic.

"I saw Liam stick out his foot to trip you. I'm sorry I couldn't warn you in time." Her lips pursed in apologetic regret.

She'd been watching him while he collected the tarts? "You saw that?" Ayanna nodded.

"He's a jerk of a brother."

"Totally," she agreed with a wave of her hand.

Bleu blew out an exasperated sigh. "Liam is not our problem, Ayanna."

"I told you I'd keep your secrets." As if he had anyone to tell. "But you both going to the Surface? That's super dangerous."

"I know more about it than you," Bleu stated as if he were some sort of expert.

"Yeah, have you ever been up there? Because technically, I have. I was in my mother's uterus up there." *Shast.* Had he actually said that? He snorted in laughter. "Okay, forget that, but still..."

Ayanna joined in his laughter. "Bleu, you better listen to him. He's seen the Surface from the window in his mom's uterus."

Bleu raised an eyebrow at them. "This really isn't funny. I can't risk my chance to get on the Expedition Team if he decides to yack that I think the cure is on the Surface."

"Right." Ayanna stifled her laughter. "Atsushi, give us your word that you'll keep it all secret."

"I promise."

Worry twisted Bleu's face. "Why should I trust you?"

"Swear on something big," Ayanna persisted. "Like…" She furrowed her brow and turned to her brother. "What should he swear on?"

Bleu shrugged and turned to stare off across the meadow. "Not sure anything he swears on would reassure me."

"I swear on Japan," Atsushi said.

"What?" Bleu glared at him. "What does *that* mean?"

"It's important to me, like—" Atsushi lowered his voice. "Like reaching the Surface is to you."

Bleu glowered at him for nearly half a song before something shifted in his eyes. "Fine. That good with you, Ayanna?"

"Yup." She held out her hand, and Atsushi happily grasped it to seal the deal. Their gazes met for a second before Bleu attempted to backhand their hands apart.

"Come on, hurry up," Bleu said. "I don't want people wondering what we're up to over here."

They dropped hands.

Bleu, his face again clouded with worry, quickly shook hands with Atsushi. "Don't screw us over, okay? I have to get up there," he said with a hint of distrust.

"I swore on Japan. What more do you want?" Atsushi glared at him.

"Sorry. I didn't mean it like that. It's getting too overstimulating in here. We gotta go." Bleu gave a tight smile and then turned. Taking Ayanna's hand, Bleu led her through the dancers toward the door.

Atsushi frowned. *Overstimulating?*

# Chapter 7

Peleguin-Rookery-By-The-Lake: Rana

    Rana jerked awake, wincing at the bright sunlight piercing the edges of her hut's door. *Ugh. Overslept again.*

From outside her ice hut came shouts and revelry. She glanced to her left. Her family's sleep spaces were tidied and empty, their furs folded against the walls. The bright sun sparkled like pastel jewels on the frozen concave walls, but its late morning beauty only filled her with a sense of failure. She was sixteen summers old, certainly old enough to get up in the pre-dawn like everyone else.

Shoving layers of furs aside, she stood to slip on her boots as Dala, her little brother, careened through the entrance of their small ice hut.

"Rana!" He panted. "Sohana is Crowned. She's Crowned!" He pranced from foot to foot, doing a little dance.

Rana's still sleepy eyes opened wide. "Sohana what?"

She shook her head, unable to comprehend this sudden manifestation of her worst fear. The odds were she'd never Crown, and being developmentally left behind when all her peers Crowned petrified her. You must have misheard. She's too young." She clasped her hands together to hide their trembling.

"No, seriously." He stopped his dance and stood up tall. "We were returning from the sunrise sit when Sohana's fathers began yelling. They said she went out for a walk and came back with the white hair of the Crowned." Dala gave her his imploring "I-know-I'm-younger-but-believe-me" look.

Rana took a step back and squinted at him. She rubbed her sweaty palms on her sleep clothes. This was bad. She would end up like Sunila, the one aged star being in their village who had never Crowned.

Almost every star being Crowned, transforming somewhere between their twentieth and fortieth summer. While the Crowning transformation itself often only took a few hours, by Rana's age they usually showed signs of the coming emergence.

Not her. She was way behind. She'd keep aging and would never master communicating without words or travel in her own star-shaped flash of light. Never. Because she had been born different. Her heart pounded furiously against her ribs as she studied Dala's face for signs that this was a joke.

"Seriously, she's Crowned." He panted cloudy puffs of breath as he danced about like a fawn. He had nothing to worry about—he had normal biological parents. She was adopted, and her birth parents were never meant to have offspring.

Rana sank back down onto her bed of furs. *Oh my Oneness! She's only three summers older than me, and I haven't displayed any signs. What if I never Crown?*

With trembling fingers, she reached up the ice wall beside her sleep mat and stroked the only decoration in the hut—the family door weaving from her birth parents' hut. Every family had a unique weaving that covered their entrance during the warmer seasons, and this weaving was all that remained of her parents. It hung on two carved sticks that she and Desna, her new mother, had knocked into the ice wall. The salt deer and a white lion lay together on a grass-green background and returned her stony stare.

"Have you seen her?" Rana nibbled the end of her amber braid and imagined Sohana with the newly whitened hair of a Crowned One, glittery and sparkly as snowflakes. She had never known any of the current Crowned Ones before they were Crowned. Star beings lived long lives and only reproduced when they needed to increase their numbers. They hadn't produced offspring for many summers before her cohort of friends had been born.

"No," Dala said, still leaping around the open hut. He danced well for his six summers, his wild brown hair swinging over his shoulders as he pranced around the floor. "Aren't you excited?" He held out his hand, inviting her to join his frolics. "This means Sohana goes to Mount Syeti. We all do!"

"I guess…" Ignoring his invitation to dance, Rana scowled at her own dull, amber braid and tossed it over her shoulder. This bad attitude was exactly why she would never Crown. Crowning required an enlightened mind.

Then Dala's earnest excitement overrode her moodiness. She jumped up. They would need the animals' help for such an extensive ceremony. "Maybe I can watch the Calling of the furred ones."

"Maybe," Dala teased, "but you should probably get dressed first." He waved his arm at her current state.

She glanced down at her rumpled sleep clothes and laughed. Her loose braids, knotted from the night's tossing, tumbled to her waist. He was right. She appeared nothing like the glorious Crowned Ones.

"Yeah, no one needs to see this mess."

The benefits of Sohana's Crowning dawned on her. "I bet our studies for today are cancelled," she said, grinning. The preparation for Sohana's celebratory ceremony would be extensive and maybe teach her more about Crowning.

He stopped dancing and shrugged. "Probably?"

"Mmm." Her eyes drifted close in dreamy anticipation of the new opportunities. An upcoming ceremony meant meeting other villagers and spending more time at the Lion's Circle.

Technically, she could always visit the ceremonial ring of humming boulders at the edge of the lake, but with an upcoming ceremony the circle would be fully activated by the Crowned Ones.

The Lion Circle's activated energy connected Rana to everything she cherished—the Web of Oneness, helping furred ones, and her parents. Her real parents, not Desna and Gandhapalin, whom she lived with now.

Spirits of the dead sometimes visited when Crowned Ones activated the circle. Her parents had only shown once and remained silent pillars, smiling at her. Perhaps, having never Crowned, they could do nothing except smile?

At the time, she'd asked Desna if her parents' lack of Crowning meant their spirits would never speak. Desna's words, meant to comfort her, still haunted her.

*"It's rare for star beings to not Crown. None of us had parents who didn't Crown, so none of us know how it will affect their spirits' behavior in the Lion Circle."*

*Or how it will affect me*, Rana had thought. Star beings never had kids unless they were Crowned. It was an unspoken expectation, based on the knowledge that Crowning gave them skills to be the best possible parents.

With two uncrowned parents, Rana was an anomaly.

"Rana?" Dala knew her too well. "You're doing it again," he teased.

Rana glowered at him. "I'm fine. I was thinking."

Of course, he was right. It irked her to no end when he detected her mental wanderings before she did. She knew the murmurs about her, that it was her parents' fault she struggled so much with focus and fidgeted at sunrise sit. Then again, sunrise sit was only a morning chanting session. Maybe she had different talents.

*Or I'm messed up and will never Crown.* A heaviness settled upon her shoulders.

Dala's small fingers grasped her own. "I like your hair the color it is."

She nodded, not trusting her voice.

"Everyone that's not Crowned is meeting now at the gathering hall." He released her fingers and stepped toward the door. "See you there?"

"Yeah." Would they all be discussing who would Crown next? Could she face that?

Dala disappeared under the swinging mat and then rushed back inside. "Oh, this morning, the peleguins started arriving at the rookery." He grinned. "You know what that means." He held up his hands like claws and imitated a lion's roar.

CHAPTER 7

"Oh." Excitement rippled through her.

He nodded and dove under the woven mat outlet.

Her heart soared in anticipation. Her village was named after the peleguins who returned every spring for nesting. The feathered ones themselves weren't exciting. But when the peleguins returned, the lions returned as well, following their favorite food. If the peleguins had flown back to their annual breeding ground, Sandor and Sinhika the Lion Masters were sure to return with their cubs.

Quickly, Rana folded her sleep furs. She had always loved the lions, but last time they visited her village she had bonded with Sukti, one of Sandor's three cubs. And since the lions taught the Crowned Ones, it made sense that Sandor and his mate Sinhika would soon arrive with their cubs for both peleguins and the ceremony.

Grabbing her clean clothing, Rana wondered how much Sukti would look the same since she's last seen her. Last summer, Sukti's white fur and mischievous blue eyes had held the camouflage advantage during their nonstop game of Hide and Sneak. One warm night, the two of them had gotten all the lions and almost the whole village playing in the dark.

With Sukti here, maybe she could face Sohana's Crowning and her own pending failure.

Rana turned to leave and paused before her adopted family's thick mat that blocked the elements from entering their hut. When she was younger, the lion and salt deer mat of her parents had protected her. Now, her new family's mat wafted in the morning breeze, its green tree with wildflowers marking it as the residence of Desna and Gandhapalin.

She glanced back at the lion and deer. They remained silent, as always. As silent as her parents had been when their spirits had appeared in the Lion Circle.

*On my own as usual.*

She threw on her cloak, grabbed her clean leather clothing, and pushed through the mat into the damp morning air.

Sprinting through well-trodden paths between huts, she nearly lost her footing several times. The early spring sunlight had warmed the air enough to cause a silvery mist to drift in from the lake. It slowly tumbled over the village huts until Rana could barely see the path before her. The only sign of other star beings came from the skittering of loosened rocks as Dala climbed the trail toward the Gathering Hall.

Her stomach rumbled. Steeling herself against the enticing scent of the morning meal, she continued toward the round cleansing hut. No steam surrounded it. The Crowned One who usually heated the water must've already left. That's what she got for oversleeping—an extra quick cleanse.

She drew a bucket of icy water and shook herself out of her dirty clothes. Wincing, she splashed the water over her body. *I really need to get up earlier.* She grasped a handful of wood shavings, rubbed them against her wet skin, and dropped them in the discard bucket.

The door crashed open, and her friend, Daman, stood in the entrance, grinning. "Slept through sunrise sit again, eh?" His round face lit with humor as he cocked an eyebrow at her.

Even though Daman was sixteen summers like she was, his round head, full cheeks, and upturned nose made him look much younger.

"Oh!" His round cheeks blushed. "Aren't you freezing?"

Rana attempted to nod her head, but her whole body trembled from the cold, and she burst into laughter at her predicament. Self-conscious at her shivering, she grabbed her clothing and quickly dressed.

"You heard about Sohana, right?" she asked.

"Yes. Didn't see that one coming." He paused. "Then again, she's so quiet, you never know what's going on with her..."

"Unlike Balavati, where the whole village knows." Rana chortled at her own joke.

"True." Daman turned and waved her toward the door. "Come on. We're missing all the fun!" He pushed the door open.

The mist, having overstretched its tendrils, had retreated from the united forces of sunlight and a light breeze. How long had she been fiddling, mentally unfocused, in the cleansing hut? A shiver passed down her spine; she wasn't close to being Crowning material.

"Where is she? I mean, Balavati," Rana asked, smoothing back her long braids as she exited the cleansing house.

"Somehow, she got her mom's permission to go to Sohana's hut. It's weird. We have all these Crowned Ones around us, but they've always been Crowned, and now, Sohana's one of them."

Rana agreed. Lately, Daman, Balavati, and she shared thoughts a lot. Sometimes, words became redundant. Mind talk often became stronger at her age, so maybe she was on schedule with something.

They strode around huts and up the narrow, rocky path toward the gathering hall. "Do you expect Balavati will become as quiet as the other Crowned Ones after she's Crowned?" Rana frowned as she imagined her friend changing that dramatically.

Daman slowed and turned toward her. "You worry too much." Then he shrugged. "But a quiet Balavati would take some getting used to."

"Oh!" Rana stopped walking, suddenly perplexed. "How does the food part work? I mean, did Sohana know her last meal would be her last regular meal?" Crowned Ones, while all around them, were still mysterious. Rana couldn't imagine ever getting to the point where she didn't need to eat regularly.

"You and food," Daman scoffed.

They continued in silence toward the gathering hall, which stood on a small rise above the settlement. Like the rest of Peleguin-Rookery-By-The-Lake, the gathering hall consisted of ice blocks for the majority of the year. During the short, warm summers, the ice blocks were replaced with blocks of earth or skin tents. This allowed the star beings greater mobility, as Peleguin-Rookery-By-The-Lake never stayed in one place. It rotated around the peleguin breeding ground, sometimes being a day's walk from its current site. Star being villages were placed far apart to respect the needs of the furred, feathered, and finned ones.

This morning, a restrained thrill hovered over the village. The circling hawks quivered their wings in the rising excitement as if they too were conscious of the Crowning. Was she the only one who had slept through it?

They continued on, the only sound the crunching of their boots on the packed snow. The closer they got to her friends, the more panicked she became of her uncrowned parentage. For her friends, this would be the first of many Crowning celebrations to come. To her, Sohana's Crowning meant her peers were about to start transforming into something she likely would never become.

Carefree Daman sped toward the gathering hall, and Rana, with a sigh, matched his pace. Reaching it first, he lifted the entrance mat marked with a green circle, and savory scents wafted out. Despite her hunger, Rana stalled until Daman excitedly yanked her through the door.

To the right, fires glowed and stews bubbled in the big pots. The star beings on duty stirred, chopped, and retrieved supplies from the large stores of dried fruits, vegetables, and dried meat.

Ignoring the gurgles in her stomach, Rana turned left and scanned the crowd of young star beings. Kahali, Sohana's younger brother, flashed Rana a full grin and waved them over.

"Kahali, why are you here?" Daman asked as he slid onto the mat next to their friend.

"What do you mean? Where should I be?" Kahali's dark eyes twinkled. His high cheekbones and thick, perfectly tied-back hair made a sharp contrast to the relaxed grin that played across his face.

Rana elbowed him. "Come on, admit it, you should be home." Was he jealous of his sister, Sohana? What would Rana do when Dala Crowned and she didn't?

"Oh, you mean the Crowning that happened while some of us were still asleep?" He gave Rana an impish, knowing look. "Well, *someone* in my family still has to eat."

Laughter erupted around them.

"I see." She motioned good-humoredly at his loaded plate and sat beside him on the mat. "You're really okay with it?"

"Of course. Now I get first dibs on all the food."

"Right, you get it all." Rana laughed, yet it rang hollow.

How could he stand it? He alone in his family had not yet Crowned. His fathers and Sohana could now star travel together and had little need of food. Didn't he feel left out?

She glanced sideways at him, and he put his hand on hers. "I know what you're thinking…" His voice was low, meant for her only. "You'll probably Crown before me."

She snorted her disagreement.

Grinning, he motioned with his hands toward her. "Rana, the first snorting Crowned One."

She chuckled despite herself, but her appetite had disappeared. The food on her plate proved her ineptitude. She would remain uncrowned and needful of food forever. No, she would never Crown—like her parents who had broken the rules to have her.

# Chapter 8

*eleguin-Rookery-By-The-Lake: Rana*

P The next morning, nightmares of being the last Uncrowned star being woke Rana before dawn. Early enough to make it to sunrise sit and complete most of the morning chants. Maybe she *could* do this enlightenment thing.

At breakfast with Balavati, she drank the horrible tea tonic that supposedly helped awaken one's awareness.

"Ugh. This is"—Rana scraped her tongue against her teeth to rid herself of the taste—"nasty."

"Warned you." Balavati giggled and handed her the bowl of berries. "Any great insights?"

"Only that I never want that disgusting brew again." Rana shoved a handful of berries into her mouth.

"Sohana has it three times a day," Balavati quipped, tucking her long, dark curls behind her ear.

"Oh my Oneness." Rana held her hand to her stomach, willing the tea to stay down.

"I'm joking," Balavati said, shaking with laughter. "You should see your face."

Rana glared at her. "Not nice."

Balavati's dark eyes sparkled with humor as she stood. "Come on. Next activity—the Welcoming Ceremony. This is much better than classes."

They left the hall and joined the excited villagers walking toward the Lion Circle. By the time they came within sight of the Circle, everyone

66

had sorted themselves out into families.

Rana couldn't resist grinning at the stone ring surrounded by tundra. The snow season was nearly over, yet even during blizzards, snow and ice never built up in the Lion's Circle. The intense energy inside created its own warmth.

As she approached this area, the fine golden hairs on her arms rose. Then began the familiar stirring of energy emanating in a steady pulse; first, it was on her arms, then as a gentle warmth pulsing in her tailbone. Her whole body smiled and woke up.

Rana turned toward her adopted mother, Desna.

"Maha?" It had taken years for Rana to be comfortable using the traditional title for mother with Desna. "Why don't we do the welcoming ceremony with the other villages?"

"Why come if there's no feast?" Kahali ran up from behind them, laughing, and threw his arm around Rana's shoulders. He pulled her closer and whispered, "I hear there's dancing..." His warm breath tickled her neck.

She laughed and pretended to adjust her cloak. All she needed was Maha to notice her blushing.

"The world does not revolve around your stomach, Kahali." Desna chuckled, her warm brown eyes sparkling with humor. And maybe, with noticing Rana's blush. "To answer your question, Rana, the welcoming ceremony is immediate, the next sunrise. It's more intimate—only for the village of the newly Crowned. And there is dancing." The ends of her lips twitched upward momentarily. "The neighboring villages participate in the Spiraling Ceremony at Mount Syeti. It requires a lot of preparation and travel time, so it occurs seven suns after the Crowning."

"Hmm." Rana took in this information as Kahali danced over to her little brother. He really could move. "So..."—she arched an eyebrow at Kahali—"there will be lots of others for Kahali to dance with at Mount Syeti?"

Desna nodded.

Kahali froze mid-step. "I don't want to dance with others." He gave Rana a pointed look, grinned, and then picked up her little brother and twirled him around. "Only with Dala."

Rana snorted. "Then it's a good thing I'll be able to find others to dance with."

Desna raised her eyebrows at them and continued. "We'll have two suns to prepare, though Sohana leaves today after the welcoming ceremony." Desna chuckled at the swirling boys. "Careful, Kahali, he's going to fall."

Kahali spun Dala to a stop and then whirled himself toward Rana, bowed, and held out an arm.

"Not now, Kahali." Rana crossed her arms with exaggerated sternness. "I wouldn't want to make Dala jealous." She winked at her little brother.

Kahali smirked and then wove his way, still dancing, into the crowd. Dala sprinted after him and Desna followed in their wake. As Kahali lost himself in the group, her feet almost followed him of their own accord. When had her admiration of his humor changed into…whatever this was?

She sucked in a long breath of air and exhaled slowly, willing her heart to slow. *Forget Kahali. Research Crowning.*

The sky was a brilliant hue of blue, though some storm clouds gathered over the far side of the lake. Maybe the bright sun signified the warming season would start early this year? She tugged her warm cape away from her neck and joined the mass of milling bodies around the circle. They waited for Sohana and the Luminaries, the chief male and female star beings who revealed the silent discussions of the Crowned Ones to the villagers not yet adept at mind talk. When the Luminaries arrived, the ceremony would begin.

Two drums began pounding out a complicated rhythm that vibrated deep in Rana's belly and stirred her every cell to dance. No one could resist such a temptation to move. Star beings swayed around the circle and chanted traditional songs to gather energy.

Rana lost all track of who danced next to her. They became one in body and voice. The drums wove through the rhythmic chanting, creating a common heartbeat.

A warm moistness nudged Rana's hand. Startled, she opened her eyes.

A lioness' warm, white muzzle nuzzled her palm. Rana stopped dancing, confused by the nearly full-grown lioness.

"Sukti?" Was this her cute lion cub friend who had left with her family last fall?

The lioness' cobalt eyes stared into Rana's. Time stopped. The crowd's singing faded to nothing. Star beings twisted around the two of them like a wild river passing two islands. All that existed was Rana's own breathing and Sukti's intensely fierce eyes.

Pictures began tumbling before Rana. Ice cascaded down on top of her. Huge frozen blocks fell onto her head and shoulders. She was smashed to the ground. Her chest was shoved onto the floor, knocking the breath out of her. Gasping, she reached for open space, but the weight of the collapsed ice pinned her down. She was being buried alive. Sukti roared, Rana screamed in terror, and…a man called her name.

A hand grasped her shoulder, and the voice of Gandhapalin, her adopted father, pulled her to safety.

"Rana…Rana…"

Rana's heart beat frantically as her lungs screamed for air. And then, the ice turned blue…the cobalt blue of the lioness' eyes. Rana gradually tore her gaze away from Sukti's and stood blinking, taking shallow breaths. The young lioness affectionately rubbed the full length of her body against Rana's hip and then turned to rejoin her two siblings. Rana remained surrounded by star beings, but hadn't she just died? She listened to her own erratic breath. Breath meant she was alive…

"Rana, are you okay? Sukti said she had a message for you," Gandhapalin said.

His gray eyes, silver beard, and white braids blended before her teary eyes until he was a gray-white smudge. She blinked, trying to see him clearly. His look of concern was a blanket covering her in safety again. She sucked in another ragged breath.

"What happened? Did she gift you with a vision?" he asked, putting an arm around her.

"I was dying…" It came out a strangled whisper.

"Nonsense, child. The lion masters and their offspring bring only love. Their visions are powerful gifts meant to guide us. You must've misinterpreted it." His lean face glanced at Sukti as her white tail disappeared in the crowd. "What exactly did she say?"

"One moment I was looking into her eyes, and the next I was having a vision. I was dying, crushed by falling ice. And then a voice…yours… called me. I'm going to die, because I shouldn't have been born." Tears stung her eyes.

"Nonsense." He rubbed her arm in comfort. "While the conditions of your coming to this world were not the norm, your birth was as much a kiss of the Divine as any other baby's arrival. Your parents brought you here out of love."

Rana's heart drank up his words of comfort. The warmth of his love mixed with the burning pain that he, not her real father, was offering it. She missed her father so much, needed him. She wiped her tears and offered Gandhapalin a weak smile.

He studied her knowingly. That's how it always was with the Crowned Ones. They knew every thought. It was awkward yet also kind of comforting. After all, he hadn't run away in horror of her inner emotional chaos, had he?

"Thank you," she mumbled, then turned and vanished into the intoning crowd.

Instinctively, she wove through the throng until she reached Balavati's side. Her friend's curly black hair bounced as she danced, mouth open wide in song, eyes sparkling. As soon as she noticed Rana, Balavati's dark eyes quickly shifted to puzzlement.

"What's wrong?" Balavati stopped dancing and stood still within the jostling throng.

"I…I ju— just saw…Sukti."

She was disoriented and numb to the humming energy of celebration around her. How much longer did she have to live? She glanced upward for dangerous, overhanging ice.

"Rana…" Balavati pulled her to the crowd's outer rim. She picked up a piece of ice and squeezed Rana's fingers around it. "Feel the ice melting," she coaxed.

Rana's gaze dropped to her wet fingers, and she smiled weakly. This had been their game since childhood, created when they were mere girls. Samasti, their tutor, had taught that when emotions threatened to overwhelm, they should remind themselves of their own inner power and connection to all things. Students identified their main problem emotion and found a tool to center themselves when overwhelmed. As always, Rana and Balavati had been partners.

*Balavati had blurted out, "Rana's always angry at something."*

*Rana blushed, while Samasti nodded in agreement and then kindly informed Balavati that she herself was always impatient and blurting things out. Daman and Kahali had laughed at that for days.*

*Their assignment was to each find a way to center their minds quickly, something that would work in any situation. After a lot of failures, Rana said, "This is infuriating. The only thing we always have around us is ourselves and ice."*

*Balavati's dark eyes lit up, and thus, their tool was born—the holding and melting of ice. They used their body heat to melt it and observed how their presence affected the ice.*

After all these years, it still worked: Rana observed the ice melt, swallowed, and attempted words. Her tongue was dry and lumpish.

"Sukti... She had a message for me..." She croaked out the premonition.

Balavati listened wide-eyed but didn't appear appropriately disturbed.

"Can't you understand?" Rana implored her. "I'm going to die."

"You can't die, Rana." Balavati smiled and pulled Rana back into the crowd.

"Where are—?"

"We're going to Sukti. She'll explain. You're her favorite." Balavati refused to release her grip on Rana's arm.

"We can't interrupt the ceremony," Rana whispered. One of Balavati's troublesome schemes was in the works.

The group was now quietly chanting and swaying as the Luminaries and lions entered the Circle.

"She'll notice us, realize you're upset, and come over, right?" Balavati whispered as she continued to gracefully weave through the undulating crowd.

Rana followed, unsure. Her feet were heavy, and Balavati pulled so hard she almost fell headfirst.

As they neared the center of the press, Rana spotted the great masters, the adult lions who had agreed to carry on the Lion Master Lineage, the teaching of universal wisdom to all beings. Lion Master Sandor sat erect, his proud, fair muzzle directed toward the center of the circle. Waves of magnetic push-pull energy rolled from him, causing the whole crowd to rock back and forth in unison. Lion Master Sinhika, his mate, stood glowing in the center of the circle with a star being that must be Sohana, though she was unrecognizable from this angle.

As they approached the great masters, Rana paused, seriously doubting Balavati's plan. Sukti sat alert next to her siblings, her ears twitching. As much as Sukti and the other young lions had grown, they were dwarfed by their father, Lion Master Sandor.

Rana gasped as the star being turned, and she glimpsed her newly-Crowned friend. Sohana was radiant. Her glowing oval face and fine features were draped by long, ivory-white locks. Her skin, brown like Kahali's, appeared lit up by an internal golden glow. And her eyes—love flowed from them so strongly that Rana was lost in the splendor.

Her heart fluttered at the magical and terrifying change in her friend. How could such a thing happen overnight?

As Rana stared, Lion Master Sinhika approached Sohana. The crowd grew still and quiet, barely chanting. Sohana knelt as Sinhika circled her three times. Each time, as she came back to Sohana's front, the lioness licked the girl's brow as if she was cleansing the forehead of a small cub.

After the third pass, Sohana raised her hands to the sky, saying, "For the One In All!" She bowed to the Earth, saying a phrase Rana couldn't hear.

Balavati grinned back at Rana, who gaped, wide-mouthed, at Sohana's transformation. This was supposed to happen to all her friends? She grasped Balavati's arm for balance as a wave of lightheadedness washed over her.

The Luminaries, Samasti and Vadin, approached from the western and eastern edges of the circle. Samasti graciously gathered up Sohana's long white hair and began the traditional braid that the Crowned Ones wore. After Sohana returned from Mount Syeti, it would be wound into a spiral. As Samasti stepped back, Vadin moved in front of Sohana and handed her a long, spiral horn from the venerable narwhal. It stood as tall as Sohana's brow and would now be her ceremonial walking stick.

"May you always love to serve and serve to Love," Vadin recited.

Sohana again raised both palms, singing, "For the One In All!"

Without releasing her horn, she touched both palms to the Earth. She exited the southern edge of the Lion Circle to begin her private journey to Mount Syeti.

The crowd erupted in joyous cheers. Balavati grabbed Rana's sweaty palm and pulled her toward the great masters. The closer they got to the clearing with the masters, the more Rana's body tensed. Balavati's plan was a bad idea. She attempted to wriggle her hand free of Balavati's grasp, but her small, lithe friend had remarkable strength. And stubbornness. She was going to get them in serious trouble.

Balavati burst into the clearing with such force that the lions twisted toward her with a speed and grace only felines could attain. Caught in the lion masters' stare, the self-confident Balavati deflated. She glanced back at Rana, who fought the urge to disappear into the crowd. Balavati's usually large eyes were now huge, pleading with Rana for help.

Despite her racing heart, Rana smiled and shook her head at her friend. Balavati's impulsivity always created messes that Rana had to clean up.

"Excuse us, Your Grace, but we were in a hurry to see our friends," Rana said as she motioned with her chin toward Sukti and her siblings, "before you left. I'm sorry if we're a bit excited."

Rana smiled at Master Sandor with an expression she hoped was appropriate. A trickle of sweat rolled down her neck and back as she met his gaze.

Master Sandor's ice-blue eyes burned into her with a searching intensity. She felt naked in such a gaze. Rana sensed his mind meeting hers, observing her panic after Sukti's message, her desperate confusion, and her current false, calm front. Her gaze fell to his huge massive paws, each larger than her own head. She was puny and afraid not of him, but of her future.

*Let go of your fear, young one. You are here for Love,* Sandor mind spoke to her. He swiftly contracted his chest, creating a sudden powerful exhalation. "Harrrr." Turning, he exited the Lion Circle, his pride of lions following him.

Rana pondered the message. Yes, she lived to give and receive Love, but if Sukti's vision was correct, how much longer did she have?

# Chapter 9

Outside *Peleguin-Rookery-By-The-Lake: Rana*

Preparations for the journey to Mount Syeti were more challenging than Rana had expected. Mindful of Sukti's vision, she completed each task as far from overhanging ice as possible. No reason to tempt fate.

Today, as part of the preparations, she and Daman were meeting a sea bear. A real, fully grown, male sea bear. After they assisted with this final feat, they'd travel with the rest of their village to Mt. Syeti.

They lifted the final basket onto the wooden sled carrier, tied it on with the leather straps, and awaited the fearsome creature. Rana attempted to copy Daman's nonchalance. After all, if she was to die from falling ice, the sea bear couldn't be a problem, right?

"Which way do you think he'll come?" Rana scanned the distant fir trees for movement. She turned, and her gaze swept the rolling ice plains dipping to the sea.

Daman shrugged, his round face careless. "We'll know soon enough." He tossed a rock. It splashed in slush. The spring softening had arrived.

"Can you believe Desna thinks communicating with furred ones might be my special capability?" Rana grinned and played with the end of her braid. "She explained the process yesterday, but I can't imagine how it works."

"Most of what the Crowned Ones do seems impossible. They're like butterflies to us caterpillars." He chuckled, making his cheeks round like peleguin eggs.

The horizon glowed with the first light. Could sea bears understand time of day? Her stomach rumbled.

*Smoosch, Smoosch, Smoosch.* The sound drifted down from the hill-top—heavy paws flattening the slush. Rana rose on her toes and searched for the giant yellow pelt amidst the sparse evergreens. The sound grew closer. She stepped nearer to Daman as her heart thudded in her chest.

Malakut the Sea Bear's head and shoulders appeared over the crest of the dirty gray hill. Desna had said it would be Malakut. The closer he got, the larger he grew. He stopped a stone's throw away, and his small black eyes examined them. He tossed his massive head, bared his finger-length teeth, and blasted them with a long guttural rumble.

"Where's Desna?" Daman whispered.

Trembling, Rana whispered back, "Hopefully about to appear." She was supposed to observe, not tether him alone. She and Daman stumbled backward. Malakut continued to jut his massive blood-stained jowls toward them.

A burst of brilliant star-shaped light shone in front of Malakut. The light vanished, replaced by Desna. Every time Crowned Ones appeared in a radiant blast, a thrill shot through Rana's spine.

Malakut stopped his challenge. He stood his ground but pulled his head back and glared.

"Everything is ready?" Desna nodded toward the carrier.

"Yes, Maha." Rana squinted as the bright rising sun framed Malakut's muscled shoulders. Even Lion Master Sandor would be small next to him. She shivered. Few stood this close to a sea bear and lived.

"You two move toward that ridge while I do the tethering," Desna said over her shoulder while keeping her body centered toward the massive beast.

Tethering a sea bear demanded a Crowned One's full concentration—the capability to communicate with furred ones while maintaining an extreme level of awareness of their surroundings.

Daman and Rana backed away as Malakut ambled down the hill. He circled the carrier, snorting as he sniffed the cargo.

All the Crowned Ones communicated with nature, yet Desna excelled at furred ones. Yesterday, she had entered the Lion Circle and Called for a furred one to be tethered. Malakut had answered and entered the sacred Lion's Circle, agreeing to pull supplies to Mt. Syeti.

Now, Desna pushed back her hood and smiled at Malakut. She had been older when she had Crowned, and small lines crinkled around her sparkling eyes as she faced the sea bear. She hefted her walking horn and drew a circle in the snow around Malakut, the carrier, and herself. This action acknowledged their prior agreement at the Lion Circle. Outside this agreement, their meeting might not be peaceful. After all, sea bears must eat, even if Crowned Ones don't.

Malakut eyed the snow circle and then lowered his head and shoulders, bowing toward the circle, not toward the Crowned One. Desna bowed toward the circle, facing Malakut.

Desna stood extremely close to the huge creature. One swipe of his massive paw could instantly kill. Rana held her breath. *Relax, she's a Crowned One.* She exhaled.

The great sea bear snorted as Desna approached and gently lifted the heavy harness. Malakut thrust his massive head and shoulders into the openings, and without a backward glance loped toward Mt. Syeti.

Rana, legs trembling, sat down on a rock.

Daman whistled a long single note and plopped beside her. "Impressive."

"I hope she doesn't expect me to do that anytime soon." Then Rana realized Sukti's vision meant she may not live long enough to do a tethering.

Daman chuckled. "Yeah, that's a bit dangerous for my taste. I'm glad Desna didn't notice *me* showing talent with furred ones. Next time, talk to the narwhals when no one is around."

"We weren't mind talking. I don't know why she thinks I was communicating with them. I was just talking out loud, and they seemed to like it."

They dropped the conversation and rose as Desna joined them. Desna glanced at their expressions and laughed. "It's not as hard as it looks."

"For you, maybe," Daman replied.

"Maha? Has a furred one ever attacked after entering the Lion Circle?"

Desna smiled, eyes twinkling. "No. Malakut always resists tethering. It's his way." She turned toward the small lumbering dot in the distance. "But when we Call, he always comes."

"Won't he get to Mt. Syeti before us?" Daman, rarely a worrier, furrowed his brow.

Rana pictured the possibility—Malakut arriving early and ripping the harness off in a single swipe. Their supplies would be ruined.

"While we all travel for the Spiral Ceremony, we come from different distances. The villages on the far side of Lake Missal will be there by moonrise tonight, and they'll untether him. Let's go. They'll be waiting for us."

*  *  *

The hike home with Daman and Desna was silent except for Rana's stomach protesting its late breakfast. The others' silence encouraged her souring mood to grow. She wanted to be excited for Sohana's Crowning, but a small, vocal portion of her mind was jealous. All this preparation for today's journey to Mount Syeti reminded her of how far she herself was from Crowning.

*The enlightened are not pulsating with jealousy,* she reminded herself. To drown out her negative thoughts, she focused on matching her breath to her steps. Three steps to an inbreath, three steps to an outbreath.

As they neared home, excited voices carried across the frozen field. Everyone had congregated near the Nest, a large boulder near the village's entrance that received its name from its resemblance to an oversized peleguin nest.

Someone belted out a rousing song, and soon, everyone had joined in. Their mood was infectious, making Rana smile. Leave it to her village to turn the journey itself into a celebration.

Balavati burst from the crowd and ran to them. "Falling stars! Isn't this exciting?" She beamed at Desna, then at her friends. "You saw the tethering?"

Rana nodded, smiling at her bouncing friend. Balavati's long spiraled hair pulsed around her face in a mesmerizing rhythm.

"Dala should have both your stuff ready." Desna nodded toward where Dala sat with his father, Gandhapalin, and two extra packs. "And, Rana?"

She stopped and turned. "Yes, Maha?"

Desna glanced at her yowling stomach. "Breakfast's in the pack."

As the crowd moved across the ice, the early sun bathed everything in gold. Samasti and Vadin, the Luminaries, led the singing caravan south, the long way around Lake Missal.

"Why not north?" Rana asked Desna as she riffled through her pack.

"The northern route is shorter, but this crowd would arouse the cave diggers. Since they never come to the Lion's Circle, it's best to avoid them."

Rana nodded. There was too much to learn, and while most star beings had centuries, she might only have days. She shuddered and pulled her long tawny braid around her shoulder for easy fiddling access. When she was young, her mother had brushed and braided her hair every day. Fiddling with her braid somehow kept those morning braiding sessions alive.

Progressing away from the village, the Crowned Ones encircled the others, both joyous and protective. Rana and her family walked. The very young rode on sturdy salt deer, which had begun their seasonal shedding. White tuffs of fur floated off them and tickled Rana's nose.

She wished she was still allowed to ride. Salt deer allowed riders in exchange for the salty seaweed the star beings harvested along the coast, but she was old enough now to walk and wouldn't take advantage of the helpful furred ones.

The journey progressed without mishaps. They sang continuously and stopped only for meals and sleep. At night, the Crowned Ones constructed simple ice block huts to block the gusty wind.

Rana had only one gnawing concern: Sukti's vision. As a result, she remained in the open, away from any cliffs or overhangs. Desna agreed with this safety precaution, while Gandhapalin told her she had misinterpreted Sukti's message.

When Rana shared her worries with Balavati, she said, "Stop worrying, Rana. You're not going to die. You're my best friend."

It was a dubious guarantee.

Two uneventful days later, they reached the base of towering Mt. Syeti. Its indigo summit disappeared behind the cold mist. Somewhere up there, in a sacred cave, Sohana had started her ceremony: she now fasted and meditated for her vision.

Scanning the mountain's many crags, resentment twisted in Rana's gut. She might not live long enough to Crown and have her own Crowning Spiral Ceremony. *Better enjoy this one.*

Laughter and cheering interrupted her brooding. She followed the arms pointing high above to where Crowned Ones had painted a humorous picture with their energy—a blue sea bear chased dancing peleguins. The peleguins flapped their wings but couldn't rise fast enough to avoid the colorful bears.

"They're sky painting!" Balavati jumped, arms raised, as if to save the peleguins from the painted bears.

Rana knew what sky painting was; she had watched the Crowned Ones practice the art form her whole life. She simply hadn't expected it to suddenly appear overhead. She marveled at the incredible focus it must take to project one's mental energy into the moving, bright displays. Another skill she wouldn't have time to master.

The entire caravan stopped, and all necks craned at the wonders above. The salt deer pranced in excitement. Every time the painted bear appeared to swing its massive paws through a peleguin likeness, it reappeared as two more peleguins.

"Whooo!" Balavati squealed and danced in circles, her arms flung skyward.

"That's amazing." Rana stood wide-eyed.

"No, that's the best two sky painters having fun." Gandhapalin grinned like a little child and hurried past Rana and her friends toward the gathered villagers.

The neighboring villagers stood outside ice huts, enjoying the camaraderie. More Crowned Ones lined up to sky paint humorous scenes in the darkening sky.

Rana greeted old friends and then observed Desna and Gandhapalin skillfully move blocks of ice into the shape of a small hut. Gandhapalin used his Crowned One abilities to slice blocks of ice, and Desna directed them with her mind into the proper shape. Rana pulled the thickly woven mat from her pack, and Desna attached it as a door. All around her, ice homes rose into being. Plants grew during the growing season; ice huts grew during the cold season.

That evening, Rana and Balavati sang and danced under the brightly painted sky. Daman joined the fervent drummers.

Kahali seemed to be everywhere, doing everything, but he kept returning to dance with her. His feet moved like lightning, keeping up with even the most rapid and complicated drum rhythms. Rana was a good dancer, but this tempo was impossible. After she had tripped for the second time, and for the second time had been caught by Kahali, she began to suspect he had requested Daman and the other drummers to accelerate to this ridiculous speed.

Not that she minded. Everyone was laughing and tripping up. And Kahali's arms were quite pleasant. He danced only with her but never closer than necessary. Surely if he was only spending time with her it meant something. *At the next song, I'll...*

But what if she leaped the chasm between their friendship and the possibility of something more and she had misread everything. Kahali wasn't exactly shy, so wouldn't he be clearer if he liked her? As the song ended in a flurry of footwork, she hugged him, laughing. The exhausted drummers began to pack up their drums to leave.

"Given how early the ceremony is tomorrow, and how horrible you are at waking up, perhaps we should call it a night?" Still holding her, he gave a soft laugh into her hair.

"Regretfully, I agree." With a wistful sigh, she stepped back. "You were wonderful to dance with, as always, even though the drummers were a bit wild." She shot him an accusatory grin.

He chuckled, his dark eyes sparkling. "Yes, they were, weren't they? Whatever was Daman thinking?" He flashed her a grin, bowed, and then turned and left.

*That was a quick exit.* With a grunt, she turned and wove through the dispersing crowd to her family's makeshift hut. Despite her excitement over Kahali's possible flirting, when she finally reached her sleeping furs, she collapsed in exhaustion.

\* \* \*

It seemed only moments later that Desna shook her awake.

"Rana, it's time."

"I wish we could at least wait until the sun is up." Rana yawned.

Beyond the door flap, her brother pranced in the darkness. How could they all wake up so easily and be cheerful about it?

Groaning, she forced herself to rise, braid her hair, and visit the cleansing hut. The temporary setup allowed chilly drafts in that gave her goose bumps. She cleansed and dressed, stomach growling. There would be no food until after the ceremony. Cold, hungry, and wishing for more sleep, Rana searched out her family.

They merged with families from all five local villages on the plain beneath Mt. Syeti. Today, the Crowning Spiral Ceremony would replace their usual sunrise sit. Like a flock of birds turning as one, the large crowd silently formed a massive spiral of seated bodies. Each individual turned toward the center.

In the spiral center sat Kalakanya, facing the peak of Mt. Syeti. Kalakanya, known as the Daughter of Time, hailed from Rana's village and somewhat creeped her out. *Should have guessed she'd lead.*

Kalakanya had never aged physically past the age of seventeen, an exceptionally young age of Crowning. She was now over twenty summers and possessed powers no star being had ever possessed before.

All Crowned Ones had some precognition, or pre-knowing of events yet to occur, but Kalakanya alone could read the strands of time like a book: past, present, and future. Rana had once seen Kalakanya stare at a woman in her village for a few moments and then tell the woman about her past lives and suggest the best course of action in a specific current situation. Usually, she didn't share what she saw, but that day Rana had witnessed Kalakanya's incredible power.

For Rana, that was the creepy part, knowing Kalakanya knew more about Rana than she knew about herself. Instead of mentally preparing herself for the ceremony, Rana wondered if Kalakanya had already seen her failure at Crowning.

A drum resounded, and Rana joined the others in a rhythmic, monotone chant. It invoked the ecstasy of connection to the One In All. As the chanting continued, sections of star beings broke off and chanted the same chant at a different pace and accent. Rana knew no one directed this, and she marveled at the evolving rhythmic intricacies. This experience far surpassed the meditations of sunrise sit. Was it the ceremony, or the larger group of star beings joined as one, that made it wildly powerful?

While she sat in stillness, her spirit danced higher and higher. Now, the different groups took on different tones that resonated off the mountain. Was the mountain chanting, too? Periodically, she'd lose concentration and fall back into her body, stealing a glance toward the mountain. Sohana, waiting on its peak, would receive her message for the community soon.

The sun rose and set in the sky, and everyone continued chanting tirelessly. Everyone except Rana. Were any others struggling like she now was? Her nose twitched, her eyes opened and wandered, mouth silently yawning, her legs completely numb. Normally, she'd be angry at herself, but immersed in the ceremony's energy, she found herself filled with only amusement at her mind's and body's fiddling. Even so, as the day wore on, her muscles cramped, and her mind became as numb as her legs. When she couldn't hold still another moment, the words she'd been waiting for all day came.

"She comes." Kalakanya's whispered words carried across the plain to all.

As one, the whole spiral stopped chanting and rose to standing. Rana wobbled upward on her stiff legs and strained to see Sohana's descent. Unfortunately, Rana was positioned too far out in the spiral's arm. She could spot Kalakanya, but she couldn't see where Sohana must be climbing down the mountain.

A wave of shifting star beings led her gaze as Sohana stepped between them. When she reached the spiral's center, Kalakanya yielded the center position to her.

Sohana entered, gazed out at the gathered star beings, and closed her eyes. Stillness descended like a blanket. Time passed. Rana leaned toward the spiral center. *Why isn't Sohana sharing her message?*

Kalakanya touched Sohana's shoulder and nodded encouragingly. Sohana opened her eyes and only stared at her. All around Rana, star beings shifted to see what kept Sohana quiet. Even though this was Rana's first Spiral Ceremony, something seemed wrong.

Kalakanya nodded to Sohana again.

Sohana cleared her throat and spoke, her shaky voice magnified by the mountain's echo. "The One In All has granted us a great undertaking. The Earth's children, after a long sleep in her womb, are returning to the planet's surface. They are young and volatile. We must Call them and provide assistance, or they will perish." She paused to breathe deeply. "There's more...If the three blues meet, and we do not act wisely, all life as we know it will perish. We are given this warning so that we may protect the Web of Life." Her intense gaze swept out the entire spiral as she clasped her hands in front of her heart and bowed.

Kalakanya blanched. "Your message is highly unusual."

Sohana nodded. "Yes, the three blues are exceedingly dangerous. If the Earth's children do not answer our Call, and the three blues meet, extinction will threaten all of us."

# Chapter 10

*The base of Mount Syeti: Rana*

Rana held her breath, waiting for the reassuring part of Sohana's message. Silence loomed over the spiral, broken by a hawk's scream and the clambering of some small creature over the rocky field behind her.

*Messages aren't supposed to be ominous, right?* Rana glanced at Desna. Her maha's furrowed gaze remained locked on Sohana.

Everyone sat back down except the ten Luminaries, the male and female leaders from each village. They appeared to be mind talking to each other and Kalakanya.

Kalakanya nodded and then said, "Thank you, Sohana, for your message given in love from the One In All. Let us adjourn for our feast, and then the Crowned Ones will meet. This"—Kalakanya paused to draw in a deep breath—"this message of the three blues is not new to me, but its meaning strangely eludes me. We will stay another day to formulate our plan."

The villagers soundlessly exited the spiral and then burst into excited murmurs. Rana searched the crowd for her friends, hoping Kahali might have more insight into his sister's message. Despite her efforts, she ended up wandering around alone, lightheaded from the day's fasting.

The crowd thinned as many drifted into the task of feast preparation. Fires were lit, and Rana's stomach rumbled as foods began to sizzle around her. She wandered among the strangers, jealously watching children convince cooks to give them early treats.

As a cluster of villagers parted, Daman, Balavati, and Kahali appeared.

85

"Here!" Rana waved and ran to them.

"Where have you been?" Balavati threw her arms around Rana in a bear hug as the guys motioned for them to follow.

"Come on, or we'll lose them." Rana pulled Balavati after the other two. "What's the plan?" she called to them.

But Daman and Kahali had already woven through the crowd, away from feast preparations. Rana had lost them.

Kahali reappeared, flashed a worried smile, and reached for her hand. "I need to get out of here, okay? I can't deal with anyone else asking me what she meant."

Rana took his hand even though her gut twanged with guilt. They should help with the feast preparations instead of walking away from the fire pits. Skirting the crowd, the four of them settled onto supply packs near the resting salt deer.

"Leave it to my sister to be the messenger of doom," Kahali joked, his voice strained.

"Who are the Earth's children?" Rana asked, perching next to him.

He shrugged.

"If it's dangerous…" Balavati looked away, twisting her fingers through her long ringlets. "I mean, I want to help, but…"

"The Crowned Ones will figure it out." Daman glanced toward the crowd.

Rana shivered in the rising wind and pulled her hooded cape tighter. She huddled closer to Kahali on the packs. The sky began to unleash its snowy minions. No one spoke.

Then, Kahali chuckled to himself.

"Are you going to share?" Daman prompted as he brushed snow off his legs.

"Maybe we can skip the cold cleanses now? Or have only two cold people in there at a time, so we don't have three blue ones together. That way, the world doesn't end." Kahali's grin looked sickly beneath his furrowed brow.

All Rana could do was shrug. When Kahali lost his ability to joke, things were bad.

"Blue is a pretty uncommon color," Rana said, frowning. *Why was the three blues part elusive to Kalakanya? She reads the meaning in everything.* "There's blue eyes, blue ice…"

"Blue sea bears last night," Daman added.

"The sky's blue sometimes," Balavati whispered as her eyelashes blinked away snowflakes.

"Okay, stop. As brother to the Prophetess of Doom, I insist we stop this. Let's go eat and stuff ourselves before we Crown and don't need to eat anymore. It's contagious in my family, you know." Kahali threw his long arms around them and shoved them toward the delicious smells of food and warmth. Tucked close to Kahali, a strange comfort radiated through Rana.

He ushered them into the throng, but a blast of snowy wind rushed them. Rana, temporarily blinded, extended her hands in front of her. Beside her, Kahali tripped, and she fell forward into the crowd.

Arms flailing out to catch herself, Rana toppled forward. A tall, lean stranger turned and attempted to catch her.

"I'm sorry," she said, laughing as she struggled to stand. The ground was icy from the huge wet snowflakes, and she slipped again, this time falling completely on top of the poor guy.

He chuckled. "I think the fasting slowed my reflexes. Are you okay?"

"Yes. You?" Blushing, she slid off him, and righted her hooded cape.

He nodded, but his face was veiled by his long black hair blowing in the wind.

Beside her, Kahali and Balavati also lay on the ground, cackling with amusement. Hanging onto each other, they finally managed to stop laughing long enough to stand.

"Sorry, we weren't paying attention." Rana glanced down at the guy as he tucked his locks into his hood, and her heart raced. Oh, he was stunning.

His dark brown eyes danced above a pointed nose and full lips, and his long hair swung free and unbraided. From his sprawled position, he gave her a lop-sided grin.

His massive friend yanked him off the ground as if he weighed nothing, and complained, "Nice work, Sakhe. You've nearly crushed my eggs." He motioned toward his pelvis.

Rana furrowed her brow in confusion. *Did he say eggs?*

The guy she'd collided with ignored his friend's strange comment. Instead, his bright gaze touched Rana's, and he bowed to them all. "I guess the snowstorm wanted us all to meet."

"Collide might be more accurate," Rana said with an awkward laugh. She stood too close to him, unsure what to do with her arms and hands.

"I'm Kahali. This is my friend, Rana." Kahali cast his arm around her shoulders, pulling her close. "And Daman, and Balavati." He gestured to the others with his free arm. "We're going to eat now before we perish saving the muddy Earth children."

"Kahali"—Balavati thumped his arm—"don't you take anything seriously?"

The stranger raised an eyebrow at Kahali, the corner of his mouth tugging in a half-grin. "Nice to meet you. I'm Eka, and my bird-obsessed friend is Tejas." Eka nodded to each of them, but his full smile fell on Rana like the sun's warmth.

"Didn't your friend just call you Sakhe?" Kahali asked a bit suspiciously.

Tejas threw his arm around Eka. "Yes, it's my special name for him. Because, you know, he's *special*" the big guy teased, motioning that Eka was the odd one, despite his own earlier strange comment about eggs.

"Eggs?" Rana asked, still baffled by Tejas' earlier statement.

"Yes, I have a nest with two eggs here." Tejas said, patting his heavy coat. "Not sure if they'll make it, but I'm doing my best momma bird impression." He grinned proudly as if carrying around a nest was the most normal thing in the world. "Some of us must walk responsibly," he said, grinning and smacking Eka playfully on the head, "and not fall all over the women." He turned to Kahali. "Or this poor, hungry man."

Kahali snorted and gave Tejas an approving smirk. "Come on, I can't be the only one who's starving."

"Shouldn't those eggs be with their parents?" Balavati asked.

"An eagle got the mom, and dad didn't return. It was me or an early demise." Tejas held out his hands, palms up.

"If you keep asking him questions," Eka said with a grin, "he'll talk all night about his little egglings."

Tejas harrumphed, pouted, and dropped his arm from Eka's shoulder. "They're cute."

Rana laughed. "Show us."

Tejas happily opened his coat, allowing each of them to step forward and peer down at the eggs.

As Rana stepped back to allow the others a peek at the eggs, she caught Eka watching her. "I warned you," he laughed. "He'll tell you all about how they wobbled during the ceremony and talked to him in his dreams..."

"Seriously?" Rana giggled. "Sounds like he talks as much as my friend." She motioned to Balavati, who was rapidly exchanging stories with Tejas. Daman stood between the two talkers, amusedly looking back and forth at their exchange.

Eka nodded in good humor. "Yeah, we could be here a while."

"What?" Tejas frowned over at Eka.

"Nothing," Eka said. "Rana and I were just observing..."

Kahali raised an eyebrow at Eka and her.

Rana wasn't great at reading minds, but Kahali's gaze lingered on the space between her and Eka, or rather, the lack of space. In a flash Kahali returned to his exuberant self.

"Foooooood..." Kahali groaned. "Come on. Eggs don't need to eat, and I'm starving." He threw one arm around her shoulder, and another around Daman's, and called to Balavati, "Let Tejas' eggs sleep." He led them past Eka and Tejas and into the sheltered eating area.

"You fell right onto him." Balavati giggled to Rana.

"Yes, he was quite... *nice*," Rana muttered, laughing so hard that she tripped over the rough-hewn entrance.

Without missing a beat, Kahali steadied her. "Yes, he kindly caught you. So *heroic* of him." he rolled his eyes at Daman, and they both guffawed.

"He was beautiful." Balavati waved her hands in the air. "We have to find him again. Did you see how he watched you?"

Rana nodded. The blush thing was happening again.

"How could you see him under all that outrageous hair?" Kahali chuckled, and Daman joined in.

Balavati narrowed her eyes at the two of them, but they ignored her.

"I liked his hair. It's like a lion's mane." Rana turned away and scanned the hut for an empty mat with enough room for all of them. The large number of closely seated diners and the giant pots of steaming food that lined one wall created a pleasant warmth.

Finding a suitable mat in the corner, she picked her way through the seated crowd toward it. She yearned for a break from the crowd, and a corner was as close as she'd get to her wish.

Removing her heavy cape, she folded it as a cushion and sat on it against the back wall. Her friends settled beside her. Kahali remained standing, stone-faced, next to her. Rana smiled up at him and pulled on his hand. "Eating? You've been talking about this feast for several suns."

"Yeah." Kahali paused and scanned the room. Seemingly satisfied, he finally sat beside her. "That guy was weird."

"I think its sweet that he's trying to save those eggs," Balavati said.

"I meant Eka," Kahali said. "He stood awfully close to Rana."

"Because I'd just stood up from falling on top of him?" Rana chuckled and leaned into his shoulder. "Is someone jealous? Don't you know you'll always be my favorite drummer? And dancer? No one could ever replace you"—she squeezed his hand—"even if he does have an amazing lion's mane."

"I don't know," Daman teased, "those eggs were awfully cute. You better watch out, Kahali."

Both guys cracked up, breaking the tension, and they became four friends again.

Some days, Rana wasn't sure if whatever was blooming between her and Kahali would surpass their friendship or ruin it. Lately, she'd caught him watching her, and things between them seemed ripe with a new tension, but every time she hoped something romantic was about to happen between them like last night, he'd crack a joke or suddenly leave.

Maybe it was all her imagination? All she knew for sure was that she never wanted anything to ever come between them.

Except maybe a plate of food. Her stomach rumbled, as she inhaled the savory aromas surrounding them. Someone served their neighboring mat elk stew with marsh tubers, snowshroom soup, seaweed and nut salad, and flat cakes with cinnaberries on top.

The first to arrive were served first, and since they had arrived late, they waited. Fingers tapping her knees, she reminded herself that impatience must be overcome before Crowning. Maybe if she focused on her friends instead of food?

Daman wrung his hands as the next mat received food. Balavati was licking her lips. No help there. She turned to Kahali, and her heart skipped a beat—his sparkling eyes had been fixed upon her. She smiled and self-consciously smoothed her cloak.

Her impatient stomach had never been this empty. *I bet Sohana's not hungry...*

As a Crowned One ladled stew and glanced toward their group, her hope arose. He smiled and approached them. She greedily accepted the bowl filled with steaming elk stew and began shoveling it in, burning her tongue on the hot broth.

They ate in silence, and more food was delivered as they emptied their bowls. Her stomach purred in satisfaction.

Abruptly, two Crowned Ones stood and left. Then more followed.

Rana watched the rest of the Crowned Ones leave.

Kahali tipped his bowl to get the last bits and then turned to her. "We should get going, too."

"Definitely." Daman wolfed down his last bite and jumped up. He turned to Balavati and Rana. "Coming?" He collected Kahali's and his dirty bowls to turn in.

"No." Balavati remained seated and cast a sideways glance at Rana. "We're still eating." She looked down at her last spoonful of cinnaberries, shook a few off the spoon, and proceeded to eat very slowly.

Daman missed her ruse. "Later, then." He shrugged and turned.

"You sure?" Kahali addressed them both, but his gaze sought out Rana.

She nodded, and Kahali, clearly disappointed, followed Daman out of the shelter.

"What was that about?" Rana raised an eyebrow at Balavati's cinnaberries. "Oh, no…you're not going to—"

"Why not?" Balavati interrupted. "Let's go find him. We could start a conversation, get to know him…" Her face shone. "And his friend was hysterical with his nest—"

"No, not this time. I'm staying right here!" She pounded the mat with her fist.

"Oh. So, I guess you can't walk to the meeting with us?"

Rana and Balavati's heads jerked up in unison to see Eka and Tejas.

"We could. Definitely." Balavati sprang up, abandoning her cinnaberries and nearly crashing into Tejas in her haste.

"Whoa." Tejas held up his massive hands between himself and Balavati. "Watch the nest, my friend."

"Oh. Sorry." Balavati caught herself on Tejas' arm. "I get a little enthusiastic sometimes."

"Like always." Rana laughed.

She walked past them to deliver the bowls to the growing dish stack on a nearby mat. As she returned, she mentally debated how upset Kahali and Daman would be if she and Balavati didn't join them. As cute as Eka was, she'd probably never see him again after tonight, and her friends came first.

"We can join you, but we're supposed to meet Kahali and Daman, too." She was suddenly unsure where to look. Eka's long, untied hair flowed in sensuous waves, and the sparkle of his dark eyes contained entire constellations.

"Oh, they already went?" Eka asked. "I was going to ask if we should wait for them."

"They didn't want to miss the beginning." Rana kept her gaze on Balavati as she straightened their mat.

Self-conscious, Rana tucked a strand of hair that had escaped her thick braid behind her ear, and silently urged Balavati to hurry. On one side of her, Tejas cooed down his coat to his eggs.

Eka rolled his eyes at his friend and mumbled, "You look like you're talking to your privates."

Rana snorted.

Eka turned toward the exit and broke the silence. "Looks like the snow has stopped..."

"Hmm." Rana nodded and glanced sideways at him, only to find him grinning at her. She turned back to the icy ground, pretending to pick at the ice with the toe of her boot. Her blood was on fire. *What's wrong with me? I barely know him.*

Thank the One In All it would only be a short walk to the meeting space. She carefully shielded her thoughts, self-conscious of her sudden inability to think, let alone speak. Standing in awkward silence, Eka's intense gaze scorched the side of her face. Electric static built around them like a gathering thunderstorm.

Balavati finally finished with the mat as if it had needed more than a quick tug. With a too innocent grin, she grabbed Rana and Tejas' arms and led them all out the door.

"That was the best food ever." Balavati, as Rana expected, filled the silence with chatter. "What village are you both from?"

"Conifers-Greet-Mountain's-Shadow."

"Oh!" Balavati gave a little hop of excitement. "You have trees *everywhere*, right?"

"Trees and birds," Tejas replied.

"We're both woodworkers." Eka held up his walking stick, and the moonlight glinted off delicate, intertwined carvings.

"You're an artist?" Rana leaned in and gasped at the detailed furred ones.

"Eh." Eka shrugged. "More of a storyteller. I carve stories into wood—walking sticks, beads, that sort of thing."

"How"—Balavati twirled and gave Rana a dreamy look—"romantic."

Tejas laughed, encouraging her antics, but Rana glared at her brazen friend.

"Not really." Eka chuckled at Balavati's ridiculous behavior. "But I suppose it could be. If I carved the right story," he said, flashing Rana a mischievous grin.

Heat flushed her face, but she was saved by the meeting. "Shh." She pointed toward the gathered adults sitting on the ground before them. "They've already started."

# Chapter 11

*he base of Mount Syeti: Rana*

Rana, Balavati, Eka, and Tejas hushed their conversation and sat cross-legged on the icy ground with the silent crowd, hoping to catch up on what they'd missed in the meeting. She scanned faces for Kahali and Daman, but if they were present, the night's darkness had swallowed them.

At the beginning of meetings, Luminaries announced the issue or question, and then the Crowned Ones connected in a silent, meditative linkage. The uncrowned joined in at whatever level their abilities allowed. The linkage gave Crowned Ones instant access to all sides of an issue. Since Rana and her friends had missed the beginning question of this meeting, which served like an anchor to the group mind, she couldn't join in at any level.

The hair on her arms rose. The linkage must have already occurred several times as the area hummed with energy. If she were Crowned, she'd know the question, but instead, she had to be patient. Her fingers tapped her thigh, waiting.

The electric humming of the air stopped as the linkage broke for another question.

Luminary Samasti addressed them all. "Are all villages willing to participate in this Calling of the Earth's children?"

The silent linkage ensued again. This time, Rana and her friends dove into the experience.

The intense energy created by five villages of Crowned Ones made the cold night air ripple so that the starry night above them appeared to dance. Between the energy before her and Eka's warmth next to her, Rana became woozy. She swayed forward.

Eka leaned toward her and silently mouthed, "You okay?"

She nodded, but her heart fell. Was it because her parents hadn't Crowned that only she was affected by lightheadedness?

Suddenly, Kalakanya stood up and turned to look directly at Rana. Despite the energetic heat generated by the meeting, an icy shiver passed down her spine, and the back of her neck tingled. Her heart skipping a beat, she cupped the back of her neck with her palm.

*Oh, no.*

These weird tickly neck sensations happened when Kalakanya performed a transtemporal scan on someone. *Why is she scanning me?* Rana rubbed her neck, trying to convince herself it was only a coincidence. The prickling intensified, as did Kalakanya's stare.

Rana met Kalakanya's steady gaze, her heart pounding. A transtemporal scan meant only one thing—Kalakanya was searching Rana's past and future for information pertaining to the current issue. But what did *she* have to do with Calling the Earth's children?

"The linkage shows all villages will participate." Kalakanya's gaze remained on Rana. "Our young ones will be the bridge. But first, we must discover where these the Earth children dwell."

"Can you locate them?" asked a guy from another village.

Only Kalakanya was skilled enough to locate a being that wasn't Calling, and the Earth children weren't exactly Calling them.

Kalakanya smiled but kept her gaze on Rana. "Of course. I believe I have already met two of them on the inner planes—a mother and son. But they do not understand those inner dimensions and do not realize I'm real. We must meet them here, in the physical world, because that is all they believe in. I'm not sure of their physical location. However, our group linkage will allow me to locate it. Let us rejoin..." She remained standing but finally closed her eyes, releasing Rana from the nerve-wracking transtemporal scan.

CHAPTER 11

Rana exhaled, and her heart stopped clamoring. Panting, she refrained from joining this linkage and instead caught her breath.

A moment later, everyone's eyes opened.

Kalakanya announced, "They are nearest our village, underground, and it's not clear when they will break from the Earth's womb. They have not decided. If we wait outside their door, it will scare them. Our young ones will find them."

"But the danger… Couldn't a Crowned One beam to their home and speak with them?" Sunila, an uncrowned woman from Rana's village, asked.

The silent linkage began again. Sweat trickled down Rana's back as the pulsing energy swept her up. Stealing a glance at Balavati and Eka, she frowned at their blissful peace. Frustrated, she swiped her brow and dove back into the energy.

Gandhapalin, Rana's adopted father, said, "No, they have great fear. Beaming a Crowned One into their space would seem like an attack to them." Deep lines furrowed his brow.

As he closed his eyes to restart the linkage, Balavati nudged Rana. The others joined in the linkage, but Balavati and Rana abstained.

"Did Kalakanya shoot a transtemporal scan up here…at you?" It was barely a whisper.

Rana shivered. "Maybe she saw my death, too. Ow!" Balavati had given her a quick jab with her elbow.

Eka furrowed his brow at them.

A Luminary from another village stood up and straightened her braid. "It's decided. We'll send out young ones, uncrowned, to make first contact with the Earth children. Kalakanya sees this path as the safest time thread. Due to the danger involved, volunteers must possess advanced skills. Each village will coordinate their own volunteers."

Everyone murmured agreement, and the meeting concluded. Though the meeting was over, many lingered in the warmth, discussing the day's strange developments. Eka and Tejas hunched together deep in a hushed conversation about the meeting while Rana rubbed her still-tingling neck.

97

Dread permeated her being. How did Kalakanya's scan of her relate to the Earth children?

Balavati sidled up close. "Maybe she was trans-temporally scanning someone near you?"

Rana blinked and leaned into Balavati's warmth. "No, I felt it on my neck."

"Oh," Balavati sighed.

Everything seemed surreal. Rana had to focus and regain her wits. She gazed about the lingering crowd. Across the gathering, Daman and Kahali laughed with Sohana. Daman waved, and both guys rose to make their way toward them.

Someone tapped her on the shoulder. *Eka.* She'd forgotten he was even there. "Sorry, long day," she said, giving him an embarrassed smile.

He nodded. "Tejas and I decided to volunteer to Call the Earth children. What about you two?" He glanced first at Rana, then to Balavati, then back to Rana.

"I'm not exactly *advanced.*" Rana brushed the end of her braid against her fingertips. One brush, two brushes...

Eka grinned. "Why would you say that?"

"I'm..." Rana paused, then shrugged.

"She's a bit scattered," Balavati said, covering her mouth as soon as the words were out. "That's not what I meant," she mumbled through her fingers.

Rana, teeth clenched, shot her a scathing look. Balavati had to be impulsive now? In front of them?

Daman and Kahali joined their little circle. Kahali, sensing the tension, shot her a questioning look. Rana shrugged. She sent to him mentally: *Balavati being Balavati again.*

He cracked a slight smile and said nothing.

Eka, missing all this, continued, "You're underestimating yourself. Kalakanya transtemporally scanned you—you're already involved."

"She what?" Kahali's eyes widened at Rana. "You?"

She nodded. "Kalakanya may want me involved, but I only want to focus on Crowning. Nothing extra."

"You can't stop living to Crown. Besides, nearly everyone Crowns eventually, so why focus on it all the time?" Eka grinned. "It takes all the fun out of being uncrowned."

"Being uncrowned is extra fun?" Balavati challenged. "How so?"

"Well." Eka's eyes sparkled mischievously. "For starters, there's eating. And then there's the star beaming. I mean, once you're Crowned and can do that, you lose your excuse to be late for classes, right?"

"No." Rana laughed. "There's still oversleeping. I can sleep through everything."

"Not the time we buried your sleep mat in snow." Kahali smirked.

"You didn't!" Eka said, biting his lip to keep from laughing.

"Yup. And you, *traitor*"—she mock-glared at Balavati—"helped him."

"Nice!" Tejas gave Balavati an approving grin. "And you thought my songs were bad, eh, Sakhe?"

"Songs?" Kahali asked, eyes alit. Anything musical got his attention.

"We're talking about a guy obsessed with birds. Don't get him started," Eka warned. "My point is, you'll miss a lot if you only focus on Crowning as a chore."

"It worked for Sohana," Kahali joked. "She makes everything a chore. But you, birdman"—Kahali threw an arm around Tejas' shoulders—"you and I should chat about songs."

"Aw, he likes me." Tejas tilted his head down to rest it on Kahali's shoulder and batted his eyelashes playfully.

Kahali snorted. "Sorry, dude, I'm already committed." He pulled away from Tejas and tossed his other arm around Rana's shoulders.

"Hmm. I seem to have missed that commitment?" Rana raised an eyebrow and grinned. "Was this commitment professed while I was buried in the snow?"

She realized Kahali's and her antics had earned Eka's keen attention.

"Every day, Rana." Kahali's grin became earnest. "And I do believe Balavati and I then lent you our furs and treated you to cups full of tea?"

"Yes, you did. But, just to be clear, this commitment you've supposedly professed to me wasn't about burying me in snow again, right?"

Kahali turned a questing look Balavati's way and then shrugged. "We could arrange it if you'd like, right, Bal?" His arm was still slung around Rana's shoulders, but not in the same way he had done since they were youngsters, holding each other up on the ice. This strange more-than-a-friend element now mysteriously seeped from him, making her warm and giddy as well as unsure.

This was her best friend, Kahali. Everything was a joke to him. Was she misreading all this? She reconsidered his dancing only with her the previous night, until his arm shifted on her back as he stepped a bit closer.

Kahali: *This okay?*

Falling stars, she hadn't imagined his interest. *Mmmhmm,* she sent, her heart soaring. At his stifled snort of amusement, she poked him in the ribs with her elbow.

Thank the One In All, the others hadn't noticed. They were all laughing about something Daman said.

"What do you think, Rana?" Eka's dark, gorgeous eyes sparkled with amusement.

Oneness, he expected an answer. They all awaited her reply. "Uhm, sorry. I spaced out there."

"Oh." His gaze fell on Kahali's arm around her, and he frowned. "It's been a long day. Tejas and I should get going."

"Yes, its past our eggs' bedtime." Tejas smirked. "They get very cranky." He rose, one hand on his belly like a pregnant woman.

"You're taking this egg thing too far, my friend." Eka snorted at Tejas' pretending to take offense, then stood and picked up his walking stick. "It would be fun if we all volunteered. It's the adventure of a lifetime, don't you think?" His words included them all, but his gaze lingered on Rana, hopeful-like. "We could all do it together."

Rana grinned despite herself. She couldn't even stay focused on their conversation. She couldn't imagine the Crowned Ones would consider her skill level *advanced.* "Maybe...?"

Balavati, hooking her arm around Rana's, said, "We'll talk about it. Have a good night."

"I already have." He gave a roguish bow and followed Tejas off toward their village's camp.

* * *

Rana turned toward Kahali. "So, are you leaving too?" She smiled expectantly at him, and then to be polite glanced at Daman as well.

Kahali took a deep breath as if working up the nerve to say something, and his arm around her tightened slightly. "I was hoping—"

"For a good night's sleep, right?" Daman interrupted. "Come on," he said, pulling Kahali's free arm. "We all need to rest before starting home tomorrow."

"I guess…" Kahali said and after giving Rana a strained smile followed Daman down the trail toward their families' temporary huts.

As they strolled away, Rana wilted. What should she have done differently to get him to stay behind?

Balavati remained at her side, shooting her strange looks until after both Daman and Kahali were out of hearing range. Then Balavati lit into her.

"What are you and Kahali doing? Eka likes you!"

Rana's mouth dropped open. "Huh?"

"Kahali's joking around like he always does, but Eka doesn't know that. You two looked like you were together."

*Kahali's joking around like he always does.* "Uhm…" Rana had no response. Was Balavati right?

"Unless…" Balavati waggled her eyebrows. "Something's changed? Has it? Are you and Kahali…?" She bounced up and down, her excitement contagious.

"Maybe? I mean…" Rana blushed terribly and hoped the darkness of the night hid it. "I like him, but I'm not sure he's serious. Tonight, he mind spoke when he had his arm around me, and it seemed like he was serious. But then he just left with Daman."

"Wow." Balavati performed a happy dance. "I always thought his flirts seemed a bit different with you, but still. This is *weird*. Happy weird, but *weird*."

"Yes. And Eka's intense eyes—did you notice? He seems close to Crowning..."

"Aha. I noticed. He also noticed you." Balavati snickered.

Rana's heart danced a little. Soared. Until her parents' faces flashed in her mind's eye, neither of which had the white hair of the Crowned Ones.

"And then there's... my parents." Rana dug at the packed snow with her boots. "I can't ever be with any guy unless I Crown. I mean, I can date, but we can never, you know...couple?" The cozy energy and fun of dating was more than enjoyable, but someday, she'd want *more*.

Balavati smirked. "Don't get ahead of yourself. And no one knows how your parents' lack of Crowning will affect you. You're already great with the furred ones."

"Star beings don't couple and have offspring before Crowning." Rana had always defended her parents' uncrowned coupling, but now she seethed with anger at the situation they had left her in. She needed to know why they'd had her, and they'd gone off and got themselves killed.

Guilt added itself to the tornado of emotions swirling madly within her. Oneness, what was wrong with her? This anger felt traitorous. Her parents had loved her and had died through no fault of their own. But what had they been thinking when they had her? A dull ache filled her chest.

Furred ones mated every spring without much thought. But for star beings, conceiving a child was always a conscious decision. They didn't have accidents.

Had her parents' decision to conceive her without being Crowned doomed her to an uncrowned life? Because if that were true, then no guy would want to be with her. Not seriously *be* with her, or they'd be condemning their children to also be uncrowned and limited for the rest of their lives. She heaved a great sigh of resignation.

"Rana, both guys like you. It's not a great tragedy. It's an *opportunity*." Balavati had grasped her shoulders, ready to shake sense into her if she had to.

"Eka doesn't know that I may never Crown or be able to have offspring," she said.

Balavati doubled over laughing. "It's a bit early to worry about kids."

Rana glared at her, unamused. Eka had already shown his potential to Crown soon. What would he want with her if she didn't?

Balavati made a poor attempt to control her mirth. She straightened, a hand covering her huge grin. "Okay, here's an idea. Maybe you and I should volunteer, too."

Rana raised her eyebrows, still fuming. "How could that *possibly* help?"

"Remember our lessons? The five kinds of love before Crowning?" Balavati ticked them off on her fingers as she continued, "Love of family, self-love, romantic love, love of community, and love of all." She tilted her head. "If you're worried about Crowning, we should practice. You know, volunteering for our community, or"—Balavati grinned—"exploring romantic love?"

Rana narrowed her eyes, and her mind raced. She'd do anything to Crown. Maybe Balavati had a point. Then she remembered Sukti's vision, and a deep heaviness smothered her heart. It wouldn't be fair to start dating someone if she were to die soon. "Maybe, but forget the romance."

"You're impossible," Balavati said with such fervency that the lingering adults turned to her. She gave them a weak smile and then stalked closer to Rana and whispered, "Fine. Then let's still volunteer. You're not the only one that wants to Crown."

"Fine." Rana spun and clomped off toward her hut, puzzled at the intensity of her own reaction. *What's my problem?*

As if in response, Eka's incandescent grin filled her mind's eye. And then Kahali's laughter.

# Chapter 12

Northern Haven: Bleu Reinier

Bleu's father, Tadwell, gave him a your-turn-to-keep-Ayanna-safe look from behind Stamf's back. The ever-darkening circles under his dad's eyes told of sleepless nights with Ayanna that haunted his family. Grabbing the remainder of his lunch in one hand and slinging his tool bag over his shoulder with the other, his dad again motioned—this time more emphatically—for Bleu to get rid of Stamf and then hurried out the door to work.

Yeah, Stamf shouldn't be here, but how was Bleu supposed to keep his best friend away without arousing his suspicion?

Stamf whispered, "What's up with your dad?"

Bleu shrugged, the awkwardness of his family's new clandestine life settling over him like fine dust. Ever since Stamf and he had started daily training for the second expedition, Stamf had assumed they would hang out at the Reinier module or the gaming rooms the rest of the day.

"What time is your helicopter training starting today?" Bleu asked his friend. *Translation: How long do I need to appear busy?*

Bleu surveyed Ayanna. She seemed pretty good today. She sat on the couch and sketched Picasso and Frida dancing under the stars.

The helicopter assignments had been a real disappointment. When the Council tested candidates for piloting, Stamf and Bleu were the first in line. Who wouldn't want to fly the sleek wonders to the other Havens? But they had opted for Commander Savas, Stamf, and Neviah. It still irked him to not have been chosen. Was it truly his scores or that Stamf was the prime minister's nephew and Commander Savas was, well, a commander? Neviah, he didn't doubt. She had always been the best at anything technological.

"We don't have regular practice today. They shortened it for your mom's sanative concert. In fact..." Stamf's eyes lit up as he ran his fingers through his hair.

Bleu knew that look. He would need an amazing excuse for whatever was coming...

"Bleu, it's your chance to see the helicopters. Commander Savas has a meeting, and Neviah and I only have to practice some flight programs. No one will be there. I can give you and Ayanna a tour."

Ayanna leapt off the couch. "Ah, Stamf. That would be awesome."

Bleu stared at the two of them, his heart racing. This was a nightmare. Stamf knew he had been itching to see the simulations, and he had no reason to decline Stamf's offer. None. "I don't know. Today's not the best day. I need to get some stuff ready for Mom. Fold programs for the concert..." But there was no reason to say no to such a great offer. Folding programs? Could he get any lamer?

"Man, I can't do this any other day. Commander Savas is out today. You know how rare that is, and Neviah always practices in the mornings. Come on, you'll both love it." He pulled Bleu toward the exit, where Ayanna already waited.

"Bleu, chill." Ayanna practically danced in her excitement. "Stamf is officially part of the helicopter training program. If he takes us in, I'm sure it'll be okay. We'll fold the programs quickly." She gave Bleu her don't-be-protective look.

Bleu teetered on the brink between fury at Ayanna's sudden denial of her condition and terror that it meant she was getting more severely ill. Hands clenched, he held his ground. "Mom asked me to do other stuff, too."

Ayanna narrowed her eyes at him. "Okay, fine. Stamf and I will go without you."

Bleu's heart raced. Had she forgotten she had the Sickness? He couldn't say anything in front of Stamf, but what was she doing? "Ayanna, may I talk to you alone a minute?"

"No. Stop being such a bore. We're going. Right, Stamf?" Ayanna grabbed Stamf's arm and exited the module.

"I give him two seconds to follow us." Stamf laughed and raced ahead of Ayanna.

"Arghhh." It took less than two seconds.

Bleu checked he still wore his expedition pass to enter the third floor and followed them into the hall. Stamf must have a plan for sneaking Ayanna onto the floor. He couldn't let her out of his sight, needed to keep her calm, and had to get her to return home as soon as possible. He was screwed.

As he caught up and they slowed to a walk, Bleu glanced sideways at his sister. She stuck out her tongue.

*Please let today be a good day.*

They took the elevator to the third level, which housed the gaming rooms and the areas where the expeditions were planned. The Council met on level two, and Bleu had no idea what was on one since it was restricted. Stamf went ahead, checked, and then waved them forward. He had been correct. The gray hallway stood empty.

As Stamf swished his card through the door's security check, the lock clicked open, and the lights inside turned on. Bleu leaned forward, heart thumping, and strained to see the training room set up. The real helicopters, which would never fit inside the Surface elevator box, were being built in sections to be assembled on the Surface.

"It's just the insides?" Ayanna's disappointment was tangible.

"Yeah, but when you fly it, the rest appears as a hologram." Stamf waved them over to one of the two interiors. "This is the one I usually fly. If you squish on this platform that mimics the floor, I'll turn it on and show you." Stamf's voice rang with excitement as he stroked the platform with affection.

"Don't we need safety belts or something?" Electric anticipation coursed through Bleu's body at the temptation, yet reason nagged him to get his sister out of here. He glanced at her again. She was having fun, and there were still no signs of tremors.

"If I fly it. But I'm only turning it on to show you the whole thing in the hologram. It's incredible." Stamf climbed up into the seat and swung a robotic arm out from the panel. He attached it around the back of his neck. The copter whirled to life. "Hurry up. Get in."

Ayanna and Bleu jumped aboard. They squatted to Stamf's right on the narrow floor and stared out the front panel. The arm around Stamf's head lit up, and the whole holographic copter appeared.

"How'd it do that? You don't need a key or something?" Ayanna asked.

"No, she recognizes me." Stamf wriggled his eyebrows dramatically. "She and I share a special connection."

"She?" Ayanna giggled. "You turned down the lions to date a helicopter?"

"Lions?" Stamf asked, laughing. "I think I'd remember if a lioness asked me out." He gave another awkward laugh and shot Bleu a baffled look.

Bleu's stomach back flipped. Was Ayanna about to lose it? A desperate hopelessness descended around his body like a blanket about to smother the life out of him.

"You and the lions…" Ayanna's voice trailed off.

"Huh?" Stamf gave them both a puzzled look.

"You know Ayanna. Always joking." It didn't even make sense, but Stamf laughed, seeming eager to move on.

"She recognizes me by the computer chip in the back of my neck. The arm goes around the back of my neck and recognizes me as an approved pilot, and then it acts as an interface."

"You put something in your brain?" Bleu stared at his friend, his innards recoiling. "Like, permanently?"

Stamf shrugged. "It's safe and lets me do some cool flying stuff, but I can't show you until we're in a real one." Stamf sighed and turned off the flight program. Everything was silent except the humming of the lights overhead.

"It's in your brain?" Ayanna shivered.

As they sat crammed up next to each other on the floor, her tremor shook Bleu's body. His heart raced. As shocked as he was at Stamf, he turned to Ayanna in greater horror. "You okay, Yanna?"

"I guess..." Her right arm had begun trembling.

Stamf was disconnecting the interface from his head. He hadn't noticed.

"Well, thanks, Stamf. We need to get going." Bleu stood up and pulled Ayanna from the machine. She landed awkwardly on the floor.

Bleu began leading her toward the door. "We'll see you tonight at the concert. Okay, Stamf?"

His friend still sat in the chopper. "Man, what's the hurry? There's more...and no one is here." He arced his eyebrows at her. "You okay, Ayanna?"

"She's fine. See you later." Bleu rushed through the doorway and hurried her toward the elevator. His sister remained thankfully quiet, but now, her whole body shook. "Just a few minutes, Ayanna, please? Let me get you home."

He smashed his sweaty palm against the button for the elevator. The door opened, and he turned to pull in Ayanna, but Stamf had caught up.

Stamf stared in horror at Ayanna, who leaned wild-eyed and trembling against Bleu, then raised his gaze to Bleu. The horror in his friend's eyes as he recognized the symptoms made Bleu nearly topple over. He had failed her. His whole family.

His best friend knew he'd been hiding a dangerous secret.

"Stamf, please. Help me get her home." He sucked in a jagged breath and pulled Ayanna into the elevator.

The door started to close, but Stamf stood frozen in shock. At the last minute, he launched himself in. "You knew? This is why you've been avoiding me?" He scowled from sibling to sibling and then glared at Bleu. They stared at each other.

Cold sweat trickled down Bleu's neck as he nodded. There was no denying it. "Stamf..." Words failed him. "Help us, please?"

Stamf fingered his flight pass. "You know what you're asking?"

Bleu nodded and swallowed the lump in his throat. It wasn't fair to ask this of him, but the Sickness didn't play fair. Ayanna shook against Bleu's chest, and he pulled her closer.

"If I'm caught hiding this, my uncle could lose everything. We'll never be trusted with anything." Stamf's voice had become a whisper.

"I know, but this is Ayanna."

She moaned, her voice muffled against his chest.

Bleu said, "Look, if we get caught in the halls, I'll say it just started. You were only trying to help me get her home."

Stamf groaned in frustration and then slapped his palm over the elevator camera that was used in emergencies. "Bleu, people with the Sickness have killed before. It's not safe."

Nothing was safe anymore. Humanity was going extinct in this hellhole, and he should at least be able to keep his sister at home while she died.

He stared at the elevator door, blinking back tears of fury. "Stamf— She's not going to hurt anyone. Help me keep her out of the unit a few more weeks. Buy my mom some time. She's onto something, a new way of using nanotechnology to fight the changes in the mitochondria. You heard Commander Savas yesterday at training..." Bleu's voice caught. "He wants to eliminate everyone in the Sickness Unit."

Stamf shook his head. "He's not right. My uncle would never allow that."

"According to Commander Savas, the Council said they'd consider it." A chilling shiver ran down Bleu's spine, and he clutched Ayanna tighter. "Please."

Stamf's gaze softened as it fell on Ayanna, crumpled against Bleu's chest. He raked his fingers through his hair, looked about desperately, then sighed. "Okay. But promise me only you and I take the blame. I won't let this ruin my family."

"I'll take it all. It shouldn't touch you."

The elevator had reached the floor for the Reinier module, but he had no way to get her through the hallway to their home. Her back arched, her head lolling. *Shast.* She'd start screaming next. What could they do that might make her screeching look normal?

"Hey, remember when we used to play that game with Ayanna? We'd pretend we were monsters fighting over her, and we'd both tickle her, and she'd play scream?"

"Huh?" Stamf turned from the door and gaped at Bleu as if he, too, had become ill.

The door dinged and began to slide open. "We need to get her through the halls, and she looks ready to blow." Bleu supported Ayanna against him, tensed as if his strength could hold her together.

Stamf surfaced from his shock. "Oh, you mean pretend we're teasing her, and if she shrieks, it looks like part of the game?"

Bleu nodded. "Or I could carry her and just run. Mom said stimulation makes it worse, so tickling's probably not the best."

Ayanna let out a scream as the door slid fully open. The two friends stared at each other.

Bleu grabbed his sister. "Mine. I caught her."

He pretended to tickle her as he raced down the hall. *We look like fools.*

Stamf reached for Ayanna, and Bleu batted him away. "Mine, fiend!"

A few workers exited a door and shook their heads at them, eyes rolling. *It's working!* They raced down the corridor. Given the time, most people were already be at the dining hall.

As they turned into the final stretch, they ran smack into Liam Collins.

"Watch out, you fools," Liam hissed at them in annoyance. His voice was extra loud because, as always, he had his ear buds in and was listening to music.

Bleu and Stamf paused and Ayanna let out a shriek. Liam jumped, startled, and stared at her contorted face.

"She really doesn't like being captured." Bleu forced a grin, roared like a wild man, and raced down the last bit of corridor.

Behind him, Stamf laughed and threatened to capture Liam, who huffed and stomped away.

Bleu raced through the door and into Ayanna's room. He slid her onto the bed and grabbed his communicator. This episode would need his mom's tranquilizers to quiet down. Behind him, Stamf panted.

"Do you think Liam knows?" Stamf sounded scared.

"If he does, I'll make sure everyone knows you didn't. But if my mom can get her quiet, maybe we can buy more time..." The full reality of what they faced hit him. "*Shast.* The concert's tonight, and Ayanna's supposed to sing in it." He blinked back his tears as he struggled to tuck in Ayanna as she writhed. Couldn't they catch a break?

The irony of tonight's sanative concert smacked him in the face. His mother, determined to strengthen teens' brain health, had organized the teaching of choral music. Tonight's concert was meant to be a fun way to prevent the Sickness, not a display of his sister's illness. Bleu ground his teeth to keep from shouting out the unfairness of it all.

He looked over his shoulder to Stamf, who was pacing outside her bedroom door.

Bleu said, "No matter what happens, I owe you a big one."

Stamf stared at Ayanna as if she would explode and kill them both. "What do we do now?"

"Keep her quiet, and somehow, get us all to the concert."

Bleu sank to the floor beside her bed, crushed by the knowledge that she and Stamf would pay for his carelessness. He should have kept Stamf away, kept her at home, and avoided all this. He was the worst brother and worst friend ever, and his parents would be furious.

# Chapter 13

*orthern Haven: Atsushi Collins*

**N** Atsushi slouched at the empty cafeteria table and poked at his now cold lunch. Images of Ayanna risking her life on the vast Surface wasteland had deadened his appetite. He'd hoped that learning her plans for the Surface might draw the two of them closer; instead, she seemed to be avoiding him. His entire Ayanna Engagement Plan had backfired in the most epic way possible.

Then again, if he hadn't overheard Bleu's suicidal plan, he wouldn't know their secret. Sometimes, sharing secrets brought people together, right?

He blew out a long breath and rubbed his eyes, tired from scanning files all morning in the Records Room. He'd double-checked Bleu's account of human survival during previous ice ages, and the guy had been right. Shouldn't history classes cover that? And why were the only records of it contained in brief summaries in the ancient online encyclopedia? Something about that was off.

One would think that as humanity scrambled to survive the impending mass extinction, the world-wide web would be buzzing with information about past human survival. He'd found nothing on past ice ages that might help Ayanna and Bleu survive up there.

If only his painted mural friends could talk. The artist had supposedly based them on actual people left behind on the Surface, who would've had access to the unedited web. They probably had access to real food as well. With a disgusted grunt at his congealed protein loaf, he trod up and deposited his tray. Turning, he spotted Educator Girak across the nearly empty cafeteria in the café area with couches and comfy chairs. Mural characters couldn't talk, but his educator could.

Atsushi stood, undecided if he should interrupt his teacher. It was the weekend, and maybe he didn't want to talk to his students. Then again, everyone in Northern Haven constantly saw each other and knew each other's business. Commander Savas sometimes played the holographic games with Stamf. Every diner in the cafeteria last night witnessed Zach and Katrina's cringe-worthy break up. Anyone with a broken gadget knew Neviah would fix it in exchange for choco.

Since Educator Girak and his wife, Josefina, often opened the labs to students during cool experiments, he probably wouldn't mind an interruption in his weekend reading.

Before he changed his mind, he hurried over to the café seating area and stopped beside Educator Girak. His sock-covered feet were propped up on the orange-and-green striped couch, his shoes placed neatly on the floor below him. Enraptured by his reading, he remained oblivious to Atsushi's presence.

"Hey," Atsushi muttered.

Girak startled, then his blue eyes softened as he gave a welcoming smile. "I should pay more attention to my surroundings, shouldn't I? That's the danger of a good book."

Atsushi shrugged. "It's not like there's predators afoot."

"There are in this tale," Girak said as he held up his comm device and chuckled. "What's up?" He swung his feet down, freeing up the cushion beside him. "Have a seat."

"No, thanks." If he was caught hanging out in the cafeteria with his educator, the teasing would be brutal. "I have a question. That okay?"

"I love questions. Fire away," Girak said as he turned off whatever horror story he'd been reading.

Atsushi's stomach unclenched. He should have known Educator Girak wouldn't mind. "Do you remember when you told me the records had all been curated by SHAST, and things may have been left out on purpose?"

Girak furrowed his brow. "Yeah…" He glanced about the cafeteria to check who else might be nearby.

"Is there any way to tell if stuff has been deleted? I mean, I know they saved the world-wide web the year before Descension Day for us, but what if—"

Girak jumped up and shook his head in warning. "Why don't we go back to my module, and I'll find the SHAST explanation for that. All teachers have it, and its *excellent* reading." He chuckled and waved his hand for Atsushi to follow him.

"Ah…" Atsushi frowned. "Okay?"

"Great," Girak said and hurried from the public space into the closest corridor. They walked in awkward silence until they reached the residential modules, and the Giraks' front door swished open and then shut behind them.

Educator Girak blew out a long sigh. "You asked an excellent question, but the Prime Minister has had his eye on me since I showed you all that unapproved Descension Day video in class." His mischievous grin reached all the way to his eyes. "What makes you think stuff has been deleted?"

He walked over and shoved a collection of printed datasheets off the couch. "Sorry. Have a seat. Ever since Josefina joined the expedition team, we have a deluge of extra research floating around here."

"It's okay." Atsushi laughed. "You should see my room, and I don't have any expedition excuses."

"Well, technically, neither do we. I mean, we have the extra bed-room"—he waved at the closed door off the living room—"where she's been stashing all her stuff, but it keeps spilling out." He shook his head as he placed his comm on the side table and sat down. "What mystery were you researching today?"

Atsushi sat in a matching blue-and-yellow flowered chair opposite him. "I was researching whether humans had survived any past ice ages on the Surface."

"Hmm. What did you find?"

His face scrunched up as he tried to put words to his suspicion. "I found they had…but there seemed to be very little on it. Especially considering, you know." Atsushi waved toward the ceiling like Bleu had at the festival to signify the Surface. Before Bleu had done that, he'd never considered the Surface as a world only kilometers above them. It had always seemed mythological, like the old stories of hellfire in the underworld.

"Yes, you'd think that might be important to us, but then again, we were the lucky ones tucked away down here." His educator's face drew in with guilt.

"Is there a way to tell what's been cut out of SHAST's web recording? Are there traces in the code or something?"

"Ha! I get you questioning a few things, and now, I've unwittingly created a monster. I can only hope when Jos and I have children they're as bright as you."

Atsushi's face flushed at the unexpected compliment. "You must have fathered kids already, right? I mean, your genetic rating is nearly as high as mine, and you're older."

Girak shrugged. "I'd guess so, but they don't usually tell us. Women know, but us guys give sperm and never know if it's used or stored." He grinned. "I haven't seen any unfortunate toddlers cursed with my red hair, so if they're out there, they must take after their moms."

Atsushi furrowed his brow. Someday, he'd be in the exact same situation, except maybe his kids' Japanese features would be noticeable. Would they know they were Japanese? Would he even know what that meant by then to teach them? "I never thought about how weird that must be."

Educator Girak nodded and held up his palms in surrender. "I may not recognize them, but someday, I'll have them as students. We'll at least have that, and it'll have to be enough until Jos and I are approved for our own kids." His smile faded.

Atsushi shifted on the chair cushion, unsure of how to respond.

He was saved by the doorbell, and Educator Girak jumped up in joy. "Jos always forgets her comm and can't get in." When he opened the door, however, he paused. "Oh. Hello, Bleu. What's up?"

"Mom told me to bring this to Josefina." Bleu sounded exhausted, almost mechanical. "It's something medical, for the expedition or something?"

As he held out the box to Educator Girak, he noticed Atsushi and narrowed his gaze. "What are you doing here?"

"I had a science question," Atsushi answered, being as vague as possible. Bleu's gaze darkened.

Girak asked Bleu, "I thought you and Jos had training today." His freckled brow creased with concern. "She's not with all of you?"

"We got the day off. I'm in a bit of a hurry," Bleu said, shoving the box toward Girak. "Mom needs help getting ready for the concert."

As soon as Girak accepted the box, Bleu spun on his heel and hurried away.

"Hmm," Girak mumbled. "Guess her stash is growing again." Holding the large, sealed box, he turned toward the spare bedroom. "Mind getting the door?"

Atsushi sprang up to open the door, then jumped back as it opened from the inside and Josefina leaned out.

"Hello," she exclaimed, a bit perkier than normal. She blew a loose strand of black hair out of her face. "Thought I heard someone come in."

Girak's face scrunched in confusion, then looked from Josefina to Atsushi. "This door isn't soundproof." His face scrunched even more. "What's going on in here? Do I smell something cooking?" He gave her a mischievous raised eyebrow and leaned to see over her shoulder.

Atsushi glanced over both their shoulders into the room. Tables stood covered with beakers, heaters, and an unusually high pile of batteries.

"It's nothing," Josefina said as she herded them backward into the living room.

"Jos, what are you hiding?" Girak, instead of getting angry like Atsushi's father, had amusement splashed across his bearded face.

"Nothing." She grinned, her dark eyes flashing with excitement. "Just a little surprise, Diggory. I'll explain *later*." At *later*, her gaze flicked to Atsushi.

Thrown by the use of his educator's first name, it took him a moment to realize that she wanted to talk to her husband in private.

"I should get going," Atsushi said. "We have another practice before tonight's choral concert." As he headed toward their front door, he spun back toward Josefina. "I'm sorry, but was that a stack of AZ batteries in there?"

AZ batteries worked on everything A to Z and were in high demand.

Josefina's smile faltered. "Yes."

"Oh, phew. I'm glad you found them. Neviah's been searching everywhere for them. She had them piled on her desk and then they disappeared, and she's, you know, a bit disorganized and thought she'd misplaced them..." His voice trailed off at Josefina's frozen expression.

"Forget about it. I'll talk to her. I had to borrow them for something," Josefina said defensively.

Girak, his face full of mirth, crossed his arms. "I suspect she'd like them back unused, Jos. You don't want to be up there with depleted batteries." He cleared his throat. "Since you clearly don't want Atsushi or me telling Neviah that you *borrowed* them, I think we deserve an explanation for our aiding and abetting?" He laughed.

Josefina flashed her husband an annoyed look. Atsushi took another step toward the door.

"Oh, come on," Girak teased. "How big can this secret be? Are you distilling alcohol for the expedition team?"

"No, we'd smell that," Atsushi said. When Girak shot him a suspicious look, he added "You taught us that alcohols are volatile, remember?"

"Right." Girak agreed, then turned back to Josefina. "So? What is my delightfully devious wife concocting this weekend?" He chuckled. "In her secret lab...off our living room..." He frowned. "You did check the venting?"

She rolled her eyes. "I'm devious, not a fool."

Atsushi snorted. Whatever she was up to, she had captured his full interest. Despite knowing he had to leave, his curiosity pulled him back toward the lab like a magnet.

"You're always welcome here." Josefina smiled at him. "But Diggory and I need to discuss this in private. Can I trust you to not breathe a word of this?"

"Of course, but what about Neviah? She's tearing her office apart, looking for those batteries." He wouldn't leave Neviah in a lurch like that.

"My work hit a little snafu, and I needed the batteries to finish. I'll get her others."

Atsushi frowned. AZ batteries were rechargeable, but he wasn't a fool. They were hard to come by. Lately, everything was. As he glanced from Girak to Josefina, a small *ding* came from the bedroom-lab.

"Oh," Josefina sprang up. "I'll be right back." She hurried into the temporary lab. She had clearly expected them to wait, but when Girak followed, Atsushi trailed him, hoping to convince her into giving him at least a few batteries to return to Neviah today.

The room had ample expedition supplies stacked against the walls and a long table in the center. With the tubes and the large containers of clear liquid bubbling, it resembled a distillation setup, with the addition of a few things he couldn't make sense of. Heaters beneath the boiling liquid were hooked up to a single AZ battery. She must have been running these heaters nonstop to need Neviah's whole pile.

Josefina spun to face them. "I told you both I'd be back."

Girak's blue eyes widened in horror. "You're clearing water? In secret?"

"Our drinking water is bad?" Atsushi whispered.

"Atsushi, I think you need to leave." Josefina gave him a firm smile. "Now."

Behind her, the water bubbled through the equipment. "I don't mean to be rude, but if the water's bad, I need to know. We all do." Ayanna drank water like a fish. Was that why she'd missed classes lately? Bad water?

"Atsushi," Girak began, "Maybe Jos and I should—"

"Continue lying?" Atsushi asked. "Because I'm not going to keep a secret if everyone's in danger."

Josefina blew out a huge sigh. "O-kaaay, I guess we're doing this conversation now." She glared at Atsushi. "You better honor your word about keeping this secret, though it's none of your business."

He inwardly squirmed at her glare yet stood his ground. "It puts no one in danger?"

"Of *course* not."

At her exasperated tone, he nodded. He'd just committed himself to another secret.

"Our water supply is fine." She put down the beaker and touched Girak's arm. "I wanted to surprise you, Dig."

"With an illegal lab?" As Girak studied the equipment, his expression grew more and more grim. "You know you can't clear the birth control from the women's water. If the Council discovers you're going against their policies—"

"Dig, we were *approved*. We can have a baby!" Her face lit with joy. "I got permission to surprise you the day I left. I thought it would distract you from worrying and give you something to look forward to on my return." She winked at Girak, whose face lit with joy as he leaned forward and kissed her.

Ugh. He shouldn't be here. He crept a few steps backward.

"Hold on," Josefina snapped.

Atsushi froze. He needed Neviah's holographic disappearing corner.

"I don't want you to think I'm breaking the law like a Deplorable, so hear me out," she said. "The Council ordered me to wait until after the expedition, but all the other women said it never works the first month off the water. So, I…" She shrugged. "I took matters into my own hands."

"Why?" Girak grasped both her arms. "Why would you risk everything we have?"

"Because I want a family, and Northern Haven needs our kids. It's not fair that other women get your children while, despite our perfect genetic match, they make us wait. Don't you think that's odd? Don't you think maybe Kern has something to do with that?"

Girak paled at the mention of Commander Savas.

Atsushi's mind scrambled to keep up. "Why would Commander Savas care?" *Shast.* He hadn't meant that to be out loud.

Josefina turned and seemingly realized he was still present. "Because he hates the fact that I married Diggory instead of him. You'd think he'd be happy with all his girlfriends, but he's become such a jackass."

"He's always been one," Girak groused.

"Back when he first started talking about leaving Northern Haven, he was different." She cast her husband a warning look. "And I wasn't naïve. I never fell for his games."

Girak shook his head. "No, but he's always thought those science discussions you two had meant something."

Josefina rolled her eyes. "He believes every woman wants him."

"Maybe I should just leave? Can I?" Atsushi backed farther toward the door.

Girak looked up, mortified. "I'm sorry. You wanted my help, and now you're involved in…" He waved his hand around the lab. "Ugh." He groaned and covered his face with his hands.

"It's okay," Atsushi said, itching to get away. This conversation gave him the heebie-jeebies. "I won't tell anyone. Just tell Neviah something about the batteries, okay?"

"We can trust you about all this?" Josefina's dark gaze penetrated Atsushi to the core. "Because if you screw us over on this…" She didn't finish, only glared.

"Yes. I gotta go." He spun and hurried through the living room.

As he opened the door, he instinctively touched his pants pocket to confirm he had his comm, but his hand slapped only fabric. He spun, scanning the living space, as the front door slid shut. From inside the illegal lab, Josefina whispered something, and Girak gasped.

"Already? You're already—"

"Four weeks," she whispered, giggling.

*Four weeks pregnant? Where the shast is my comm?* He hurried to the chair he'd sat on and slid his hand around the sole cushion. Nothing. *Shast. Shast. Shast.*

"You shouldn't go up there. It was risky before, and now…" Girak said to her from the other side of the wall as Atsushi spun around their living room.

*There.* His comm was next to his educator's on the side table. He tiptoed over and snagged it.

"Dig, I'm still going. We both know how important this expedition is for the children. For humanity's survival."

Atsushi crept toward the door.

Jos said, "You're not going to forbid it out of some supposed masculine right to protect me, are you?" That edge that had scared him before had resurfaced.

"Never. I just—"

Not wanting to hear anymore, Atsushi dashed through the door and skidded into the opposite wall.

"Atsushi?"

The door slid shut.

He considered running, but instead stared at the closed door, willing it to stay closed. Willing the Giraks to not check.

The door slid open and Girak sprang out nearly running into him. "Atsushi? I thought you'd already left. His educator's eyes were wide with fear.

"I started to, but my comm wasn't in my pocket. I can't enter my module without it, and explaining where it was to my parents would mean explaining why I was here, and you didn't want people to know—" Aware they were in public, he swallowed the rest.

Girak's panic softened to a frown. "Hmm." He glanced up and down the hallway. "Can you keep this a secret until I figure something out?" He whispered, "Please?"

He nodded.

Girak checked the hallway again and whispered, "I'll let you know as soon as we have a plan, okay?"

Atsushi nodded, unsure how to respond.

Would knowing their secret upset them both so much that he'd lose the connection he'd always wanted with Girak? Despair crept into his chest, and he could only stare at his educator, ashamed to crave his approval.

Girak smiled and clasped him on the shoulder. "Thanks." He checked his comm. "You better get going. Your concert starts soon."

"It's that late?"

Girak nodded. "Have fun. We'll be there."

As Atsushi hurried down the corridors leading to the auditorium, he wondered what sort of plan the Giraks could concoct. Yes, the expedition was vitally important, but was it safe for her to go on it? He knew little of pregnancy, but if anything happened, the council would blame Girak. They thought women never did anything on their own without their husbands' consent.

The council had clearly never dealt with Ayanna. She'd never listen to anyone, not even Bleu. That fire attracted Atsushi, but he feared the Giraks might soon get burned by Josefina's rebellious sparks.

# Chapter 14

*The base of Mount Syeti: Rana*

By the time the salmon-colored sunrise framed Mount Syeti, their temporary camp had been completely dismantled. The only signs remaining of the multi-village gathering were the stamping, pack-loaded salt deer, the stretching white lions, and the star beings milling about exchanging final farewells with friends from other villages. Somewhere out there, Kahali, Balavati, and Daman were having fun, whereas she'd been pulled aside by Desna for an ill-timed parental chat.

"Do you think you'll volunteer to Call?" Desna asked.

Rana groaned. "Do we need to do this now? Can't we talk on the way home?" She still couldn't spot her friends.

"No, you need to make a decision."

"They want Callers with advanced skills. That's not me." She laughed. "Come on, you know that."

Desna pursed her lips, then shrugged. "Okay. I thought the experience might gain you skills toward Crowning. But if you're not ready, you're not ready." She hefted her pack onto her shoulder.

"Wait." She grabbed Desna's arm. "You really think it's that important?" Desna nodded.

"Then I'll consider it." She pulled her cloak tighter against the wind. "Can I go now?"

Desna frowned. "I'd love for you to return with us, but after her transtemporal scan on you, Kalakanya has a...request." The unease in Desna's tone gave her shivers.

"O-kay?"

"She saw two time threads for you. In one, you return today with us to the village. In the other, you return the shorter Northern-most route around Lake Missal—alone." Desna sighed. "The second option is dangerous, with predators, but if you choose that path, you'll meet someone vitally important to our community and the changes we face. It's your choice."

"Changes?" Rana asked.

Desna raised her palms in a gesture of not knowing. "I think as a result of Calling the Earth children."

Rana looked away, her eyes burning. "This is Sukti's vision, isn't it? If I go, I'll likely die?"

"She said you have equal chances of death and success, and that the success would be very important to us. She wants you to go." Desna put her hand on Rana's shoulder. "But she's not a maha. I couldn't bear it if something happened to you."

"Who is this star being I'm supposed to meet, and how will I find them?"

"You know how her gift works." Desna sighed in exasperation. "Telling us would change the outcome."

"I either stay safe and selfishly don't help my community or die trying? Why me?" she demanded. The only reason she was different than her peers was her parents.

Desna chuckled and shook her head in amusement. "So much fire. Look, this has nothing to do with your parents. That's not the way of the One In All. Every child is dreamed into existence for a beautiful purpose, and that purpose is not to face the consequences of your parents' behaviors."

"Then why me?" Rana kicked an ice chunk.

"Oneness knows! I have never understood how Kalakanya's time threads work, but they do. We all have our paths, and today, you get to choose between two."

"What should I do?"

Desna cupped Rana's chin in her hands and kissed her forehead. "You must make the choice."

Rana backed away and looked from the crowd of family and friends toward the northward icy desolation that she might soon face alone. "I need to go the Northern route around Lake Missal, the faster route, to meet someone?"

"If you so *choose*. No one will think less of you if you come home with us instead."

"*I will*." she said, nearly growling with frustration. "If I want to Crown, I need to face my fears, right?"

"Yes, but not recklessly endanger yourself. She's giving you an option. Why don't you come home?" Desna held out her hand, waiting.

Rana frowned. She had always sensed something between Kalakanya and Desna. Her maha didn't seem to quite trust the younger Crowned One, always questioning her transtemporal readings.

"I'm equally as likely to succeed as to fail?"

Desna swallowed. "Yes."

"Then I'm going." She watched as the Lion Master Sandor allowed his large cubs to topple onto him. "The lions have always guided us, which means Sukti gave me that vision for a reason. She wants me to know what to avoid to stay safe. If I can do that and stay alive, I'll be closer to Crowning."

Desna pursed her lips, in deep thought. "I'm not sure I agree with your logic, yet..." She gave a tremulous smile. "I accept your decision."

"Wait. What if I meet Malakut? He's no longer bonded by the Lion Circle and still might be in the area." That sea bear was scary.

"You have talents with the furred ones and have already travelled alone before. Remember your skills and trust the One In All." Desna pulled her in for a hug. "I'll let your friends know what you are doing, and Sohana already packed you some food and supplies." Desna gestured to where Sohana waited with a pack. "It's kind of exciting, right? Knowing your community needs you?"

"I guess," Rana said.

A true heroine would happily help her village, not begrudgingly help for fear of not Crowning. She wasn't a heroine, but she'd do anything that increased her likelihood of Crowning.

She gave a parting bow. "Wish me luck."

"My heart and blessings are always with you." Desna's face tightened. "Be careful, okay?"

Rana nodded and bowed farewell and then sulked over to Sohana.

"Here." Sohana extended the pack toward Rana, her new, radiant form like salt in Rana's wound of self-doubt. "I even snagged you some of that amazing sweetbread from the feast." Sohana's grin carried the same mischief as her younger brother's, Kahali. "A certain *friend* told me you especially enjoyed it."

"Thanks. I didn't even get to tell him I can't walk back with him," she said.

"He'll forgive you." Sohana gave her a knowing smile.

Standing next to her newly Crowned peer, Rana found own grumpiness childish. She sucked in a deep breath and straightened her shoulders. "Okay. See you back home."

Rana shouldered her bag and scanned the crowd one last time for her friends. For Eka. Desna didn't know to tell him.

As she walked alone across the field, the misty snow swirls blew across her path, churning like her emotions. Not only would she miss all the fun of traveling with her friends, she now faced two days of hiking alone in an unknown wilderness.

"Rana. Wait," a guy said, his shout punctuated by distant crunches of boots on iced snow.

She spun around. Eka had broken away from his village's group and ran across the field toward her. His long black hair whipped about him in the wind.

He cared enough to search her out. She beamed and tapped the snow off her boots, grinning at the ground.

"Why...are you...going off on your own?" Eka breathed hard from his long sprint across the snow-encrusted field.

She shrugged. "I've accepted a special assignment."

His brow furrowed as his gaze followed Desna and Sohana's figures merging with the laughing crowd. "From the Crowned Ones?"

She nodded. "From Kalakanya."

"Oh." He watched as Desna disappeared into the group, biting his lip as if considering his next words. "Um, I wanted to ask if…if Tejas and I visit your village to trade, could you and I maybe meet?"

*He wants to meet again!*

A huge grin burst forth before she could squash it. Ugh. She was doing this all wrong. She shouldn't encourage him, especially when she might die before he ever made it to her village. It was plain mean to lead him on.

She shrugged and went for a matter-of-fact look. "You don't need my permission to visit my village." It came out all wrong and offensive, making her want to hide under a rock.

He frowned. "Okay." Tilting his head, he asked, "Are you okay?"

It would be kinder to end this now. Let him be offended and leave. But that wasn't right, either.

"Sorry, I'm a bit out of sorts with Kalakanya's request to…" Her voice faltered as she met his gaze and blushed at its intensity. She blinked to recover her brain. "They said I need to meet someone on my way home. But I have to go alone, the short way."

"By yourself?" His eyes widened. "The whole way?"

"Yes." Anger surged through her body. *He thinks I'm incapable.*

His eyes flashed with mischief. "You're anything but incapable."

She snorted and looked away. In her outrage, she hadn't kept her thoughts private. This is why she'd never Crown.

"What I meant is, are you okay with what they're asking?" He glanced back at his villagers disappearing into the distant tree line. "With doing this?"

"They gave me a choice." She scowled at her defensive tone. "I'm a bit worried, but I chose to help out." *And Crown.*

"Okay." He frowned and worked his jaw as if he had contracted her worry. "I get protective of my…friends when they order us around, you know?"

"I'll be okay," she reassured him, hoping it proved true.

"Right. Of course." His amazing grin burst forth, the one that warmed her to the core. "Call me if you need anything. Anything. I'm very good at hearing others."

"Yeah." she laughed. "I may have noticed that."

"Right." He shook his head, chuckling. "It's not my fault you didn't block your thoughts."

Raising an eyebrow in feigned offense, she retorted, "You didn't need to listen."

He tapped his walking stick on the ice. "I like your thoughts." That grin spread across his face. "Anyways, I can't star beam, of course, since I'm not Crowned. But if you run into trouble, I could get help, okay?"

*Oh, yes.* That grin would keep her warm the whole walk home. She blinked, breaking the intensity. "I'll be fine. I hope."

"Right. Of course." Clouds of some turbulent emotion dimmed his previous brightness. "May the One In All keep you safe." Bowing, he took a few steps, looked back, and then tore off toward his villagers.

She stood alone. The wind whistled through the vacant campsite, pushing her toward the lake. She flipped up her hood and shivered. *I can do this.* She grimaced, unsure whether she meant her journey or ignoring her attraction to Eka.

\* \* \*

"Meet this mystery someone and get home safely," Rana grumbled, trudging toward the still icy lake.

Past lessons on the dangers of spring flooded her. It was risky, especially around the lake, because the melting could bring shifts in the ice. Hypothermia was a danger if she got wet from the melting ice and snow. And furred ones became more territorial, either because it was mating season, or they were already protecting young ones.

She prodded the ground ahead with her walking stick and stepped toward Lake Missal. Prod. Walk. Prod. Walk. She found her groove and soon only had to make sure she proceeded in the correct direction.

The lake's vast shore could be distinguished by slight differences in the

# CHAPTER 14

drifted snow. It lay flatter on the lake but became clumpy near the shore, where the snow's fluttered flight had been interrupted by protruding boulders and vegetation. The tops of scattered bushes peeked out from below their snowy blanket.

She trudged on, grateful for the well-trodden salt deer paths and the company of the gusting wind. As the sun rose higher, an eagle soared overhead, and she wondered if its higher vantage point allowed it a glimpse of the lake's other side.

The shore wound north and eventually east and south toward home. If she was lucky, she'd meet this person soon and gain a traveling companion. As the sun passed its zenith, the glare on the ice became unbearable. Squinting, she untangled her leather snow-glare mask from her hood and allowed it to hang over her face. Bless those two little slits that let her see without going blind.

The shoreline rose until it formed a rim surrounding the frozen water below. She edged farther away to avoid plunging downward. Desolation surrounded her. Who could she possibly meet out here?

Whoever it was, she'd be a better companion if she wasn't grumpy from hunger. Digging through her pack for the promised sweetbread, she stumbled on a buried stone and fell downward. As she slid down the rim toward the lake, her arms flung out to catch herself. There was nothing to grab.

Her left foot smashed against something but found no foothold. As she slid lower, she twisted and grabbed at whatever her foot had hit. Her left hand coursed over the rock. Her right hand found a sharp edge and held on, halting her plunge toward death.

She clung to the rock, panting. Her arm shook as it held her weight. Carefully, she dug the tips of her boots into the snow. How could she have been that careless? If she had fallen through the lake's frozen surface, she'd have drowned in its icy depths.

Carefully extracting her dagger from her pack, she used it to climb upward until finally she slid over the ridge and lay panting on the deer track. *See? Rana takes care of Rana.*

129

She rose on shaky legs and stomped on, not in the mood to meet anyone. *This was my own brilliant choice, so I should get on with finding this star being.*

The far-off call of wolves drifted across the plains to her and she shivered. She wasn't the best at shielding and had no weapon except the dagger. *Great. The wolves can use it to pick their teeth after they're done with me.*

Darkness would soon edge out the fading daylight, and she still hadn't reached the caves on the northern shore. As the rising moon crested the distant treetops, she sped up and then broke into a trot.

Something was wrong. The hair on her neck rose as she sensed a furred one following her. Her only chance was to reach the shelter of the caves before the predator attacked.

# Chapter 15

*nknown Wilderness: Rana*

Unknown Wilderness: Rana

Rana ran at an even, maintainable pace toward the rising, dark hulk of the ice caverns. Her assumption had been that the caves and a fire meant safety, but as she sprinted, another fear hit her. If Sohana hadn't packed the soaked wood, she wouldn't have a fire. The caves would offer no safety.

At a sudden scraping sound behind her, she burst into a sprint. Risking a quick glance behind her, she saw nothing but boulders.

Lions stalked. Wolves ran down their prey. Sea bears? She poured every bit of strength into reaching the caverns. If she could pick an unoccupied cave and light a fire to drive off predators, she'd survive.

She ran, struggling to center her mind. She would need intense focus to pick the right cavern. Just as she gained the right mental clarity—oneness with her breath, the steady rhythm of her pounding feet, and the expansiveness of the darkening indigo sky—she heard the scratching of paws on ice behind her. Her focus shattered, and adrenaline flooded her limbs in preparation of whatever furred one stalked her.

*One In All help me.* The Lion Circle, her safety zone, appeared in her mind's eye. Its pulsing energy connected with and slowed her racing heart, reminding her of her innate power. Her senses were magnified. All became clear.

*Desna said to trust.* Her eyes were drawn to a cave entrance ahead and a few feet off the ground. *Okay, I trust.*

Breaking every safety rule she had ever learned, she launched herself up and through the opening. Her left shoulder slammed against the icy ground as she rolled to pull her lower half into the enclosed space. She spun around and whipped off her pack. The rising gloom made vision difficult, so she riffled through her pack, trusting her fingers to find her fire kit.

Dried meat. Twine. Dagger. Finally, two soaked logs. She yanked one out of the pack and grabbed her flint, fire stone, and tinder pouch.

The logs were treated by the Crowned for the Uncrowned in situations like this. If she could only get a good spark, its special soaking would make it catch quickly and remain ablaze all night. She'd be safe.

As she smashed the stones together, scratching came from the darkness outside the cavern's mouth. Something was coming closer, maybe a stone's throw away from the entrance now.

*Kalakanya gave me an equal chance at success. I must find it.*

Her grip relaxed on the flint, and her hands glided together in a fluid motion. Sparks appeared. She repeated the movement, keeping her hands close to the tinder that rested within the carved log. The log burst into flame.

Scooting backward, she dug through her pack for the gripper, two interlocking carved bones that grasped a log like a torch. After scrutinizing the distance between the cave entrance and the burning log, she put the gripper down. The fire's current location would prevent predators from entering her cavern.

She glanced at the yawning blackness that made up the back of the cavern. A slight air current brushed her cheek. *Where's the air coming from?* Her eyes were useless in the darkness, and she wasn't eager to blindly enter the cavern's depths with only her questionable shielding abilities and her dagger.

She crouched, ready to lunge if necessary. Still holding the dagger, she inhaled deeply to awaken all her senses. She unfurled her awareness and prodded the darkness for a rear wall but couldn't sense one. Did the cavern curl back out like a ram's horn? That could be a good escape route...or another way in for whatever stalked her.

CHAPTER 15

Rana glanced around and pondered her best course of action. The cavern was large enough for her to stand erect, but in the near darkness, the uneven roof was treacherous. The burning log cast everything in flickering yellows and grays. Was it a trick of the light, or did strange, lateral lines mark the far wall?

She approached the marked wall, careful not to trip on the murky, rutted floor or smash her head on the jagged roof. The lines congregated in series of four, all over the wall. She traced their depth with her dagger. Horizontal lines…not from melting. An icy cold chill ran between her shoulder blades. *Claw marks. Oh my Oneness! Why was I pulled to this cave?*

Her heart thumped wildly in her chest. She could Call a Crowned One, but she was supposed to do this alone. From farther back in the darkness came animalistic grunts and whimpers. A vocal timbre that deep required a large body, probably a cave digger.

Falling stars! This was beyond her abilities. She needed help. Focusing all her attention inward, she resisted her instinct to fight or flee and Called the Crowned Ones. She'd mastered this in class, but never while in mortal danger. Every time she centered, and the energy built up, another growl made her lose focus. *I'm going to die because I can't focus*, she thought as she backed closer to the lit log.

The Crowned Ones should have already star beamed here. She wasn't Calling properly. No one had heard her.

She was on her own.

She knelt, and with trembling hands, she grabbed the extra piece of soaked wood. If she put one log in the back of the cave and kept one in the entrance, then maybe she'd be safe between them until daybreak. Of course, that assumed whatever predator lurked outside lost interest in her by daybreak.

Two fires were her best chance. Her only chance. She quickly placed the second piece of wood, filled its opening with tinder, and grabbed her stones.

The growling grew closer. At this rate, she'd never get the log lit in time. Her mind raced through possibilities, but they all required skills she lacked and ended with her death.

*Wait. Furred ones sense energy.* In desperation, she expanded her energy to appear larger and hoped her fake size might give the predator pause.

In this enlarged-energy state, she struck the flint and fire stone together. They sparked, but the log remained unlit. Long claws scraped against the floor. She peered up from the flint. The pale light of the first log reflected off two eyes.

Her body tensed, but she had nowhere to run or hide. She tried to create a shield, but in her panic only managed a brief spark. The furred one snarled. Her heart hammered against her chest as her gaze darted to the small dagger lying between her feet. She abhorred violence.

*Light the log, and neither of us will get hurt.* She continued madly striking the rocks together, but her hands shook too much.

Then Balavati's nonstop chattering and Kahali's laughter echoed through her mind, and the world made sense again. Their training mantra flowed through her... *Trust. Focus. Breathe.*

Everything came into ultra-clear focus as if time had stopped. The flint seemed to light itself before she noticed her hands moving. The tinder caught fire, lighting the log, and she exhaled slowly, afraid of extinguishing the new flames. Keeping the log aligned between her and the beast's eyes, she snatched the dagger. Could she hurt another being to preserve her own life?

She raised her gaze, and the shifting firelight revealed her worst fear—a full grown, teeth-bared cave digger. Its black lips curled, revealing a muzzle full of dagger-like teeth that reeked of musk and rotten meat. Her log formed a pathetic defense.

Everything she'd learned about cave diggers tumbled through her mind—long claws that dug huge tunnels through solid ice, intense strength out of proportion to their size, and incredible aggressiveness. In short, not the best company she could hope to meet.

Snorts and whimpers came from behind the furred one. *Oh my Oneness! There's more than one of them.*

She reached behind her and grasped the gripper. If she could hold up the flame, maybe it would back up. Her instinct was to mind talk, but cave diggers despised star beings. Since its broad head was waist high, she thrust the flaming log in front of her at its eye level, hoping to set a boundary. She didn't stand a chance against an enraged cave digger.

But the high-pitched whimpers that were increasing in frequency meant this den contained pups.

"Okay, momma." She struggled to keep her voice calm. "Let's work this out. I'll back up." She took a step backward and tripped over her pack.

A blur of noises and movement followed. A yelp escaped her throat, and she fell backward, landing on her shoulder. A loud crack sounded overhead, and the cave digger leapt forward, slicing the air where Rana's head had been.

Something fell on Rana's stomach, and she screamed, throwing her arms up protectively around her neck and face. But the thing on her stomach didn't move. Behind her, the cave digger also screamed in pain as more thunderous noises came from above.

Rana shoved the large thing—ice?—off her chest, scrambled to her knees, and began half running, half crawling toward the cavern entrance. Her arm snagged on something made of soft leather—her pack. She looped it around her shoulder as she strove to escape the chaos.

This was either a very unlucky earthquake, or the heat from her two logs had started a cave-in. She screamed as something sharp fell on her boot, sending hot, searing pain through her foot. The acrid smell of her own blood tinged the air. Lethal ice chunks fell all around her.

Sukti's vision had arrived.

# Chapter 16

The Ice Caves: Rana

Rana pulled herself toward the moonlit mouth of the cave, dragging her injured leg over and around the fallen ice blocks, ducking lethal-sized chunks as they crashed down from above.

"Ranaaaa! Rana, where are you?" a man's voice yelled.

Another block hit her shoulder and slammed her against the ground, knocking the breath from her. Snow and ice covered her head. Something grabbed her wrist and pulled. Her face plowed through the loose ice as she burst into fresh air. She tumbled downward onto the snow, landing face first on her rescuer.

Loud crashing and animal screams echoed behind her, and then silence. Her lungs screamed for air. Her throat burned as she coughed out snow and sucked air into her lungs.

"Are you okay?"

*Gandhapalin?*

The moonlight reflected on the snow-covered ground, giving her enough light to make out his features. She blinked, disoriented. It wasn't Gandhapalin. She squinted and tried to focus her blurry and wavering vision.

"Rana?"

"Eka?" She gagged out more snow.

"You okay?" Eka's face was masked in concern.

She nodded, causing pain to slice through her shoulder. "I'm...alive."

"Yes, it would appear so." His eyes crinkled with humor, then narrowed.

"Your foot!"

Grimacing, she pulled her bloody foot closer. Her shock evaporated, and the full pain returned. "Oh, that's not good." The snow near her foot blossomed red. Shards of collapsing ice cave had sliced through her boot and had torn her foot.

"We need to stop that," Eka said as he unwrapped his scarf to use as a bandage. "Do you think you can get the boot off?"

Rana began to pull, but she couldn't get her foot close enough, given the injury, to get a good yank. "You do it. The quicker the better." She looked away, waiting for the inevitable pain.

"Sorry." He grasped her torn boot and yanked.

At the searing pain, she roared like a sea bear. Ice cold water splashed over her foot, and then the softness of his salt deer-fur scarf wound tight.

She grimaced at her partially wrapped foot. "Is it ruined?"

"It's fixable, but you need a healer. That was quite the growl." He nodded in approval. "Was that all you in the cave?"

Rana snorted and blushed at the same time. "Wait. That was you behind me?"

"They said you had to go alone, but they didn't say I couldn't follow."

"That's a unique take," she muttered and shook her head, but the pain stopped her short. Everything spun again. "I thought I was being stalked by wolves."

"Sorry." He frowned as he brushed ice from his furred coat. "I couldn't let you know it was me, or you wouldn't be going alone." They were both silent a moment, catching their breaths.

"So…" She scrutinized him. "Do you often ignore the Crowned Ones' wisdom and stalk others like a predator?"

A dark expression washed over his face, and he narrowed his gaze back toward Mount Syeti. "No." He grimaced and shook his head. "I've never ignored their wisdom before, but I should have. And I wasn't stalking you. I…I had reason to believe they messed up. Sorry I scared you." He cast her a sideways look. "Forgive me?"

She nodded. Of course she would forgive him. Holding onto anger was useless. Also, he'd just saved her life. But was he serious about not trusting the Crowned Ones' decisions?

"Can you sit up?"

She nodded. He put his arm behind her and supported her as she sat up. The flat frozen field tilted at strange angles. "Whoa..."

Only his arm around her kept her from toppling over. His warmth seeped through her cloak and into her trembling body. Annoyed at her weakness, she jutted out her jaw and put her hands onto the ground to support herself.

This was *her* quest. Everything around her still spun, but she refused to let on to it. However, she couldn't ignore that he believed he should disregard the Crowned Ones' advice. No one did that. It made no sense to avoid advice that was always correct and well-intentioned.

"Why ignore them?" It came out accusatory.

"What?" He sat back on his heels and blinked in confusion.

"You said you thought the Crowned Ones had messed up. I get questioning them, because they annoy me too with their lack of explanations. But why would you not trust them when they said I'd be safe? Why follow me? It makes no sense."

"Oh." He stared at the snow-laden ground, biting his upper lip as if to keep himself from saying more.

She waited, too tired to move on.

"Sometimes...once..." He sighed and gave her a searching glance. "They're not always right. Everyone thinks they're perfect and infallible. My own parents said I misunderstood, but I know I didn't." His words had tumbled out like rocks down a mountain, gaining speed as he went.

His accusation against the Crowned Ones hung awkwardly in the air between them. How could he experience them so differently?

"I don't understand what you're trying to say."

He gave her a sad smile. "I sound a bit off, don't I?" He searched her face for a reason to continue. It seemed that whatever he was about to say had been held to his chest in silence a long time.

"Maybe start at the beginning?" she suggested.

"Right, of course." He stared at the ground a moment longer. "My older cousin, Gian, was a bit different. He avoided others, was moody a lot, and preferred furred ones to other star beings. But the two of us were real close." He motioned toward her bandaged foot. "Is that really okay?"

She nodded. "Thanks. What happened to him?"

"Last spring softening, the Crowned Ones said he needed to figure out what was bothering him. I don't know what that meant, because he told me everything." He shrugged. "Anyways, they sent him into the mountains for seven suns to perform a specific ceremony. Before he left, he'd said he had a bad feeling about going, but he had to trust them. On his fourth night away, I awoke from a nightmare where I was him and fighting off a strange predator." Eka closed his eyes. "He was supposed to be safe."

She gasped. "He died?"

Eka nodded, his eyes still closed. "When you'd said they were sending you out, and said you were worried..." He grimaced and rubbed his face with his hand before casting her a tentative glance. "I know I should trust them. Usually I do. But the two situations seemed similar, and I promised myself I'd never let that happen to anyone else..."

"A predator killed him?" Rana reeled from his revelation. It echoed the strange tragedy of her parents' deaths.

"Yes, despite his ability to shield and to mind speak with furred ones. It made no sense. I've always felt like our special connection had given me the nightmare—like a warning. If I had acted faster, and been able to star flash, or gotten a Crowned One..."

"Eka." She touched his arm. "Please, don't blame yourself."

"I should have listened to my dream..." He sucked in a shaky breath.

"But you didn't know. It's not your fault..." But she had blamed herself for years after her parents' deaths. How much worse would it have been if she had dreamed their deaths in real time?

She said, "Wait. Isn't your family wondering where you are right now?"

His lips cracked a smile. "I told them what I was doing. That I had to make sure. Ironically, they said it might help me regain my trust in the One In All." He shook his head. "But I was right. You would've died."

Rana frowned. "Not necessarily. If I hadn't mistaken you for a predator, I would have picked a cave more carefully."

He covered his face with his palm. "Falling stars, I caused this?"

She shrugged. "Maybe? At least you meant well." She grinned.

"Right…" He sighed. "I'm sorry. Look what my anxiety has caused." He motioned to the ragged, ice-covered mess they both were in. It *was* a mess, but the guy needed to chill.

"On an interesting note," she teased, hoping to lighten the mood, "your hair is freezing in wild spikes." She batted the ice off one of his long strands.

"Oh." He frowned at his frozen locks and then seemed to recognize the humor there. "This is my new Tejas-approved style."

She snorted.

He motioned to her own hair. "Your braid is frozen solid."

She glanced down and groaned. "That will be cold later." She shook it out, showering him anew with ice.

"Right." He gave her an approving nod. "I deserved that for my failed attempt to not interfere." He turned to look at the collapsed cavern. "What was that in there?"

"A cave digger."

"Oneness!" He shook his head in disbelief. "When you get in trouble, you really go big."

She laughed. "It's my specialty, though I don't know how I'll finish my mission now."

"I'm not a healer, but I can work on your foot. That might at least get you moving again."

She nodded and shifted her foot onto his lap. "Thanks."

As he cupped his hands over the tied-off wound, a healing warmth filled her foot. Energetic first aid. She sighed as the pulsing pain gradually lessened.

"Better?" he asked.

"Much. Thanks."

He flashed his lop-sided smile. "The least I could do after scaring you into a cavern with a cave digger. What do you want to do now? I'll help if you want."

"Think it's dead?" She gestured with her chin toward the collapsed cave. The adrenaline was wearing off, and she was exhausted, too tired to talk.

He narrowed his gaze at the collapsed cavern. "I suppose one could dig its way out of that mess, assuming it survived being crushed."

"We should be good. The biggest pieces of falling ice were behind me." She sensed she'd omitted something, but a brain fog had descended. After yesterday's strenuous Spiral Ceremony, the long day's walk on her own, and the attack, she was crashing from exhaustion.

He sighed. "Its death is my responsibility, too."

What kind of star being was she that she hadn't even worried about the cave digger's life? "We should be good" was a horrid thing for her to have said.

"I'll give you my left boot. It should fit with the wrap on." He pulled it off and handed it to her.

"No, I'll be fine."

"Fine to sit here and freeze to death." He mock grimaced. "I doubt that's what the Crowned Ones had in mind for you—survive the cave digger attack, refuse help, and then freeze to death unable to walk."

She rolled her eyes. "Fine." Taking the boot, she braced herself and pulled it over her torn foot. "What about you?"

He rifled through his pack and retrieved a bundle. "Extra socks. I'll be fine as long as we avoid water. Or should we Call for help?" He clearly hadn't heard her attempts at Calling earlier, and he had been right outside the cave.

"I haven't met anyone yet," she responded.

He raised his eyebrows, motioning to himself.

She laughed. "You don't count. I already knew you."

He shrugged and grabbed another thick sock from his pack and pulled it over his already socked foot. "Then what's the plan?"

She wobbled into a standing position, wincing as she touched her torn foot to the ground. She scanned the direction she had to travel. The sky was still dark, and only a weak, silvery light shone from the slivered moon.

"I have to continue." Her glance went down to her foot, then to his supplies. "Could you please lend me your walking stick?"

"Of course, but I'm not thrilled about you out here alone, bleeding. The smell of fresh blood will get you lots of unwelcomed company." He gazed past her to the horizon. "I could follow like before, and then you'd still be following their instructions?"

"Why bother when I'll know you're back there? I suspect everything's changed." She frowned. "Should we spend the rest of the night in a different cave?"

He studied the endless pockets of darkness in the pale moonlight. "Since cave diggers are territorial and have huge territories, the caves nearby should be pretty safe."

"Because my burning logs killed the local one," she whispered, flush with guilt.

"We share that responsibility." Standing up, he handed her his walking stick.

Rana grasped it, and even in the watery moonlight, its beauty was clear.

"Wow. You made this one, too?" She yearned to raise it and examine its geometric patterns, but feared she'd fall.

"Yes, it took a nearly full moon cycle." His face lit with pride. "That's the only one I won't trade away, though if you really like it, I could attempt a replica." He grinned. "Come on, we should find a cave before your blood attracts the sea bears." They turned back toward the caverns and approached the entrance next to the collapsed one.

"Maybe we should skip this one in case it was weakened by the collapse next door?" She wanted no more trouble.

"Good thinking." They moved on to another promising entrance.

Eka entered the cavern to check for signs of furred ones. If only she had been able to check the first cave before diving inside. Instead, her mistaken panic at being stalked by a predator had resulted in a loss of life. Such reactive behavior would never get her Crowned.

He hurried back outside to her. "This one will do." He grinned as he lit one of his logs and helped her into the cave.

They had just settled against one of the cavern's walls when a strange high-pitched noise pierced the night.

"It's probably the wind." Despite his confident tone, his hand slid to his dagger.

"Eeeeeek." Pathetic whimpering soon followed.

Rana's heart thudded hard in her chest again. "I forgot. I think I heard babies in the cave."

"Cave digger pups?" he asked, jumping up.

She nodded.

"But the mom was right behind you when the whole thing collapsed." He glanced toward the back of the cave, using his gripper to hold up the flaming log. "She had to be killed...right?"

"She screamed. It happened quickly, but she must have. If you hadn't pulled me out right when you did..." Her heart quickened at the memory.

"We should move on, just in case. Let's go." Eka helped her up and pulled her toward the entrance.

"Wait. Please?"

*What am I doing?*

Reason urged her to follow Eka outside, yet she was drawn toward the pathetic whimpers coming from the cave. "If this cave connects to the one that collapsed, we should be able to go back there."

"No. It's a deathtrap. Come on." He motioned toward the front of the cave.

"No." Why was she being reckless and pulled toward the sound? Her poor choices had already probably killed the mom cave digger.

Desna's face loomed in front of her. *Sometimes we must trust in our journey.*

"I can't explain it. I need to check it out."

"Rana, we need to leave. Now." He urgently waved his arms in circular motions, motioning for her to follow.

"Eka." She caught his arm. "I know it makes no sense, but I have to go back there. I can't explain it. I *know*."

Eka stood still and tilted his head, reading her.

*He sure has that penetrating look down.* She glared back at him, daring him to argue.

"All right," he muttered and shook his head, as if engaged in an internal argument with his own better judgment.

With his lit log held aloft in a gripper, he led them deeper into the ragged cavern. When they turned a corner, the stink of death nearly knocked her over.

"You sure about this?" he asked.

"Yes," she replied. Deep down, she knew it was the right thing.

"And you claim Balavati is the one dragging *you* into trouble," he teased as he created a small shield around the two of them.

Rana hobbled behind on her injured foot. The tunnel split.

Eka peered back at her, eyebrows raised in question.

"That way." Rana pointed with her chin, one hand gripping the walking stick while the other trailed along the wall for support. The smell grew worse. She needed a third hand to cover her nose.

They rounded another corner, curving back out toward the entrance, and were met with a wee growl.

"What?" Eka jumped back, his shield flickering.

Rana giggled and strained to see over his shoulder, but her giggle faded away.

The now-dead mother cave digger lay before him, her crushed bloody head and shoulders protruding into the opening from a pile of collapsed ice. In front of her lay more ice with the tails of two small bodies sticking out. Their mother had not reached them in time.

How had she not cared about this beautiful creature's survival?

"What's growling?" she asked. Everybody appeared lifeless.

Eka backed up. "It's coming from the mother. Go."

"Wait."

The growl was pitiful. Could a dying adult even make that high-pitched a sound?

A small snout jutted out from under the adult's throat, vibrating with a tremulous growl.

"Oh my Oneness." Rana gasped. "It's dangerously cute."

A young cave digger pup, smaller than her forearm, struggled to emerge from its shelter under its mother's throat. It growled fiercely, protecting its fallen kin. Newly opened eyes struggled to focus on them as its whole body shivered.

"Are you going to attack us, little one?" Eka dropped his shield. He flashed a grin back at Rana. "Now what?"

Rana paused. This was a cave digger. A very cute little cave digger. Its brown, black, and white striped fur betrayed its helplessness by trembling. She leaned down to examine the pup more closely. It was young yet already displayed legendary claws. Straightening up, she winced at the pain in her foot.

Its mother had almost killed her, but this shivering mass of fur was too young to survive on its own. "We can't leave it here."

Eka grimaced.

Rana pulled at the pack on her shoulder and removed some dry meat. She bit off a small piece and tossed it at the trembling mess. The pup froze, and then stretched its head forward. It made snuffling noises, licked at the meat, and then tumbled into a heap. It made another yowl and raised its quivering head.

"It doesn't eat meat yet. How could we even feed it?" She watched Eka, hoping he'd share her compassion for the young creature. She didn't know him that well.

"You could take it to the Lion's Circle and have the Crowned Ones Call for an adult cave digger."

Rana sighed. "They never come to the Circle."

"They never help other species, but they might come for one of their own," he reasoned, stretching the limits of believability.

"Hmm." She painfully squatted and opened her pack. Using Eka's walking stick, she gently pushed the pup's rump until it half-crawled, half-tripped into her pack.

"Well, then, that decides it." He shook his head. "You know it's going to tear its way out of there and shred your shoulder with its claws, right?"

"We'll see," she said, beaming. He was probably right, but she was giddy with happiness. She murmured to the ball of fierce fur and gently closed the pack, careful to not make any sudden movements. She fiddled with the closing strap. The pup needed air, but she didn't want to freeze her new little charge. It grunted as she shifted the pack to her right shoulder, away from her heart, in case it panicked and clawed her.

Fortunately for her foot, the pup weighed little. Strangely, its desperate plight had evaporated her exhaustion. "We better get moving. We have a pup to save."

"What about the star being you're supposed to meet?"

Rana froze. He was totally right, yet she knew she had to save this pup. Was it her guilt over killing its mother or something else that guided her?

"Kalakanya never specifically said a star being. Maybe I'm supposed to meet this wee one?" She pointed at the stowaway in her pack.

Eka chuckled. "You really believe they'd send you to find a cave digger?"

"Desna said to trust in my journey, and Sukti gave me a vision of the collapsing cave that killed her mom." She grimaced. "Is it that too wild?"

"Hmm." He stared at her pack. "Maybe not, now that you put it all together."

"Or if there is still someone to meet, maybe they're along our direct path to the Lion Circle."

"We'll need the Crowned Ones to return before you Call the other cave diggers," he reasoned.

"Uh-huh." But Rana wasn't fully listening. She was alive. She had survived Sukti's vision. She had a cave digger pup to save. And, most importantly, she still had a chance at Crowning.

# Chapter 17

*Northern Haven: Bleu Reinier*

After another rough night with Ayanna, Bleu dragged himself from sleep by remembering that he had to reach the Surface and somehow find a cure. And to do that he had to first get his butt to training and act as if everything were fine. His family had hidden Ayanna's Sickness during the concert by claiming she'd eaten bad food and needed to stay home, but someone would soon notice the pattern of her absences. He grabbed a breakfast bar and strode through the halls toward practice, hoping his friendly greetings to teammates hid his exhaustion.

Today and for the last two weeks they trained daily in the largest gaming room, now a holographic nightmare of subfreezing temperatures and extreme winds. As Commander Savas hit the button on his remote control, the bitter wind stopped churning through their campsite. Bleu teetered in the immediate lack of opposing force and fell forward onto his orange tent, its canvas billowing around his fallen body. Stamf and Zach snorted in laughter as he tried to free himself.

"It's all fun and games in here, men, but out there, I can't hit a remote to save your butts." Commander Savas focused his glare on Zach, though Stamf had also chortled. Zach was not Prime Minister Pridbor's nephew.

*Sometimes, Lee's a bit too good in his programming,* Bleu thought as sensation returned to his frozen cheeks.

"I'm not taking you softies up there until I'm confident you'll have a rat's ass of a chance to return alive, so we're having an extra session tonight after dinner." Savas glared at Abdul. "And yes, you'll show up in full gear."

Abdul smiled a good-natured toothy grin at his commander, not the least bit rattled. Bleu warmed at his teammate's skill at taking their commander in stride.

If only he could do the same. He despised Commander Savas' ability to elicit efficiency at the cost of human decency. Last week, he'd tried to convince the Council to "kindly kill" the teens afflicted with the Sickness, and then he'd bragged about how his policy would save resources in their next expedition training.

Commander Savas' pulse was as frozen as his icy blue eyes, and while Bleu would follow his orders to reach the Surface, he'd never trust him.

"Should we repack this now, sir?" Abdul motioned to the limp tents.

"Last I checked, they weren't self-packing tents." Savas muttered something about lack of time, turned abruptly, and crashed into Josefina.

"Sorry, sir." She squatted on the ground and repacked her equipment, which had been scattered by their collision.

Bleu marveled at Josefina's apology. *It was his fault.*

Commander Savas nodded to her and removed his headpiece to run his fingers through his perfectly trimmed hair. He knelt, assisting her with the cleanup, and said something to her, his voice too low to hear, but whatever he said got Josefina to laugh with him.

Savas stood and assessed the others, and his smile evaporated. "Maybe I should have you clean this up in the wind? I said *move*."

Bleu glared at the camp supplies still scattered despite his efforts. He groaned under his breath and gathered the gear.

"Perhaps you have forgotten the importance of our mission?" Commander Savas was on a roll.

*Here comes the lecture.*

Stamf, apparently agreeing with Bleu's assessment, rolled his eyes behind the commander's back. Bleu returned a grin.

"If we do not find other humans, humanity is done. We must defend our door, map the area, and confirm the pole readings to allow the next expedition to fly to the other Havens. All of this while you breathe air so foreign, it's as if your brain is flash-frozen with every breath." Savas spun toward Bleu before he could drop his grin.

"Bleu, let's see how amused you are when teammates die. Did you forget those who died on the first expedition?"

Bleu glowered at the floor. He hadn't poked fun at their mission, rather at the constant lectures. He knew what was at stake—Ayanna.

"Abdul, list the priorities and assignments." Commander Savas wouldn't let it go.

*How dense does he think we are?*

Abdul's grin faded as anger flashed in his eyes, yet his response came measured and calm, "One: Set up the base camp. Assigned to all of us. Two: Assess topography and dangers—that's Bleu, Stamf, and I. Three: Confirm magnetic poles and samples—Zach and Josefina. Four"—his voice dropped to a whisper—"keep an eye out for any Undescended."

The room went still as death. The Undescended, those not chosen to enter one of the four SHAST havens, had become more and more radical as the ice age increased and the havens were completed. Many had joined radical terrorist groups and vowed to survive, find the havens, and slaughter all those within. Every Northern Haven kid had nightmares of the Undescended attacking them.

Everyone in the room had ancestors who had been chosen to nestle in safety while the ice age ravaged the Surface. There were no expectations of survivors, but if any had survived, who knew how dangerous their radical fury had grown after centuries of being deserted to die.

The door whizzed open. Prime Minister Pridbor stood in the doorway with his lordly bearing. He visually assessed them all, scowling slightly at Bleu.

Turning to their commander, Pridbor said, "Commander Savas, a word with you."

"Of course, Prime Minister." Commander Savas bowed in respect, and then said to the team, "I want this neatly repacked. Now."

As Savas exited, Bleu exchanged concerned looks with the others. The Council had never shown up at training. What was going on?

"Do you think they've monitored us?" Abdul voiced everyone's concern.

"I can't go back to my old job. If I clean another slimy, eyeless fish, I'll scream."

"They won't replace us." Stamf gave his winsome smile. "We were all handpicked—they said that themselves."

Murmurs of assent answered him as the team strained to repack the bulky orange tents into their impossibly small bags. The tension remained too thick, the silence too long.

"If they were watching, it wouldn't be fair to judge us on today. Savas created that unrealistic wind storm just to test us. We won't have such a bad storm—its spring up there, right?" Bleu motioned with his chin toward the ceiling.

When Josefina remained quiet, he glanced over his shoulder to see her face shrouded in fear. *Of Commander Savas? But she's clearly his favorite.*

As Josefina caught Bleu's glance, her face became a mask. She jumped up, startling the others. "Get that packed up, Stamf." She threw her research gear over her shoulder, stood by the door, and glowered back at them. "This team isn't losing anyone up there."

When they exited the arena, Prime Minister Pridbor and Commander Savas stood against the gear room's far wall and conferred in hushed voices.

"Bleu." Commander Savas glared at him.

Pridbor slowly shook his head, causing his ample jowls to waggle.

*What did I do?*

As Bleu paused, shifting his pack, Stamf clasped his friend's shoulder. "I'll meet you at dinner. Good luck."

Bleu nodded slightly and then turned to join his superiors. Stamf and the others began stowing the tents and other gear against the wall. It was a small room, so his would be a public chew out.

"Yes, sirs?"

"You will not join us this evening," Commander Savas began. "In fact, you will not join us again. You are cut from the expedition team."

Bleu's jaw dropped. He glanced at Prime Minister Pridbor and was met with complete disdain. His teammates hushed and turned toward him, alarm flooding their faces.

*Ayanna.* No, this couldn't happen. Not when he was so close.

"The council held an emergency meeting this afternoon with your family as *guests.* It is clear Ayanna has the Sickness. We cannot risk you developing symptoms and endangering the team."

"But I'm fine." Then he added, "Sir." He desperately searched his commander's cold eyes for a change of heart. But he didn't have a heart.

"Doubtful. You and Ayanna are siblings." Prime Minister Pridbor regarded him like a grenade about to explode. "We will determine your future status by standard protocol. Until then, you are a risk and are cut from the team. You are quarantined to your module."

Bleu stood before all of them, grasping for a way to combat their decision.

"Dismissed, Reinier." Commander Savas shook his head. Whether in disgust or in self-pity for losing a team member, Bleu couldn't tell.

He wiped cold sweat from his brow. His mind spun, his thoughts unraveling. *What chance does Ayanna have now? And my vision...was it all for nothing?* His heart slammed against his ribs. The dagger bumped against his leg, a solid reminder of his vision of standing under the sky.

"Sirs, please." He knew it was futile to beg, but he had to save Ayanna. He was useless in quarantine.

"Do you need an escort, Reinier?" The contempt in his commander's voice hit him like a fist.

"No, sir." He forced himself to breathe normally despite the adrenaline coursing through him. He needed to get home. Was Ayanna okay? He spun to leave but then stiffened.

*Not too fast—they'll think I'm becoming symptomatic.* Bleu put back his shoulders and stared straight ahead as he strode toward the door.

"Leave your gear, Reinier," Commander Savas said.

Bleu froze and stiffly shrugged off his pack. It landed with a thud at his feet. He couldn't meet Stamf's alarmed gaze. Even his connection to Prime Minister Pridbor was useless when the Sickness was involved.

"The parka, too. Everything."

Was Commander Savas going to have him strip in front of everyone?

Bleu ripped off his parka, snow pants, and boots.

"All the layers. Someone worthy will need them." By Savas' tone, he'd already tossed him into the "kindly kill" category.

He shed the three layers of special thermals and socks until he stood in his underclothes. Could they see his heart thudding under his bare chest? Stamf left the group and hurried around the corner of the room, deserting Bleu. *He warned me if Ayanna's Sickness became known, he'd choose his uncle.*

Prime Minister Pridbor tsked and turned away.

Bleu shot a defiant glare to Commander Savas, turned, and forced his feet toward the door.

"Bleu, hold up." Stamf ran up behind him and handed him his regular pants that he must have just retrieved from the lockers.

"Thanks," Bleu mumbled. Unable to bear eye contact, Bleu looked away as he slipped on the too short pants and then rushed through the door. As it hissed shut behind him, all dreams of saving Ayanna and visiting the Surface were extinguished.

# Chapter 18

*eleguin-Rookery-by-the-Lake: Rana*

P
Rana sat on the great hall's floor, her legs splayed out straight with the trembling cave digger pup crouched between them, sniffing at the various foods Eka had retrieved from the food stores. Eka squatted beside her, eyeing the pup's every move. Distant singing alerted her of her fellow villagers' imminent arrival.

"They're back." She grinned at Eka.

Relief washed over both of their faces. The pup still hadn't eaten any of the food they'd placed before it.

"Raaaa-naaaa!" Balavati called.

Rana snickered. Of course, her loquacious friend was the first individual voice heard in the village.

"She should be the one Calling the Earth's children." Eka chuckled, and the pup cringed against Rana's leg at his laughter. She stroked calm energy into the striped head. Eka watched, his face tightening as he stared at the pup.

"What?" she asked.

"I ruined your mission, and now your community will pay the price."

She sighed. "There wasn't anyone out there to meet. You saw that."

"Hmm." He shrugged and cast worried looks from the pup toward where Balavati's voice had come from.

"Do you mind?" she asked, gesturing toward the approaching noise. She feared the pup's reaction to the loud crowd's entrance. Its small claws were still lethal.

Eka understood and sprang up to prevent the noisy villagers from scaring the pup. She'd only known him a few suns, and he already understood her as well as her lifelong friends did. Contentment seeped into a few of the empty holes inside her, holes created when she had been told her parents weren't coming home. Suddenly, she wished Eka hadn't left.

But she didn't have a long wait. Rapid whispers floated through the doorway and then a beaming Balavati tiptoed into the hall, closely followed by Eka, an oddly stoic-faced Kahali, and Daman. Curious others followed close behind.

Rana waved her friends closer. Balavati, never needing a second invitation, sprinted toward her.

"Rana," she whisper-squealed in delight, barely sliding to a stop before Rana's bandaged foot. She gasped. "What happened?" Then Balavati's eyes widened as they caught the pup's movement. "I leave you alone for a few suns, and not only do you get hurt, but you convince Eka to visit and rescue this fluffball?" She cooed at the pup.

Rana grinned and beamed at her new little charge. The squirming bundle of fur emitted strange grunts and whimpers at the newcomers.

"What is it?" Balavati circled closer.

"Isn't she cute?"

"Falling stars!" Balavati squatted, examining the pup. "Yes. But…what exactly is it?"

Rana smiled at the crowd. "It's a cave digger pup."

Gasps erupted from the group. Balavati jumped back. The pup hissed and scrambled closer to Rana.

Several Crowned Ones appeared, including Desna, who knelt next to Rana. "You know we need to take it to the Lion Circle immediately, right? In a year, this cutie would eat you without hesitation." She paused, her eyes softening. "She hasn't scratched you?"

"No, it's the weirdest thing. Eka and I thought she'd shred my shoulder, but she's fine."

"And the only star being you met was Eka?" Desna appeared unchar-

154

acteristically baffled. Behind her, Kahali and Daman made humorous motions about her having *met* Eka.

Rana ignored them and nodded. "No one else was out there."

As she related their escapades, the others oohed and ahhed at her adventures, but Desna's gaze never left the pup.

"I'm grateful you're safe." Desna gave Rana a look of such tenderness that she had to look down. Her real mother had often held her in such regard.

Desna moved closer to Rana's injured foot and hovered her hand above it. Tingles and heat washed over Rana's foot and ankle. The pain evaporated, and the slashed skin knit back together, so not even a scar remained. Like all Crowned Ones, Desna excelled at healing.

"Oh, Maha. That's much better. Thanks." Rana had been in pain for so long that the absence was a new delight. She gingerly tested her foot, first wiggling it on the ground, then standing.

At Rana's rising, the pup whimpered, and she crouched back down immediately. "Do we need to go to the Lion's Circle right now?" She dreaded giving her little sweetie over to a violent cave digger adult.

Desna nodded. "We need to do it before they send out the Callers. Did you decide to volunteer, dear?"

Rana shrugged noncommittally, scooped up the pup, wrapped it in her pack, and followed Desna to the door. Eka, Balavati, Kahali, and Daman trailed behind.

Kahali tapped her arm, his hand lingering there a moment longer than usual. "I'm glad you're okay. It wasn't the same without you on the way home."

"I'd give you a hug," she said as she grinned, "but my furry friend wouldn't like that."

"And I'd also prefer to stay in one piece." His eyes sparkled. "I can't go to the Lion's Circle with you because Kalakanya wants to talk to me. Good luck there with your little monster." He chuckled as the pup's snout emerged from her pack. "Catch up with you later?"

She nodded and hurried after her maha.

155

As she caught up, Desna turned. "We need to know who wants to Call and then make a plan. There's a bit of a rush on this decision, it seems."

Rana's mind swirled as she recalled her epic fail in the cavern with the cave digger. Was she capable of Calling?

She remained silent as they strode toward the Lion Circle, allowing Desna to access her turbulent thoughts. Her qualifications for Calling were questionable. She didn't want to relinquish her sweet pup to a violent adult cave digger. Her journey hadn't led to meeting anyone. And then there was Eka. Ah, Eka.

*Eka!*

Rana snapped her mind shut. *Oh My Oneness! Is he close enough to Crowning to follow my thoughts?*

Eka chuckled from behind Rana, but Daman and Balavati didn't. Were they joking back there, or had he read her mind again? Her heart began to race.

"Rana, let's focus on Calling the cave diggers." Desna was always the voice of reason.

"Okay." She wasn't sure she could focus on anything, but cave diggers seemed a safer focus than Eka.

"They've never come to the Lion's Circle before, but for another cave digger, they may." Desna paused, then said, "I want you to help me with this."

"Me?" She slowed her pace. Why was everyone expecting such difficult things of her lately?

"Clearly, I was correct. You're gifted with the furred ones." Desna gestured toward the pup in Rana's pack.

She blushed. Between Eka's presence and the compliments, her face would remain in a constantly reddened state.

"Do you remember the three scales of consciousness—sentience, capability, and awareness—from your classes?"

Rana nodded as she stepped carefully over some rocks to avoid jostling the pup. Sentience was the ability to differentiate oneself from others. Most of life had this ability, though sometimes, star beings lost all sense of themselves in deep meditation. Sentience was easy. It certainly wouldn't keep her from Crowning.

Capability was Rana's nemesis. Capability covered all inherent and learned skills. Inherent, like her having fingers to weave when a salt deer couldn't, and the birds flying when she couldn't. But the learned skills covered stuff like differentiating when she was being followed by a gorgeous guy from being followed by a pack of wolves, how to Call under all circumstances, or to hold a strong shield.

And then there was awareness, the ability to understand how one affects the whole of existence and how to utilize that interconnectedness. Trees rated high in awareness since they shared nutrients with others through their roots and changed their growth based on their surroundings to benefit all. Rana could do this a bit. She had expanded her awareness to the back of the cavern and noticed it continued in the darkness. But that was child's play. For Crowning, she'd need much more.

"What do sentience, capability, and awareness have to do with taking her to the Lion Circle?" Rana kissed the top of the pup's head.

As the pup murmured in delight at the kiss, Desna's eyes widened. "Incredible. Cave diggers aren't like other furred ones. They don't mind talk with us, and they've never come to the Lion Circle. We don't know if they lack the capabilities or the awareness. You should know that they may completely ignore us."

Rana selfishly hoped they did, so she could keep her. "I know. But it's not lack of awareness, because she knows I'm helping her. And she certainly has the capability to stop me—her claws are huge."

"This world is full of such delightful surprises. Did she let Eka carry her?"

Rana smirked. "No, only me. But she let him stroke her head between her ears. She likes that."

"Ah. Interesting." Every few steps, Desna stole glances at the pup. "Did you see any signs of other star beings along your path?"

"Nothing." Her stomach twisted. "Did Kalakanya say anything? Did I totally mess up?"

"No, I'd call this"—Desna motioned between Rana and the pup—"a miracle. Let's see if you have another miracle in you today. Think we can be the first star beings to successfully Call a cave digger?"

# Chapter 19

Peleguin-Rookery-By-The-Lake: Rana

Rana and Desna continued across the ice field in silence, with the others following behind. Distant squawking of nesting peleguins filled the air. As the Circle came into view, Rana's steps slowed, and she held her pup-filled pack tighter. The Circle's pulsing energy seemed to whisper to Rana, *Let her go. Let her go. Let her go.*

She glanced at the sleeping pup, sighed, and forced her heavy feet onward.

When they reached the outermost stone of the Lion Circle, Desna reviewed the plan. She herself would Call. When Rana sensed the approaching cave digger, she would remove the pup from its warm pack, put her into the center of the circle, and then stand behind Desna. Hopefully, the adult cave digger would adopt it.

As they got into position, two other Crowned Ones joined them.

"Backup," Desna explained. "Just in case. We've never had a cave digger come near the village."

Desna raised her arms in invocation and began the chant to connect herself to the Web of Oneness. Instantly, the circle hummed with warm vibrations. Then Desna put out the Call, a silent, energetic wave tuned to the vibration of cave diggers. It pulsed, throbbing like a beacon. Normally, animals of the Called species would mind talk in response, and Desna would then send them images of the issue. The Called species would then send one of its members to help.

After a short time, there was a slight change in the circle's energy as if

Desna had made contact. Rana searched the horizon for cave diggers.

Nothing.

Rana turned back to Desna.

Her maha's eye twitched slightly as she squinted in concentration. Desna slightly shook her head once, and then the energy shifted back to its original rhythm. Why was she Calling again?

The pulsing continued. Finally, Desna began an ending chant, lowered her arms, and backed out of the circle. Rana followed her lead, as did the other two Crowned Ones. Eka, Balavati, and Daman appeared confused as well.

"Sorry, Rana." Desna shook her head. "They're not coming."

"Why?"

"As far as I know, they've never cooperated within themselves or with other species. We're stuck with her, but..." She frowned. "I'm not sure it's safe to keep her."

The pup wailed as if aware that her fate hung in the balance. This time not even rubbing the patterned fur above the pup's eyes helped. Rana shot her friends a worried glance, hoping for support, but they were too busy gaping at the mini cave digger to notice her silent appeal for help.

"It's my fault she doesn't have a mother. I'll take full responsibility." Rana gave her best pleading look.

Desna narrowed her gaze at Rana and the pup, then sighed. "I guess if anyone can pull it off, you can."

"Thank you!" She rushed forward to hug her, but then remembered the pup and stepped back. "Can we make her a stew? She didn't like any of the samples Eka and I tried. It'd be warm."

"We'll try, dear. But she needs her mother's milk. Let's hurry back and see if I can convince a salt deer to share some."

As they all hiked back to the village, Gandhapalin strolled out to meet them. He glanced at Desna and then at the mewling pack cradled in Rana's arms.

"You two will figure this out." He patted Rana's arm. "I'm glad you're back safely." He kissed her forehead.

"Me, too. I'm glad Eka showed up at the right time."

Gandhapalin nodded soberly. "Thank you, Eka. You have our deepest gratitude. We'll be seeing you around?"

Eka's dark eyes sparkled. "Hmm. Maybe? Do you have any woodcraft mentors looking for a student?"

Gandhapalin chuckled. "Compared to Conifers-Greet-Mountain's-Shadow, we're a bit lacking in wood." He motioned toward the mostly flat land accented with bushes and some lone trees. Beyond that rose the rocky ridge that led to the peleguin breeding ground. "But I can make some inquiries."

Rana's brain froze. What were they doing? She and Eka just met, and her dad was already asking Eka if he'd like to stay in their village? She turned her back to them and noticed Desna studying her.

*Have you made up your mind?* Desna's question was sent to only Rana.

*You mean the Calling?*

*Of course. You have only just met him.* Desna chuckled, her brown eyes twinkling.

Rana groaned at her adopted parents' embarrassing attitude toward Eka and pulled her cloak hood lower over her face.

"I know it's the right thing to do, but I couldn't Call properly for help when her mom attacked." She nodded toward the fur in her pack. "My mess-up caused her family's death. I don't want anyone else to get hurt because of me."

Desna considered this, but Gandhapalin broke in. "You'll be in no danger Calling them, Rana. It's the reaction of the Earth's children that could be dangerous. Look at how well you handle her." He nodded to the pup. "You are tuning to a species that star beings have always struggled with—a capability we've never seen before."

Rana's heart thudded. Obviously, she should help, but her gut twisted like a tornado. Eka's proximity didn't exactly calm it.

"You need to decide soon, dear. They're planning for it as we speak," Desna added.

Rana closed her eyes. To Crown, she'd need to take risks and act enlightened.

She blew out a long breath and opened her eyes. "Okay, I'm in." The pup's wet nose nuzzled her hand. Rana frowned. "But, Maha, I have Digga to care for. Who'll watch her?"

"Uh-oh. She has a name now, does she?" Gandhapalin stroked his mustache to hide his obvious grin.

"I have to call her something. If she survives, we'll go to the Lion Circle and get a real name, right?"

"If she wants one, Rana." Desna smirked as the pup extended its snout into Rana's massaging hand and snuffled. "We need to figure out what to feed her, and then you can take her with you. That's what mothers do. Having her close by when you meditate and Call might even moderate her innate fierce nature. This connection is so unusual that I'm amazed she hasn't eaten your fingers."

Rana smiled, her chest warming at the praise.

Just then, Kahali raced up to them and slipped on a patch of icy snow. "Whoa." His arms flew up to balance himself as he nearly plowed Rana over.

Digga growled at the sudden intrusion into her space. Spittle flew from her tiny mouth as she lurched forward to grab a piece of Kahali.

*Digga, Digga. Shhhh.* A swoosh of intense power rushed through Rana's body. The air sparked to pink and gold around her chest. The pup froze in surprise and then slumped back down peacefully.

Rana let out a long sigh and realized how quiet everyone had gotten. She peered up to wide-eyed looks of her friends and family.

"What? I had to calm her down, didn't I?" Heat spread over her face.

"Rana, that was beautiful." Desna stared at her with moist eyes. "You're displaying all kinds of new capabilities since your journey. I'm immensely proud of you."

Desna gingerly hugged Rana off to the side while watching Digga's reaction. The pup ignored her and burrowed her snout into Rana's chest in the most adorable manner possible.

"Um...yah...wow, Rana." Kahali had regained his composure. He grinned at Rana and Digga until he noticed Eka behind her. His smile faltered. "I guess you've attracted us two new villagers, Rana." He glanced from Eka to Digga. "Sorry to upset your fur-child, but Kalakanya wants you, Balavati, Daman, and me to see her immediately about volunteering."

Desna said, "I guess Kalakanya reached the same conclusion as you did, Rana. Go to the meeting, and I'll make a few stews for Digga to try." Desna beamed at her, took Gandhapalin's hand, and the two Crowned Ones strolled back toward their home.

As the small group of friends turned toward Kalakanya's home, Rana paused awkwardly. "Eka, will you stay with us, or are you returning to your village?"

"I'd love to stay and visit. But…" His gaze met Rana's then shifted around to everyone. "But I probably should go Call for my own village. I already volunteered."

"Do you need to leave right away?" Rana's voice wavered. She'd hoped they could spend some time together without Digga between them.

"Yeah. May I speak to you alone for a moment?" Eka motioned to a lone evergreen as their intended spot for privacy.

"Sure." Had she responded too quickly? She nervously tucked the loose strands of her hair behind her ear.

"No." Kahali stepped closer to Rana.

The whole group turned to him, surprised.

"I don't mean to be rude, but Kalakanya will leave soon. She has a meeting south of the Earth Belt and will be gone for days. That's why I ran."

"Of course," Eka said, annoyance flashing across his face. "I'll be in touch. Be safe out there." Eka touched his palm to his heart, slightly bowed his head, and extended his hand toward them all. But his gaze was only on Rana.

Rana returned the gesture, wishing her friends would give them a moment's privacy.

They didn't. Eka headed toward the great hall for supplies he needed before heading off, the loose flow of his dark hair swishing with every step. Daman and Balavati smirked as she watched him and then left for Kalakanya's ice hut.

As Eka disappeared over the hill, she sighed at his absence.

"Let him go, Rana. His village needs him, and we need you," Kahali said. "Come on."

\* \* \*

As Rana easily kept pace with Kahali's jog, Digga made grumbling growls of protestation, but then adjusted to the rhythm. Village huts appeared on the horizon, their ice block construction reflecting pastel colors as the sun lowered behind them.

She adored the extra sparkle her village gained from its winter ice blocks. In the summer, the huts were made of earthen blocks, or tents if they were travelling. Crowned Ones could easily levitate blocks of earth or ice, and Gandhapalin joked that hut building was the physical counterpoint to their deep, meditative work.

From this distance, all the huts appeared nearly identical. But as they drew nearer, family huts could be identified by rectangles of color emblazed in the thickly woven mats that allowed entrance to the huts while keeping out the cold. Kalakanya's hut greeted visitors with a blue-and-yellow rendition of the night sky.

Rana slowed her pace, falling behind Kahali. She had passed Kalakanya's hut daily but had avoided entering it since the morning she had sat on her mats and learned her parents had both died in an avalanche. Crowned Ones would have survived such a disaster.

That day, that avalanche, had ripped holes in her heart. She couldn't deal with it today. She stopped, staring at the mat and blinking away tears.

Kahali took her hand. "Come on. This is totally different. We're going to do something good and help others. Your parents would be proud."

She nodded, not yet trusting her voice, and followed him to stand before the star-strewn mat.

Before entering, he called out the traditional greeting, "The One In All brings Love."

"The One In All receives Love." Kalakanya's voice rang within the frozen walls.

A moment later, her head and shoulders appeared from behind the mat. As usual, her white hair was immaculately braided and her green eyes shone with mischief. She bowed and held the mat aloft for their entrance.

Kahali's warm grip on Rana's hand tightened in encouragement, and they entered the tiny hut together.

Kalakanya's hut, sized for only one star being, was a cozy fit. As far as Rana knew, Kalakanya had never dated. Would knowing how the relationship would end beforehand ruin her relationships before they started, or allow her to enjoy the moment? Rana, enjoying the warmth of Kahali's hand around her own, briefly wanted Kalakanya's gift to know their potential.

Balavati and Daman were already crowded together on thick floor mats facing Kalakanya, who perched on her sleeping furs. Rana and Kahali squished in beside them. Every possible space on the mats was occupied, and this difference from that other lonely day Rana sat here alone helped keep her memories of that day at bay.

Rana loosened her fur cloak and tugged her braid free from her hood. Kahali sat close, still holding her hand.

He leaned over. "Okay?"

She nodded.

With a nod back, he let go of her hand and loosened his own cloak.

As soon as they had settled themselves, Kalakanya began. "I'm glad you came quickly. As you know, our village is closest to the underground home of the Earth's children, and therefore, each of you have a very important and possibly dangerous role to play. Are you all sure you want to Call?"

They all nodded.

A chill passed down Rana's spine. She had agreed despite her gut warning her this was not a good idea. Her mind went to Eka's cousin and his unexplained death by a violent predator. She shivered, and Kahali's hand found hers.

"Good." Kalakanya gave them a strained smile. "Also, I remind you that you need to be aware not only of the Earth's children but also of the normal, environmental dangers, primarily the predatory furred ones and weather changes."

They nodded again.

Rana's breath froze in her chest. *Falling stars! She just mentioned predators.*

Kalakanya laughed. "I've never seen you all so grave."

"Because we don't want to end up in one." Kahali grinned, and the tension lifted.

"I hope my skills have eliminated all threats of that, Kahali. Now, we'll need shifts, because I can't get a clear sense of how long it will take before they respond to our Calling. All beings understand mind talk as it's the common language, but if they don't use it, they may be confused by inner hearing."

"It sounds a bit like communicating with cave diggers," Rana joked. "Wouldn't Crown Ones like Desna be better at this?"

Kalakanya didn't laugh. "No, all the time threads suggest your age group will be less threatening and better able to communicate with their fearful mental state than Crowned Ones would be able to. Rana and Balavati, would you two prefer to go together?"

Rana startled, surprised at Kalakanya's offer. *She senses my fear.* Rana glanced at Balavati and they both nodded.

"Okay, we can do that initially, but if this takes more than a few days, we may need you to do separate shifts to ensure everyone gets enough sleep." Kalakanya looked anything but sleepy herself. "Questions?"

"Kahali and I go alone?" Daman asked.

"Are you okay with that?" Kalakanya asked.

Daman nodded.

"Yes!" Kahali shifted his feet under him, ready to charge out the door and start immediately.

"Okay, Kahali, you may have first shift." Kalakanya laughed, shaking her head. "Rana and Balavati, you take the next, and then Daman. Then we'll keep cycling through until we reach them. May the One In All bless this with a graceful and peaceful solution."

She held her hands to her heart and then swept them toward them. Her blessing floated down upon each of them as light as a peleguin feather.

Rana's friends all smiled.

But Rana only wondered if they would all be together again and smiling in the future. Her gut twisted with anxiety. This wasn't like her. She clasped Kahali's hand tightly, fearful that he or one of her other friends would be taken from her. Was she the only one who sensed something was about to go terribly wrong?

# Chapter 20

*orthern Haven: Bleu Reinier*

Northern Haven: Bleu Reinier. If frustration was lethal, Bleu would have died days ago. He paced a small circle from the front door, through their living quarters, into Ayanna's bedroom, and back. This quarantine endangered his teammates because now they somehow had to carry out his work as well and were down a man if the Undescended attacked. And how could he find the cure his vision had suggested the Surface held if he was stuck down here?

Clenching his fists, he rounded his circle to enter Ayanna's room again. While his parents worked, he guarded her from herself. They never knew when to expect another episode. He took a deep breath and unclenched his hands before she could notice. No use upsetting her.

She sat on her bed and doodled on her computer while she absently fingered her blue pendant, his family's only heirloom from the Surface. It had been passed down mother to daughter for centuries. Their mother had given it to Ayanna when it was clear she had the Sickness, as if she needed to complete the tradition before Ayanna was taken from them.

His mom's decision to give it to her now was just another thing that angered him.

As he rounded her room, he glanced at her screen, a sketch of characters from the hallway murals. Sometimes, her artwork became secret sibling messages, like the time she'd needed to talk and had left him a picture of Frida crying. Today's drawing featured Frida and Renoir trapped inside a cube. Maybe it symbolized them stuck in their module? Reassured that her artwork seemed normal, he continued his pacing.

"Bleu—stop it. You're driving me crazy," Ayanna said without looking up.

Bleu froze and stared at her. *Crazy?* His heart skipped a beat.

She glanced up, grinning. "Oh, come on. I'm not that far gone yet. It's a joke."

"It's not funny." He gripped his head with both hands as if that would shield him from this cruel reality. "Don't talk like that."

"Well, if I'm going to go insane and die, I deserve a few laughs while I can still comprehend them." Bitter anger underscored her tone.

Bleu sighed. He had never lacked words with Ayanna. Now, he had no idea how to talk to her. "I'm sorry, but I don't know what to do. I should be going up there, looking for a cure."

She narrowed her eyes at him. "Just sit." She patted the edge of her bed.

Bleu perched on the mattress's rim and stared bleakly at her drawing. The air circulator hummed overhead as Ayanna's pen resumed its scratching across the screen. The module's front door chimed and they both startled, but her startle turned to trembling.

"Don't worry"—he protectively laid his hand on hers—"it's probably a medic doing a quarantine check. I'll be right back, okay?" His mother had warned him tremors may signal an oncoming episode. He stood and paused, unsure whether to answer the door or stay.

"Go. If I'm going to freak out, it won't stop because you're standing there." She gave him a weak smile.

His throat constricted, and he turned to hide his damp eyes. He couldn't lose her. He walked to the corridor door, took a deep breath, blinked a few times, and opened it.

"Hi, Bleu." Ayanna's classmate, Atsushi, smiled at him as if it were totally normal to visit a module on quarantine.

"Oh, it's you." Bleu remained in the doorway, blocking Atsushi's entrance. Ayanna hadn't mentioned Atsushi since his eavesdropping at the Spring Reigns Festival. Was he here to get the latest gossip on her? His unspent frustration coiled for a strike.

"Uhm, well…I came to see how Ayanna is doing." The kid awkwardly shifted from leg to leg.

"Why?" Bleu stared down at him. Atsushi was four centimeters shorter, and Bleu intended to use it to his advantage.

"I was worried…you know, when I heard. Is she—"

Bleu's glare silenced him. "Who sent you here on your little information gathering trip?" Days of exasperation edged him near fury.

Atsushi's mouth dropped open. He gawked wildly around the corridor as if searching for his backup friends. Over Atsushi's head, Renoir's painted face glared at Bleu with that soulful look. It always made him uncomfortably self-conscious.

"No one sent me. No one even talks to me. And I never told anyone your secret, so you have no reason to be mad." Atsushi's voice had risen as well.

"Secret? Oh, you're referring to your overhearing us at Spring Reigns?" Bleu snorted in disgust. "No wonder no one talks to you." He glared at him, waiting for him to admit he had only come for gossip.

Atsushi glared back. "I used to think you were cool."

Bleu blinked, surprisingly bothered by that.

"Bleu. Let him in." Ayanna had wobbled up behind him.

He turned, grasped her arm, and helped her back to bed and pulled the blanket up over her legs. "You want me to let him in?"

Ayanna nodded and then smiled at something over Bleu's shoulder. "Hi, Atsushi."

Bleu twisted. Atsushi had followed him into their module and now watched them through her open door.

Fury swelled inside him. *The little jerk.* He strode toward Atsushi as Ayanna yelped.

"Bleu, stop. Go talk and b—be nice." Her trembling increased.

He frowned at her shaking limbs.

"I'm fine." She panted. "Let me sleep. Talk to him. He's the only one brave enough to come." She lay back and closed her eyes, clearly not open to negotiation.

*What do we have to talk about?* Bleu strode out of Ayanna's room, past Atsushi, and collapsed in a chair. The only thing keeping him awake right now was his fear for Ayanna. Last night, he had sat by her bed for hours while her brutal tremors had kept her from sleeping.

He'd become a makeshift nurse while his parents worked nonstop to create viable options to counter Savas' movement to terminate the Sickness patients to save resources. His mother only slept a few hours a day, spending all her time in the laboratory or in the Sickness Unit. Tadwell spent all his spare time organizing the other families touched by Sickness. They couldn't keep this up much longer.

He sighed and closed his eyes, wishing Atsushi would take the hint and leave. But he didn't want to kick him out and upset Ayanna. What if the tremors turned into an episode while he was here?

After a few minutes of silence, Bleu gave up and opened his eyes. Atsushi had rose to gawk at the shifting old Surface photos projected on to the wall—a lush mountain forest, deserts teeming with cacti, the face of a deer. It made most guests to his family's module uneasy, but Atsushi seemed fascinated.

"Can I sit?" he asked.

"You didn't ask to come in. Why start now?"

"Look, I'm sorry." Atsushi walked across the small room and knocked into the desk. A statue wobbled off the edge. He sprang to catch it, repositioned it, and then sat in the nearest seat.

Bleu ground his teeth together and swallowed the fury screaming its way up his throat like a rocket. *Just leave so I can sleep.*

From his seat, Atsushi frowned at the nature photos. "Who do you think picked these pictures for the database?"

"What?" Bleu was so tired he saw two screens with two pine forests.

"Don't you ever wonder how they decided what to include? Like are these all scenes from a powerful nation's ecosystem? Did they really include stuff from all countries?" The guy had too much energy. He probably slept at night.

Bleu groaned. "I don't have time for philosophical debate. Does it matter? It's all we have. Can't you simply enjoy it?"

Atsushi looked down at his hands. "No," he mumbled. "I want the truth. Not just what SHAST wanted us to know."

Bleu heaved an exasperated sigh. "I can't deal with this right now. Why are you really here?"

Atsushi balanced on the edge of the seat and glanced toward Ayanna's room for the tenth time. He leaned forward to whisper, "I get you don't like me. I can deal with that. But she trusts you to find a cure, and she said I could stay. What's your plan?"

Bleu stared, his jaw open. "My plan? I'm in quarantine. My team will leave tomorrow without me. I have no plan." His voice had risen to a shout.

At the words *no plan*, Atsushi widened his eyes in alarm, and he gestured wildly toward Ayanna's room.

*And now, if she heard that, I've upset Ayanna.* Bleu dropped his face onto his palms.

"We'll make one," Atsushi said loudly, probably for her benefit. Then he leaned toward Bleu and whispered, "Do you still believe the solution is on the Surface? What does your mom say?"

Bleu was confused. How well did Ayanna know this guy? Why was he interested? He stared at Atsushi so long that the kid started to fidget. "What's it to you?"

Atsushi turned bright crimson. "I just…care. She's nice. No one should have to suffer."

"Have you gone to the families of the other teens with the Sickness to offer your services?" Bleu had a theory about Atsushi's "caring."

"Uh…no. I wasn't friends with them."

"But you're *friends* with Ayanna?" If this guy was thinking of hitting on his little sister in her current state, he'd throttle him.

"Kind of…I have always liked her." Atsushi's blush darkened as he shifted on the edge of the chair.

Bleu sprang up. "You think you'll get her to like you now?"

A loud thump came from Ayanna's bedroom. Bleu's heart pounded as he raced to her sleeping quarters. Atsushi smashed into him as they both grappled to enter. Bleu shoved Atsushi to the floor, and he fell in a heap of arms and legs.

Bleu ran to his sister. Spasms rocked her body and strange noises gurgled from her mouth.

"Ayanna." Bleu pulled her small frame to his chest, hoping to calm her. She continued thrashing.

"Ayanna, it's okay. Shhh...."

Her fist smashed into his nose, and she pulled free. Bleu grabbed at her arm, but she was faster.

Atsushi jumped up and blocked the bedroom door as Ayanna ran at him. She threw herself against him, knocking them both to the floor. Oblivious to her surroundings, Ayanna whipped her head backward as Atsushi threw out his hand, preventing Ayanna's head from hitting the door frame. Instead, his hand smashed against the metal-edged door frame. Blood dripped from his hand to the floor.

Bleu dove in to keep his sister from pummeling Atsushi as her fingers tangled in his black hair, pulling Atsushi's neck into impossible angles.

"Ayanna, stop." Atsushi kept his voice calm, though every muscle on his neck was taut with pain.

Together, they slowly untangled Ayanna's hands from Atsushi's head. Bleu held her as Atsushi sat on the chair, his bloody hand wrapped in a towel he had snagged from the bathroom. Bleu held her as she sobbed herself to sleep. Atsushi's gaze never left his sister's face.

*He really does care.* Bleu jerked his chin to get Atsushi's attention without awakening Ayanna.

Atsushi locked eyes with him, his expression grim.

"I owe you one. Thanks," Bleu whispered.

Atsushi's whole face morphed through a series of contortions. Finally, it settled into a slight smile. "It's the least a...a *friend* of Ayanna's can do."

Bleu chuckled. "We both know you don't think of her as a friend."

Atsushi grinned. "If I agree, do I die now?"

"Only if you try anything." Bleu stared and tried to look fierce, but there was something too engaging about the guy.

"I'm not like that." Atsushi's brow furrowed. "How about a deal? You find the cure, I'll help however I can, and then we'll see what she says."

Bleu smirked. "Unless the cure is hidden in my module, you've made a hopeless offer."

"I have a plan." From the hope in his tone, he really did.

Bleu hadn't realized until that moment how defeated he had become. First being cut from the team, then Savas' public shaming, the quarantine, Stamf not being able to convince his Uncle Pridbor to help, and seeing Ayanna suffer—it had been too much. With Atsushi's simple statement, a spark of hope quivered into existence.

Bleu slowly slid Ayanna's body onto her bed and tucked the blanket tight, willing the tightness to prevent her tremors' return. He motioned for Atsushi to follow him, and they both tiptoed out of her sleeping quarters. Bleu carefully pulled the door shut.

"What's your plan? They leave tomorrow." He was careful to keep his voice low as he motioned for Atsushi to sit on the nearby chair.

Atsushi sat with a sigh, still holding the towel around his injured hand. "They're replacing the topography equipment you were to carry with head cameras on each team member, so they'll still be able to create their computerized maps."

"How do you know what they're doing?" Bleu asked.

Atsushi looked him straight in the eye. "Promise you won't tell. I need to protect my source."

"Seriously?" Bleu hit the cushions beside him. "I have all this going on, and you want me to swear to secrecy? I mean, who'd believe me anyways? I'm on quarantine."

Atsushi stared at him, unmoved.

"Fine. I won't tell anyone. Can we hurry this up a bit?" Bleu needed action. His body was a tight spring about to explode.

"I'm friends with Neviah Thanh. She's training to be the backup pilot for Commander Savas and Stamf."

"I already know that," Bleu snapped and began pacing his module. It had become their prison. And Ayanna had a death sentence.

He was cognizant of Atsushi scrutinizing his every movement. The kid had moved to the edge of his chair as if Bleu might turn on him. *Do I look that out of control?* Bleu stopped pacing.

"I'm trying to explain," Atsushi said. "Since you aren't going, they needed another way to map the Surface. Everyone will wear a head camera, and Neviah and her father are writing a program to use the data for mapping."

"But you have a plan for me to go, right?" Bleu held out his palms, waiting.

"Not to go, but to watch."

"Huh?" Bleu's excitement ebbed.

"If you could get to the data room, Neviah can hack into the two-way radios on the headpieces, allowing you to watch and listen. You could talk to Stamf while he's up there. It wouldn't be as good as going, but you would see and learn..."

Bleu considered this new information. "Why would Neviah risk that?"

"She's cool, and we've been worried about you and Ayanna."

Bleu snorted. *"You* were worried about *me?"*

"Neviah was." Atsushi flashed him a knowing smile.

"I don't know how any of this would help Ayanna." Bleu's gaze drifted to the sleep chamber and his sister's muffled snores.

"You'll be learning and seeing what's up there, and when the doctors clear you, you'll be ahead of the game for the next expedition." Atsushi raised his eyebrows, clearly expecting praise for their plan.

"Wait. I can't go to the data room." Bleu groaned in frustration. "Who would stay with Ayanna?"

Atsushi blushed.

"No." Bleu shook his head.

"Look. When you go up there, someone needs to stay with her, right? And both your parents have critical jobs. I could skip a few days of school. The council wants me to keep my exclusive genes healthy, and I think I feel the sudden need for a vacation." Atsushi grinned sardonically, then became serious again. "Bleu, you can trust me. I swear I'll take good care of her."

"She barely knows you," he argued, but did he have any other options? Did Ayanna?

"She told you to let me in, and her only other option is that she goes to your mom's unit."

Patients went there as a last resort. They never returned home. Ayanna had only been allowed to stay home until she grew too dangerous because of their mom's expertise.

He considered it in silence, staring at the floor while footsteps and laughter drifted in through the corridor door. The normalcy of life outside his module was surreal.

"Okay, fine." He was desperate, and this was the first glimmer of hope in days. "But first, we need to get Neviah's help."

# Chapter 21

Bleu frowned at Atsushi. "How are we going to get Neviah's help? I'm stuck here on quarantine."

Atsushi, sitting across from him on the couch, grinned and pulled out a small device and held it up. "Neviah's brilliant. Made this to message me during classes. She sends me jokes so I can tolerate Liam and his friends." He snapped his mouth shut.

Clearly, he had not meant to say that out loud. So, it had been the truth that no one would send him for gossip.

"Sounds like she's a good friend. Go ahead," Bleu said, motioning toward Atsushi's device. "Message her."

The kid nodded and hunched over his device. Bleu waited for several minutes, then began pacing again.

Finally, Atsushi straightened up. "She'll get her father out. You need to meet her in ten minutes in the data room."

"Now?" Bleu froze mid-pace and glanced back at Ayanna's room. "It's the middle of the day. Everyone will see me." If he got caught running around during quarantine, they'd assume he had the Sickness. He scanned the room for ideas. A disguise? An excuse? Nothing seemed adequate.

Atsushi narrowed his eyes at the ceiling and then ran to the corner. He jumped on the furniture and began to fiddle with the module's environmental and safety settings.

"And I'm the one on quarantine?" Bleu scowled. "Get down."

"Hold on...I'm disabling your fire alarm.

"Why?" Bleu started to doubt Atsushi's sanity.

Suddenly, the lights began flashing.

Bleu's eyes widened in understanding. "That's Neviah's way of clearing the halls?"

Atsushi nodded. "Told you she's amazing."

"She's scary."

In two minutes, everyone would have followed protocol and cleared the halls, but he'd still need to avoid emergency workers. He ran to the door and listened. Footsteps pounded past and then the hallway became silent.

Bleu turned. "I have your word? You'll contact us through that thing if Ayanna needs me?"

"Of course. Go." Atsushi waved him off.

Bleu rushed through the door. He paused, listening for footsteps, and then raced toward the elevator that would take him to the data room. He skidded around the corner and stopped in front of the elevators. How would he avoid the emergency crew if they were on the elevator when it opened? He turned around. searching for a hideout as the elevator opened. Two men stepped out.

"Sorry." Bleu shoved past them and into the elevator, his arm over his face as if shielding himself from their bulky equipment. Alarms still echoed throughout the corridors and lights flashed. Had they seen who he was?

They spun to face him, but the door was already sliding shut. Would they follow?

He smashed his fingers against the correct number. It took forever for the elevator to respond. *Is it turned off for the alarm?* His heart pounded out the seconds. When it finally lurched into motion, he rocked against the wall.

The elevator stopped, and he threw himself into the hall. He faced a painting of the man Ayanna had nicknamed Bada Shanren screaming at the lightning-filled sky.

"I share your frustration with the powers that be," Bleu mumbled.

He reached the data room and paused, heart thudding. Would Mr. Thanh be gone? Pressing his sweaty palm to the button, he peeked in as the door began to slide open.

He faced a wall covered with computer consoles. Neviah had wires wrapped around her shoulders and bent under an open panel. She clearly hadn't heard his entrance over the ongoing alarms.

Bleu cleared his throat.

"Oh!" She jumped, hitting her head on the console. "I didn't know if you'd actually come." She rubbed her head and flashed him a shy smile. "Give me a minute to make this all look like an electrical system malfunction." She turned and furiously tapped on the opened console with a small tool.

"That should do it." She turned and attempted to stand, but the wires on her shoulder snagged the panel. She stumbled and nearly fell on top of him.

Bleu grabbed her arm and steadied her. "You okay?"

"Yeah, sorry." She snickered and pulled free from him. "Sorry about you being cut from the team. I'm sure you would have been great up there." Her dark eyes met his.

"Next time." His voice quavered with emotion, but she didn't seem to notice.

"Next time, I might be flying. We could both go." She blushed. "Well, I'm only the backup pilot. But still…"

"Did Atsushi tell you his idea?"

"Of you observing? Yes." She grinned. "It was a mutual idea." Her dark eyes sparkled as she tucked her long black bangs behind her ear. "I'll have to find something to keep my father away. The technology is no problem. But we need to either *borrow* Stamf's headpiece or let him in on our plan. And you'll need to find another way to sneak here and back while they're up there." She appeared to be mentally checking things off on her fingers.

Unlike everyone else, she acted nonchalant about Ayanna's illness. Bleu frowned at her relaxed body language. "Why are you doing this? I'm on quarantine. Aren't you scared of me?"

She peered up and a series of expressions struggled to dominate her face. The blankest of them all claimed victory. "No, we were in classes

179

together."

He knew he was okay at the moment, but her lack of regard for her personal safety alarmed him. "As far as I know, I'm fine, but if I'm wrong, our having been in classes together won't protect you from me."

"I'm safe with you. You won't get the Sickness," she said with complete confidence.

"I never thought Ayanna would get it. Know something I don't?" he asked, crossing his arms.

She gave him a sad smile. "You won't. Everything always goes perfectly for you and Stamf."

Bleu grimaced. "Ayanna getting the Sickness isn't perfect. You should be more careful. We need you." She side-eyed him with such joy that he quickly added, "Especially since you'll now be a pilot."

"Right," she said and stared at her desk. "Glad to be needed…as a pilot."

He inwardly cringed. "Come on, that's not what I meant. I'm super stressed and rambling like a drunk. Ignore me."

She raised an eyebrow in his direction. "Not likely," she said, her lips curling upward.

Bleu cleared his throat. "Okay. You need Stamf's headpiece." He grabbed a piece of paper and jotted a note. "Give this to Stamf at dinner. He'll bring it. He'll love this."

He wished he could tell Stamf himself, but Stamf had no time for social visits before he was slated to leave.

Neviah took the note, her fingers brushing his.

Was she being more careful with this plan than she was with exposing herself to people on quarantine? Everyone knew how quickly someone with the Sickness could turn violent. "No one else will be here watching? Not the Council or anything?"

Neviah shook her head. "No, they were happy my father and I would handle it." She tilted her head. "It's like they fear they'll be contaminated by seeing the Surface."

"Contaminated?" He grimaced.

She nodded. "Too wild and unrefined."

He snorted in laughter, but then noticed she hadn't. "Do you feel that way?"

She tucked her hair behind her ear in consideration. "Not really, but I've never seen it."

"Then why did you volunteer for the pilot program?"

She rolled her eyes. "I didn't. My father mentioned to the Council that I was a shoo-in, and next thing I know I'm doing it. Honestly, it terrifies me. How can we fly real helicopters in unknown conditions around the world after only simulated flying programs? I'll probably crash the first time."

Bleu snorted. "Thanks for the warning. I'll make sure to get in Stamf's copter."

Neviah snickered. "They'll never let me fly for real. Savas thinks all women are incapable."

"He's letting you train and is letting Josefina go up there. Maybe he's changing?"

"Him?" Neviah scoffed.

"I like to believe people can change. Become better." Bleu chuckled. "But, yeah, probably not him."

The alarms had stopped, and footsteps sounded in the corridor again. He needed to get back.

"Well, thanks." He leaned forward, hugged her in appreciation, and turned to leave.

"How are you going to get back?" she asked.

She was crimson. As crimson as Atsushi had been talking about Ayanna, and her beaming gaze met his, a question in her eyes. Yes, she'd just asked him a question, but she clearly now had a second question. A hope.

Bleu wanted to smack his forehead. *What was I thinking hugging her?* Sure, someday he'd like a girlfriend, but he wasn't obsessed over physical stuff with girls like Stamf and the other guys. He risked a glance at the beaming Neviah who still waited for an answer.

"I was thinking camouflage," he said.

"Oh..." she murmured, sounding disappointed. Then, her face scrunched up in confusion. "I'm sorry, cama what?"

"Blending in. No one's specifically looking for me, and if I walk normally and disguise my looks, no one should notice." He held up his hands, palms upward. "It's the best I've got."

Neviah tilted her head and studied him "Blend in how? You can't change your face."

Bleu surveyed the room. "Those boxes. Do you have more?"

She nodded and opened a closet full of supplies.

"If I pile them, like I'm carrying supplies…." He picked up a box and opened it. "Ah. I'll leave the top one open. I'll position my face around the flaps so the flaps block others out."

"That's great as long as everyone approaches from the same angle. But what if they don't? Or someone talks to you?"

He shrugged. "Then I'm sent to the unit. Got another idea?"

"No," she said, frowning. "We need a better system. Otherwise, this will never work."

"I'll figure something out. See you then." He scooped up the boxes, grinned, and ducked out the door.

# Chapter 22

**N**orthern Haven: Commander Kern Savas

Commander Savas surveyed the families and dignitaries who had gathered in the small, hastily decorated room. It was the last room on the corridor prior to the huge elevator to the Surface. The second expedition's send-off party had a good turnout, small enough to appear intimate but large enough to justify all the councilors' presence.

Prime Minister Pridbor said, "Our hearts go with these fearless heroes, our second expedition, as they ascend to the Surface." He dramatically extended his arm toward the team members. "We know they'll be safely guided by the experience of Commander Kern Savas, who in his forty-two years of life has faced death and won many times over."

The gathered families hooted and clapped. Many more viewers had gathered in the assembly hall for the live streaming. He nodded into the cameras and flashed his best you-only-live-once grin. According to Northern Haven's bored wives who frequented his module, his well hewn jaw, startling blue eyes, and scar from the first expedition made quite the impression. *If you've got it, use it.*

After all, it had taken every skill he possessed to convince the council to let him lead expeditions to the Surface. If he hadn't come along to shake them from their stupor, humanity would have rotted down here for fear of Nature's icy wrath and the terror of facing any surviving Undescended.

"Let's give a round of applause for Zachary Adelstein and Josefina Girak, our Science Officers." He paused for applause. "And Stamf Herrick, our Gunner." Pridbor winked at his nephew as the group hooted. "Abdul

Zinnas, our Medic." Another pause. "And most importantly, Commander Kern Savas." The prime minister beamed and added his dignified claps to the tumultuous cheering.

This time, Savas gave them a trust-me-with your-future smile. He'd go down in history as the man who saved humanity by re-establishing human dominance on the Surface. Of course, the crowd loved him.

Savas stepped forward. "This expedition will lay the groundwork for finding the other Havens. We humbly offer our services for the benefit of all."

The crowd nodded and cheered.

Savas turned to his team. "You have five minutes."

His team rushed to hug loved ones in a final goodbye. Family members cheered and patted shoulders with frenetic jubilation and confidence. Only their gazes, taking in every last detail of their relative, betrayed the truth—their loved one may never return. Savas basked in the tension. It was more nourishing than breakfast.

His gaze sought out Josefina. Her pathetic husband, Girak, looked terrified. What did she see in his ridiculous red hair and beard? *He's an overgrown, mythical leprechaun.*

As Girak kissed Josefina and released her, Savas caught his gaze. Girak set his jaw and glared at him.

Savas grinned. "*We* leave in one minute." He sauntered away and thanked the council for the opportunity to serve.

His exhilaration was only marred by his team being one man short. He had suspected Bleu all along. What fool studies hunting and tracking skills while living underground? Was he hunting worms? And seriously, who studies hunting techniques? Just take out a gun and shoot. He should have cut him from the team then. The council's quarantine had saved him the trouble.

Five minutes was up. *Time to shine.* "Line up."

His team bustled from their families to form a line. Savas strode down the line and tugged here and there, checking the connection between the soft headpiece and the parka. It flopped back hood-like until pulled up and attached to the parka. The headpiece served as a warm hood, would ease breathing the cold air, and contained a radio and camera. They'd had to add the camera to compensate for the loss of Bleu's topographical research. His team was already compromised, and he'd spent the last few days obsessing over how to keep them all safe with one less man.

He stopped in front of Josefina and motioned to where her hood hung back over her shoulder. It was attached properly, but he lingered.

"Don't attach the head piece to your chest." He gently hovered his hand above Josefina's shapely chest, designating where the hood attached to the parka. "Not until we reach the top of the shaft system. It will help you adjust to the pressure changes if it's open." He flashed her the grin she used to love.

She gave him only a tight nod.

His grin faltered, and he dropped his hand to his side. *I didn't even touch her. What's wrong with her?* Hiding his puzzlement, he proceeded to check the rest of the team. He reached the end and nodded his approval.

"Abdul, you first."

Abdul flashed his toothy grin, strode to the snow rover, and backed it into the large metal elevator box. As he turned off the engine, Savas led the rest of the team inside. With a dramatic wave to the crowd, he pressed a button, and the door slid shut.

He grinned at his team. "Time to prove your worth."

The elevator box lurched upward, and they all swayed in tandem. It rushed ever higher, making his stomach lurch.

"Remember your bags." Savas held up a small vomit bag. He had warned them that the elevator ride was brutal on the stomach. As their ascent accelerated, an invigorating rush surged through him.

"Bet my dessert rations Zach loses it first." Abdul grinned expectantly at Zach.

"Dessert is the last thing I want to think about." Zach groaned, holding his stomach.

Savas watched Josefina. He'd always been taught women were the weaker sex, but his own mother had shown him otherwise. She had outwitted them all until they caught her.

He shoved that horrible memory aside, instead seeking Josefina's gaze. Her normally radiant face wore a greenish tinge. She attempted a smile while keeping her lips pressed together as if that would prevent her need for the vomit bag. Everyone did their first time.

Savas gave her a nod of support. He had four days before she returned to her husband. His smile broadened. Every second, the elevator brought them farther from Girak.

"Rest stop."

The box slowed and paused its ascent. The short break facilitated their adjustment to the pressure changes; they must arrive on the Surface ready for action.

As they waited, his team shot each other nervous smiles. They were all young—Josefina was thirty-four, while Zach and Abdul, the next oldest, were still in their mid-twenties. And Stamf would be the youngest to reach the Surface at eighteen. His first team had been older and had trained longer, and they hadn't survived the storm. After that, only these kids had risked volunteering. Everything in Northern Haven had fallen to hell, and he was the only one willing to risk the Surface to save them all.

"Breathe deeply. It'll help settle your stomach and your nerves." He modeled sucking in a dramatic breath while admiring the rifle strapped to Stamf's shoulder. He had wanted that beauty, but the council had insisted Stamf's standing position as the number one gamer justified him taking the only completed rifle. If only production wasn't severely restricted by the lack of new raw materials. It was amazing they'd lasted this long underground.

Around him, the others made heavy breathing sounds as resignation replaced their nervous grins. They understood the danger they'd soon face.

Savas touched his hip briefly, unimpressed by the too small handgun that hung there. It matched the others' guns, having been reconstructed from the databases left by their ancestors. The only adjustment their engineers had made was in adding nanotech to keep the weapons from freezing or getting too damp and jamming in the unpredictable arctic weather.

If only he led a well-equipped military team like the Surface used to have. He trusted his instincts and his team, but if the ancient military generals watched their sorry asses on this elevator, they'd fear for humanity's future.

The elevator surged upward again—its final rising. Josefina moaned and grabbed her stomach. She turned and lost her stomach contents. A moment later, Stamf and Zach joined in.

"Sorry, man. Didn't mean for you to see that." Stamf muttered his apology still facing the wall and no one else.

Commander Savas frowned. *Who was he apologizing to?*

"Dude, the wall doesn't have cameras." Zach grinned.

"What?" Stamf replied, then widened his eyes. "Oh, right. Of course it doesn't."

"Jos." Abdul smacked her shoulder playfully. "You lost me the bet. Couldn't you have held it in a few seconds longer?" Then he lost his stomach.

Josefina laughed and clapped Abdul on his back. "Forget your dessert rations. We need breath mints."

A twang reverberated deep within Savas' chest. Ever since their first practice, she'd been playful with the others and purely professional with him. The only woman in Northern Haven he cared about could now barely tolerate his existence. What lies had Girak had told her?

He threw back his shoulders. "Headpieces and goggles on before I open the door."

The box was slowing its upward speed, and he was the experienced one here. *She jokes with the boys, but on the Surface, she'll see the value of experience.*

They shuffled to do as told. Savas strode past each one, re-checking them. They were as prepared as possible. The rest was up to him.

"Soon, you'll understand the need for shade goggles under the head piece. Everyone wants to see the Surface, but don't look right away. You'll be temporarily blinded. First, look only at the box's floor. Give your eyes a chance to adjust. Stamf, get to the front here with your rifle just in case."

Savas waited for Stamf to shift near the door and checked that they all focused downward. His hand drifted to his handgun. He was determined not to be surprised again by this alien terrain. He stepped to the safety lever, pulled it, and then pushed the button to open the door.

# Chapter 23

O n the Surface: Commander Kern Savas
As the internal mechanisms that opened the colossal door groaned to life, he raised his gaze to the door's embossed symbol of SHAST and instinctively touched his gloved hand to his chest. His cushioned fingers sought out the hidden compass with the near-matching seal hanging from his neck, and he nodded his silent acceptance of the massive responsibility he now bore for humanity.

He was ready. "Look at the floor. Don't get blinded," he warned them. The ancient door clanged open, revealing a brilliant line of light on the floor. It widened as the door opened.

His nose hairs curled. Even after the Surface air passed through the air warmer in his headpiece, it smelled wild. It moved with a life of its own, constantly wafting endless foreign smells toward him and pushing against his hood at ever shifting angles. Its chaos enthralled him.

"Eyes down." Savas winced as the intense white light bore deep into his skull. His toes clenched against the soles of his boots until the stabbing in his head receded.

He glanced up only for a moment, checking for dangerous movements in the brightness beyond the door. "Take quick looks. Not too long at the brightness. Keep returning to the ground until you're used to it."

The initial view and sudden lack of mechanical humming always disoriented him. The team lingered in the large opening, acclimating to the bizarre Surface. Its vast openness was breathtaking. Apparently, literally breathtaking, because as Stamf emerged, he sputtered and gasped for breath.

"Breathe, Stamf. In and out. Takes some getting used to, eh?" He assessed Stamf with rare amusement.

Savas was the only one on this expedition with prior Surface experience. No one else from the original expedition was brave enough to return. To be fair, the other three had died, but in a way, they had chosen that fate. He had been in the same storm and survived.

Catching his breath, Stamf straightened his posture. He stepped outside and leaned back, craning his neck to see the incredible expanse in all directions.

Josefina stood unmoving in the door well. Her arms rose to the sky, her face upturned.

"We made it." Her face glowed.

"We're only starting." Savas chuckled, his heart racing with excitement. The Surface did that to him.

Abdul sprang onto the ground and experimentally stamped his boots. It produced an irritating scrunching sound. Stamf and Zach responded by launching themselves out and imitating the ridiculous sound. Horrible squeaks arose around Savas.

*They've sent me up with a pack of children.*

"Playtime's over! Abdul, get the rover out."

His growling tone immediately subdued them. Driving was one of Abdul's tasks. After all, they wouldn't need a medic's expertise unless there was an emergency.

Abdul sprang into the driver's seat of the snow rover. "Ready, sir."

"Hmm." Savas glared at him a moment. "You sure?"

Abdul nodded. Indeed, he did appear to have reached adulthood again. "We have to stay focused up here. It's too dangerous to play around."

He paced forward and scanned the endless horizon. Not a dark cloud in sight. *Now this weather I can deal with.* Like an instant challenge, the thin layer of snow was blown off the ice and onto his head piece visor. He growled and wiped it clear.

The first thing Savas always noticed was the endless sky, then the colors.

Everything in Northern Haven was obnoxiously bright, but the whites, grays, blues, and rusty yellows of the Surface soothed him. They shifted and glowed under the ever-changing sunlight.

Their door opened at the base of a flat-topped cliff and faced down a long, frozen valley with steep cliffs to their left and right. Beyond the valley, the drones had shown open, barren ice fields, dotted with scraggly bushes and trees.

Savas reached up and adjusted his head cam, making sure it pointed straight ahead. "Everyone, get in the rover and check your head cam and radios."

His team stumbled toward the rover, tripping over their own boots because they couldn't tear their gaze from the endless space above them.

"The sky's not going anywhere, but we are. Get in!"

The rover rolled out of the shaft's box, and he radioed the Council. "We're out. Seal the shaft. Radios are on, cameras synched. We'll contact in thirty."

Abdul stopped the rover, and they turned as the heavy doors clanged shut behind them. The doors stood at the bottom of a long, steep cliff of frozen rock, a gray rectangular bastion of humanity in an unyielding arctic wasteland. They would only open from the inside or with the command remote zipped into Savas' parka. The locking system protected Northern Haven from the wrath of the Undescended.

"It's so quiet," Josefina whispered. "Only wind."

"Eerie, isn't it?" Savas turned and smiled at her. "This snow rover and the snowmobiles they're finishing up were designed to have relatively quiet engines. We don't want to attract unsafe attention. But in this silence, they still seem loud."

"Unsafe attention from the Undescended?" Zach glanced around uneasily. "They could attack from anywhere out here." He shuddered. "We're so...exposed."

Abdul sat stiffly at the wheel beside him, while the rest of his team huddled close together in the back of the rover. Spatial anxiety, the doctors called it. Living in enclosed spaces and then exiting to endless openness caused an overwhelming emotional reaction no matter how accurate Lee's preparatory holograph programs were. He needed to restore their confidence.

"Remember your training and look around. Your cams help with the mapping."

They all looked upward.

"Not the sky." He rolled his eyes in exasperation and clenched his teeth. "We're. Not. Mapping. The sky. If you want to be safe, then focus."

He gave them a moment to visually sweep their cameras left and right of the door. They could travel only south, as three steep cliffs protected Northern Haven's door. According to the robotic probes sent out before the first expedition, the top of the cliff led to a plateau. Savas' plan for the elevated land included construction of a small, armed camp to defend and overlook the door.

The two side walls rose straight up hundreds of meters in the air, as if a giant swordsman had split them apart to create a wide road out of Northern Haven. Between the walls, a vast open valley extended many kilometers to the south. It seemed an odd geographical layout, though he'd never experienced any others. The first expedition hadn't gotten far.

He glanced at the monitor. "Keep your eye on the display, Abdul. I don't want to fall down a crevasse."

With a fearful glance at the nose of the snow rover where the sensor was located, Abdul nodded.

"Let's move out." Savas pointed toward the endless white-and-gray valley. At some point, the left-side cliff leveled out to the valley level, creating a switchback that they might travel up to the plateau above the door.

Savas turned to his team. "I proclaim this The Valley of Ice." He grinned as they nodded in agreement.

As they drove farther into the valley, Savas kept hearing whispering. He turned. Stamf was mumbling to himself.

"Man, did you see that? This is cool... I can see forev—"

"Stamf, you okay?"

Stamf stiffened and then laughed. "Sorry, sir. Just a bit excited."

"I hear that. Mind keeping it down?" Savas shook his head disapprovingly. But inside his hood, he grinned. *Had the same thoughts on my first expedition.*

The high cliffs on either side grew shorter as they progressed down the Valley of Ice until they reached an open frozen field spotted with boulders, distant evergreen trees, and small, scrubby plants.

They continued about twenty kilometers south when Abdul pointed out a massive boulder, large enough to be a substantial wind block. Savas decided it was as sheltered a spot as they would find. He jumped over the side of the rover.

"This is the real thing, team. Let's make good use of this weather." He scanned the sky. No clouds.

As trained, the guys divided into two teams to secure the two tents. Stamf, Zach, and Abdul would share one, and since Bleu was cut from the team, he and Josefina had the other. Maybe with Girak out of the picture, she'd remember she had always wanted a real man who shared her dreams of adventure, or at least appreciate that he'd called in his political favors to get a woman scientist on his team.

As he radioed back to base with an update, the others got distracted. "Abdul! Stamf! Stop obsessing over the sky and focus on setting up camp."

Josefina, however, was all business. She efficiently divided scientific equipment into what would stay on the rover, what would go in the tents, and what equipment would be left out to gather data. She began setting it up and moving happily about, almost skipping.

Watching her, Savas realized she was his sky. He kept having to remind himself to pull his gaze away from her and to focus. His camera recorded everything he saw. He forced himself to watch the others for a few minutes, while wondering how hard it would be to sabotage the camera later if he got lucky and she remembered how things had once been between the two of them.

The team pulled together and made camp in under two hours. Despite the smooth camp set-up, unease filled him. He scanned the sky again, but it remained clear. The first expedition had been lost within hours of reaching the Surface, swept up in a sudden explosion of frozen fury. Instruments had failed, and the team had gotten separated and lost. He alone had made it back to the door.

*Never again.*

A strange noise reached his ears. *Music?* He turned slowly, searching for the source. His headpiece made everything sound odd. He followed it until he spotted Josefina and Zach moving their heaviest equipment past the tents. They were collecting data on the earth's magnetic field.

The melody grew louder as he approached. Was there a bird near them? Savas had never heard a real bird sing. When Josefina stood and waved, the music stopped.

"Enjoying yourself?" He couldn't resist teasing. Dr. Reinier's concert must have inspired her.

"This is a dream. It's not every day I get the opportunity to do research like this." Josefina returned to her equipment and humming.

"Anything useful?" He stepped closer to view the equipment but not too close. He didn't want to upset her like he had at their send-off.

Her humming stopped again. "Commander, if this equipment is correct, the poles have shifted. Navigation to the other Havens will be complicated."

He grimaced. Was Nature determined to thwart his every move? "You both better confirm that." He'd hoped to have the helicopters ready to leave within weeks, but they'd need a new navigational system if the poles had truly shifted.

"Yes, sir," Zach said.

Josefina, already humming again, nodded.

Savas considered this new information. "We didn't just travel twenty kilometers *south?*"

Zach shrugged. "I guess we went twenty kilometers in the direction of the new south?" he held up his palms in surrender.

Savas scowled. "Great." *As if I don't have enough to deal with, now all the maps are wrong.*

"Sir, we believe that over there"—Zach pointed to a distant area where the ice became bluer—"may be meltwater."

"Meaning?"

"It's a possible water source. See how that mountain is white and then there's that bluer part than comes down onto bluish ground?"

Savas nodded. *Water will be useful for my future command post.*

"We'd like to investigate it later, once this is set up." Josefina grinned at him. "When we build our base camp, it'd be lovely to have fresh water."

"Sounds good. But stay together at all times." Savas again checked the sky. "I'm going to lead Stamf and Abdul on the reconnaissance trip to the west. The new west." He sighed, looking over his team. An urge tugged within his chest to stay put at camp with Josefina. He hadn't seen her this happy and glowing since she'd attended his speech about the need to find the other havens, and that had been over a decade ago.

He frowned. "This is when we need Bleu's replacement. I don't like leaving you two unguarded."

"We're fine, Commander. The water's not vicious." Her beautiful smile had the power to melt the Surface.

"All right. Keep your radios on and your eyes open. This isn't a lab." He scanned the horizon, reluctant to leave, then turned and strode back to the snow rover. "Stamf, let's find some wildlife."

Abdul started the engine. The mechanical vibration was a little piece of home in this vast wilderness.

As the rover turned, Savas yelled, "Zach. Josefina. Keep your guns nearby at all times, understood?"

Josefina nodded, waved her gun in mock threat, and went back to her work. Zach patted his hip and nodded, never taking his eyes off his instruments.

Leaving them alone filled him with dread, but perhaps his growing concern was a touch of spatial anxiety or some strange emotional reaction to the failure of his last mission. In any case, a commander shouldn't be controlled by his emotions. Ignoring the warning in his head, he directed Abdul to head off into the unknown.

# Chapter 24

*On the Surface: Commander Kern Savas*

Savas turned in his rover seat and watched as Zach and Josefina shrunk to small specks behind them. Soon, they blurred into the gray horizon, engulfed by the deserted gray wasteland around them. Wind crackled the fabric of Savas' hood, as if the souls of the Undescended were warning him that nothing could live up here.

Stamf startled. "Look!"

They all followed the extension of his arm into the sky. A small black speck circled high in the endless blue.

"What the *shast*?" Abdul swerved and nearly tipped the snow rover.

"Focus," Savas warned as Abdul gained control of the vehicle.

"I think"—Stamf stared upward a moment more, lips pursed in concentration—"it's a bird."

"I saw something like that last time before the storm, but it was a lot bigger." Savas rested his hand on his holster. No, the bird was way out of range.

"It's growing. We should get out of here." Abdul sped up the rover.

Savas examined the bird. It *was* growing, and quickly. "No, it's an optical illusion. It's simply getting closer." Yes, that was it. "Our eyes aren't used to seeing stuff at such distances."

"Oh." Abdul slowed down and then stopped to reassess the bird. "That's weird."

Stamf guffawed at him. "Thought it was going to eat us, eh, Abdul?" Then Stamf muttered something like, "Man, did you see that?" He began laughing again to himself.

"What?" Savas narrowed his eyes and examined Stamf.

"Hmm?" Stamf raised his eyebrows and smiled at Savas. "Oh, just warning myself about the dangers of carnivorous birds." He smirked at Abdul.

They watched the bird rise and fall in the sky, shrinking and growing but always out of range. Savas had the eerie sense of being observed. Observed by something other than the bird.

He shivered. "Keep moving, Abdul."

As the snow rover rolled across the snow-blown plain, his sense of foreboding grew. It had to be spatial anxiety, because the horizon showed no signs of life. Only boulders, ice formations, and the lonely patches of scraggly wind-ravaged trees surrounded them.

A few minutes later, Abdul pointed to their right. "Look at that. It's like an entire glacier or mountain or something." A hill or unusual ice formation of some sort loomed on the horizon.

Something about it promised intrigue, as if it *wanted* to be explored. Everything begged to be studied in this new environment. Savas also knew his team, and Abdul noticed details. They turned the rover to investigate.

A kilometer later, a sharp wall of ice rose on their right, taller than anything he had ever imagined. They drove along the strange ice wall until it ended sharply like the external corner of a building. As they drove around it, a large opening became visible.

Abdul slowed the rover to a halt and glanced at Savas. "Should I drive it in, sir? The place looks huge."

The gaping hole was indeed massive. Savas nodded. Awe-filled, he examined the beautiful yellow-and-clear ice that made up the entrance. "Slowly, Abdul."

The cave was mammoth, like an ancient cathedral of ice. He'd taken virtual holographic tours of ancient Surface architecture in school, and the eerie peace this place exuded reminded him of those long-gone buildings. Light from the entrance reflected off the roughly shaped walls, turning them into masterpieces of art.

Unlike cathedrals with their idyllic stained-glass saints creating warm patterns of light, the reflected light here created cold shadows that lulled him to sink sleepily against his seat. He rocked with the rover's movement as Abdul drove in for about two hundred meters and then killed the engine.

"It's too narrow to go any farther." Abdul gestured with his gloved hand.

For some reason, they all turned in their seats facing toward the tunnel branch to the left, ignoring the larger area to their right.

"All right, get out, men." Savas had never experienced such peace on the last mission. This was truly pleasant. They climbed out of the rover, and he tripped on his own feet as if drunk.

Laughing at himself, he reminded the others, "Guns out. Stamf, take the lead. I'll bring up the rear."

He paused, swaying a bit, while the other two men passed him and then proceeded slowly down the left branch. Sparkling light from farther down the tunnel lit their way. With a quick glance back toward the entrance, he took up the rear.

Then a voice as ethereal as the wind sang, "Caaaaaahm heeeeeeeere… caaaaaaaaaahm heeeeeeeere…"

*What the hell?*

Savas shook his head, blinked, and tapped his ear communicator. Stamf and Abdul, farther ahead, had frozen and appeared confused, swaying in place.

Something was terribly wrong. Was this cave filled with noxious fumes? Had they all gotten cold sickness? The databases talked of arctic workers becoming weak and confused by the extreme temperatures.

*Think! Think.* Savas wanted to lie down and nap. *What's wrong with me?* Images from his childhood tumbled through his head. *Not now. Not again. I control my own mind.*

"Caaaaaaaaahm heeeeeeeeere," the voice lulled, endlessly peaceful.

They all mindlessly continued forward, as if in a dream. A small part of Savas' brain screamed in warning. *I. Control. My. Own. Mind.* He grunted with the effort. Fighting the urge to relax, Savas forced his hands to raise his weapon.

Ahead, Stamf froze, while Abdul continued past Stamf.

Savas forced his lips to move. "Sta...Stamf. What's up there? Your rifle!"

Stamf jumped and his hood shook as if he was trying to rid himself of the trance. He raised the semi-automatic and aimed it at something.

"Abdul, get back! Get back!" Stamf wildly gestured toward Abdul, trying to get him to snap out of his trance.

Abdul continued forward, unresponsive to their shouts.

Savas warred with his relaxed muscles, that refused to move. Something horrible had paralyzed them. His heart hammered a wake-up call to his body. Thanks to his screaming survival instincts, he managed to gather his wits and stumble around an ice formation. He lumbered down the tunnel.

How long had he stood frozen? Stamf and Abdul were way ahead of him.

Savas stared over Stamf's shoulder. A large, brown, hairy creature like the two in Neviah's video, squatted on the cave floor. Savas instinctively knew the lulling thought control came from this monster. An unfamiliar sensation rose like nausea from his gut to his throat.

Terror.

This creature was luring them to their deaths. It raised both forelegs toward Stamf and Abdul, rising up on its hind legs.

"Shoot! Shoot now, Stamf! Shoot," Savas yelled as he pulled his own gun and fired. In his strange mental state, he slipped on the ice, and his second bullet careened toward the ceiling.

Stamf fired, hitting the monster squarely in the chest. As it bellowed and blood flowed onto its belly fur, Savas glared in horror at its head. The thing had a completely flat, brown face— no eyes, no mouth, nothing. Its strangeness repulsed him. What the *shast* was it?

When the injured creature crumpled forward, the eerie peace shattered; clarifying that the strange lulling had indeed arisen from the beast. A sudden, sharp light flashed from the creature, and a loud roar came from the cave's ceiling.

*Weaponry.*

Stamf and Savas fired toward the blinding light flashes. Savas covered Stamf as he edged forward, screaming at Abdul to move backward toward them.

Above them, yellow-and-white ice cracked and began breaking loose. The weapons had started a cave-in.

"Back to the entrance. Run!"

Savas stopped firing, turned, and ran, grabbing the closest parka. Screaming, he pulled the man backward. They fled toward the bright white of the cave entrance. Huge boulders of ice rained down on every side.

Savas turned momentarily to see one of his men pausing, still entranced by the creature's luring call. His man still appeared confused by the surrounding chaos.

"Run," Savas yelled, but he couldn't wait any longer. Turning, he hoped they both followed. He raced, dodging the falling blocks of ice.

Savas reached the larger tunnel with the rover and risked looking over his shoulder. An orange parka dodged the falling debris, running after him. Savas turned and ran toward the rover, and then reared back as an ice boulder landed on it, nearly crushing him.

Someone pulled him to his feet. Stamf. *He's alive.*

With a final horrified look at the crushed rover, they darted toward the entrance, arms held above their heads. They burst into the light, stumbling.

"Where's Abdul? What was that? Abdul? Do you see him?" Stamf yelled and spun in circles, scanning for his teammate.

Savas panted, his hands on his knees. He faced the collapsing cave entrance, waiting, but Abdul did not appear.

"We have to get him! Where the *shast* is he?" Stamf raced in frantic circles.

Savas struggled to his feet as Stamf acted out his own confusion. It was strangely comforting. Sudden accidental death rarely occurred in Northern Haven. It was as incomprehensible as rain below the Surface. Eventually, Stamf stopped spinning, quieted, and turned questioningly to Savas.

Commander Savas shook his head. "He didn't make it, Stamf." He shivered. "You saw that, right? Some sort of freak predator?"

Stamf nodded, eyes wide.

"Did you feel…" He hesitated. "It lured us in like we were prey? Like mind control?"

Stamf shivered, his face pale. "Yes."

They stared at each other for a long moment, and Savas knew he should say something, be the strong leader, but words failed him. It was too much. They had nearly been reaped for dinner.

Stamf sniffed. "Maybe there's another way in? We need to find Abdul."

Savas sighed and shook his head. "He was standing right in front of that thing, and the ice was crashing all around him. We should get back to camp." He was glad that his tinted goggles and face protection hid his horror.

*We lost not only Abdul, our medic, but the rover as well. Gone.*

"Wait." Stamf grabbed Savas' parka sleeve. "His radio. Does it still work? What if he's trapped?"

No one would have survived that much crashing ice. Stamf's naïve hope touched something in him, so he tried a few times to reach Abdul over the radio in his head piece, but there wasn't even a connection.

"I'm sorry, Stamf, but he's gone." He put his arm around Stamf's shoulder. "We need to go warn the others about that thing."

When Stamf finally nodded, Savas turned and began leading the way back to camp. They were in for a long walk, and because Nature seemed to have a personal vendetta against him, the wind had picked up as well. *Perfect.*

Savas looked about and realized how vulnerable they were in this open ice plain. "We need to be prepared for more of those creatures. How's your ammunition?"

Still in a daze, Stamf checked his magazine and reloaded it.

"Good. Now try to stay sharp," Savas said.

The poor kid was in shock and only grunted that he'd heard.

Savas' fury fueled him as he stomped across the icy field. He'd lost Abdul, the snow rover, and his hope that Neviah's video monsters had been a digital artifact of her program. As if humanity could afford more loses. The council would not be happy that another life had been lost, and Abdul had been a good team member. *If our luck doesn't change, humanity will become as extinct as the dinosaurs.*

No. His hands fisted at his sides. He'd do anything to keep that from happening. He *would* reestablish humanity on the Surface. Though, first, he had to demonstrate humans could survive up here. Today's losses wouldn't help his case. He growled inside his hood.

Stumbling alongside him, Stamf seemed too lost in his own shock to care.

Savas shivered again as the wind buffeted against him, yet he somehow continued his brisk pace. They hustled for several hours in silence, their only distractions being the terrible keening of the wind as it whipped around ice formations, boulders, and a random, straggling tree. Every few minutes, Stamf talked to himself, probably muttering in grief.

The sun sank toward the horizon, and Savas' legs grew sore. It was much harder to walk in the snow than on dry ground, and no one should ever need to walk this far.

When they reached the ice plain where they had built their camp, he spotted Zach furiously waving for them to hurry with his one arm, while the other arm fought to control the large tent that had collapsed and threatened to be blown away.

"Great," he grumbled to Stamf, "things just keep getting better and better."

Exhausted, they broke into a slow run.

"Curse these heavy packs," he muttered to Stamf, but the kid remained silent as if his earlier yelling had drained him of words.

"Stamf, do you see Josefina?"

Savas saw no movement other than Zach's frenetic waving. Then his gaze fell on the orange silhouette on the ground near the waving Zach. *No.* He surged forward, his exhaustion forgotten.

# Chapter 25

On the Surface: *Commander Kern Savas*

Josefina lay curled on the ice, trembling and holding the emergency blanket to herself, while Zach tried in vain to control the billowing tent that whipped at both of them.

"What happened?" Savas grunted, out of breath, as he knelt by Josefina's fallen body. Dread gnarled its way through his intestines. "Jos." He gently shook her shoulder.

She turned her head to look at him, a mask of grim resolve on her face. "I was wrong. The water was vicious." She attempted a smile but then gasped and wrapped her arms tighter around her abdomen.

"What—"

"It's my fault." Zach cut him off. "We were getting water samples, and I slipped. She caught me, but then lost her balance and fell in. She got soaked and freezing, and then the wind kicked up and the tent came untied. I had to catch this tent while trying to get her to the tethered one.

"Then, a few minutes ago, she doubled over, and I thought she was trying to warm herself, but she says its abdominal pain. And I tried radioing you but..." Zach paused for breath but then suddenly straightened and began pivoting on the spot. "Where's Abdul?"

Savas growled. Totally unprofessional, he knew, but he couldn't take two catastrophes in one day. He didn't have the extensive training of the ancient military men to remain cool and collected.

"Commander, where's Abdul?" Zach's voice rang higher than usual.

"He's dead. A creature attacked us. We'll do without him."

Zach paled and spun to Stamf for confirmation. As if he'd lie about Abdul's death. Stamf gave a silent nod.

"*Shast shast shast shast shast!*" Zach cursed.

"Zach, you can freak out later. Now, we need to act. Radio below. Get contact."

If one of the doctors could give them more information, she'd be okay. He had read everything he could find in the databases on cold survival—remove wet clothing; warm with body heat if nothing else is available; and seek medical attention. But he'd never read about abdominal pain.

"Dead?" Zach stood uselessly as if they had all the time in the world to grieve.

It was all Savas could do not to slap the fool. "Pull yourself together. Let's keep the rest of us alive."

He stood, hoping to appear more commanding in this precarious situation. "Zach and Stamf, fix that tent. Then call Base. I'll get her to the other one and warm her."

She was still in wet clothing and held an emergency electric blanket, but it was a poor solution in the whipping wind. Savas cursed, wrapped his arms around her, and lifted.

She whimpered at the movement.

"Sorry, Jos. I'm going to get you to the tent and warmed up." He raced across the slippery ground toward the tent, trying not to jostle her.

Josefina was tough. She should be fine, but she didn't look it. Her gaze looked through him, barely registering his presence.

He dove into the tent and rushed to get the wet clothing off her shivering body. He frantically tugged at her parka. It had already frozen into a stiff mess. His heart sank, its frantic beat thrumming against his ribs. This was not the way he had wanted things to be between them; he had always envisioned her removing her own clothing in a vastly different scenario.

"Sorry." He pulled out his knife and sliced open the parka, grimacing at the loss of the valued clothing. Inside the parka, her clothing was damp and clung to her skin, making its removal difficult. As he finally removed all her upper layers, he gasped. Her skin was already becoming mottled.

He stripped off his own jacket, coughing as he removed his headpiece. The bitterly cold air stabbed into his throat and lungs. He pursed his lips and slowly breathed through his mouth, allowing the air to warm briefly as it passed over his tongue. Still coughing, he put the headpiece on her and then pulled the electric emergency blanket from his sack.

Once he'd wrapped her top half in the blanket, he began removing her lower layers, but she pulled the blanket from her back and hugged it tight to the front of her.

*What is she doing?* He rewrapped it around her shoulders and grabbed the sleeping bag for her lower body. Then he encircled her with his own body, hoping his body heat would be of some additional help.

"I've got you, Jos. They're calling for help. Hang in here with me."

She lay nonresponsive and limp against his chest.

"Jos?" He couldn't see her chest moving. Quickly, he loosened her headpiece and held his fingers near her nose. Moist air blew against his ungloved finger, making him sag with relief. He left her helmet loose to give her the benefit of the air warmer and head covering yet still be able to observe her breathing.

Desperation clawed at him. What else could he do to warm her? Struggling to breathe in the frigid air, he watched his warm breath condense as he exhaled. Could his breath contribute warmth? He had read that the most heat is lost through the head. Did that include one's own breath?

With her headpiece askew, he breathed in her scent and exhaled his hot breath into her dark hair. It tickled against his nose. *Please let this work.* For years, he'd wanted to be this close to her, but now, he could lose her forever.

*Please. Keep her alive. She's the only one who gets me.*

Her hand jerked to her belly, and she moaned in pain.

Outside, the wind screamed, and Zach and Stamf yelled at each other as they pounded in the metal tent pegs. The cold air sent another round of spasms through his throat and set off another coughing fit.

*I need to reach base.* He had no radio; Josefina was wearing his headpiece. He stretched to where he had discarded her wet one and tried to activate it. It sputtered static. *Too wet.*

Just then, Stamf and Zach pushed through the flap, bringing in gusts of cold air. It rattled through the tent, puffing out the sides.

"You're freezing her!" Savas fought the urge to smack them.

"Sorry, sir." Stamf sounded truly distraught. "How is she?"

"Did you reach base yet?" He ignored Stamf's question. She had been quiet too long. His gut twisted at the possibility that she wouldn't warm.

"No, the wind is too loud out there." Zach swung his arms to warm them, oblivious to their cramped quarters.

Savas forcibly grabbed his arm. "Do it. Now."

As Zach's icy fingers fumbled with the radio, Josefina tried to stand.

"What are you doing?" Savas gathered her stumbling body in his arms and attempted to force her to use the blanket.

She wasn't in her right mind. She tore off the blanket and tugged at the sleeping bag.

"Too hot…" she mumbled.

"No, you've got hypothermia." Savas motioned for Stamf to help him and rewrapped the blanket around her. "You need to stay covered, so you can warm up," he explained.

Stamf seemed to remember his training, because he quickly assisted Savas. The archives had described such frantic activity to cool off in hypothermic people.

They all huddled around Josefina, trying to use body warmth, all the emergency electric blankets, and the pellet stove Stamf had just set up. But she remained listless and pale, moaning in pain. That symptom hadn't been reported, had it?

"Commander, they have doctors on the line. I reported what happened. They want us to keep warming her and to get a temperature reading." Zach's voice shook.

"Zach, we lost our only medical equipment with our medic. It's under an avalanche, and there are armed creatures near there. We can't retrieve

206

Abdul's body or our supplies."

Zach relayed the information, paused, grimaced, and turned to face them again.

"Sir, they want us to bring her back on the rover. Immediately." Confusion flooded his face. "Did you bring the rover back with you?" Zach reminded Savas of a young boy asking his father to tell him everything was a misunderstanding and that his friend would be fine.

Savas sighed. "We lost the rover in the cave-in. We need other options." He squinted with the effort of analyzing everything he knew about their current status. "Can they send another rover out to get us?" He knew the answer, but Josefina needed a miracle.

Zach waited for an answer.

"They say it will take a minimum of an hour for them to ready the other rover, but they don't have any trained people."

A deathly silence hovered in the air.

"Bleu is trained." Stamf stated only part of the obvious. Bleu was also possibly insane and violent.

Savas grunted. Josefina shifted again, this time curling into him. He stared at her pale face.

"Tell them we need Bleu."

He was grasping at straws, but Bleu Reinier *had* trained, and they had expedition gear that would fit him. Would they risk an eighteen-year-old potentially doomed to develop the Sickness to save a celebrated scientist?

*We're all at risk if we must carry her the whole way back. And if that creature shows up again...*

He tapped his gloved hand against the electric blanket he held to Josefina's body.

Zach relayed his suggestion, and from the way he winced at the response on the radio earpiece, Savas could only imagine the yelling and chaos his request had incited.

Zach adjusted his earpiece. "They're conferring."

Their silent wait dragged on. They remained huddled around Josefina, her breath shallow and unsteady.

That new feeling of terror began to build in Savas' stomach again. She was running out of time. He shook his head at how horribly wrong everything had gone.

"Commander?" Stamf must have noticed his movement.

"Nothing." He contorted his face into a neutral expression.

Moments dragged on. "Zach? What the *shast* is taking so long?"

Zach shrugged.

Finally, the crackle of a radio response came from Zach's headphones. His furrowed brow frustrated the hell out of Savas. It gave no information.

"Really? Can you repeat that?" Zach questioned as the wind howled against their tent.

"What? Tell me." Savas shook the younger man.

"They're sending Bleu. They want us to relay our position."

# Chapter 26

*arlier that morning: Kahali*

Kahali grinned as he recognized the massive cave ahead from Kalakanya's description. The wind whistled its bitter breath against his hood and blew icy crystals in his eyes. His long black hair had come untied under his hood and stuck to his frozen lashes. As he stumbled into the cave's mouth, the wind faded to a distant howl. Relief flooded his body, and he straightened to better examine the place.

Sculpted ice rose around him in subtle shades of blue, yellow, and orange tinged with silver from the reflected moonlight. Kalakanya was correct as usual; the place appeared ideal for Calling the Earth's children.

He stopped, sensing for furred ones, but found nothing. Excitement danced through his body at being the first from his village to Call. He wandered into his discovery, trailing his gloved hands along the icy walls in wonder.

The cavern split. Silver-blue radiance beckoned him up the left path, and he meandered toward it. After a narrow section, he entered a small opening lit by streaming moonlight. This spot was perfect for Calling. Overhead, the moon and stars watched through uneven openings. In a few hours, warm sunlight would filter through. He'd take any additional warmth he could get.

Proud of his find, he couldn't wait to share it with his friends. Balavati's chatter about its perfection would be eclipsed by Rana's slow smile. He loved that smile.

Ever since the two of them had watched the summer meteor shower together last year, her smile made him breathless. If he could successfully make contact with these beings that needed help, maybe in the congratulatory excitement he'd get a kiss.

"Time to Call the Earth's children," he announced to the surrounding darkness, and dramatically settled himself on the flattest part of the floor. Chuckling, he imagined small children created from frozen mud dancing toward him as he meditated. This would be interesting.

Re-tying his icy hair, he flipped his hood up for warmth and began deep breathing. He breathed consciously, pulling in the energy of the One In All with every breath. The excitement coursing through his body transformed into pure joy. When he was fully charged, his gaze gently fell on the opposite wall, and he Called by putting out a mental pulse.

Because no one knew where these children fell on the awareness scale, he'd need to experiment. While each type of furred one could be reached by its own peculiar vibration, not even the Crowned Ones knew how to reach these unknown children. Kahali fiddled with new vibrations until he found one that intuitively felt right for lost, muddy little children. His heart leapt at the opportunity to help them.

Hours passed. Years of training had honed his concentration. Periodically, he shifted his body, but his focus remained constant. Determination fueled his intense fixation. Sweat beaded his brow as shafts of midday sun pierced the overhead openings.

The sunlight ricocheted off the walls so brightly it pained his eyes. He needed the leather face covering worn to prevent snow blindness. He paused, slowly reached for the face covering, and attached it to his hood. He moved calmly, careful not to shift out of his peaceful mindset. As he lowered his hands, the soft brown leather fell over his face. His eye muscles instantly softened. The two slits allowed him to see but blocked most of the harsh glaring light as it reflected off the ice.

He reentered the deepest parts of himself, Calling with renewed vigor. Suddenly, his awareness noticed a strange flicker...a slow, heavy energy that steadily drew nearer. Kahali's heart skipped a beat. The new vibration was unfamiliar—fear-based, perhaps? He struggled to maintain his intense focus, but the excitement of a new energy rushed through him.

Shivering in anticipation of his discovery, Kahali grinned. Was this an unknown furred one or the Earth's children?

Cold sweat dripped down his spine. He locked his Calling onto the frequency, rocking his body back and forth with the push-pull rhythm of it. The new energy grew closer, and soon, strange vocalizations and extremely noisy walking came from the front of the cavern. No furred one made that much noise.

Three upright beings appeared—unlike anything Kahali had ever seen. They had shiny, brightly-colored pelts and huge, dark, reflective eyes. They walked like star beings but were smaller and denser. They approached him warily.

*These must be the Earth's children.* Kahali stood in greeting, extending his arms in a nonthreatening welcome. One of the creatures yowled. The fear energy overpowered Kahali's senses. He stopped the meditation and peered about for the source of their terror. *Did I do something threatening?*

The first one quickly raised a stick to its shoulders, and Kahali was blasted backward.

*What?* Searing pain flooded him as he Called for help. Ice cascaded down around him. A millisecond later, in a flash of light, Samasti appeared and threw up a wall-like shield of energy between them and the attackers. As she pivoted to grab him, a large chunk of sharp ice fell from the upper cave and sliced viciously downward.

Kahali had never screamed before. It was primal and horrid. It did nothing for the pain in his chest and his arm, but it burst forth like a waterfall with no ending.

All went black as his scream faded to nothingness. He drifted in the endless void of unconsciousness.

* * *

Sometimes awareness grips you and tears you from the comfort of not knowing.

So it happened for Kahali; it wound him in agonizing pain. A rattling echoed in his ears. His breath. Each movement of his lungs caused convulsions of dagger-like pangs throughout his body. When he opened his eyes, he lay on furs in his own hut. Pain tore at his chest, and his arm burned. The blurry faces of both his fathers hovered above him.

"You're safe, son." His father, Luminary Vadin, had tears in his normally bright eyes.

Kahali attempted to speak, but opening his mouth increased the spikes of pain. He resorted to mind talk.

*What happened? Am I dying?*

His father shook his head. "No. You're safe now. They..." He turned to Kagni, his other dad, and held up his palm in confusion. Nothing ever baffled his fathers. Kahali sensed their minds trying to find the correct word. Each passing moment, he fell deeper into the darkness that had claimed him before.

*What?* He tried to grab his father's arm, but nothing happened. As he gasped for breath, black spots appeared in his vision. He blinked furiously, trying to not lose their faces.

"You Called well, Kahali. We don't know why, but they...they hunted you." Kagni's grip on his arm tightened. "You did everything well, but they were too full of fear to hear properly. Rest."

Hunted? His words made no sense. Kahali closed his eyes and exhaustion pulled him into the depths of unconsciousness. Macabre images danced through his mind. The Earth children's fear had infected him. He moaned and screamed, seeing ghastly sights he previously would not have imagined.

The image of a beast gnawing off his arm woke him. Sweat ran down his face. The saltiness of it made it difficult for him to keep his eyes open. He reached for his arm, but something was horribly wrong. His brain couldn't understand as his heart thudded in his ears. Was this still a nightmare?

Kagni quickly appeared at his side. Powerful undulations of calm flowed from his palm to Kahali's chest. Despite Kagni's skill at healing, his energy was a drop of water on a burning inferno of pain that ripped through him.

Kahali stiffened and screamed, but that only increased the burning pain. He collapsed back into a useless heap on the pile of furs.

"What happened?" he gasped.

Kagni and Vadin sat on either side of him, sending him waves of healing energy. Vadin's jaw tightened and he exchanged a look with Kagni.

Kagni said, "They hunted you. They hurt your chest. Their hunting sticks created a cave-in, and a sharp piece of ice fell on your arm." He paused, holding his gaze with a steady calmness. "It sliced it off."

Kahali's eyes widened. *Off? Like its gone?* He frantically turned his head, straining to see his arm. Pain nearly blinded him, but he had to know.

"Yes." Kagni's voice wavered.

"Forever?" Kahali knew it was a strange question, but he couldn't grasp what had happened.

Vadin nodded.

"Crowned Ones can re-grow their own, not yours. Your chest is healing, but your arm is gone. Perhaps when you Crown..." Kagni smiled encouragingly as tears ran down his cheeks.

"But why? I Called to help them." Kahali had known there would be risks, but why would they hunt him? Were they starving? Is that why they needed help?

"Fear and ignorance are the real problems, Kahali. They are very young and do not understand Life. They react without sensing."

Kahali, trembling with fury, pressed his lips together. There was nothing appropriate to say. But his mind screamed. *They're rabid. Diseased. Walking Death.*

"Kahali, stop." Kagni had never yelled before.

*You yelled. They're infecting us all. We must stay away.*

"Kahali, listen with your heart. They don't understand what they did, and this anger hurts only you. You must forgive them."

"Never." With his good arm, he painfully pulled a fur over his shoulder and face, blocking both his fathers from view. An immature act, but he couldn't tolerate their talk of forgiveness or garner the strength to leave.

He had loved the Earth children. They had hunted him and taken his arm.

He squeezed shut his eyes and heart. Everything he had believed was wrong... Love was not the most powerful force; their weapons were stronger. The dark sap of hate seeped around his closed heart and spread its nebulous form over him. It flowed about him like a new, powerful cloak, protecting him from whatever was out there.

# Chapter 27

*orthern Haven: Bleu Reinier*

N Bleu and Neviah had been helplessly watching events unfold on the Surface from the cramped data room. When Commander Savas said, "We need Bleu," Bleu stared at Neviah, open mouthed.

"*Shast!* I have to get home now." Bleu's heart thudded against his ribs.

With no time for sneaking, he punched the button to open the data room door and raced home. As he careened through the halls, his only camouflage was his speed. Fortunately, nearly everyone was at work or school, and the halls were clear. He burst through his door and collapsed on the chair. He had beaten them here, but would he leave for the Surface before his sprint through the halls reached authorities?

Atsushi raced into the living room still holding his mug of tea. "What happened?" He looked around frantically.

Bleu shook his head. "Too… much." He panted. "They're coming."

The door chime rang.

"Who's coming?" Atsushi asked, his face full of alarm. He turned back to Ayanna's bedroom door. "Do we need to hide her?"

Bleu shook his head. "Get…the door." He panted, trying to slow his breath. He had to act like he had been in his module, bored and ignorant of the dangers his friends faced. His body trembled in anticipation of finally going to the Surface, but he still had to pull this off. He sat back, put up his feet, and plastered what he hoped was a wearisome look on his face.

Atsushi glanced back as he approached the door. His tea-free hand grabbed his own black hair. "Bleu, your head."

Bleu's hands flew to his crown and pulled off the headphones from the data room. In horror, he rose, checked himself for other telltale signs, found none, and threw the headphones behind the chair. He turned as the front door hissed open and a council guard entered.

The guard stepped across the threshold, nodded to Bleu, and then glanced nervously at Ayanna as she traipsed into the room wearing pajamas.

"What's going on?" Ayanna moved to stand behind Bleu.

The guard said, "The Council has reconsidered its ruling, Bleu. They need you to report for duty immediately. You're needed on the Surface." His gaze twitched to Ayanna.

"I don't bite, you know." Ayanna glared at him.

Bleu shot her a warning look. Her attitude would get them all in trouble. If she mentioned his recent return to their module…his gut clenched.

He glanced at Atsushi for assistance, but he was messaging Neviah on his hacked comm.

"What?" Bleu hoped he sounded genuine to the guard. "They want me?"

"I need to bring you *now*." The guard stepped forward.

"Okay, give me a second." Bleu turned and hugged Ayanna. "Don't worry, I'll be back soon. Promise." His throat tightened at the other alternative. His arms lingered, not wanting to let go. Would she still be herself when he returned?

The guard cleared his throat. "The council said if you delayed, your sister would be taken to the Sickness Unit immediately." The guard pointed his chin to Atsushi. "He'll keep her under control?"

"Yes. He'll *stay with her*." Bleu glared at the guard over Ayanna's head and then turned to Atsushi. "Remember our deal."

Atsushi nodded. "Neviah's going to let your mom know to meet you in the Control Room."

That's what he'd been doing. "Thanks, man."

Atsushi nodded. "Be safe up there."

Bleu nodded and held Ayanna tightly as he gazed at his family's module one last time. Would he return? His insides revved in anticipation of what he'd encounter on the Surface, but what if he failed to return?

Ayanna pulled back and gave him a grin. "Imagine you're as tough as me up there, and you'll be fine."

Laughing, he followed the guard into the hall but whirled as they passed through the door.

"Love you!" He and Ayanna blurted it out at the same moment as the door sliced between them. The closed door slammed him with the reality of what he faced, and the danger hit him like a sucker punch.

*Teams can't handle it, and they want me out there alone?*

The guard grabbed Bleu's arm, pulling him toward the Control Room, but he shrugged free. He didn't have to be coerced to ascend to the Surface even if this particular mission seemed suicidal.

They strode to the Control Room, which neighbored the door to the Surface shaft. A whirlwind of assistants checked his vitals and updated him. He didn't have to act shocked. Josefina had gotten worse since he had watched with Neviah, and it'd be dark when he reached the Surface. Alone.

He listened to the details while others brought him his layers and helped him dress. Suddenly, his heart skipped a beat, and he turned about, trying to locate his regular pants. His dagger. How could he sneak it into his parka? He'd kept it on him since its surreal appearance. Despite his layers, he felt naked and exposed without it.

He waited until the people stopped fussing over him and returned to their regular tasks. One assistant remained, and Bleu's discarded clothing lay thrown on a chair nearby.

"I'm worried about the darkness. Could you grab me an extra light?" he asked.

"No problem. *Shast*, you couldn't pay me to go up there in all that openness with no idea what's around me." The assistant cringed in horror, then caught himself and smiled. "You'll be fine. I'll get that extra light." He left for the equipment room.

Bleu darted to his pants, extracted the dagger, and shoved it in his parka pocket.

The man returned with an extra light. "Checking out the pockets?"

"Oh, yes. Just like I remember." Bleu looked down. *Just like I remember? I sound like a fool.*

"It's okay to be nervous. Everyone gets nervous." The guy patted his shoulder.

Bleu nodded. "Have you reached my parents? They don't know any of this is going on." *Or that Ayanna's alone with Atsushi.*

"I think someone called the Unit," he said as he walked around Bleu and inspected his clothing as if he hadn't trained for this expedition.

Getting his parents was clearly not a priority. He wouldn't get to say goodbye, and despite his age, he could use a mom hug before facing the dark Surface alone.

They reviewed the snow rover controls, rechecked his pack, explained the tracking device that would lead him to the team, and then, finally, radioed Commander Savas for one last update.

"Don't get distracted by the sky. Utmost urgency, Bleu." Commander Savas' voice was strained.

"Yes, sir." *Ugh. Stop reviewing everything, then.* He looked around. Still no sign of his parents.

"And, Bleu, there's one more thing." Commander Savas cleared his throat. "You have to come straight here to the base camp. No stopping. No matter what."

"Of course, Commander. You don't need to tell me that." Bleu glanced up at the others in the control room. They mirrored his confusion at this odd statement.

"Bleu, this is vitally important. The creature that attacked us...it was like nothing in the Records. Not of this world. Remember the video Neviah showed you and Stamf? Like that. The creature was covered with hair, stood on two legs, and tried to lure us to it. It affected our ability to think clearly. We couldn't react to protect ourselves. Keep your gun ready, and get here as soon as possible."

"Yes, sir. But...it lured you?" Bleu had noticed the team reacting too slowly. Is that what he meant?

"It made noises." The Commander paused again to confer briefly with another man. "Stamf and I heard it imitate human language. But it's definitely not human. It's dangerous. Shoot on sight. That's a command. You understand?"

"Yes." The hairs stood up on Bleu's neck.

"And Bleu?"

"Yes, Commander?"

"Don't lose your meal on the elevator ride up. You'll need all your strength to do this."

The instant Commander Savas had finished his instructions, the team hurried Bleu from the room.

As he entered the last set of doors leading to the elevator, a familiar voice yelled his name. He turned as his mother burst through the gathered Control Team.

"Mom." He grinned. Someone had found her.

"Bleu." She threw her arms around his bulky Surface gear. A mom hug, but too tense, as if she were holding him back from leaving. When she pulled away to look at him, fear shone in her eyes.

"Bleu." She leaned in close and whispered, "I had to fight the whole council to name you something other than Jean Paul. You're Bleu—same as the sky over the Surface. It's your destiny."

"You named me after the Surface?" He couldn't fathom it. Everyone in Northern Haven was assigned a name from a different culture—Bleu from France. How could he have been named after the Surface in general?

The team leaders approached, mumbling about the time constraints.

She nodded, her eyes sparkling with tears. "Ayanna insisted you take this. It's on a cord, so it won't break and get lost." She placed her closed fist above his palm, and a hard object fell onto his glove. It was the large, blue stone pendant Ayanna wore, passed down from their Surface ancestors.

Bleu's breath caught in his throat. Ignoring the impatient staff, he quickly undid his three-layered suit and put the cord around his neck. He tucked the cord and stone between the layers to prevent the metal from freezing

219

to his skin.

The pendant hung heavily on his neck as if all his ancestors were collectively resting their hands on his shoulders. A wave of lightheadedness passed through him.

"Trust your instincts, Bleu. You can do this."

Her confident attitude warmed him. "Thanks. And thank Ayanna."

He turned away then, because he was about to lose it at the thought of leaving his sister in her current state. He swallowed his guilt and nodded to the edgy Control Room staff.

"I'll bring them all back. Alive." He stepped into the shaft with the rover. The doors clanged shut behind him with a finality he hoped wasn't prophetic.

*Next stop, the Surface!* Heedless of the danger, his heart clamored its joy. Soon, he would stand beneath the sky, his feet resting on the ground his ancestors had fled centuries before. Alone. His stomach clenched. Was he ready for this, especially at night? He had always pictured a blue sky, not total darkness.

He shivered and checked the handgun holstered to his thigh. His hidden dagger was in his pocket. Since the camera and radio were already activated in his headpiece, he refrained from checking the dagger. The moon woman's voice came back to him. *Keep it with you, always.* He studied the sturdy snow rover as if its solidness proved he'd be safe.

The box shuddered to a stop just in time, allowing the rising bile to settle. Commander Savas had not exaggerated the nausea induced by the ascent. Bleu swallowed and tried to calm down, but his anxiety for Josefina made relaxation a distant dream. He counted his heartbeats, distracting himself from his rising awareness that the box had not yet restarted its ascent.

Finally, the box lurched upward. He focused on the noisy, churning, mechanical sounds to divert his attention from his stomach, which turned itself round and round like a gear.

*Just get to the camp, man. Rescue them before Josefina dies. Just get to the camp.*

It was strangely comforting to reduce his bizarre day and solo mission to five syllables. *Just get to the camp. Just get to the camp.*

He had started to settle into this repetition when the elevator stopped.

His radio clicked and someone from the Control Room said, "Bleu, put on your hood and turn on the breath warmer. We're opening the door."

# Chapter 28

O n the Surface: Bleu Reinier
Knowing how many lives depended on his success, Bleu rushed to activate his breath warmer and then rechecked everything.

"Okay, ready." He could open the door himself, but, apparently, the Control Room wanted to live up to its name.

The door cracked open, and the temperature dropped. *I hope this outfit is as good as they promised.* He leaned forward in his rover seat to get his first view, but the door crept too slowly. He jumped out, unable to stop himself, and peered into the widening space.

Bleu stood still, jaw dropped, head tilted upward. Time and space lost all meaning. The whole universe opened before him, dark and luminous at the same time. Light from somewhere made the snow and ice sparkle like millions of miniature silver candles glowing, lighting his way. Above, Nature had strewn stars across the sky like diamonds on velvet.

He slowly turned his head, taking it all in. The light came from the moon, a full, round glowing orb of beauty. A warm sensation began in his chest, and, despite the cold, it spread throughout his body. When it reached his face, it blossomed into a smile.

*I'm home.* The expansiveness of the sky overpowered his senses. It was like nothing he had ever experienced; the sheer intensity of his joy threatened to explode him into a million elementary particles that would surge upward into the star-strewn heavens.

*Just get to the camp.* He snapped back to normalcy. With the door fully open, he needed to get the rover out.

He tore his gaze from the sparkling stars and forced himself to turn back to the metal and machinery of his home. He checked that no gear had fallen out of the rover and then climbed back into the driver's seat.

As he turned it on, the engine's familiar vibration grounded him in the mission ahead. *Just get to the camp.* As the rover lurched forward, the treads shifted from metal to the crisp crunch of the ice. His smile returned.

"I'm out." He hoped his enthusiasm sounded appropriate. They might suspect him of the Sickness.

"Good luck, Bleu. We're closing the door. Head straight to camp."

"I'll radio in half an hour." This was the agreed upon protocol during training.

"No. Maintain constant radio contact. Just in case."

"Yes, sir." Apparently, Neviah wouldn't be the only one listening now.

Bleu headed the rover in the direction indicated by the detector. He wanted to push the vehicle to its limits and go at top speed, but he had strict orders to go slower. If the engine went, there would be no rescue.

*Just get to the camp.* Still, urgency to reach Josefina as quickly as possible coursed through his body, and he itched to test the vehicle at higher speeds. *Why build a rover with higher speeds if I can't use them?*

He felt strangely alone in the darkness. No, not alone. Isolated. Another strange thought. *Isolated from what?* He continuously swiveled his gaze, peering into the deep-blue darkness around him. The thrum of the rover's engine pulled him from the majesty around him. He checked the gauges, rechecked his direction, and then allowed his gaze to wander upward toward the blanket of stars covering the cold Earth.

He had seen stars, of course. Pictures in books. Holographs of night skies. But seeing them in person had a very different effect. He became puny and insignificant and surrounded by vast swathes of emptiness.

A bloodcurdling howl pierced the darkness nearby. He startled, and the rover lurched to the side, the treads grinding against the ice. In all his years of secret studies, he'd never considered studying animal vocalizations. Anything, including the Undescended, could be making the howls beyond the range of his snow rover's headlights. As much as he had longed for this world, he was lost here.

As he scanned the inky horizon, a large dark blob drew his gaze to an elevated area of ice. *Did it move?* He narrowed his eyes, straining to confirm reality. *Just get to the camp. Just get to the camp.*

It moved.

"Base, something's out here…pacing on a hill above me. I'm maintaining course, but I'm going to have to pass below it. Should I change course?"

"You heard Commander Savas. Shoot it as soon as it's in range. Continue course."

"Continue course. Got it, sir." Bleu hastily checked his gun, wishing for Stamf's longer-range rifle. *It's not close enough yet…*

His hand tightened on his gun. *I don't even know what it is, and I have to kill it?* The rover sped along as his indecision churned within him. *Trust your instincts, Bleu,* his mother had said. *It lured us,* Savas had said.

In his mind, Bleu replayed Neviah's terrifying video footage. That creature could be stalking him right now. Orders were orders. He raised his gun.

*Just like in the games with Stamf.* He steadied himself, slipped his right index finger out of the slit in his glove, and readied it near the trigger as he'd been taught. He waited. It wasn't attacking or luring him. He stood ready.

In an instant, dark movement flowed alongside the rover. Large shaggy animals raced alongside it, surrounding him. *There's too many…* He aimed at the closest and pulled the trigger, vaguely aware of voices shouting over the radio. Like a crowd in the gaming rooms…

A spine-screeching scream echoed off the hill. This horror was nothing like shooting the stoic lions in holographic games. He pivoted to the next closest thing running alongside. Something huge galloped along on four legs, yellow teeth flashing in the moonlight. *Giant wolves?* He quickly glanced around him.

Four more. He aimed at the closest and again pulled the trigger. As the dark shape yelped and fell, a force slammed Bleu forward. One of the creatures had jumped on his back and grasped over his shoulder for his throat. His headpiece detached from his chest, and he gasped as the cold air stabbed his lungs. His arm flew up to protect his neck. The massive jowls locked on his upper arm, and the gun dropped to the rover's floor.

"Base!" His yell sputtered as pain rippled through him. Stamf was too far to help even if he could hear. *I'm going to die...*

The dagger. His good arm yanked it from his pocket, shook off the sheath, and thrust it at the giant, wolf-like beast's throat. Hot blood exploded all over his face. He gagged, coughing and spitting while the thing collapsed and fell off the rover.

Another one lunged and grabbed Bleu's boot. He slipped and twisted, trying to pull himself back into the driving seat. He coughed as the frigid air constricted his lungs. He yanked the steering wheel as the creature again grabbed his leg and pulled him from the rover.

He grasped for something to hold onto, but his mangled arm was too weak. He slipped from the rover just as it flipped on its side. The toppled, spinning rover caught a different wolf in its treads. The last wolf grabbed his booted foot in its maw and pulled him into the endless darkness.

He was still grasping the dagger, but, in his bulky clothes, he couldn't reach the snarling beast dragging him across the ice, and he couldn't get enough air into his lungs. Waves of lightheadedness washed over him. The wolf-thing stopped, dropped his foot, and suddenly was airborne. Bleu lay on his back as it arched through the air, its massive jowls aimed for his exposed abdomen. In slow motion, he raised the dagger toward what he hoped would be its incoming throat.

The head hit his arm, but the dagger struck the wolf's shoulder. Startled, the beast jumped to Bleu's side. Bleu crawled to a crouch and roared from his gut, a foreign but animalistic threat. The wolf creature paused, growling at the bloody dagger Bleu raised in its direction, and then raced off into the night.

"Bleu! What? Are you—" Panicked voices thrummed in his headpiece from both the team and the Command Room.

Bleu grunted, stood, and examined his damage. Despite his injuries, he'd make it back to the rover. He reattached his head piece, slipped off his pack, and wrapped his ankle and arm to minimize blood loss. The voices in his radio still screamed, and they finally came into focus.

"Bleu! Bleu! What's going on? The cameras aren't working. Bleu, are you there?"

He sucked in a deep, shuddering breath. "Still here. Five huge wolves attacked. I'm walking back to the rover."

He bit his lower lip to distract himself from the pain in his leg. The voices of Base continued to yell, but they seemed far off, almost unimportant. Background noise to the main event. They couldn't help him, so he focused on each placement of his throbbing leg.

Limping back toward the lights of the snow rover, he hesitated at the giant wolves lying in the snow. Were they truly dead? Not wanting to find out, he hurried to the rover, which in its spinning had miraculously restored itself to an upright position. Its engine groaned as it attempted to free the treads from the two bodies crushed beneath. Bleu jumped inside, grabbed his gun, and reloaded it. The wolves on the ground still hadn't moved. *Dead.*

"Bleu? Bleu? Are you there?"

"Uh..." Bleu sat straighter, even though they had said the cameras weren't working. "Yes, I'm okay. I found my gun and got back to the rover."

"Where are the creatures?"

"Four dead, one ran away." The urgency returned. He had to get moving.

"Dead? Good. Are you still moving toward base camp?"

"No. The rover is stuck. Hold on." Bleu glanced at the instrumentation, then down at the treads. "The rover looks okay. I just need to get it loose from the bodies."

He turned off the rover and ground his teeth to keep from yelling as he climbed down and yanked dead body parts from the treads. As he pulled out the last one, he collapsed, waves of dizziness nauseating him. He barely got his hood off to throw up and then crawled back toward the driver's seat. Everything was distant, numb...

Blackness engulfed him.

# Chapter 29

On the Surface: *Bleu Reinier*

"Bleu..."

Distant voices called for someone, but heaviness pulled Bleu under the waves of darkness. He floated in a cold sea of blackness.

"Bleu?" Voices yelled in his head piece. "Bleu?"

"Huh? Uh..." He blinked at the spinning world around him. He lay crumpled in the driver's seat of the snow rover, bleeding. "I passed out."

He wanted to kick himself for losing consciousness. How much time had he wasted? He used his last strength to sit up, adjust the direction, and start the engine. The vibration of the engine threw spears of pain into his neck and back. *Just get to the camp.*

The snow rover rolled toward the flashing beacon on the display. His eyelids drooped from exhaustion as he examined his arm. Blood had soaked through his makeshift bandage. Biting his cheek to stay awake, he drove on, checking his heading periodically to make sure he was still on course. Stay awake and...just get to the camp.

Finally, the scanner showed he was nearing the camp. He pressed the button on his radio.

"Commander Savas, its Bleu."

"Where are you?" The relief in the commander's voice was clear.

"About a half a kilometer away. Do you see my lights?"

"We're in the tent with Josefina. Stamf, go out and see if he's within sight."

There was a pause. Bleu fought a rising panic that he had somehow read

227

the equipment wrong. There wasn't any room for error. The rover only had enough power to get there and back. *If my lightheadedness from blood loss made me mess this up...* He bit his cheek to stay conscious.

"Visual confirmed," Savas' voice said over the radio. "Nice work, Bleu."

Bleu drove over the other rover's tracks in the moonlight. *The one crushed with Abdul.* Bleu shook his head to clear the image from it. *Maybe it had been a mistake to watch?* He leaned forward, willing the rover to go faster.

A figure that must be Stamf waved enthusiastically, directing him to the second tent. He slowed the rover and killed the engine. Bleu stumbled from the rover as Stamf threw his arms outward to hug him but froze, his arms dropping.

"Man, you look like hell. Did you battle the whole Surface to get here?"

Bleu smiled weakly, too drained to compose a witty response. He swayed on his feet. Stamf startled and grabbed his shoulders to steady him.

"Let's get going." Commander Savas came toward them, carrying Josefina. His hood was missing. Instead, he had wrapped a blanket over his head and face. Only his eyes showed.

Zach was already throwing the surviving equipment, including the damaged hood, onto the rover.

"How is she?" Bleu searched Josefina's face as the Commander passed him.

"Not good. Zach, drive."

"Man, Bleu. Wolves?" Stamf assisted Bleu into the rover's back seat.

"Five. Looks like I'm winning this game. You shot, what? One?"

Stamf harrumphed and climbed into the front seat with his back to Bleu.

As Zach circled the rover back toward Northern Haven, Bleu and Savas leaned over Josefina, protecting her from the wind created by the moving rover.

"Stamf, be ready. No telling when those reaper-things will reappear." Savas repositioned himself to cradle Josefina's head in his arms. Through the headpiece, she appeared ghostly pale.

The return trip was beauty laced with fear. Fear that time was passing too quickly, and the beauty of Bleu's first sunrise with hues shifting from black to indigo to cobalt to combinations he couldn't even name. The ever-increasing light burned his eyes, but he wanted to see it all. Yet his fear for Josefina gnawed through the glorious light, turning it into a clock. The appearance of each new shade decreased the odds of saving her.

"Zach, go faster." Savas got to his knees, knocking over supplies. "Josefina? Jos?"

Bleu peered down at Josefina, the commander holding her head in his lap. Savas' voice had faltered. *Is she...?*

Savas straightened and shouted over the radio, "Base, we are at the door. Open it. Now!" His hand slid inside her headpiece and checked her breathing, then he brushed a strand of hair from her eyes. "Hold on, Jos."

There was the tremor in his voice again. Bleu had never seen this side of him. Savas never showed concern for anyone's welfare except his own.

As the door opened, Zach slowly drove in and turned the rover off. The doors closed.

*I made it, Yanna.* Bleu rested his head on the seat back in front of him. The now-familiar gut twisting sensation began as the elevator system lowered him to safety.

"You surprised me, Bleu. Didn't think you had it in you." The Commander gave him a wry smile.

Bleu bobbed his head up and smiled, but that small movement roiled his stomach. He jerked away, dry heaving over the side of the rover. Now that he was safe, his pain sharpened while his vision blurred. He collapsed against the seat.

In his distant awareness, the elevator stopped, the doors opened, and people hustled around him. Strong arms pulled him from his seat and carried him to the medical unit. He was numb. His eyes refused to stay open.

After some brief questions, they accepted that he couldn't respond. Voices expressed horror at his wounds. The word "surgery," and then nothingness.

* * *

Bleu first awoke to pain reverberating throughout his body. His mother argued in hushed tones with another doctor. Bleu's eyes flew open. His mom's colleague, Dr. Medicci, held a syringe, and his mother was furious.

"No, he won't want that. He'll want to keep his memories, trauma included. I know my son."

"Given the trauma he faced, the medical team recommends that we use the new serum."

She crossed her arms. "No, he's my son."

Dr. Medicci snorted and shook his head. "You know it's safe. You're the one who created it."

"I never meant to. I was looking for a cure to the Sickness." She turned to Bleu, and her eyes widened. "Bleu, you're awake. Tell him. You want to keep your memories."

"What? Of course. It was beautiful up there." Horrible, too, but he never wanted to forget that open, sparkling night sky. It existed every night...

"You were attacked and maimed. Why remember that?" Dr. Medicci approached him, syringe ready.

"Don't you dare." Bleu rose, his good arm swinging toward the approaching doctor to prevent his approach.

"Bleu, calm down." His mother stepped between them. "See? He clearly declines. Now, please leave us alone."

Dr. Medicci left, and Bleu fell back on the bed. His ankle and arm sent piercing pains throughout the rest of him. Sweat beaded his forehead.

"Rest, Bleu. If you need any other meds, I'll draw them up myself. You're safe." She gave him what Ayanna called her doctor look. "You need more pain medication."

She stepped away and returned with a needle, but he couldn't even detect the stab over the constant hammer of pain. She pulled the sheet to his chest as his heavy lids squeezed off consciousness.

Undulating clamor awoke him. Cries drifted in—was Ayanna okay?

Bleu jerked up and furrowed his brow in confusion. The medical suite surrounded him, not his family's module. The room spun in circles while his body adjusted to its sudden upright position.

His small unlit room was quiet, yet beyond it medical personnel, family, and Control Room staff crowded the hall and adjoining suite of rooms. Stamf and Zach rushed into an adjoining room. The beeping of medical equipment drifted from it. Apparently, the whole team was still on the medical floor, as well as their families and staff.

A pained moan drifted from the busy room. Someone was in trouble. Bleu stumbled off his bed, and using the walls for support, shuffled to the door well of the adjoining room. His pain had lessened, though now a heavy grogginess filled his limbs. He leaned against the wall and strained to see through the crowd.

Josefina lay on the bed surrounded by tubes and strange pillow-like heating devices. She was terribly pale. Educator Girak had collapsed on her chest, sobbing as Dr. Medicci pulled Prime Minister Pridbor out into the hall.

"Whath's happening?" Bleu's tongue was swollen and uncoordinated.

His mom shuffled over and held his shoulder.

"She's dead, Bleu. The doctors followed the Records' treatment for hypothermia, but that wasn't the real issue...she was bleeding internally too."

Bleu stood, stunned, and stared at Josefina. *Dead?* He stumbled under the weight of it. His mind went blank and he stood perfectly still, a statue with a floundering heart.

Unexpectedly, he was pushed against the doorframe by the returning Prime Minister Pridbor, who stormed into Josefina's room. Dr. Medicci, the doctor who had threatened Bleu with the serum, followed.

"She was pregnant, you fool!" Prime Minister Pridbor's jowls shook with rage.

Everyone stared at him.

*Who was pregnant?* Bleu glanced at the others, but they appeared just as baffled.

"That damn educator allowed his wife, his responsibility, to explore the Surface pregnant," Pridbor fumed. "Pregnancy is obvious grounds for dismissal from the expedition team. Letting her go was murder!"

The silence was deafening. All faces turned to Educator Girak, who held Josefina's hand to his face. Tears ran freely down his cheeks into his beard. He appeared oblivious to the accusations flying around him. He uncurled Josefina's fist. Slowly, with great tenderness, he traced in and out of the spiral tattoo on her palm.

"He didn't know." Bleu's mother moved protectively to the educator's side. "It was early. How could he?"

"The women's water with birth control must have been eliminated. She would have told him. If she was here and her pregnancy had been documented, this could have been prevented. No one dies of ectopic pregnancies anymore." Dr. Medicci shook in his fury.

The other doctor accused, "What he allowed is *criminal.*"

"Get out!" Girak roared, glaring from one onlooker to another.

Tears glistened in Bleu's mother's eyes as she put a hand on Girak's shoulder. "They think you knew she was pregnant. It was a mistake, right? Explain it to them, Diggory."

Girak gave her a blank look. "A mistake to accidentally get my wife pregnant?"

Rage gripped Commander Savas' face. "You killed her, Girrr-rrrrak!" He growled Girak's name like a wild beast, grasped him by the collar, and smashed him against the wall. "Couldn't you at least have protected her?"

*Isn't anyone going to help Girak?* Bleu wobbled forward to intervene but lost his balance. Stamf caught his arm and pulled him upright.

"You knew before she went up there, didn't you, Girak?" Prime Minister Pridbor's face was contorted with fury.

Girak merely stared, then gave an almost imperceptible nod and collapsed as Commander Savas dropped him.

Gasps of horror spread through the room. Girak clambered back toward Josefina, while Commander Savas remained facing the wall, eyes closed, breath shuddering.

"Guard." The Prime Minister called to the only visible guard.

Bleu's mom, eyes wide and her hand covering her mouth, stepped away from Girak as Bleu reeled over it all.

232

Girak and Josefina would never risk a child's life. He had dedicated his whole life to teaching. And risking a member of a dying race...a child whose father has near perfect genes? Bleu clenched his fists as the anger swelled within him. How could an educator forget how desperate they all were for the birth of more healthy humans?

A half-groan, half-laugh nearly choked him. Healthy humans in the Haven? The next generation might be the one that no longer had enough healthy people to run the Haven. Maybe Josefina and Educator Girak had hoped her Surface research would save their baby, like Bleu hoped it would help Ayanna.

"Arrest him." Prime Minister Pridbor directed the guard in the doorway toward Girak.

Zach, Pridbor, and the doctors surrounded him and pressured him away from Josefina.

"No, stop. I have to be with her," he pleaded, begged, tried to hold onto her hand, the bed. Anything.

"She'd be alive if you had done your duties as a husband and forbidden her from going." Spittle flew from the Prime Minister's mouth.

Savas yanked Girak's hands from the bedpost. "You never deserved her, Girak."

The angry crowd dragged the broken man from the room. The throng shoved him down the hall, and his red hair disappeared among the crowd. Only Bleu and his mom remained in the empty room. Empty, except for Josefina.

As the mob stormed down the hall, Stamf stood alone in its wake. He turned and stared through the doorway at Bleu and his mother, and then disappeared down the corridor.

Bleu turned to the bed. To Josefina... No, Josefina's body. Her mottled skin and cold stillness barely resembled his vivacious friend. Only her long dark hair seemed right. He stumbled to her side, sat on the bedside, and brushed her cold forehead with his trembling fingers.

"I'm sorry, Jos. I tried to be quick." His voice caught on the last word.

His breath shuddered and his vision swam as he blinked away tears. The pain of his injuries faded under the shredding sensation in his chest.

His mother grasped his shoulder, but it was too late for consolation. He had failed to save her. If he had only finished off the wolves faster, more efficiently, she might still be here. If he had shot right away, they wouldn't have injured him. He wouldn't have passed out.

He hunched beside her, drowning in his mistakes.

His mother's communicator dinged. She checked it and then sighed. "It's your father. Ayanna's getting agitated. I hate to leave, but..."

"Go." He dropped his face into his palms, overcome with the potential loss of his sister as well. *I can't let her die, too.* As unsuccessful as his first visit to the Surface had been, he still had to somehow find a cure to save Ayanna.

His gaze returned to Josefina's body. No one else would die on his watch. He sucked in a determined breath. "Next time I'm up there, Josefina, I'll pull the trigger right away."

# Chapter 30

*eleguin-Rookery-By-The-Lake: Rana*

Rana sat on the frozen ground beside Balavati and nodded in approval as Digga finished the stew her maha had concocted. "We're gathering now?" Rana asked, gingerly picking up the satiated Digga and brushing snow from her fur.

Digga yawned toothily, squeaking a little in the process, her breath sweet and meaty.

She patted Digga's head and tore her gaze away to face her friend.

"Yes, now." Balavati's tone was oddly annoyed. "Kahali finally agreed to the healing ceremony, so we're doing it as soon as everyone can gather at the Lion Circle."

Rana nodded. "Good. I hope it helps. He still hasn't let me see him."

Balavati remained silent, her almost black eyes squinting as she stared past the spindly evergreen trees that lined the clearing. From her perch on the rock beside Rana, she twisted her hair around her fingers.

Balavati's rare quietness created the perfect opportunity to get Digga asleep. Rana began wrapping the furry body in a bundle, careful to leave room for her short tail to wriggle. Otherwise, she cried and squirmed, and she'd need to re-swaddle her.

"I don't think he wants a healing," Balavati whispered.

Rana looked at her, surprised. "What? Why wouldn't he? It's horrid what happened to him..." She shivered at the horror of his lost arm.

When he had asked his dads to keep visitors away, Rana had assumed he had meant everyone but her. The day after his attack, she had sat outside

235

his ice hut with only the wall of ice separating them. She had felt his energy, lying right on the other side of the wall, but he had refused to acknowledge her. She had stubbornly sat there all morning, attempting to mind talk to him, to no avail.

The Kahali she knew would never ignore her. She had cried herself to sleep that night.

"He wants to be left alone." Balavati sighed. "It seems like everyone wants that lately…"

"Huh?"

"Kahali doesn't want visitors, and all your attention's been on her." She glared at Digga, then hopped off her rock. "She's all you care about anymore."

"What?" Heat surged through Rana and she tensed, ready for an argument.

While holding Digga, she found her usual anger uncomfortable. The irony of a species known for its rage and violence assisting her with her anger was not lost on her. Digga had turned everything she had *thought* she knew about cave diggers upside down.

Unclear what to do with this newfound wisdom regarding her own anger, she pursed her lips to keep from blurting out an impassioned response. If she refrained, would the feeling pass? The Crowned Ones didn't always respond immediately…

Rana tucked the now sleeping pup into her cloak, her hands shaking. Desna had sewn a carrier that allowed her to walk hands free with Digga tucked into her heavy cloak. It was meant to be worn during the Calling, but that would probably be cancelled given what had happened to Kahali.

"You're jealous? Of Digga?" Rana glowered at her friend as the words burned through her lips.

"She takes a lot of time," Balavati fumed, hand on her hip. "Time we used to hang out."

"Well, I guess that's why we don't have children until after we're Crowned. We have to prepare ourselves for such a responsibility. You know, this isn't all fun and games for me, either. She's a lot of work," Rana informed her.

"As if you mind. You're always cooing to her and making her new toys." Balavati's eyes flashed as she tossed her head and flipped her long dark curls out of her face.

"Yes, it's such a joy to clean this carrier after she relieves herself in it. Or to chase her around, or to wait for hours outside a tunnel she's dug, hoping she'll get hungry enough to come out." Her anger, which she tried so hard to moderate, began to boil, so she bent forward and touched the icy ground, focusing on the coldness.

"She does that? And you just sit there?" Balavati smirked but then narrowed her eyes at Rana's hand on the ice. "That must really rot," she said, her tone less barbed.

Rana nodded, unclear whether or not her friend meant to be supportive. "It does. And so does the Crowned Ones' laughter when they see me waiting."

Balavati considered this in silence. Her shoulders dropped, and her demeanor completely shifted. "Maybe I could help? It'd be easier to catch her with two of us." She tucked her curls behind her ear.

"You'd do that?" Relief flooded Rana's body. She despised arguments with her best friend.

"We'd be hanging out. I don't care if it's with Digga." Her lips curled upward. "Just don't ignore me, okay?"

Rana nodded. "I'd love help. Only not now, because I finally got her to sleep." She glanced down at her chest, beaming at the resting pup, and lowered her voice. "She hasn't slept much. Desna said, now that she's eating, the next most important thing is that she sleeps."

"Which apparently involves snoring." Balavati giggled at the snuffling noises.

Rana nodded and stood, Digga completely hidden within the folds of her cloak. She glimpsed her enlarged torso. It appeared she had eaten too much, not that another life nestled on her chest.

"You're bringing her to the healing?"

"To quote Desna, 'Take her everywhere you go. Keep her warm, and hopefully she bonds enough to not eat you when she grows up.'"

"Or your friends. We don't taste good, either." Balavati released her impish smile and grabbed Rana's hand. "Come on, or we'll be the last ones."

As she approached the Lion's Circle, Rana's heart beat erratically. The last healing ceremony that wasn't for illness had been eight springs ago, when she was only eight springs herself. Her village had come together for her after her parents' sudden deaths. The lethal avalanche had crushed her heart as well.

As she joined those gathered at the Lion Circle, its usual joyous tingling effect was drowned out by her memories of that healing circle and the sight of her friend at this circle's center. Still too weak to stand, Kahali sat in the center of the gathering, his normal grin and comic jibes replaced by stern eyes above a rigid jaw. His cloak sleeve hung limp below the shoulder.

Rana managed to catch his glance, but he turned away as if her gaze burned him. Tears ran down her cheeks. Was her jokester friend, the Kahali she loved, gone forever?

Today's ceremony, like the one eight years ago, passed in a blur. She tried to focus, to be there for Kahali, but she kept finding herself trembling at her own losses. *It's been eight years. Why aren't I doing better with their deaths by now?*

After the ceremony, Kahali and his dads left. Rana struggled to a stand, hoping a good, warm dinner would clear her head, yet everyone else remained seated, including Sohana. Her heart pounded as everyone turned quizzical expressions to her upright stance.

She dropped back to the ground, realizing she was out of the loop. *How much have I missed while taking care of Digga?* As her stomach growled in protest of its lost early dinner, she studied the lingering crowd and gave Balavati a questioning look.

"They scheduled a meeting of the Crowned Ones," Balavati whispered. "We need to decide what to do about Sohana's message. You and I are the next to Call."

"I had assumed it was cancelled." Rana's stomach squirmed. She leaned close to Balavati's ear. "They still expect us to go?" She fiddled with the end of her amber braid.

Balavati shrugged and pointed to the center of the Lion Circle. The community's leaders, Luminary Samasti and Luminary Vadin, entered. Luminary Vadin must have helped Kahali home and then returned.

Rana closed her eyes and sighed. *What have I gotten myself into?* She held her thick braid in her lap like a lifeline.

The meeting flowed around her while all sides were expressed. After eight silent linkages, her eyelids became heavy. She wanted the Crowned Ones to handle the violent Earth's children. She was too tired from Digga's antics to even focus...

"Rana." Balavati nudged her.

Rana straightened, jerking her braid. "Oh My Oneness. What did I miss?" All around them, people were leaving.

"It's decided. It's still us. But we can back out if we want..." Balavati's face tightened as she waited.

"Oh. Uhm..." Rana's head spun. How could she agree to such a risk when she still couldn't understand why the Earth's children had decided to hunt Kahali? *How do I call them with love if I'm scared of them? But if I back out, won't that be letting fear win?*

Struggling to stand on legs that had fallen asleep, Rana stumbled away from Balavati's question, away from the questions tumbling through her mind. As her fears raced faster, her legs did as well. She climbed the rise that divided Peleguin-Rookery-By-The-Lake from the actual peleguin breeding grounds.

"She said volunteers only. We could withdraw." Balavati had caught up with her.

Rana kept up her brisk pace uphill, nearly running. "I don't know."

She had nearly reached the top of the plateau. She said over her shoulder, "How was it better to have Kahali out there alone than to have Crowned Ones who could've defended themselves? Maybe Kalakanya's wrong. Maybe they're all wrong."

*Maybe Eka was right; the Crowned Ones could make dangerous mistakes.* She thudded upward; this steep path was something she could handle.

Rana stopped short, having reached the end of the cleared trail. She'd need hooves or daylight to proceed any farther up the rocky summit. She plopped down on the frozen ground and gazed out over the darkening vista. The icy plains below were showing signs of the softening. The meltwater had attracted sea-faring feathered ones by the thousands. They squawked overhead, giving voice to Rana's own internal conflict.

Balavati ran up and settled beside her. "Kalakanya consulted the time threads. How can she be wrong?" She shook her head, sighed, and lay back on one elbow. *"A lot* of what the Crowned Ones say doesn't make sense. Like why did you need to journey back from Mt. Syeti alone? How has meeting Eka again changed things?"

Rana scrunched her eyebrows in dismay. Her best friend should know the answer to that one.

Balavati grinned and lay back on the ground, staring up at the sky. "Changed things for the community. I know you like him."

"He saved my life." The peleguins squawked louder as if they, too, were annoyed at Balavati's lack of insight.

"Which wouldn't have been in danger if you hadn't gone." Balavati sat up. "See? A lot doesn't make sense." The fussing feathered ones preened their wings and squawked out warnings to stay away from their stone nests.

Rana shrugged and sighed. "I met Digga. I think she's the one I was meant to meet."

Balavati laughed. *"She's* going to help our village?"

"Well," Rana chuckled, "Kahali certainly doesn't think it's Eka." She sighed. "I don't know. Desna told me sometimes we need to simply trust in our journey."

Her friend's face lit with excitement. "So, you're in?"

*Trust in your journey.* She had trusted enough to go on the risky assignment to meet someone, and her skills with animals had blossomed. She needed to increase her capabilities to Crown. Not a single part of her wanted to do this, and yet she couldn't let fear get the best of her. Determination flowed like a molten river through her veins. She would do whatever it took to overcome her shortcomings and Crown. "Yes, I'm in."

* * *

After a night of nonsensical dreams, Rana awoke to Balavati's impatient shaking of her shoulder. Rana groaned and rolled over, not wanting to leave the warmth of her sleeping furs. "Already?"

"Yes. Up like the sun..." Balavati held out Rana's clothing. "Come on."

Rana blinked wearily. "The sun isn't up."

"Then up like the moon. Just get *up*," Balavati yanked off her sleeping furs.

"Argh."

Rana looked around her empty hut. Her family had already dressed and left for sunrise sit. She threw on her clothing, making sure Digga was secure in her pouch, and they traipsed through the village. The morning air turned their breath to misty white clouds in the blackness. They trudged to Kalakanya's hut, too tired for conversation.

"Try to look awake." Balavati grinned.

"Why can't we Call at night? Maybe the Earth's children are nocturnal..." Rana despised early mornings. She walked slowly, pausing to feed Digga small chunks of cooked salt deer. Her fingers grew sticky from handling the cold stew, but at least she still had fingers.

She bent to wipe her hands on some snow before they reached Kalakanya's hut. "The One In All brings Love," Balavati sung out the greeting.

"The One In All receives Love." Kalakanya's grinning face appeared under her starry mat, and then the rest of her slid out. "You made good time for getting up so late, Rana."

"Does it get annoying to know everything?" Rana winced at her nasty tone. "Sorry."

241

Kalakanya laughed. "Annoying? No, I'd say amusing." Her green eyes twinkled in the moonlight. She stretched her arms overhead and swung them as she strode off into the gray morning. Rana and Balavati hurried to match her pace.

They hiked in silence as the horizon blazed the color of fresh salmon. Rana's stomach grumbled in protestation of skipping breakfast.

Kalakanya stopped and turned back toward Rana, a mischievous grin on her face. "Is your stomach doing the Calling today, Rana?"

Rana blushed and stroked Digga's head. Kalakanya sure was amusing herself today.

"This new spot for Calling is pretty open, so you'll see them from a distance, unlike Kahali. I've shown this spot to the other Crowned Ones, and we'll be standing by if you need us. I suspect they'll approach from that direction." She pointed across the plain in the direction the Earth children's den was believed to be located.

Rana and Balavati nodded solemnly.

"If it's warm enough, keep your hoods down. I believe our hoods and face coverings scare them. Remember, once they're within sight, one of you vibrates love, while the other observes for signs of danger. Shield and Call us immediately if they touch their hunting sticks. Got it?" Kalakanya's mouth smiled, but her eyes emanated concern.

"We'll be okay. They probably won't even be coming out of their hole today." Balavati radiated confidence.

Rana nodded. Maybe they'd be okay. The frozen tundra remained calm; the only life in sight was lichen, evergreens, and a small scurrying furred one that soon disappeared below the snow.

"May the One In All be with you." In a starry flash, Kalakanya left them.

Balavati and Rana stood alone. They turned in place a few more times, and then like wolves settled themselves onto the ground and began Calling.

# Chapter 31

Northern Haven: Atsushi Collins

Atsushi jumped to his feet as the front door of his module crashed open and his father hurried in.

"Sarabella," his father shouted, then glared at Atsushi as if his mother's absence was his fault. "Where's your mother?"

He shrugged, but when his father's glare deepened, he added, "She didn't tell me, though usually about now she's with her friends in the solarium."

"Better. Was that so hard?" He hung up his work bag and then turned in circles as if lost.

"Are you okay?" He clearly wasn't, which meant he'd better tread lightly.

"You didn't hear?" He studied Atsushi as if mind-boggled that a son he raised had turned out so dense.

"No, I've been studying physics for our test tomorrow." Atsushi gestured to his computer which he'd barely had time to open.

He'd been with Ayanna when her dad had come back and told him he could go home. The halls had been unusually empty, but he'd been so relieved to get home before his parents and not get caught skipping school to help Ayanna that the empty halls hadn't concerned him.

He sprang to his feet. "Is this about the expedition? Is Bleu back with Josefina?"

"How did you know he left?"

His stomach dropped. "I— I heard it in the hall this morning."

"Nothing stays secret in this place." His father harrumphed with professional councilman disdain. "You can stop studying. School will probably be cancelled tomorrow. Girak won't be testing anyone. Josefina died."

"What?" He fell back onto the couch, gasping for breath. It couldn't be. He must have misheard. He couldn't imagine Josefina, so full of life, gone. Panting, he struggled to remember his meditation practice and managed to slow his breath enough to speak "She's...dead?"

"And Girak is to blame. After a highly deserved beating, the council declared him a Deplorable. He's under module arrest."

"What? They beat him?" Atsushi sprang back up and rushed toward the door, filled with righteous fury.

"Where are you going, young man?" his father hollered.

Atsushi froze. "He's my Educator..." he mumbled.

"Not anymore. We read him his loss of rights. He can't leave his module, and he's to have no visitors except for medical treatment and food delivery."

"Medical treatment?" His fury collapsed into panic. "What did they do to him?"

Josefina was dead and Girak was alone and beaten in his module? He couldn't get enough air. He put his hand on the front door, steadying himself.

His father droned on. "...but he'll survive, not that he deserves to. How the *shast* excellent genes can create such an ass is beyond me. Atsushi, I don't want you having anything else to do with that man. You understand me?"

Atsushi understood, but his whole focus was on staying upright. Josefina dead? Girak a Deplorable? His fellow Northern Haveners had beaten him? Like in a poorly constructed dream, nothing made sense.

"Atsushi! Are you listening to me?" His father's voice roared.

He managed a nod.

"You are not to see him. Do. You. Understand?"

"Yes." His voice sounded simpering, like he actually would go along with the parental order. *Let him think I'm a wimp. First chance I get, I'm checking on him.*

* * *

All that night, Atsushi waited for Liam to fall asleep and his parents to go to bed. His parents had sent them to bed early, so they could discuss the day's horror while emptying a bottle of something strong. When his father finally shuffled into bed, his mother stayed up and fiddled around in the kitchen, making tea and sobbing. She hadn't exactly been friends with Josefina, but they had all known each other since birth, and every death hammered another nail into humanity's casket.

When he snuck across the living room at 4:00 a.m. to reach the front door, he was horrified to find his mother still seated in the kitchen, watching him.

"Oh, there you are," he said, trying to cover for his failed escape. "I was worried about you."

She wiped her tears, apparently too upset to argue with the likelihood of his lie. He'd never been uncaring toward her, but it was hard to care for parents who cared little for him. "Let's all go get a few hours of sleep before the day starts," she murmured.

And so, he was stuck in his module until they both went to work and Liam left for an impromptu no-school party at one of his friends' home. Finally alone and fearing no one had brought Girak any food, he grabbed his bulky sweater and rushed to the cafeteria.

Since the only transportable food was rolls, he snagged five, wrapped them hastily in his sweater, and then grabbed a mug of tea. Turning to leave, he nearly ran into his classmate, Sera.

"Watch out," she grumbled, her hair a mess and clearly having just crawled out of bed. She eyed the caffeinated tea he'd grabbed for Girak and pouted. "That's not the last one, is it?"

"No, you're good." He shifted to hide the bulk in his sweater.

"You heard about Educator Girak?" she asked, yawning as she found a mug.

He stiffened. "Yeah. Listen, I gotta go meet someone at the Records Room." He strode away before she could share the morning's gossip about the Giraks.

He scurried toward Girak's module, keeping his head down to avoid being asked where he was going or dragged into a discussion about them. What if Girak didn't want his help? What if, when Girak opened the door, he only saw the annoying kid who'd upset his wife?

When he reached the hallway, he waited until everyone was gone and then knocked with his elbow, his only free body part not holding stashed food. No one answered.

Was he too injured to answer the door? Atsushi knocked again. And again. Still nothing.

He didn't risk all this to not even see him. He pounded. "Hey, are you in there?"

Shuffling feet approached the door, and then the door slid open to the dark pit within. "At—thushi?" croaked a man's voice.

"Yeah, it's me." Atsushi stepped into the darkness before the door closed behind him. "Where are you?"

There was a light on somewhere in the back, but everything was so dim that he nearly missed the hunched silhouette leaning on the wall.

"Oh." He had no idea how to help, but he had to try.

"You shouldn't be here," Girak slurred.

"Can I turn the light on?" Before Girak could protest, he flipped on the light with his elbow. It was in exactly the same place his family's light switch was.

He'd been expecting a black eye, but Girak's entire face was discolored and swollen. No wonder he hadn't been able to talk properly. "*Shast.* I can't believe they did...that."

"I messed everything up. Everything..." Girak took a teetering step toward the couch.

Atsushi dropped the rolls onto the couch and grasped his arm to steady him. "Come on. Sit down. Have you seen a doctor?"

Girak collapsed back onto the couch and shook his head. "Dr. Reinier gave me ice and some pain meds, but I don't want to sleep."

"You could probably use some," Atsushi said as he shoved aside untouched food trays to make room for his fresher stash. "Here."

He handed Girak the tea, the world's most pathetic offering ever. The guy had just lost his wife and his entire career, and all he could offer was a cup of cooling tea?

But Girak, oblivious to the tea, stared at a recorded moving photo of Josefina in a frame across the room.

"I'm really sorry. I tried to come earlier, but my parents said—"

"You should go. You have enough going on without getting in trouble for associating with me."

"Associating?" Atsushi blinked away tears. "You are not an *associate*. When I heard they attacked you, I tried to hurry here to help, but my dad wouldn't let me."

"She's dead..." Girak's voice broke, and he sucked a shaky breath as if to steady himself.

"I know." Atsushi clasped his hands together in his lap, desperate to do something but unsure if he should hug him or give him a back slap or reoffer the tea. "I don't know what to say. I'm really sorry. I brought you food, but I can't stay long, and I don't know what else to do to help."

"It's already done. She's dead. I killed her and my child by not forbidding her from going. But I couldn't. It was who she was. I couldn't..." He dropped his head into his hands and sobbed uncontrollably.

Atsushi had never felt so helpless. Well, no, he felt this helpless around Ayanna, too. Lately everything was secrets and helplessness. He wanted to *do* something. Anything. Instead, he sat awkwardly on the couch beside his sobbing teacher, his leg jittering up and down.

Finally, he blurted out what had been circulating in his head since he'd heard the news. "Do you blame me for her death?"

"What?" Educator Girak wiped his face with his sleeve and looked up. "Of course not."

"But I knew she was pregnant, too."

Girak grabbed his arm and shook it. "Don't you *ever* say that out loud again. Do you hear me?"

Somehow, that shake released everything Atsushi had been holding in.

247

Silent tears streamed down his cheeks. "But...but it's true. You can't hate yourself without hating me, too."

"I was her *husband*." He choked backed another sob. "It was my business, not yours."

Girak was going to pull rank? Then Atsushi could do the same. "Well, I'm..." He sucked in a shaky breath. "I'm a councilor's son. I should be extra law-abiding."

Girak snorted in amusement, then cringed at the pain. "There's a claim I never thought to hear you own." His expression sobered. "I'm an adult, and you should not have known any of that."

Now he was pulling rank as an adult? Fine. "Do you remember that message you wrote me? The one about not letting the records on Japan define me? That my truth could only be found inside myself?"

"Yes?" Girak's attempt to smile ended up a wince.

"You shouldn't let the council records define you as a Deplorable. My educator once said something like, 'who you are is inside you.' Did I get that right?" He gave him a shy smile.

"Hmm. Sounds like a wise educator." He sighed. "They'll never let me teach again. I have no way to help, trapped in my module and shunned by everyone."

"Not me." Atsushi handed him the tea again, and Girak lifted his swollen lip out of the way to drink. "You need a medi-straw."

"Hmm." He was gulping the tea like it was the first thing he'd drunk since everything happened.

"I'll see if Dr. Reinier will give me one."

"No, you won't." Girak took a final slurp of tea and set the mug down next to the untouched trays. "I won't have you risking everything to help. I'll figure out something."

Atsushi glanced around the mess of a module and his untreated bruises. "Not to be rude, but I think you need some help. What will they do with you long-term? They're not going to hurt you again, are they?"

"Let's hope not. We've never before had that sort of breakdown of civic law that I know of..." Girak frowned, as if remembering something.

"What?" Atsushi handed him a roll.

"I just remembered something my mother told me once. A few years before I was born, there was a breakdown like this."

Atsushi leaned closer. "People attacked each other?"

Girak sighed. "What is it about you that makes me spill my secrets?" He wince-grinned at him and popped a piece of bread in his mouth.

Atsushi was going to have to dig to get answers. "You're thirty-something?"

"Thirty-five, and don't go searching in the records." He gave another wince-grin. "I've already tried that."

"Maybe my parents would know? They're older than you," Atsushi suggested.

"I've discreetly searched. There's no information. As far as I've seen, they forgive Deplorables after a few years, so maybe I'll be okay. Though..." He grimaced. "They're considering me a murderer, so maybe not." He looked away at Josefina's picture, and his eyes filled with tears again.

"What would she do if she were in your situation?"

"Huh?" He continued to stare at the video cycle of Josefina giving the camera a mischievous grin and then blowing it a kiss.

"Josefina. What would she have done if you had died, and, somehow, she had been blamed?"

"Oh." He sniffed and put down the half-eaten roll. "She'd carry on with finding the other Havens. She believed their science may hold a cure. If not that, then exchanging people to diversify our gene pool might help us avoid the Sickness in future generations. That's why she still wanted to go after finding out she was pregnant. To help the kids..." Girak turned back toward him, sudden fervor burning in his swollen eyes. "I could volunteer for the next expedition. No one will volunteer after what has happened to the first two."

Atsushi nearly slipped off the couch. "But you might die!"

"My outcomes are as equally poor down here. Up there, I'd at least be useful. If I help find the other Havens, lives will be saved." He seemed super confident about this drastic change of plans.

"But they declared you a Deplorable. They won't let you go." *Forget about it. Please. I don't want to lose you too.*

"That's exactly why they'll let me go. They'd rather risk losing me than another scientist."

"Please, don't. Not to be rude, but have you looked in the mirror?" Atsushi waved at his bruised face. "You're in no shape to train. You can't even smile properly."

"Your visit inspired me."

"I came here because I was worried about you and wanted to help. Instead, I've somehow inspired you to risk your life." Atsushi studied his educator with renewed concern. "Is this you being suicidal after losing Josefina?"

"No, I'm not suicidal. You've helped me remember what Jos and I were working toward. There are still kids to save."

Seeing the determination in his eyes, Atsushi sighed and then chuckled.

"What's so funny?"

"I've unwittingly created a monster," Atsushi said, referring back to Girak's joke about Atsushi's past unapproved research. He stood and walked toward the door. "If you need me to get you anything for this new mission, let me know."

"Thank you, but you should stay away."

"But—"

"I mean it." From his sharp look, he did. "If I succeed on the mission, maybe I'll be allowed visitors. In the meantime, when you ignore my warnings and dig around the old files, be careful, okay?"

With one hand on the door, Atsushi nodded. What if he never saw him again?

Girak chuckled. "No need to memorize my face. I'm not dead yet."

Atsushi blinked. "Right. Well…if I don't see you before you go, good luck up there."

"Stay away. I can take care of myself."

Everything from Girak's bruises to his uneaten food trays said he couldn't, but he nodded.

There was nothing else for him to do. Girak would volunteer for a dangerous mission, and Ayanna had the Sickness. He could lose everyone he cared about, and he could see no way to stop it.

# Chapter 32

Peleguin-Rookery-By-The-Lake: Kahali

Kahali stood outside his hut, grateful for the thin predawn darkness. Even if his parents or Sohana returned from sunrise sit to check on him, the gloom obscured his inept attempt to dress himself. The longer he fumbled with the ties on his cloak, the louder his disgusted snorts grew. Even the simplest activities took forever with one arm, one hand, and no sleep.

At least today he had made it out of his sleeping-fur pile and out of his ice hut. As hard as it had been to let his community see him like this, the healing ceremony must have helped, because he'd voluntarily left his hut. If only the ceremony had improved his sleep.

All night, sleep had eluded him, chased away by nightmares of Rana in trouble. *Last time, she and Balavati came home safely,* he reassured himself. But his mind continued to unfurl horizon after horizon of violence—he and his friends mangled by Earth children, Rana hunted, or his village strewn with bodies. Sweat trickled down his spine, and his fingers shook. Trembling didn't exactly help his one-handed tying.

With a final snort loud enough to wake any late-sleeping neighbors, he gripped his cloak together at his chest and stomped off to the Nest, the massive boulder outside his village where he and Rana often hung out. Right now, others were on their way to the ice cave for his severed arm, and if it was found, today would be its cremation. The horror of seeing his disconnected limb nauseated him.

Leaning against the boulder's cold surface for comfort, he inhaled the crisp air and tilted his head skyward. The stars blinked down at him. They were old friends. But unlike his other friends, they were far above this Earth child chaos, safe and secure.

A breeze lifted his cloak, chilling his exposed left side. "Well, today's the day," he voiced to his missing limb. "Reunion day. *If* no furred ones ate you."

"What?"

He spun. Rana stood on the other side of the boulder, her expression hovering between amusement and concern.

Heat coursed up his neck and flushed his cheeks. "I was, uh, talking to... my arm."

Rana's brow furrowed. She glanced around. "Are you okay?" she asked in the same tone she used to calm Digga. "I mean, I know you didn't want visitors, but I feel like a horrid friend..."

*Friend.* He stood up straight and pulled his cloak tighter. "I'm fine. You're not horrid, and it was a joke."

"What happened was not a joke." She stepped closer, the puff of her condensing breath nearly reaching his own.

"I meant talking to my arm." He tensed, waiting for her repulsion at the sight of his stump.

Instead, she came even closer and her gloved hand extended toward his full arm. He yearned for her touch but was unsure of her intentions.

She pulled him into a gentle hug, barely touching his unarmed side. "This okay?"

"Very." It would be even better if there wasn't a drowsy cave digger between them.

"I missed you. Sorry for not trying to see you every day. You didn't seem to want me around, but, also, the whole cave-in thing reminded me of..." Her warm arms tightened around him.

He'd been so lost in his own mind that he'd forgotten her parents had been killed by falling ice. "It's okay. I haven't been exactly easy to deal with."

"Completely understandable." She tightened her hug momentarily and then pulled away. "Does it hurt?"

"A little. Not bad. Mostly it feels cold all the time, like it's still there." He frowned at his empty side.

"Do you think after they find it today and we hold the cremation, it'll feel better?" Her brow crinkled with hope.

He gave a bitter chuckle. "You mean, so that then it can burn instead of feeling frozen?"

"No." She returned to her earlier concerned look, a look everyone now so readily gave him. "Ah..." She twisted the end of her braid. "I left sunrise sit early because I wanted to catch you without your family around. I'm glad I found you."

"Me, too." He grinned and waited. Her returning smile emboldened him to motion toward the top of the boulder. "Join my star gazing, soon to be sunrise gazing?"

"I'd love to." She glanced at his empty sleeve, and her concern that he might not make it to their familiar hangout twisted his stomach.

"I can do it." *I hope.* He clambered up the cold rock, and she followed. "See?" He chuckled, hoping it covered how out of breath he was. Dizzy, he plopped down.

She joined him, sitting close enough that her body heat warmed him. If she were on the other side, he could rest his hand near hers. Still, she had wanted to find him alone. Maybe she'd said "friend" only to play it safe?

"So?" He turned toward her expectantly.

"Well." She reached inside her cloak to stroke Digga. "Balavati and I are up to Call again tomorrow morning, and—"

Kahali sucked in a sharp breath as the noises in his head drowned out her voice. Screams. Horizon after snowy horizon filled with dead bodies. Rana bleeding in the snow. Image after image poured forth. He gasped for breath and threw out his arms to stop the Earth child from raising its hunting stick...

"Kahali?" Someone grabbed his arm, their face up to his. "Kahali, what's wrong?"

He blinked and shook with effort to separate his inner sight from the realness around him.

Blink. Rana's concerned face.

Blink. Rana dead in the snow.

Blink. Rana a few inches from his face.

*Rana. Oh my Oneness! She's going to think I've lost it.*

He sat straight, her warm hand still grasping his trembling arm, touching his face.

He turned away, eyes burning. He should have stayed hidden in his hut. "I'm fine." He couldn't stop shivering. He took a few deep breaths and the images faded.

Rana sat beside him. Safe. They were alone.

*She's Calling tonight.*

He turned back toward her. "I'm sorry. I'm okay now. But you— you're Calling? Leaving tonight to Call tomorrow?"

She nodded, concern still furrowing her brow. The lightening sky beyond her took on new significance. The dawn of the day she and Balavati would leave to Call. "You sure you're okay?" she asked.

"As okay as anyone can be knowing those rabid creatures are out there."

She shrank back at his anger-filled words. The fury and hostility that had become second nature since his attack rose like bile in his throat. He *should* resist this dark feeling. Breathe through it. Let it go.

But it fueled him. It coursed through his weakened body and lent him the strength of a sea bear. A stronger, better star being would let it go. But not he.

Bahujnana's voice from his last healing session whispered through his mind. *You are not anger, Kahali. There is much light and laughter in you. Don't smother it with anger.*

What if he had already smothered his light?

Rana touched his knee. "Hey...I'm right here. You don't have to do this alone."

Her voice relit the dying embers of himself. Maybe he could still choose light over anger. For her.

He couldn't let her see the rage that possessed him. She had shrunk back at his earlier words, and he'd been holding back when he'd only called the Earth children rabid.

Rana knelt beside him, but he averted his gaze to the boulder's gray-and-black surface. He heaved deep breath after deep breath, trying to remember where he was. *Who* he was. The fury drained from his body, leaving him only his new, weak self.

He sighed. "Sorry." He winced at the tremor in his voice. "This is why I've been hiding out. It's why I've been sending everyone away. When my mind does that, it's embarrassing." He risked a sideways glance at her.

"But now is when you most need people you're close to." She gave him a beautiful, warm smile that made him momentarily forget how to breathe. Scooting closer, she wrapped her arm ever so carefully around his waist. "You're shivering."

"These last few days, my body's been doing all sorts of unusual things." He gave a small chuckle, making light of it for her sake.

"You know"—that lovely smile blossomed again—"it's not only you who needs your friends right now. We need you, too." From her seat beside him, she leaned in close. "I need you. It's been horrid, these last few days, not being able to see you." Her soft lips brushed his cheek in a kiss, and then she turned her gaze up at him expectantly.

"Aw, you missed my lovely face that much?"

Something in her gaze shifted and she sat back on her heels. His heart fell.

*Fool*, he berated himself. He'd missed his chance to kiss her back. She had left him an opening, and he had gone back to his usual jokes. His grin evaporated. Why was he like this with her? Could he fix it? "That day you sat on the other side of my ice hut wall, I was desperate to talk, but I was afraid that if I did, I'd mess things up."

She scowled. "Not talking at all messes things up, too." Sighing, she gazed out at the peleguins searching in the ice for small rocks for their nests. The field looked barren, yet, somehow, they always located what they needed.

If only he were as lucky.

"I wanted to ask your advice," she said, her gaze still on the birds. "But it's okay if you can't talk about…it. I don't want to upset you."

"I can talk about it." *It.* Their hunting of him. The thing he pushed to the back recesses of his mind only to have it spring out and smack him. He'd face it for her. "I had that little freakout because it surprised me that you're Calling tomorrow."

That was actually only part of the story. He'd been having these freakouts regularly since his attack. Their healer, Bahujnana, said they were normal after such a violent attack, but he couldn't bear to have others witness him having the trauma visions. He gave her the most confident smile he could muster. "Ask me whatever."

"You sure? Because whatever just happened looked terrifying."

He took another deep breath and nodded. "I'm sure."

"Okay." The warmth of her smile dispelled any remaining doubts. "I was wondering if, looking back on what happened, you noticed any warning? Anything that might help us if they show up? You know, tomorrow…" Her smile faded as she absently twisted her braid around her hand.

"Oh." He had relived that fateful encounter countless times. Had he missed anything of importance? The weird energy of the Earth children. Their appearance. Their fear. His attempt to calm them… *Boom!* He sucked in a breath. "No, there was nothing except their fear."

"Oh." She bit her lip. "Well, I'm sure we'll be okay. Balavati's not worried."

"You could not do it." He pushed down the urge to beg. "Blame it on me. Say I said something that scared you."

She laughed and batted his good shoulder. Despite his layers, the brush of her fingers lingered. "No. It'll be fine." She swallowed. "I simply thought it'd be wise to check."

He studied her for any sign that he could change her mind. No, she was infuriatingly stubborn. She would Call. His terrifying intrusive images could happen. Tomorrow.

"Subject change." She flashed a carefree grin. "Have you heard the news? Since the Earth children have emerged near us, the other villages are sending their volunteers for Calling. I think we should throw a welcome

257

party. You in?"

"Yes." He laughed at her excitement. "Though I suspect my drumming days are over."

She frowned. "Maybe. But you're the best dancer I know. Everyone will be fighting over our hero."

He snorted. "As long as you and I get to dance, I'm set." Then he remembered who else had volunteered and would be attending—Eka.

Guilt twisted his gut. How had he become such a horrible star being? He had no right to resent Eka's presence, because right now Eka and his friend, Tejas, were taking a detour from their journey here to recover his arm. They were helping him, because he was too weak to do it himself. His family was busy taking care of him and planning how to best deal with the Earth children. But Eka would also want to dance with Rana. And would she survive Calling to organize the festivities?

"You'd better dance with me," she teased. "I should get the first dance, since I allowed you to bury me in snow while sleeping."

Kahali snorted. "Allowed? Okay, point taken. You get me first, assuming I *can* dance by then." *And that you're alive.*

"You'll be fine." She threw her arm around his shoulder, friendship-style. His senseless joke had chased away whatever she had intended when she'd kissed him. "So, what were you planning to do today?"

He needed rest. His short excursion had exhausted him, but this was too important. "I'm convincing you not to Call."

"Oh, Kahali." She rested her head against his shoulder. "I can't do that. You heard the prophecy."

"Please?" Falling stars, he was begging.

She sighed. "I have to get going." She slid down the rock.

"Wait." He had to stop her.

She turned expectantly, then frowned. "Look, we'll do dinner when I get back, okay? I promise." And then she turned and left.

He sat still, heart racing as his fingers touched the spot on his face where her lips had brushed him.

*She kissed me.*

*She's Calling tomorrow morning.*

Desperation clutched him. He needed help stopping her, but everyone in the village that he'd talked to yesterday about cancelling the Calling thought he was overreacting.

An idea so ludicrous that it might work came to him. He'd have to rest, or he'd never have the focus to pull it off. Wrapping himself in his cloak, he curled up on the boulder and gave in to his body's exhaustion.

*\* \* \**

Kahali awoke to the distant voices of laughing and the sun high above him. He'd slept too long. As he sat upright, a fur blanket slipped from his shoulders, and his hand fell on Sohana's canteen. She must have decided to let him enjoy sleeping in the fresh air.

He drank deeply from the canteen and readied himself. He'd do anything to keep Rana safe, even enlist the assistance of the heroic soon-to-arrive Eka.

Kahali released his clenched jaw and extended his awareness to mind speak. *Eka? It's Kahali. Did you find the cave?*

His heart raced, though he wasn't sure if it was from fear that his plan wouldn't work or fear that Eka had the power to convince Rana to not Call when he couldn't.

*Kahali? You okay?* Surprise accompanied Eka's thoughts. *We haven't found your arm yet, even though Tejas and I are pretty far into the cave.* This came as an apology. *Still, we know it's the right spot because we found a huge mechanical thing, and...*

A flood of horror followed, and Eka's mind talk cut off.

*Eka? Eka?* Kahali gripped his hair, trying to focus. *Eka? Tejas?*

Nothing. Kahali sucked in a shuddering breath as his nightmares replayed in his mind.

*Eka!*

*Sorry, Kahali.* Shock. Repulsion. *We found a body. One of theirs. Can you let your Crowned Ones know? We can't carry it all the way there. We need their help.*

Kahali gasped for breath. How in Oneness was there a body there? *You're...you're both okay?*

*Yes. Can you send a Crowned One here to star beam it back? Don't worry, we'll find your arm.*

*Just be safe. I'll send someone.* Kahali took a deep breath. It was now or never. He had to ask Eka to convince Rana not to Call. *Uh, will you still arrive here tonight? Before Rana leaves to Call?*

*Definitely.* Eka's wave of cresting emotions regarding Rana was more than Kahali could bear.

He lost focus, and the connection faltered. Reeling, he swiped away tears of frustration with his one fist. Eka was falling in love. With Rana. His Rana.

No, she was her own, but she had no idea the danger she faced. He had to enlist Eka's help. Eka might still make a difference and convince her.

Kahali forced his mind to expand, to reach Eka, but he couldn't center. Violent images poured through his brain, washing all other thoughts away. His heart banged against his ribs, and each small breath was too little.

*It's just flashbacks.*

But the awareness held little comfort.

Thanks to the horrid Earth children, he'd lost his mind, and now, because he couldn't pull himself together, he was going to lose Rana.

# Chapter 33

*eleguin-Rookery-By-The-Lake: Rana*

P As dusk settled over her village and each moment brought them closer to Eka's arrival and to Calling, Rana's heart beat faster and faster. If it continued racing like this, it would soon be hard to breathe. "There's too much going on," she complained to Balavati as Digga dug circular tunnels around them in the snow.

"And by 'too much' you mean two guys you like. Doesn't sound that horrible." Balavati smirked, then tossed a snowball for Digga to chase.

Her friend had a way of cutting straight to the point. "There's also the danger of Calling." Rana felt the need to defend her internal chaos.

"We're going. That's decided." Balavati's eyes twinkled. "But...you still haven't picked one of *them*. I mean, Kahali knows all your secrets, and he's still totally into you. He's funny, and he dances like a stag. Then there's the lesser-known Eka, with his mane of long hair, deep eyes, and desire to protect you from wolves." Balavati shook her head in mock pity. "Oh, to have your problems, Rana."

"How could anyone make that choice? Could you?" she challenged.

"Irrelevant. But..." Balavati furrowed her brow and tapped her gloved finger on her lips. "No, it's really irrelevant. Lighten up. You're too young to couple, and you'd have to Crown first anyways, so as your advisor, I see no need to choose"—she grinned— "yet. Have fun and enjoy them both. When's Eka arriving?"

Rana looked at the evening sky, now deepest blue with the first stars showing. "He should be here already."

Her gaze followed the horizon toward the lake Eka would need to travel around to reach their village. Only a salt deer raised its head from the lakeside to stare in their direction. The rest of the herd munched on the dried lake weeds the star beings collected.

She said, "I thought we'd see them coming."

Balavati grinned. "That's why we're on the hill giving Digga playtime?"

At her name, Digga's snow-covered snout popped out of a mound.

"Look, I'll watch her. Go find him. I promise I won't lose your baby."

Rana hesitated. Not because she didn't trust Balavati, but because Digga would provide entertainment if she got too awkward around Eka. If. She always got awkward around him, but never with Kahali. That was something.

She nodded. "Okay, thanks. I'll meet you back here so you don't have to carry her."

"Have *fun*." Balavati waggled her eyebrows. "Just remember I'd appreciate a bit of sleep tonight before we leave." She smirked and then turned back to watch Digga.

Rana snorted and spun as her blush deepened. She raced down the hill and wove around the ice huts. Murmurs of conversation and singing drifted around her, but her neighbors' camaraderie held no attraction tonight. She rushed toward the gathering hall, where guests from other villages stayed. If Eka and Tejas had arrived, that's where they'd be.

As she reached the rocky path toward the gathering hall, her pace slowed. *What reason do I have for bursting in? What if he's not even here yet?*

She stopped as if the deepening darkness could calm her racing heart. Laughter drifted down from the hall. *They're here.*

She touched the empty space at her chest, feeling exposed without Digga's constant presence. The pup had almost become a part of her, and her absence felt wrong.

"Don't be a fool, Rana." Her nerves had reduced her to talking to herself. Not a good sign.

She forced herself to continue climbing. The path leveled out, and the scent of wood smoke and cooked meat grew stronger. Since the rest of the village had eaten earlier, the meat must be for Eka and Tejas. Firelight spilled out around the woven mat that covered the entrance.

*I'll say I came to welcome them.*

She raised her hand to push aside the mat when it whipped aside on its own.

"Oh!" Rana stepped back to avoid being barreled over.

"Rana?" Eka stood frozen before her, his hand still on the mat. His dark eyes crinkled into one of his glorious smiles. "We have to stop crashing into each other."

Her heart fluttered like bird wings in her chest. "Eka."

She began to bow and extend her hands outward in greeting, but *thunk.* Their heads collided.

"Sorry," They said in unison, and then stared at each other.

"Well, you found her." A humorous round face appeared over Eka's shoulder. Tejas' hair had been brutalized, cut to within a thumb's length of its life. "You two are dangerous together."

"What?" Eka shot his friend a dark look.

His wide-shouldered, round-faced friend stepped around Eka, grinning broadly. "You just smacked into each other twice in the time it took me to put on my cloak." He shook his head and began humming.

"Oh, I love that song. 'The Fool,' right?" Rana laughed. "Where the guy makes a fool of himself every time he sees the woman he likes…" Heat flushed her face as she realized Tejas' joke.

"Aw." Tejas threw his arm around Eka's shoulder. "She loves your song, sakhe." He leaned his cheek on his friend's shoulder and batted his eyelashes coyly.

Eka shook him off. "Don't you have some boots to clean or something?"

"Nope." Tejas smirked and continued humming.

Eka shot Rana an embarrassed look.

Self-conscious, she didn't know where to look. "I came to welcome you both." She stepped past them and into the hall. "Do you need anything?"

They followed her back inside.

Stew bowls and their packs had been set up by the cooking fires. She asked, "Did someone bring up the bedding?"

"Yes, we're all set up." Tejas grinned at his friend. "I think Eka wanted to go out for some fresh air, right?"

Eka's face tightened, and Rana sensed he'd sent his friend a message to stop embarrassing him.

Tejas cleared his throat. "I'm going to have one more bowl of that delicious stew." He stepped away, leaving the two of them alone.

Eka turned to her. "Would you like to join me for a walk?"

Her heart fluttered. "I'd love to."

He held the mat aside for her, and they stepped out into the crisp, starry night.

"I got the carving of Digga you sent. It was unbelievable." She caught his gaze. "And adorable. Thanks."

Eka's eyes crinkled again. "I tried to capture her not-so-innocent character."

She snickered. "Yeah, I guess you know her pretty well. And the way you worked with the natural wood color and knots. You're the best wood carver I've ever seen."

He chuckled. "Don't let Tejas hear that." He stopped and looked around them. "Where is our little monster?"

*Our?* Her heart skipped a beat. "Um, Balavati offered to take her for a walk so that I could—" She snapped her mouth shut.

*So I could meet you for a romantic walk without a vicious Cave Digger coming between us?* She wasn't about to admit to that.

"So I could have a break." She fiddled with the end of her braid.

He again had that deep, intense Crowned One look, but he cracked a smile. "She never came between us."

"Oh." She groaned and studied her boots. "I'm horrid at keeping my thoughts private."

"Well, in this case," he said as stepped closer and took her hand in his, "it makes things easier. I hoped you felt the same." His hand, strong and calloused from years of wood carving, enfolded hers in its warmth.

If ever there was a time to block her thoughts, now was it. She quickly utilized every mental block skill she had ever learned. She breathed in his evergreen resin and leather scent and allowed herself a nod. "I'm glad we found each other before I had to leave."

Was she mad? She had kissed Kahali's cheek earlier, and now she was taking an intimate stroll with Eka? Two guys might be fine for Balavati, but it made her head spin. *Get a hold of yourself. Change the subject.*

Rana studied his face while they walked, but he showed no signs of receiving her chaotic thoughts this time. Good. "Was it bad? The cave?"

His jaw twitched. "Yes. Especially finding the body. Did Kahali tell you?"

Rana nodded as she stepped closer to him to avoid a large rock. "I wish we had more time together before Balavati and I leave."

"I wish you weren't going." His grasp tightened on her hand. "After what happened with Kahali..."

"I know." She grimaced. "You found his arm?"

"Yes. His parents met us at the boulder."

The Nest, Kahali's and her boulder. Where she had kissed Kahali's tear-streaked cheek, and he had responded with another joke. Maybe there was only one guy who liked her, and Kahali was only messing around as always.

"I hope retrieving that helps him find peace." That kiss she'd given Kahali seemed like another lifetime now that she strolled beside Eka.

"How's he doing? Is he still avoiding everyone? Avoiding *you*?" Judging from his narrowed eyes, he knew it was a loaded question.

"No, we talked today. He wants me to quit Calling, but Balavati and I have already Called once, and they didn't seem to hear us. Though now that you found the body...well...Kalakanya wants us to try something different when we Call."

"What?" Eka stopped midstride and turned to Rana. "They aren't sending you into their den, are they?"

"No, but we're going much closer to it than Kahali's cave was. We're going to return the body with Kalakanya's help. She's reading the threads of time now, researching possible symbols to sky paint above the body to reassure them that we're peaceful. I mean, it's not like we killed him."

His head tilted. "We feared it was young, given its height. It's an adult male?"

"Yeah, they examined it before they took it to the Lion's Circle for prayers. They're not getting any sleep tonight." She sighed in empathy for the long night they faced.

"Well, you need some sleep. You're not Crowned," he said, touching her arm, and sleep was suddenly the furthest thing from her mind.

"I know…" She stopped and turned to meet his gaze. A sensuous wave of energy coursed through her, and she stepped closer. As she did so, the energy passed from her to him. She'd never experienced this before, but it flowed from her being as naturally as her breath.

Powerful, yet completely within her control, merging energy allowed two star beings to connect, understand each other's intentions, and confirm compatibility. But that class definition was nothing like what she now experienced.

Eka, his gaze never leaving hers, clasped both of her hands and held them to his chest, over his fluttering heart. When she sucked in a steadying breath, he did the same. Their breathing became as if they were one being. As they intermingled thus, a warm glow began to throb around them. They basked in the golden orb, experiencing one another.

Her friends had described this merging, but she'd never before understood its intensity. She closed her eyes and tilted her face upward. His breath came closer and his warm lips brushed her brow. Gasping, she opened her eyes to meet his gaze.

"Rana, I know this sounds unbelievable, but I think you're the one for me. For always…"

She smiled, her damp eyes gleaming. *Wait. Always? He's claiming this is coupling love when we're not even Crowned yet?* She stiffened, and the warm light snapped out of existence.

"No." She pulled her hands from his and backed away from him. No one ever claimed coupling love before Crowning. All your emotional attachments shifted when you Crowned. Everyone knew that. It was one of the reasons star beings weren't supposed to have children until after

266

they were Crowned.

Merging energy revealed the other's intentions. Why would he suddenly claim coupling love? Was he mocking her parents?

"What's wrong? I know that's not supposed to happen, but I mean it," he confessed, his hands over his heart.

She froze in place, determined to not make her parents' mistake.

"Rana?" Both of his hands raked through his long mane. "My Oneness, what'd I do?" He put a hand on her shoulder.

Shrugging it off, she wished she could as easily shake off the possibility of being like her parents. Oneness, she really liked him. Was he not thinking clearly?

He stepped back, giving her space. "Please, talk to me. I thought you felt the same?"

Eka's desperate tone tugged at her heart. Had she misread him? She shot him a sidelong glance and still saw only sincerity. She inhaled deeply to calm herself and decided to risk explaining to make sure they understood each other. "I have a...*situation* that makes it unlikely that I'll Crown, so stop talking about coupling love. I won't be involved in coupling with anyone until after I Crown." *I'll never do what my parents did. Please understand.*

He grimaced. "What? Of course, I meant when we're Crowned. No one would do that to a child...couple without being Crowned," His disgust at her exact situation was a punch in her gut.

She glared at him, eyes stinging. "You, you—" No words fit her disappointment in him. "Argh!" She spun and ran into the night.

All her deepest childhood fears tumbled out around her. When she was younger, she had overheard the concerned whispers of her elders. *Will Rana be affected? What were her parents thinking?* She had never expected a guy she liked to find her situation disgusting. Angry tears splashed down her cheeks.

"Rana!" Eka's voice carried across the frozen field, but she had no more time for such a jerk. She had to Call in a few hours.

# Chapter 34

*orthern Haven: Commander Kern Savas*

Northern Haven: Commander Kern Savas

Commander Savas understood the limitations fate had dealt him. The most powerful humans alive today controlled the destiny of only three hundred humans of United People's Northern Haven. Not exactly a grand prize, but it was all that remained of humanity, and he was responsible for keeping it safe.

SHAST, the Subterranean Haven for the Advancement of Science and Technology. That acronym, an expletive to most due to their survivor's guilt, was his link to the truth. Because despite their best efforts to make him forget who he was, he remembered hiding under his bed as they busted into his family's module. Stroking the antique compass tucked under his clothing, he silently repeated their vow.

*...and we will save humanity by any means.* Savas gripped the reflective metal railing on the stairwell, his vow weighing heavy on his mind, as he scrutinized the team's preparations below him.

This Third Expedition was the key; it would establish a preliminary Surface base to launch the new helicopters and protect the door from those mind-controlling monsters that had called Abdul to his death. He'd declared them "reapers" at the team's last meeting. The simple act of naming them had given his team more confidence about facing them again.

"Neviah, you only have an hour." He glared as she began deftly taking apart and rebuilding the communications devices. "What are you doing?"

"The tech guys did it wrong, sir. It'll just take a minute." She beamed a ridiculously perky grin and returned to her work.

He'd have to watch that one. Another woman on the team concerned him. Josefina had been exceptional, and look how that had turned out—her natural body had turned against her. Somehow, he'd made a mortal enemy of Nature. It had killed his entire first team and then stolen Josefina. An uncomfortable pressure built in his chest and squeezed its way into his throat, forming a lump. He swallowed hard.

*Stop thinking about her—she's gone.* As if it were that easy.

Below him, Bleu and Stamf scurried around the obnoxiously fluorescent-green room and made final checks on the equipment. The brilliant SHAST scientists who'd planned and built Northern Haven had foreseen the bleakness of living underground. Bright colors or murals covered all the walls. What they hadn't anticipated was the annoyance of such false cheeriness.

His spirit lifted when his gaze fell upon his new toys: two snow rovers with storage; two snowmobiles; two large, weatherproof artillery on removable tripods; long-range rifles; handguns for all of them; and a camouflage shelter kit for the artillery. *Perfect.* His heartbeat quickened as he imagined blasting reapers with the new large artillery.

Descending the stairs, Savas watched as Girak approached Bleu and Stamf and effortlessly joined their conversation. It was beyond him how the others had so quickly accepted that Deplorable as a team member.

The three men joked over the still-opened crate of urination tools—special bottles to urinate in so one didn't need to take off all their clothing to piss.

"Get that all to the elevator, now." Savas motioned to the urination tools. "Did they pack the small ones for Girak?"

Stamf and Bleu burst into riotous laughter. Girak shook his ridiculously red head and walked away. Neviah turned pink and ducked her head behind the computer screen. Savas narrowed his eyes and smirked. Girak had no idea of his plans for him.

His greatest urge was to "accidently" eliminate him, but between his genes and the fact that no other scientifically trained citizens were willing to risk their life to further research the Surface…well, it wasn't clear if he'd get away with it. The council had been too lenient when it only removed his educator status. The jerk had essentially killed his own wife.

Savas checked the time. "Neviah, it's time. Get that thing packed." He turned to the technicians, who had finally arrived. "Get the rest of this loaded, now. It will take three trips up the elevator. Make sure the first load has a rover, weapons, and ammo."

The technicians scurried off to do his bidding.

He turned to his team. "Your families are in the room before the door. Five minutes with them, and then the first shift leaves. Stamf and I will go first with the one rover. Bleu and Girak, you're second with the next rover. Neviah, you come up last, but Bleu will come back down and get you. The technicians know they are to help you and Bleu load the last time. Questions?"

No one spoke. Bleu rubbed his shoulder.

"Bleu, did you get that wrapped?" The kid had recovered quickly, but they had no room for weakness.

Bleu dropped his hand from his shoulder. "Yes sir. I did it myself."

"Good, we don't have a medic this time. Outer layers on, now."

They jogged to the wall on the right that contained their layers and dressed. No one spoke, all occupied with their impending expedition.

*This level of fear will hold them back. Pep talk time.*

"You have, with the exception of our newest member"—he smirked at Girak—"all been well trained. Use it. This is our planet and our rightful home. Whatever those alien reapers expect to do will fail. Last time, their mind control caught us off guard. This time, we're prepared. Let's go. We have a Surface to reclaim!"

Girak's face had become rigid and white. The coward was already losing it. This would be too easy…

"Girak, since you don't have anyone waiting in the family room, help the guards load."

Bleu gave Savas a sharp look and clasped Girak's shoulder. "My mom said to tell you to stay safe up there."

270

Savas snorted. Girak nodded and stared at his palm tattoo before sliding on his glove.

"Come on. You'll love it up there." The kid patted Girak's back as if trying to transfer his own endless enthusiasm for the Surface.

Bleu was such a bleeding heart.

"Hmm." Girak's pale skin somehow got even paler above his beard. "Which part? The frostbite, the giant wolves, or the reapers?" A smile crinkled around his blue eyes.

Bleu chuckled. "You'll see what I mean..."

With a nervous chuckle, Girak left them to help the technicians. Savas led the others in for their brief video fame and goodbyes. This time, it held no pleasure and only reminded him of Josefina's absence. Since his mother was dead and he'd never married, no one gave him any special attention. He smiled for the camera anyway, promising himself a wild party when he returned.

They exited and walked down the corridor together, Savas leading.

He spoke without turning his head. "Stamf and I will secure the entrance. When the elevator returns, get it loaded as quickly as possible. Remember, we must secure the area outside our exit and establish an armed base camp on the upper plateau above the door. Nothing can be allowed to approach the entrance to Northern Haven. Until we secure the vicinity, we can't risk sending a team to find the other Havens.

"We shoot anything remotely threatening. I challenge you all to a reaper-killing contest. Winner gets my year's choco candy ration, so keep count."

"Choco?" Neviah's eyes widened, and she glanced down at her gun as if seeing it with new eyes.

"Hope you enjoyed owning it, Commander, because after today, it's all mine." Stamf laughed.

Savas chuckled, pleased to have them joking, their fears forgotten. Plus, the contest would be fun, and if they could bring back a living specimen of their new enemy, then even better. Study them and find their weaknesses. Mess with *their* minds for a change.

Savas and Stamf entered the crammed elevator. Stamf deftly climbed on top of a stack of gear and perched. Pride filled Savas' chest. *So much like me at his age. And he's Prime Minister Pridbor's nephew. A handy connection.* He'd lucked out on that piece.

Stamf turned and grinned. "No breakfast today, as recommended, sir."

"Good." Savas returned a matching grin. "It's a bit cramped in here. Have your rifle ready when it opens. Maybe we'll get lucky."

"Good to go, sir." Stamf's fingers tapped out a rhythm on his AR-15. Years ago, Savas, as the council's strategist, had negotiated to have the gaming guns designed like this real rifle model. After all, he had no military, so he had to use any advantage toward training he could get from the council. Stamf, having grown up in the Gaming Arena, had grown up using these weapons. His comfort was the result of Savas' decades of planning.

Grinning, Savas hit the button. The skipping breakfast idea worked for both Stamf and him. The ride to the Surface passed quickly and uneventfully.

As he pressed the button to open the door, Savas turned to Stamf. "Remember to look down. A blinded sharpshooter is useless."

Stamf gave him a thumbs up and nodded, then raised his semi-automatic to his shoulder while keeping his gaze on the floor.

The door opened, and the usual blast of cold, too bright light and fresh air clarified Savas' dream—an armed Surface fortress staffed by hardened humans under his command. He could keep them alive and safe in these conditions. Humanity would reclaim its birthright of ruling the planet.

As his plans marched through his head, his eyes adjusted to the bright light. It happened faster each time he ascended to the Surface. He was already changing, hardening to the conditions.

When Stamf was ready, they stepped out and scrutinized the white land and gray sky for danger. These colors were real. A bit drab, but they sang of danger, not false cheer. Savas nodded, turned, and stood guard while Stamf moved out the rover and supplies.

His ears perked. Beyond the crunching of Stamf shifting the rover, the wind moaned as it whipped ice crystals around them. The weather droid they had sent up—his own idea after the failed first expedition—had said storms were unlikely. A queasy urgency arose from his gut. He shifted his rifle and paced, anxious to send the box back for the rest of the team.

"Done, sir." Stamf sounded pleased with himself.

"Okay, you watch. I'll send it back down." Savas strode to the door and pressed the button.

The groaning wind rose around him. *Damn it. This poor visibility will slow us down.* As the door closed, a round of gunfire blasted behind him.

"Freaking shast!" Stamf yelled.

He spun as Stamf fired into a mound of snow. The bullets exploded a snowbank roughly thirty meters to the New South.

"What?" Savas had his gun unholstered but saw nothing except encrusted snow.

Impossibly, the drift shifted. A mountainous form rose on two mighty legs. He could make out two small, black eyes and massive jaws. A bear? He fired, but his handgun was a poor match against the massive beast. It roared and lowered itself onto all fours, swung its massive white head in fury, and charged.

They both fired, and the body thundered to the ground, sending reverberations into his boots. Savas panted, unwilling to lower his gun. *This damn place is teeming with monstrosities.* For a moment, his vision of a fortress shattered.

"That was awesome." Stamf raised his hand to high-five Savas, then sobered. "Ah, sorry. Bleu and I always do that after a game."

Commander Savas glared, a bit shocked at the playful outburst. "This isn't a game, Stamf. I'm depending on you. Stay focused."

He would have chewed anyone else out for the disrespectful movement, but this was Stamf. Given Northern Haven's genetic control, biological fathers didn't know who their children were unless they had powerful connections. Savas knew, but he still wasn't allowed to disclose that information.

They slowly approached the monster's body as the door behind them clanged open.

"Bleu, look at what we shot." Stamf ran to the door. "Ah, sorry, take your time. Forgot...but when you're ready, man, look over here."

Savas kicked the body. It remained still. He peered around, searching for any additional danger. Behind him, Stamf updated Bleu and Girak.

"This time, I'm ahead. This thing *has* to top five wolves." Stamf approached with the other two men.

Bleu gasped at the massive dead bear and turned to Savas. "Sir, those used to be nearly extinct. Next time could we scare it off instead of killing it?"

Savas bristled with righteous fury. "It attacked us. Don't you *ever* question my judgment again. Understood?" he yelled into Bleu's face.

The kid nodded. Girak stood next to Bleu and glowered at Savas.

"This is our land. Threats are extinguished. Got it?" He glared at Bleu, then realized it was useless, given his headpiece and goggles.

Silence.

"Get that stuff out, now. Bleu, get Neviah up here. Pronto."

The wind's wailing had stopped. Had that been the bear all along? He needed to pay more attention to these things.

Bleu left, and when the door next opened, Neviah stood beside him, staring at the ground. After several minutes, she stepped cautiously from the box and placed herself only centimeters from Bleu. She peered around until her gaze fell on the great white body now bleeding onto the ground.

*Great. Another coward....*

"Sir?" Bleu cleared his throat.

"What?" *If he suggests we hold a funeral, I'm going to lose it.*

"I'm not questioning the need to kill that"—he motioned toward the large body—"but it might bring scavengers to our door."

"Then we shoot them, too, and have a banquet," Savas said, smirking.

Bleu shrugged, clearly not agreeing, but this time showing respect.

*Good, he's learned.*

"Remember, we have a more dangerous enemy to deal with: the reapers. Any creature that smart won't need to scavenge. They could be anywhere, so let's gather our gear and get moving. Stamf and Bleu, take a quick look around."

The team snapped into a flurry of activity. Bleu and Stamf fanned out and scrutinized the harsh surroundings.

"Bleu, try looking up. They might be watching from the cliffs." Savas didn't hide his annoyance. *Why in the world was the kid looking down at the snow?*

"But, sir, I see tracks," Bleu yelled.

Savas stiffened. "What? You see a creature?"

"No, but I see the prints of several animals that must have passed by recently. Look." Bleu waved him over.

Maybe his weirdness would be useful. Savas closed the distance between them with long quick strides.

"See? It's clearly not a polar bear. It looks pretty big...but no claw marks." Bleu pointed to the length of the tracks, measuring them against his own boots. "Bigger than mine...and they stride like humans." He stared down the length of the valley toward the switchback. "A couple of them, sir."

Savas checked his gun. "Team, we have company. Be sharp."

# Chapter 35

*orthern Haven's Door: Commander Kern Savas*

As Bleu analyzed the prints in the snow, Savas' heart quickened at the chance for revenge. "Bleu and Stamf, walk point while we move out. It could be a trick."

He turned completely around and looked up. Northern Haven's door stood in a solid rock wall. The iced gray granite rose steeply, flattening to a plateau that was the future site of his base. He strained to see up onto the flat space, but the cliff was too vertical. *That's the perfect hiding spot. What if they beat us to it?*

"Neviah, scan up there. Any heat forms?"

Neviah dropped the gear she was holding onto the rover and scrambled to find the right equipment. She withdrew it, turned it on, and paused. In the silence, Savas' heart hammered against his ribcage.

She shook her head, "No, sir." She stood there holding the equipment stiffly, unsure what to do next.

"Stop acting paralyzed, or you'll get us all killed. Use that pretty little head of yours."

She shrank, nodded, and swiftly put the equipment back in its case.

Bleu approached her and said something quietly.

Savas narrowed his eyes. *Is he undermining me again?*

Neviah nodded to Bleu, giggled, and returned to her usual quirky self. She buzzed around, opening and closing crates. In a flash, the necessary equipment was ready for them to move out.

Savas squinted up at the plateau. He wished the damn geography was different. How could he defend the door effectively while being kilometers away? Yet they had gone over it a million times. The only way to get above the door was to travel down the Valley of Ice and go up the natural switchback to the high point. If only the helicopters were already up here. They'd be finished on the Surface, but they couldn't risk bringing that technology up here until the area had been secured.

The journey to the switchback was their only option. Otherwise, he faced climbing a sheer cliff with all the supplies. Not possible.

*But if the reapers get up there first...* He growled at that possibility.

He radioed the control room and updated them. "They're nearby, headed down the valley toward the switchback. Our best option is to risk sending two men up the cliff to defend the top while we bring the equipment around. It'll split us up, but we have to defend this door."

"Who are your best climbers?" the radio technician asked.

"Stamf's the best, then myself and Bleu. But we need a hunter in both groups. I'd say we send Stamf and Girak. I can lead Bleu and Neviah around with the equipment. There's some risk in climbing, but Stamf's good." He silently eyed Girak, who stared at the icy rock cliff in disbelief.

Savas inwardly smiled at the man's impending predicament. *Perfect.*

"You're the one out there and our strategist. You call the shots, Commander. Just keep the radios on. We'll get some backup people in the shaft in case you come in hot. But they don't have gear to come out, and only handguns. They're still making the other suits. You're on your own until you hit the door."

"Understood. Commander out." Savas studied his team. "We're splitting up. Stamf and Girak will scale the cliff. We'll guard you until you reach the top. Then you have to hold the door till we come around with the big guns." He nodded at the weather-proof artillery loaded into the back of the snow rover. "Stamf, you lead climb."

As the team readied itself, Savas pulled Stamf aside. "Stamf, you're the better climber. If there's a problem with Girak that puts you at risk, cut the line."

Stamf's jaw dropped. "But—"

"You heard me. We absolutely need at least one of you to make it up there safely and hold the door. That's an order."

"Yes, sir." Stamf appeared shocked and then hardened his face with grim resolve.

Savas shifted to face both climbers. "Good luck. We'll guard the door until you signal us that you're both safe at the top." He turned and ordered Bleu and Neviah to position the rovers at the cliff base to provide some cover while they waited by the door.

Stamf slapped Girak's shoulder. "Don't worry. We can do this. Just like the climbing wall down under, right?"

"Hmmm." Girak leaned in, tapped his ears, and grumbled something.

Commander Savas sneered. Girak had overheard his comments to Stamf. *Plan engaged. Girak's anger always makes him clumsy.*

Stamf smiled encouragingly to Girak. They sat and switched into mountaineering boots and then attached the crampons—metal plates with spikes that would allow them to grip the ice. Next, they each buckled on a climbing harness, which fit snugly over their many layers. Since Stamf was going to be the lead climber, he took the larger climbing rack, which contained more nuts and camming devices to place as safety holds. They added climbing ropes, carabiners, and quick draws to their harness belt.

Stamf studied the cliff and then turned toward him. "One ice pick? There's a decent amount of exposed rock."

Savas examined the climb and then pointed. "That one section is quite icy. If you get up there and can't get around it, you might want both. Take the other one on your belt, just in case."

"Are there four?" Girak asked, stepping forward and examining at the supplies.

"There's five, in case we each needed one. Here." Neviah handed Girak two picks.

"Guys, don't forget these." Bleu held out the thin climbing gloves. "Put your others in your packs for later."

"Sir, our guns?" Stamf held his rifle in front of him. "I don't know. The pistol and ammo can go in my pack, but my rifle?"

They stood at the base of the icy cliff considering their options and wasting valuable time. Savas clenched his jaw.

"You could attach the rifle to your pack, though it might catch on something." Neviah examined the rifle. "If only we had brought a remote-control flying probe, we could fly it up."

"Next time, Neviah." Savas could see no way for Stamf to reach the top with his gun that didn't increase the danger of the risky climb. "Stamf, when you reach the top, secure a rope, toss it down, and we'll send you up the guns."

He really hoped Neviah's readings were correct and no reapers awaited them.

"I guess." Stamf grinned. "Just make sure the safety is on, or we'll all be dancing." He checked and rechecked the position of the devices on his belt and then walked the base, looking for his best starting point.

Was he making a mistake sending them up like this? He turned and gazed angrily at the tracks of the upright reapers. They left him no choice. The door was compromised and needed protection at all costs. If they guarded it from their present location, they'd be easy targets for reapers above on the plateau... Let the cost be Girak. Stamf would make it.

Savas' chest tightened at the danger to his youngest recruit. "Stamf, remember to check the quality of the rocks before you place the devices. Only use the drilling cams if you need to deal with ice, and double check it's healthy ice. We've never tested them in the field. I need you to reach the top alive. Tug from all angles before you attach the carabiner clips and your rope. A lot is riding on you."

"You mean *us*." Stamf said, playfully punching Girak in the arm. "Come on, Edu— I mean, Girak. Time to save the Haven."

Stamf walked back and forth for a moment and then began his ascent.

Savas' muscles tensed and strained as if he were climbing himself. Adrenaline coursed through him, and he forced himself to breath as the kid ascended.

Stamf made slow, steady progress, finding crevices, pausing to check them for safety, inserting the protection, tugging to check the placement, and then reaching around to grab a carabiner clip from his belt.

As Savas observed the confidence in Stamf's athletic movements, his heart swelled. *Just the way I taught him.* Stamf added an extender, hooked on his rope, and continued to the next lofty crevice. Higher and higher he climbed, and Savas found himself holding his breath. The sun was high in the sky and burned through his tinted goggles into his retinas. When Stamf finally pulled himself onto the plateau, Savas blew out a long exhalation.

He clicked his radio. "Great work, Stamf! I hope they saw that on our cameras. Anything up there?"

"N-no, sir." Stamf stood panting and waved down at them. "Come on up, Girak. The view is worth it."

"It's hard to follow a show like that, Stamf," Girak said, shaking his head as if he refused to make the climb.

Savas grinned. This was it...

Bleu approached Girak and said something quietly, his hand on Girak's shoulder.

Savas quietly groaned at the annoying do-gooder. "Bleu, let him go. We don't have all day."

Girak began his upward climb, and Savas inwardly grinned as he slipped at almost every footing and took forever to attach his rope to each hold. At about thirty meters up, he slipped completely and screamed as he fell only a few meters before his protection caught him.

*Not yet...get higher before you fall, murderer.*

Neviah and Bleu yelled suggestions and support as the out of shape jerk dangled helplessly. Slowly, he swung and dug in with his crampons to stop his swinging. He regained his footing and began again.

Savas ground his teeth in frustration. Up and up Girak went, now, strangely enough, moving with more confidence. Savas narrowed his eyes at the sight. *He doesn't care if he dies...*

He shielded his eyes from the sun and strained to see Girak's movements. He was almost there. *Slip now...* It would be a faster, kinder ending than he deserved.

But Girak continued upward, unstoppable. As he climbed up on to the flat surface, he rolled over and took Stamf's hand. Stamf pulled the older man up to standing.

Savas scowled. The bastard had made it. He clawed at the innards of his gloves in frustration.

Neviah and Bleu cheered and whooped it up for their teammates, who hooted down to them. Savas snorted. So much for surprising the reapers. "Stamf, send down a line." They still had to get the rifles up there.

The first one caught a few times on rocky crags until Bleu suggested that they tie lines to both sides of it to maneuver it better. The kid was smart. Soon, Stamf stood on the clifftop armed with his semi-automatic—a mini success for humanity.

"Stamf, you're in charge up there," Savas said. "Hold the door and don't let them trick you. We'll need about five hours. Constant radio contact."

Both Stamf and Girak acknowledged and waved as the lower team turned to move out with the equipment.

Savas loudly cleared his throat. "Follow me in the second rover, Bleu. Neviah, with me." He turned, strode to the first rover, but then noticed Bleu had frozen in his tracks. His eyes widened as he began frantically turning in all directions.

"Bleu? What is it?" Savas' heart raced as he withdrew his gun.

The kid's fearful movements ceased as he hunched his shoulders. "Ah... did you just hear a woman's voice?" Bleu looked away, as if again hearing something.

"The reapers are nearby. You spotted their tracks in the snow, remember?"

*My team's affected already, and they're not even in sight?*

Bleu nodded. "It was a conversation, not a lulling urge..."

"What are they telling you?" Savas asked, glancing at Neviah.

She shook her head. Neither of them had heard it. He turned back to Bleu.

"Nothing to me, sir. It's like I overheard them saying, 'Rona, last time nothing happened. Everything will be fine.' That's all, sir." The kid gave both of them an imploring glance. "Neither of you heard it?"

"No. They're trying to delay us. Report anything else you hear, and let's get moving." Either Bleu had truly overheard something, or he was getting the Sickness. Or maybe he was a secret weapon, able to listen in on the reapers. Or he was already falling into their trap?

Savas mulled these possibilities over as he turned his rover toward the Valley of Ice. Either the geography had been totally different centuries ago, or the Northern Haven planners had possessed no strategic sense. Travelling down the valley, they made easy targets to anyone above. A chill rose up his spine.

They had gone about five kilometers when a massive lightning-like flash appeared ahead. He slammed the brakes. Unlike lightning, the flash steadied and grew into a balloon-like shape.

"You see that, Neviah?" Savas asked, keeping his eyes on the unnatural light. Adrenaline rushed through his limbs.

"Whoa!" Neviah hissed. "Is it…?"

Bleu answered, "It's them."

# Chapter 36

*he Valley of Ice: Commander Kern Savas*

Savas knew they'd face the reapers again, but he'd hoped for more time to get their door defenses in order. Without looking away from the strange light, he shouted to his team, "Get ready. They've got to show themselves sooner or later. Neviah, get the artillery pointed at that."

He raised his gun and slipped his right index finger through the slit in his glove that allowed him to better control the trigger. "Focus. Don't let them control you."

The light continued to expand from a flash to a large luminous globe. The forcefield became transparent, and he could make out three reapers within its luminescent boundaries. The shortest one waved its forearms around and the forcefield was imprinted with a golden cross, a blue pair of stacked triangles, a green crescent moon and star, and a circle, or maybe an eye? Shapes continued to appear from nowhere.

Savas' jaw dropped. These creatures were using ancient religious symbols to communicate? Did they expect his team to worship them? Fury and peace flooded him at the same time. *They're messing with my head.*

"You both see the symbols, right?" he asked.

He'd created this protocol to reality-check anything unusual with each other. Otherwise, they didn't stand a chance fighting an enemy that could control their perceptions and body responses. These reapers were the most dangerous threat humanity had ever faced.

"I see it." Bleu said, sounding awed. He had pulled his rover up parallel to Savas'.

"Me, too." Neviah pulled out her equipment and tried to get a reading.

Savas fingered his gun and scrutinized the creatures. *Three of them, three of us...* "Neviah, you've studied communication. Any ideas about what they're saying?"

"Sir? My equipment...it's malfunctioning," she said, her voice rising in pitch.

Savas rolled his eyes. She was completely lost without her tech. "Forget the equipment. What are the symbols? Is it a threat?"

Neviah cleared her throat. "Sir, they're religious symbols. Some predate the Great Change by thousands of years. Sir, I don't know how this could be possible, but they must have been studying humanity...like forever."

"Aliens," Bleu mumbled over the radio.

"Aliens?" *How the shast do I destroy aliens? We haven't even fully constructed our helicopters.*

Then, the reapers appeared to take their heads off. Savas recoiled and gasped at the three glowing, humanoid feminine faces before him. They were almost beautiful. Something nagged at the back of his brain—an ancient story of the Greek Sirens calling sailors to their deaths.

"Are you two seeing...*giant women?*" he asked, gaping at the glowing creatures.

The others grunted agreement over their radios.

He felt odd, almost light-headed, as if their very presence oozed something toxic to human brains. How far did their mind control go? Were they all mass hallucinating?

The reapers parted, and between them lay a human body in the orange gear of the Expedition Teams. Savas' stomach fell. They'd gotten to Stamf and Girak. Rage exploded through every pore of his being.

"Fire!" Commander Savas pulled the trigger on his gun and blasted the reapers.

The noise shook the very air, but the bullets evaporated in little harmless puffs as they hit the edge of the globe. He reloaded and held his breath as Neviah hit the shield dead-on with the artillery. Another puff of smoke.

The shield barely flickered.

Two of the reapers grabbed the body and shoved it through the shield toward the team. The third and shortest reaper had her arms up and continued to gently toss about balls of gaseous light. As the balls hit the forcefield, more symbols appeared. A bright pink circle appeared, with a line bisecting it and an upside-down V.

"Sir, that's an ancient peace sign," Neviah shouted as if their guns were still firing around her.

Savas spared a glance at his team.

Bleu stood in awe; his handgun loosely held at his side. He appeared completely possessed by the aliens.

Savas clenched his fists. He had no way to know if the symbols were actual peace symbols, or if Neviah also was under their control. Or if any of this was happening at all. How did he fight an enemy he couldn't describe or even see? He growled.

"Neviah, check the body for heat. Any chance he's still alive?"

Neviah scrambled into the back of the snow rover to find the proper equipment.

"Bleu, they killed Abdul. Don't be so damn calm. Fight it," he yelled and then grunted encouragingly as Bleu put his hands up to his goggles as if to clear them. "Yes, fight it. They're lulling you."

Bleu shook his head.

*Surely, he's not disagreeing with me?*

"Bleu, snap out of it," he yelled, climbing down from his rover to smack him one if needed.

Bleu exited his own rover and stumbled forward, closer and closer to the reapers' forcefield, as if he had nothing to fear.

Savas shot a round of gunfire in front of the fool's feet.

Bleu froze and gave him a puzzled look. "Sir?" His voice shifted from confusion to fear. "You almost shot me."

"I saved you. Now, get back here." Savas pointed to the rovers.

"But, sir, they're giving us Abdul's body."

Savas didn't trust Bleu's drunken assessment. "Neviah, the readings?"

*Why is she so slow?*

"No heat. He's dead, whoever it is." She gave a small whimper.

Fear twisted his innards. If Stamf and Girak were dead, then all Northern Haven was compromised. "Bleu, don't make eye contact with them, but get the body. Quick."

*Please, let it be Girak, not Stamf.*

Bleu rushed forward, eyes downcast, running awkwardly toward the pulsing forcefield. The orange-clothed body lay outside it. He grabbed its coat at both shoulders and attempted to heave the body over his shoulder, but failed miserably. Rigor mortis had set in, or maybe it was simply frozen solid.

*How long have we been away from Stamf and Girak? How long does it take for rigor mortis to set in?*

Clumsily stumbling, Bleu grabbed the feet and began running backward, still keeping his eyes down.

"Who is it?" Savas yelled.

Bleu gave him an odd expression. "I already told you, sir. It's Abdul."

"Show me," he demanded, striding closer.

Bleu bent and pulled off the face gear to expose Abdul's frost-covered face. Savas sighed. Stamf was still safe.

Then, Neviah screamed.

Commander Savas lurched up, aiming his gun at the reapers. Or at least where they had been. The huge shield was gone, replaced by a smaller energy field with only two reapers. *Bet I can puncture that one.*

Neviah shouted a warning.

Savas spun as the third, shortest reaper, arms raised, pointed a stick at a huge, snarling badger-wolverine creature that had appeared out of nowhere. Its body shape resembled a wolverine, but the head shape and striping were those of a badger. Either way, it was bad. Behind it lumbered two more.

*Monstrous allies? Could this get any worse?*

But Neviah was pointing in still another direction where a fourth gigantic badger-wolverine lumbered closer toward her.

Savas raised his gun and fired at Neviah's attacker. The wolverine lurched slightly. *Shast it! It's almost as big as the rover.* A small patch of blood stained the animal's front leg, but other than that, he had only enraged it. It turned from Neviah and rushed him, separating her from the others. She ran backward toward the walls of the Valley of Ice and disappeared into a shadowy alcove.

Savas noted all this in the few seconds it took for the giant wolverine's dagger-like yellow incisors and lethal-looking claws to race toward him. His heart hammered against his ribs. The beast's claws clanked like small swords as it ran across the ice. He fired off another round, but the hide of the beast was impenetrable. He stumbled backward, needing to reload.

"Bleu!" *I refuse to be killed by this mountain of fur.*

"They're...everywhere." Bleu, panting, ran up behind him and plopped down the giant tripod artillery from the other rover.

Savas slapped a new magazine into his gun as Bleu fired the artillery at the wolverine. Light exploded everywhere, burning Savas' eyes. The striped monstrosity reeled back, as did Savas and Bleu. The artillery went flying over Bleu's shoulder.

With fire in their eyes, the two reapers stood between them and the monstrous animals. One faced Savas and Bleu, while the other faced the rearing animal. Each created a wall of light, sealing the two reapers between the wolverine and the humans.

"They're protecting their allies. Fall back to the rover," Savas shouted.

"Where's Neviah?" Bleu shouted, straining to see around the rippling forcefield while Savas kept up his gun fire.

"Behind the beast. Maybe while the light's distracting it..." Savas lunged left, trying to race toward Neviah.

The reaper facing them extended the energy field, and he slammed into it and was thrown backward.

Bleu pulled him up. "All right?"

Savas nodded, though pain racked his leg. He wobbled and raised his gun, but he couldn't properly aim.

Bleu began firing, covering them both. "You're injured. Get the gun on the rover. I'll get Neviah."

Savas nodded, still dazed. *The kid just gave me an order.* Part of him was furious, but Bleu's plan made sense, so he lumbered backward toward the rover, firing and reloading the whole time.

Bleu took off away from the wall of light, then zigzagged back toward Neviah.

Savas' feet stumbled over the artillery. He lifted it into the rover and growled as pain shot through his leg from its added weight. By the time he'd turned back, the two reapers had adjusted their wall of light to stay near him. Bleu still needed to reach Neviah, and it was up to him to distract these two.

He eyed Abdul's body, fearing it may be rigged or a trap. His family would want it, and they needed the clothing. Also, the reapers had touched it, and a DNA sample could be useful. The possibility of learning more about these enemies decided it.

He lunged for Abdul's body, and the reapers adjusted their shield, but not quickly enough. He grabbed the rigid body and hoisted it into the rover. The wolverine creature struggled against the wall of light, but the reapers held the massive beasts at bay *What are these aliens planning?*

In the distance, the third shortest reaper held off the three wolverines, forcing them to turn around.

*Almost like she's sending them somewhere...*

His stomach clenched. Struggling into the driver's seat, he radioed Stamf.

"Stamf. Is the door secure?"

"Yes, sir. The gunfire?"

"We're engaged. There may be some large wolverine-like animals headed your way. They work for the reapers, and our guns don't have much effect on them. Thick fur. Aim for the eyes. Guard the door. Out."

The one reaper still faced the three disappearing wolverines, and the other two tried to control the fourth. Bleu had reached Neviah, but they were cut off from the rover. Savas glanced back at the two reapers, who now both had their backs to him. *Time to burst your bubble, freaks.*

Savas aimed the large artillery at the closest of the paired reapers and pulled the trigger. The shield disappeared, and the reaper staggered and fell. A surge of hope rose in his chest.

The other reaper turned and released a loud high-pitched sound.

*Oh, Shast. What now?*

Flashes of light appeared all over as the aliens began popping up everywhere.

Desperate, Savas floored the rover and flew toward the fallen reaper and the screaming one. The second reaper's shield had collapsed when it made that hideous scream. Savas grabbed the fallen one, knocking the other over in the process.

Heart thumping, he grinned as Bleu and Neviah ran toward him, firing wildly. The materializing reapers appeared befuddled, and many were shot before they activated their shield devices.

Bleu screamed like a warrior of yore and shot with amazing accuracy. He felled at least eight of them. Neviah ran beside him, firing small pops with her handgun.

*Wow.* A new respect for the kids flowed through Savas. He fired the artillery on the shielded ones, creating a distraction for Bleu and Neviah to reach the rover.

Bleu and Neviah nearly reached him when a yellow sphere enveloped them, trapping them within it. Their gunfire disappeared in puffs of smoke as it hit the bubble encasing them. Bleu stopped firing and tried to push the end of his gun through the orb. He was thrown to the ground. Neviah yelled something to Savas as Bleu rose and again tried to shoot his way out of the bubble.

Savas turned the big gun on the entrapping orb and fired. It must have protected from the inside only, because it instantly exploded. The surrounding reapers froze, turning slowly toward Savas, their heads cocked.

"Didn't expect that, did you, bastards?" His glee, however, was short-lived. The explosion of the globe had knocked Bleu and Neviah flat. They didn't get up.

Time stopped. Savas ignored the hairs rising on his neck and calculated. He had two team members possibly dead in front of him and surrounded. He had an unconscious prisoner on his rover. And his main mission was to protect the door that sheltered humanity.

Humanity came first. Without a backward glance, he spun the rover and pushed it full throttle toward the door.

# Chapter 37

T he *Valley of Ice: Commander Kern Savas*

A clammy sweat trickled down Savas' neck as he urged the snow rover toward Northern Haven. *Forget the speed recommendations.* The Valley of Ice seemed to have grown longer. He kept glancing behind him, but no reapers pursued.

*They don't know I have one of them.* He grinned, leaning forward as if that could speed up the rover. With one hand on the steering apparatus and the other on his gun, he radioed Stamf.

"I'm coming in hot. Anything there?"

"No, sir. Should we come down and help you?"

"Stay. We can't let them take that spot. I caught one. I'll have someone meet me at the door and take it in. Cover me, then I'll help you."

He next radioed Northern Haven. The rover bucked at its high speed causing his teeth to clank together. "Bleu and Neviah are down, possibly captured. I have an unconscious reaper. Have the bravest you can find meet me at the door."

Someone would meet him at the door. That someone would remove and wear Abdul's suit to fight...with a handgun. *Like the legendary Alamo.*

Savas silently fumed over the lack of preparation for warfare. Northern Haven hadn't maintained its arsenal over the centuries. The Unde-scended—humans left to fend on the Surface—had never attacked. *We felt too safe...*

"It's our planet. Ours!" he shouted at the unconscious reaper.

He pictured the reapers killing Stamf, Girak, and himself as they stormed the door, humanity's last hope destroyed. All the lives and energy put into preserving the species and its glorious knowledge destroyed by light-wielding aliens. A desperate option thrust its way into his mind. They had survived below for years…

"Base, this is Commander Savas. We need stronger weapons. I suggest we nuke them. It's nearly impossible to get through their shields; our regular weapons are useless. I don't know how long we can hold them up here.

"Bleu shot a bunch, but only because they hadn't activated their shields yet. With shielding, we couldn't stop three, and there are tons of them. I saw about twenty appear out of thin air." He was panting, though the rover was doing all the work. His heart raced at breakneck speed. *I don't have the genes for heart attacks…*

"We've been monitoring and agree, Commander, but the nuclear weapons aren't online. It will take time to prepare them and calculate where to fire. Any signs of their stronghold?"

"No." How the hell was he to find their stronghold when they appeared out of thin air?

"Some council members want other options. Nuclear weapons limit our ability to reach the other Havens."

"I'm the council's strategist, and the other options will fail. There have to *be* Northern Haven survivors to worry about reaching the other Havens." Energy raced through his limbs, and for a moment, he considered stopping the rover to take out his frustration on the unconscious reaper bouncing in the back of the vehicle. "If they kill us all, setting off a nuke won't matter, but it may save the other Havens from being found and attacked." A strange chill fell upon him. "We may already be the only survivors. Underground may be the only option for humanity."

"I'll express your concerns."

Savas ground his teeth. "Please also convey *my concerns* for containing the reaper I caught. If we experiment on the alien freak, maybe we'll discover some non-nuclear options to kill them."

"We have a medical team ready. Get the reaper to the door, and Nahim,

Bjorn, and Erik will meet you."

"Within sight. We can still learn from a dead reaper, so if she tries to activate any technology, kill her." Savas peered behind him, but there was still no sign of pursuers. *Odd.* He glanced down; the reaper was still unconscious. Maybe it was dead already? He certainly wasn't going to check it for a pulse.

Suddenly, gunfire crackled from above. *Ambush.*

"Stamf? What is it?" Heart racing, he searched the horizon and cliff top as he tapped his headpiece. "Stamf, what's up there?"

The gunfire continued. *Shast. I need wings.*

He stopped the rover at the door and yelled at the radio, "Open up. I need to help Stamf." Did they expect him to use his remote and unload the reaper himself?

The door slid open with agonizing slowness. Three men in thin tunics covered with parkas and headpieces stood shivering and staring at the ground.

"What the hell? Just squint. We're dying out here," he shouted.

The men glanced up with terrified grimaces on their faces, and then back at the ground. Nahim, the bravest, rushed out, and the other two followed.

"Hurry. Get it restrained and drugged." He attempted to pull the hairy reaper from the back of the Rover, but its fur or boot was snagged on something, and he couldn't get it over the lip of the rover bed. The creature was taller than he was, and earlier, it had appeared feminine. He shivered. *If this is a female, how huge are their males?*

The three men ran to help him, slipping and nearly falling over from the frigid air. They had no proper layers or boots. Savas silently cursed the council for not listening to him; he had told them more clothing and weapons were needed as much as helicopters.

The reaper was still unconscious. He held his gun on it while they tightly wrapped it in a mesh net, immobilizing it. Then Nahim and Bjorn carried the thing inside. Erik fell over and had to be half-dragged in by the other two. *Pathetic.*

"Take Abdul's body. It'll give us another suit."

The men kept stopping to look for danger.

"Hurry," he shouted as he paced back and forth from the men to the door. "If you don't move faster, I'll shoot you myself."

As they lifted Abdul's body from the rover, his puffy parka got caught on a screw.

"Stop." But the precious orange parka split open to reveal its stuffing. *What the shast? Can't anything go right today?*

Inside the shaft compartment, Erik attempted to take off Abdul's insulated pants, but they were too stiff with ice to remove. He muttered apologies, shrugged, and wished them luck. Nahim slipped into Abdul's torn parka and tossed his gloves and hat to Bjorn.

Savas spun with Bjorn and Nahim at his heels and raced back to the cliff bottom.

*Climb up or stay by the door?* His radio clicked.

"Commander," Stamf yelled as he fired. "It's the wolverine things. They're backing us up to the edge. Three of them. Can you assist?"

"I can't see them. Draw them near the edge and I'll use the artillery."

"Not"—rapid fire—"an"—more gunfire—"option. They're forcing us off. Sir, we can't hold this. There's nowhere to go."

The animal screams and roars were almost as deafening as the gunfire. Savas knew he had no options, but he had to find one. He cast his gaze over the scattered gear, the underdressed Bjorn and Nahim, the rover, the guns, and the unused snowmobiles.

"Is Girak near you?" he yelled, hoping to be heard over the ruckus.

"Yes. But they're trying to separate us." Stamf's sounded panicked.

Savas could now see the tops of two human heads. *Shast. They really are near the edge.*

"Get together. I'm firing the gun behind them. If I distract them, can you get around? Make your way back the long way?" *If they could get around, maybe they could travel the switchback? Could they outrun such creatures?*

"But sir, the door."

Stamf was right about the door, but they did Northern Haven no good being slaughtered needlessly. Healthy humans were too precious. He needed other options, but what? He looked about for some way to save them.

A creature screamed as Stamf yelled triumphantly in the background. "One down. Girak, get over here." Stamf was now clearly visible near the cliff edge.

Savas aimed the gun and fired a volley of shots in the direction of the massive wolverines. Or at least what he hoped was their direction. He froze, straining to hear the results.

"It turned." Hope surged in Stamf's terse voice.

But instead of disappearing, the two heads got closer to the edge.

"Fire again," Stamf yelled over the radio, and then he said something to Girak that Savas couldn't understand.

Savas again fired a series of shots. Energy surged through him. He could do something. "What's happening up there?"

Girak stopped firing and crouched behind Stamf to attach his harness to descend.

"You bastard! Don't desert him," Savas said, moving the gun sight to Girak. *He needs to die.*

With Girak in his sights, Savas grew aware of Nahim and Bjorn yelling next to him.

He paused his trigger finger. *Killing him with witnesses won't look heroic.* He snorted, lowered his gun, and radioed Stamf, who was again firing at the giant wolverine-like monster. Both were now harrowingly close to the edge.

"What are you doing?" he asked, retraining the artillery on the now-visible monstrosity of nature. He fired as its huge claws raised an arms-length from Stamf's rifle tip. It lurched slightly and paused, turning to look down at Savas. Its muzzle was stained with blood from its wounds, but it appeared resolute.

He fired again.

"Is Girak safe?" Stamf yelled as he adjusted the rope around his own harness. His other arm struggled to balance and fire the rifle.

"This is suicide, Stamf. What are you doing?" Savas strained every muscle upward as if he could somehow will himself to reach up to the plateau and stop Stamf's heroics.

Still firmly rooted on the frozen field and determined to be helpful in some manner, Savas unleashed his fury through the gunfire. The wolverine continued pushing Stamf to the edge. Savas' heart pounded. He couldn't just watch Stamf die.

"Stamf!" Girak had miraculously gotten his harness and rope re-attached safely onto the pegs.

Would the protection pieces hold both their weight?

But Stamf had no time to descend safely.

He fired directly into the beast's face, screaming in fury. His foot slipped, and he fell to one knee. The creature's sword-like claws raked his headpiece, shredding it. The rifle dropped from Stamf's hands and fell, hitting rocks and ice on its long way to the bottom.

Fumbling, Stamf let himself over the edge, tumbling and crashing into the top rock wall above Girak. Girak lunged toward Stamf's tumbling body, missing his hand by centimeters.

"No!" Girak and Savas simultaneously yelled in horror as Stamf plummeted down the cliff, ropes unattached.

# Chapter 38

Earlier that same day, Peleguin-Rookery-By-The-Lake: Kahali

Kahali arose at dawn, aware that Rana and Balavati had left in the night to journey to where they'd Call. He'd hardly slept, and now that he was up, his mind teetered on the brink of absolute panic. No way was he lying around here by himself all day.

He needed a distraction, and he wanted to know the moment they safely returned. He was also sick of Sohana and his dads hovering around, watching him, and they would return from sunrise sit at any moment, expecting him to passively rest all day. He had to get out now.

He struggled into his clothing, snorting in self-mockery as he left ties untied and buttons unbuttoned. He'd be lucky to make it to the gathering hall without everything falling off him. Stepping out onto the path, he was stopped by Rana's little brother, Dala.

"Hi! I'm your friend today." He grinned up at him, showing the gap in his front teeth.

Kahali laughed. "Just today?"

Dala shrugged. "Rana told me to hang out with you but not to tell you she said that," he said, flashing a quick, toothy smile. "But you're too smart and would figure it out, so I'm telling you." He scrunched his face at Kahali's outfit. "Your clothes are all messed up. I know how to tie now. Want me to show you?"

"Yes, please." He took pride in his appearance and being appropriately clothed would be one less thing to stress about today. Silently thanking Rana, he waited while Dala fixed his clothing.

"See?" Dala motioned with pride at his work.

"Impressive. Thanks." Kahali wanted to hug him, but he was still a bit light-headed and feared leaning forward. He'd better avoid Bahujnana the healer, as well as his dads and Sohana, or he'd get sent straight back to his sleeping mat. "I'm going to the gathering hall. It overlooks everything, so when they come back, we'll see them. Want to join me?"

Dala's eyes lit up. "Think they'll give me a second breakfast?"

"Yup."

Starting up the path, Kahali doubted the wisdom of his plan. The walk uphill took forever, but with Dala running circles around him and shouting encouragements, they finally made it. Entering the gathering hall, Kahali stumbled to a back corner and plopped down onto an empty mat. As he caught his breath, Dala raced off to get them both food.

Kahali's stomach was too unsettled for him to eat, so instead, he downed cup after cup of tea. The little guy kept running outside to check for Rana and Balavati, and then would return with more tea. Dala's constant presence kept other well-wishers away, and in gratitude, Kahali talked the kid through some dance moves.

The sun had now been up for hours. "Can you check again?"

"Of course." Dala hopped off and soon skipped back in under the mat. "Still no sign of them. But"—he wriggled one of his new dance moves for dramatic effect—"I did see Eka and Tejas."

"Oh?"

"They were going down to the peleguin rookery to see the nests. I told them to keep their shields up, or they'd come back full of pecked holes." He giggled.

"That's not the nicest way to have put it, Dala." The wind whistled around the corners of the gathering hall. "I'm surprised they'd want to be out in this."

Dala shrugged. "That Tejas is pretty silly. He has baby birds in his cloak."

"I know. At the Spiral Ceremony, he was carrying around their eggs."

Dala giggled and leaned in. "Want to know a *secret*?"

"Sure."

"I think Rana likes Eka."

"Oh." Kahali fake pouted. "Not me?"

"She's *always* liked you, silly," he said, giggling and play-batting Kahali's chest. "You're her best friend."

"Right." He frowned and touched his cheek that Rana had kissed.

"I'm going to go let Maha know what we're doing, okay?"

Kahali nodded, grateful for the break.

"Don't worry. I'll be right back." Dala raced away.

Kahali slouched back against the wall. Somehow, his ghost arm throbbed with pain, and exhaustion threatened to topple him over. The blustery wind sweeping against the gathering hall's walls brought a steady stream of villagers in for tea and a midday snack, but no one bothered him. Lulled by the wind song as he reclined against the wall, he watched the tea drinkers through heavy lids.

Suddenly, all the Crowned Ones froze their movements.

Kahali sat up, his breath caught in his chest. He had never seen such an eerie group reaction. He extended his awareness to connect with the Crowned Ones' linkage, but his pounding heart scattered his focus. Unable to center within himself, he couldn't access the linkage. Concern rippled across their faces, magnifying his growing dread.

He jumped to his feet. "What?"

They stood and began disappearing, star beaming to another location.

"What's going on?" He waved his arm frantically at the one remaining Crowned One, Sunnia.

She turned toward him, her face echoing his own alarm.

He stumbled forward. "Are they okay? Rana and Balavati?"

"They are being hunted. Kalakanya requires help, and assistance has just left." She motioned to the near empty hall. "All will be fine."

"No, take me there," he shouted and hurried around the deserted tea bowls toward her. "Now."

She regarded him with an infuriating calmness. "Kahali, it's best if we Crowned Ones handle this. If you will allow—" She held up her hand, signaling for him to be quiet and let her mind speak with the others.

Kahali stared at her, then raced to the exit and looked down the hill. The common pathways had filled with star beings yelling for help and star beaming in and out of the village. All was not fine.

He turned back to Sunnia. "Rana? Where's Rana and Balavati?"

Her eyes cleared but the confusion remained, making Kahali's stomach fall. "Balavati just beamed back with Bahujnana. She's injured. Rana seems to be…missing?"

"What? Missing how?" Fear gripped his lungs and squeezed.

"I don't know, though…" She listened to other Crowned Ones in her mind.

But he was already out the door and running down the hill. It was his second day out of his hut, and his poor balance and weakness made him careen like a newborn salt deer. He hurried toward Bahujnana's hut, knowing the healer would take Balavati there first. She'd know what had happened to Rana.

Crashing through the hut's mat, he collided with Desna, Rana's adoptive maha. "S— sorry, Desna," he said, panting. "Rana?"

She motioned for him to be quiet and turned back to Balavati, who was seated on a mat.

Balavati, trembling and red-eyed, turned to Desna. "I'm sorry. I don't know how it happened." Tears poured down her cheeks. Her leg bled, but it was fully intact.

Desna, beside Kahali, stiffened at Balavati's apology. "What? What happened?"

In a flash, Kalakanya star beamed in between them, forcing Desna and Kahali to step backward. "Sorry to intrude. Balavati, tell me the last thing you remem—"

"You were there," Desna shouted. Kahali had never seen a Crowned One yell. Not like that. It was unnatural.

Kalakanya blanched. "I was dealing with the cave diggers."

"Cave diggers?" Desna's eyes grew wide.

Bahujnana remained quiet, but he looked up from cleaning the deep gash, a question in his eyes.

Didn't anyone else care about Rana? Pressure built in Kahali's chest and created the urge to scream and pound something.

"Where's Rana?" he shouted.

Balavati's fearful gaze flickered to him. "I don't know. She…she was just with me. And then she wasn't." She hugged her arms to her body and begged Kalakanya, "Can't you sense her?"

Kalakanya, judging by her deep stillness and unfocused gaze, was already searching the inner planes for Rana. Her brow furled in concentration. "I don't feel her…"

Outside, lamenting voices grew louder. Already positioned against the entrance wall, Kahali lifted the mat and glanced around. Crowned Ones were still star beaming in with the first responders, helping the injured flash back to the village. And returning with the dead.

Dead? Crowned Ones hunted?

Could Rana have survived when they hadn't? A new, terrible urge to lash back at the horrible Earth children gripped him. Sweat trickled down his back, and he quaked from the effort to control himself. Violent images washed over him, some from his own attack, others from his mind's own morbid creation. He sank to the floor, hands gripping his head.

*Kahali, she's okay. Breathe.*

Bahujnana had stopped working on Balavati and eyed him with concern. *Kalakanya will find her. Trust the One In All.*

He sucked in a shuddering breath and managed a jerked nod. Regaining control, he checked on Kalakanya's progress.

Kalakanya was no longer searching. "Balavati, what's the last thing you remember with Rana present?"

"We were holding our shields back to back. I was blocking the cave digger from attacking or being hunted, and Rana was protecting us. Then Rana's shield disappeared. I glanced around, and that huge metal creature with an Earth child on its back ran at us. It knocked me down…and… and…" Balavati began sobbing. "She was right there."

"She's not dead. I'd know. She must be unconscious. Otherwise, I'd be able to locate her," Kalakanya said, her face tight with concern.

*She's alive.* Kahali sagged against the wall with relief. *Rana's alive.*

"I don't know how I lost control... I'm sorry, Balavati." Kalakanya's face pinched, and her jade eyes welled with tears. "Desna..."

Desna's face remained stricken.

Kalakanya took in a deep shuddering breath, and her face hardened. "I've got to fix this."

"But—"

*Flash.*

Kahali blinked at the Crowned One's sudden departure, "If Rana's unconscious?"

Desna put a hand on his back. "Kalakanya has the best locator skills. If anyone can find her, she can." She sighed. "Though I wish she had taken me with her. She seems a bit *off* today." She narrowed her eyes at the spot where Kalakanya had been.

"So we just wait?" Trembling with effort, Kahali stood. The images had stopped, but the waves of emotional memories had leached any remaining vitality from his bones.

"Absolutely not," Desna answered. "A gathering is starting at the Lion Circle. We can send energetic assistance to Rana, even if we don't know where she is." She spun to go.

"Wait." Bahujnana motioned with his hand for her to stop. "We need all the information to make the best decisions. Balavati, what about the cave diggers?" He had finished re-growing new pink skin around her gash and now opened a clay jar of herbal ointment. It was the same stuff Kahali had been using daily on his arm. "Did they want Rana and Digga?"

Balavati shook her head. "Rana and I were returning the body when a bunch of cave diggers surrounded and attacked us. But not *just* us. The Earth children, too."

Desna furrowed her brow. "Cave diggers don't hunt in groups. Did they listen to Rana? Like Digga has?"

"No, they attacked us all. We were attacked from all sides." Balavati stifled a sob.

"Why didn't Kalakanya Call for help right away? You were in danger, and you're not even Crowned!" Desna's eyes flashed with anger.

Kahali had never seen a Crowned One's mood fluctuate so dramatically. Was his own rage contagious? Desna caught his gaze, sighed, and returned to normal. Still, her brief fury had unsettled him. Everything was different since he'd contacted the Earth children.

Bahujnana cleared his throat. "I suspect there's a reason Kalakanya reacted as she did. Cave diggers don't travel in packs. There must have been a carcass nearby, or the Earth children were carrying food…"

Desna's face softened and took on a sacred quality. "One In All, keep Rana safe."

Everyone murmured their agreement.

It wasn't enough. "We should go look for her," he suggested. "Now."

"I know you're willing to do anything in your power, Kahali, but you're barely standing. Isn't this only your second day out and about?" Bahujnana's warm smile was edged with the sternness of an experienced healer used to being obeyed.

Desna rested a hand on Kahali's shoulder. "Rana wouldn't want any of you endangering yourselves on her behalf. We need more information." For a long moment, she stared in the direction of the Earth children's den and then gave him a weak smile. "If anyone can get her back safely, it's Kalakanya. As for us, let us go to the Lion's Circle and send some healing and protection to Rana."

Kahali shot Balavati a questioning look, hoping she'd join his dissent. She glanced between him and Desna, and then her gaze dropped down to her leg. "I think maybe the Crowned Ones should handle this."

"But the prophecy—"

"Did not say you should mindlessly endanger yourselves." Desna gave him a warning look.

"Fine." Kahali threw back the mat and began staggering toward the Lion Circle. The world seemed to tip on end, spinning. He made it only a few steps before he tripped and fell.

Bahujnana pulled him up and turned him toward his hut. "Kahali, you need rest. Let's get you home."

"But…" He gave up. He was in no shape to mount a search party.

Leaning on Bahujnana, he staggered past sobbing neighbors. From snatches of conversation, he gleaned the full scope of destruction. Crowned Ones had been hunted as they star beamed to assist Rana and the others. After materializing, they hadn't had time to put up a shield.

Crowned Ones lived for centuries. To have this many killed together, on one day, in one brutal attack, was unthinkable. He was so overcome that he almost missed the star being with ridiculously cropped black hair running from home to home, inquiring after Rana. Tea drinkers this morning had mentioned the unusual haircut of one of the visiting star beings.

Maybe it was Eka's friend? Which would mean Eka was still here as well. Kahali stood a little straighter, the seed of an idea growing within him.

"Tejas?" he shouted.

Miraculously, the star being heard him over the din and spun around. It *was* Tejas. Kahali risked letting go of Bahujnana's waist to wave.

Recognition lit the guy's round face, and he hurried through the crowd toward them.

Kahali turned to the healer. "Thank you. He can take me home. I'm sure you have others to attend to."

"Yes. Take care of yourself. I'm serious." Bahujnana gave him a knowing nod. Then, patting his good shoulder, he hurried off as Tejas ran over.

"Ka— Kahali, right?" Panting, Tejas wiped sweat from his brow.

He nodded.

"Yes. Thank the One In All I found you." Tejas grabbed him in a sideways bear hug, making Kahali sway. The big guy pulled back and steadied him. "Sorry." His eyes looked as wild as a cornered hare. "Where's Rana? No one's telling me. I have to find her for Eka."

*Find her for Eka?* As if Eka owned her. "Why isn't he looking for himself?"

"He…he… Oh, I don't know." Tejas pulled at his chopped hair and looked about as if the answer floated in the chaos around them.

To their left, Kahali's father, Luminary Vadin, star beamed in holding another limp Crowned One. In his haste to begin healing, his father ran into a nearby hut, missing Kahali completely. Were Sohana and his maha

304

safe?

*What's wrong with me that I haven't even worried for them?*

Beside him, Tejas continued. "...even the Crowned Ones can't explain it. Something happened to him. Tell me where she is, so he'll live. Hurry."

"Live?" Kahali reached for Tejas' shoulder as the world tilted again. It was grab the giant or fall on his face.

Tejas steadied him. "You don't look that good, either. Yes, *live.* Is she okay? I have to get back to him."

Kahali blinked. Could he really do this? Partner with Eka and his friend? The full ramifications of his idea hit him. If Eka saved Rana, he'd be her hero.

Kahali's weakness prevented him from helping Rana himself. The obvious choice was to ask Eka for help, but that seemed like admitting he was broken. He glanced at his empty sleeve. He'd lost his arm, but not his common sense. Rana needed him, and if that meant letting Eka get all the glory, so be it.

"She's missing. Kalakanya says she must be unconscious, because even she can't locate her. But she's still alive." He pushed away his panic that things may have changed since Kalakanya's last scan. He knew how quickly the Earth children could kill.

At his words, relief swept across Tejas' face. "Okay, good. That might be enough to save him."

"From what?" Nausea rippled through Kahali's gut. What else was going on besides the hunting? The world tipped the other way.

"I can't explain," Tejas' huge arms wrapped around Kahali, supporting him. "You'll have to see him."

Kahali swallowed back the nausea and nodded. "Okay. Help me get home. Then I'll tell you and Eka everything, including my wild idea."

# Chapter 39

*orthern Haven's Door: Commander Kern Savas*

N "Staaaamf!" Savas lunged forward, possessed with the ridiculous urge to try to catch him as he fell down the cliffside past Girak.

Stamf's descent suddenly stopped, and he hovered in the air. *He's floating.* Relief, and then terror gripped Savas. *They're here.* He spun, gun at the ready.

Behind him, a golden bubble rippled. A lone reaper stood her ground, a fierce expression on her fake, humanoid face.

*What does it take to kill these things?* He fumbled momentarily to reload the artillery; he was done with his puny gun.

He blasted the bubble. It flickered, then re-stabilized. "Damn you—" he shouted. Their weapons were useless against the aliens' tech.

The untrained men beside Savas screamed something to him, but he ignored them. Warning Northern Haven of the reaper outside the door took priority.

"Base, they're here." Would the old nuclear weapons designed to protect Northern Haven from the Undescended work? Otherwise, they might as well throw rocks and clubs at these reapers.

He risked a glance up to Girak and Stamf. His heart stopped. "Where's Stamf?" He shouted to the two men besides him.

"She let him drop. When you shot at her. We tried to get your attention—"

"What?" Savas' spotted the misshapen body and crumpled rope at the

306

cliff base. The surrounding pandemonium faded. His vision narrowed to the motionless orange parka. *No.*

He glared back up where Girak climbed downward. Alone. He glanced back at the human on the ground. No one could survive such a drop...

His head pounded. He turned back to the reaper, who now wore a mask of gravity.

"You killed him!" He unleashed a fury of shots, trying to find a weak point, or at least to wear down her protective forcefield. The head pounding got worse. He fell to his knees, almost dropping the artillery. His men stood unmoving, but not gasping in pain as he was.

*She's messing with us.* Only Girak continued to climb down despite the chaos.

Girak reached the bottom, tore off his ropes, and ran to Stamf. Savas froze, hoping for a miracle.

After opening Stamf's hood, Girak moaned, "Noooo."

Savas' knees threatened to buckle under him. *Not Stamf. Anyone but him...*

A moment later, Girak stood, turned to the reaper, and slowly put down his weapon.

"No..." he said, but it was too low for Girak to hear. Wooziness made standing an impossibility. *What is she doing to me?*

Girak slowly walked forward, arms in front, palms up. *He's surrendering, the bastard.*

Savas tried to maneuver his arms to shoot near Girak. Shots like that had before snapped Bleu out of his reaper trance, but the reaper glanced in Savas' direction and he was instantly reduced to a weakened, trembling mess. Hatred for them surged through every cell of his body.

*Where is she?* The reaper's voice pounded through the airwaves.

He hadn't heard it through his ears. It had vibrated within his head.

"Where is who?" Girak asked with complete innocence.

*Didn't he know they had captured one? Hadn't Stamf told him before he...* Commander Savas' mind was sluggish. *The reaper's controlling me...knows I'm the one in charge.*

307

The reaper stared at Girak. *Where is Rana? You stole her. We come in peace. Return her now.*

"Come in peace, my ass." Fury roared through Savas' crippled body. He struggled to his feet.

"We did?" Girak turned his head to Savas. "We got one of them? When?"

"If you ever want to see your hairy friend again, leave our door now." He managed to radio base. "You hearing this?"

"Hearing what?" The voice from the control room sounded confused.

*If I sense any injury to her, I will be pressed to enter your den forcibly.* Her message vibrated inside Savas' head like a drill.

"You all hear her?" Savas turned toward his extra two men.

They nodded, their faces masks of terror.

*We want to help you. We come in peace. She must be returned to us safely. We are not the enemy.*

The more she spoke into his mind, the worse Savas' head pounded. He couldn't maintain eye contact. His eyes squeezed shut as if to shut out the sharp bolts of pain pulsing through his head.

"Not the enemy? I suppose you killed Stamf and Abdul in peace?" Through his pain, Savas barely heard the control room rumbling in his headpiece that they could get the door open in a moment, and to start backing nearer to it.

"Behind me, men." It came out hoarse, pathetic.

Their footsteps told him they were following his orders. Grunting, he forced his eyes open.

Girak stalled, turning back to the reaper. He was holding his heart, and Savas hoped briefly that the reaper was giving the fool a heart attack. Instead, Girak nodded in a trancelike manner, then returned to Stamf. Grabbing him under the arms, Girak dragged the body behind his commander.

They backed up. A moment later, the door opened with a clank of metal.

"Get...in."

He paused until they were all in, maintaining his impotent gun's sighting on the reaper until the last moment. As the door began closing, he limped in, barely squeezing through the opening.

They descended to their deep home—Commander Savas, his three surviving men, and Stamf's crumpled body. As they travelled closer and closer, the hiss of disinfectant nanotech came from all sides, clearing them from any possible Surface pathogens.

He stared at the floor, his gaze swimming as it skirted Stamf's outline. Sucking in breaths, he strove to understand, but nothing made sense except his burning fury and the heart-wrenching pain of the wasted boy before him.

He closed his eyes, willing himself to be strong…to save those still alive…

But why Stamf?

How had he lost everyone but Girak?

Girak knelt beside Stamf and reached out to do something, but it was too late. He'd fallen too far. His neck appeared broken, and blood poured from his mouth and ears.

"Get away from him." Savas pointed his rifle at Josefina's killer.

Girak jerked upward, startled, and backed away.

Savas glared as he stood over Stamf and guarded his body, his head still pounding.

He'd never told Stamf he was his son, and now it was too late. Stamf lay dead because he'd saved useless Girak. If only he'd chosen to save himself, he could have lived to help Savas save all of Northern Haven. Standing guard was the one final gift he could still give him.

There was no way he'd allow a Deplorable to touch his son.

# Chapter 40

Peleguin-Rookery-By-The-Lake: Kahali

"The One In All brings Love."

The distant deep voice reached Kahali inside his hut, but grogginess still claimed him.

"The One In All brings Love. Kahali? You still in there?"

His bleary eyes snapped open, and reality crashed in. Rana was missing. He had been deposited on his furs by Tejas, who'd then ran off to get Eka.

"Kahali? I'm coming in." The green mat was pushed up, and Tejas' head and shoulders appeared. "Can we come in?"

He nodded and sat up. Tejas was being annoyingly formal. None of his friends would have made such a big deal out of entering. Of course, he was from another village and didn't know how informally his fathers, Luminary Vadin and Kagni, ran their hut.

His brief sleep had cleared his head enough to ask, "Did they find her?"

"Not yet." Tejas came in, and then two tall Crowned Ones led Eka in.

Kahali sat up straighter. He had never seen these two identical Crowned Ones before with their neatly braided white hair. They had the same dark skin as Eka with the same reddish undertone. They also had the same nose and dark, almost black eyes.

Kahali asked, "Tejas? What's going on?"

In silence, the four guys found spots opposite him. And as Eka sat, Kahali gasped. Eka now had a wide white streak of hair hanging from his left brow. It was the color of the Crowned Ones', but Crowning was never a partial affair. In addition, Crowned Ones glowed with vigor, and Eka was pallid and sweaty.

"Eka? Are you all right?" He looked from Eka to the others.

"I told you you'd have to see it to understand." Tejas rubbed Eka's back supportively. "We were watching the peleguins, and suddenly, he started to, like, spark and disappear. I had to grab on and keep him from star beaming."

"But that's fatal if you're not Crowned." Kahali raised an eyebrow in Eka's direction. Was he suicidal?

"I couldn't control it," Eka said, gasping with effort. "I knew...she needed me, and then...it happened. A glaring light filled my vision... then blackness, and then Tejas grabbed my arm. I couldn't control it. I knew something was wrong, but I couldn't get to her."

Kahali knew he was scowling in horror, and yes, probably jealousy. He glanced from Eka to the two Crowned Ones on either side of the white-striped fool and shivered.

"I Called his older brothers for help," Tejas explained, motioning to the identical Crowned Ones. "I couldn't prevent him from star beaming by myself, and I had no idea what to do." He looked down. "I thought he was imagining Rana being in trouble, but when Jagrav and Asav star beamed us back here... Well, we found everything in chaos."

Kahali swallowed. He glanced down at himself, still covered in sleeping furs, and then at his stump. Across from him sat Eka with his heroically-streaked crown and his three supporters.

He swallowed again. "Ah...nice to meet you, Jagrav and Asav." He didn't even convince himself that he meant it.

"Sorry to burst in on your rest, Kahali." Jagrav or Asav said. Kahali didn't know which was which. "Your heroism in meeting the Earth's children has travelled far. Are you up to sharing what you've heard about Rana?"

Heroism? Was he serious? Kahali felt anything but a hero under his furs while his fellow villagers were dying. "Of course."

He related everything he had heard in Bahujnana's hut. When he got to Kalakanya insisting that Rana was still alive but unconscious, hope lit Eka's eyes. It twisted Kahali's gut, but he remained resolute in making a pact with him. Together, they might be able to do something. Find her. Maybe.

"We should go offer to help. Eka, are you okay now?" the other twin asked.

Eka nodded. "Thanks for coming. You saved my life."

"Yes, no more chasing after the one you love, okay?" The first twin laughed and slapped his younger brother on the shoulder. "She'll be fine."

Both of Asav's and Jagrav's faces tightened, and then they rose.

One of them said, "The Crowned Ones just called a meeting. We'll go get information. Tejas, if our brother gives you any more trouble, give us a holler, and we'll keep him in his place." They grinned identical grins.

*The one you love.* Unclenching his hands, Kahali managed the traditional salutation before they exited. He turned to face Eka and Tejas.

Tejas seemed like he had something to say, but he remained silent until the twins were gone and then gave Kahali a weak, hopeful smile. "So, what's your idea?"

Kahali stared at Eka, assessing him. Eka met his gaze with calmness. Or maybe exhaustion.

"The One In All brings Love."

Balavati burst through the green mat covering the door. "Kahali, I hope you're not mad. Maybe you were right—"

Her eyes widened at the presence of Tejas and Eka. "Oh." She looked back and forth between Kahali and Eka. "This is...*interesting.* Should I leave?"

"No. Sit down." Kahali patted the mat next to him.

She shook her head. "I can't hold still." She worked her lower lip with her teeth. "Kalakanya just returned. The Earth children took Rana into their lair."

Tejas' mouth dropped open in shock.

"No," Eka whispered.

"Oneness help her." Kahali shrank into himself. What would those creatures do to her? He blinked, not willing to cry in front of Tejas and Eka. "When are they leaving to get her?"

"They're not." Balavati flopped down on the mat.

"What?" all three exclaimed in unison.

"Not right now, anyway. They want everyone to gather at the Lion Circle to send her energetic help and decide what to do."

Kahali met Eka's gaze. They both stood as one.

"Then we better go change their minds," Eka said.

"Because that's not enough to keep her alive," Kahali finished. "I know them."

# Chapter 41

*orthern Haven: Commander Kern Savas*

As Savas, hampered by the bulkiness of his Surface gear, clomped through the chaotic hallways, rage flushed through every muscle fiber of his being. If Northern Haven's mission had stayed true to SHAST's original mission, they'd be prepared. Now, humanity's last bastion was at risk of being destroyed by a far superior force.

Unarmed and untrained citizens scrambled through the corridors for anything weapon-like to defend themselves—dinner knives, power tools, and even a broken chair. But he'd seen the uselessness of their guns against this alien tech. They were screwed.

If the council had just once listened to his warnings to be better prepared, Northern Haven would never be in this weak position. What was the use of being the council's strategist if they didn't take his advice?

He shoved past Councilor Bergstrom, who paced the corridor while shouting orders that made no sense with his whiny, high-pitched, panicked voice.

Savas spun in fury. "Bergstrom, stop giving our few guns to untrained people. Gather them back and bring them to me."

"But...but..." Bergstrom's mouth worked like that of an eyeless fish gasping for air.

"They'll shoot each other. Bring me the guns and the best guys you can find. I'll give them a quick lesson." *Not that it'll do any good against their shields.*

Bergstrom gasped at him, wide-eyed.

"Now, you fool!" He had little right to order a councilman, but he had even less patience.

Bergstrom nodded and hurried off into the crowd that had gathered defensively in the halls between the elevator shaft and the heart of Northern Haven. *How did humanity's best end up so useless?*

Savas continued shoving through the amassed group to the room where they held the prisoner. Its accomplice had ended his son's life, and *someone* had to pay. With an attack by these reapers hanging over his head, he couldn't even properly care for Stamf's body. He'd had to leave that up to Nahim.

If that reaper wanted her freak friend back, no problem. He'd see how she liked having a body returned to *her*. As soon as the medical team completed their examination, it was a goner.

He tossed his headpiece, gloves, bulky pants, and parka on a table outside the door and reattached his gun and holster to his waist. Picking up Stamf's rifle, he slipped the strap over his back and pushed away the image of Stamf's crumpled body at the base of the cliff.

*Focus,* he reprimanded himself. *Learn how the reapers tick and defeat the bastards.*

Excited to see what they had discovered about the reaper, he shoved open the door. "Someone's been busy," he said to a guard, grinning at the makeshift reaper lab that had been hastily assembled. The large rectangular room with the corners sectioned off for various purposes teemed with equipment and staff.

In the open center section, the clustered medical staff blocked his view of the reaper, still bundled and netted on a gurney. As eager as he was to see what they'd found, he paused to yank off his heavy boots and ordered a man to retrieve his real shoes. If the reapers flashed into Northern Haven, he'd maneuver more quickly in shoes.

The suite hummed with the sounds of medical equipment and computers and stank of a rancid musky odor that must be the reaper. To his right stood large medical scanners and rolling lab tables holding equipment, with built in cabinets underneath.

To his left the front and back corners were subdivided into a jail-like room and a computer room. The prisoner cell resembled something from an old Surface movie with cowboys and horses. Apparently, this area had been built to restrain individuals, but he'd never seen it before. Odd, because they never imprisoned people, except Deplorables, who remained in their own modules.

He swiped the sweat from his brow, combed back his hair with his fingers, and strode up to the others. He gave a perfunctory bow to Prime Minister Pridbor and nodded to Dr. Medicci and the rest of the medical team.

"What have you found?" His skin crawled at knowing that thing was in the same room. Its physical proximity made him light-headed, as if it oozed a toxic energy.

"Commander. We're just about to put the reaper through a scanner. See what it is on the inside. Machines can't be lulled."

"It's still unconscious?"

Savas was still concerned about controlling the alien once it awoke. His gaze wandered to the inert reaper, and in his mind's eye he again saw Stamf's crumpled body. Hatred coursed through his innards, and he tensed in frustration of having to stand around waiting for test results. His fellow humans were remarkably clinical and relaxed in their attitude, but they hadn't seen these things in action.

"Yes, still unconscious. About time we get some luck. They're preparing dart guns with some pretty powerful stuff." Prime Minister Pridbor motioned to the doctors conferring with the armed guards.

"It has shielding. You won't be able to get a shot."

His gaze followed the reaper's gurney as the medical staff rolled it toward the large scanner. Two men gingerly lifted it in and then sprang back. The machine clicked on.

Savas forced himself to breathe. As much as he wanted to know what the creature was, he had seen what they could do with energy. He took a step backward, half expecting the machine to blow up as his hands tightened on Stamf's rifle. Somehow, it had survived in working order. He had wanted to get the rifle, but not like this.

Never like this. He ignored the sting in his eyes. He had the rest of humanity to save.

"How long will this take?" He motioned to the scanner, but his gaze was on the medical team with the tranquilizer.

"Not long, maybe ten minutes."

"Excuse me for a moment, Prime Minister." Savas turned from him to approach the medical staff and asked, "If we put the creature in that cell there, and she puts up her light shield, how are you planning to get her with a dart gun?"

*Damn fools. How do doctors not have more intelligence than that?*

"Commander Savas." Dr. Medicci nodded deferentially. "We plan on removing the shielding device before we let her gain consciousness. The scanner should tell us the location of any metal devices."

Savas turned and scowled at the scanner. "You didn't see them in action. I'm not sure that will work. What if..." His mind raced back to the size of their smallest bubble. "What if you hide darts in the cell with it, very close, maybe in the floor? How quickly could we do that?"

"Sir? I'm not sure I follow. The scanner will locate its technology. What's your concern?" Dr. Medicci scowled at him.

"And if it doesn't? They've continued to outsmart us. Once she's scanned, get her in the cell, and then if she activates a shield or tries anything, the darts will be close enough to be inside her shield. We could fire them remotely from here. See?" He motioned to the computer control panel behind the blast door.

The medical staff looked at each other, clearly impressed.

"We need engineering immediately. I'll get them." The younger medic ran from the room.

"What's the status on our weapons, Prime Minister? Is the nuclear option viable if we don't find an exploitable weakness?"

"It's viable, but delayed. Engineering needs twenty-four to forty-eight hours. In the meantime, we are exploring other options—biological weaknesses, how to counteract their technology, other ways of wiping the

Surface clean." Pridbor's watery eyes gleamed at the possibilities.

Savas stepped aside as the summoned engineers rushed into the room. "If we have enough time, Prime Minister. But if the reapers attack now, our weapons are useless. Humanity will be done."

Dr. Medicci tapped impatiently on the computer screen as an image formed. His eyes widened in alarm. "What the hell is that?"

The other medical staff leaned in, horrified.

Savas strained to see over the closest doctor.

"Is that two spinal cords?" Savas asked, shuddering.

"Yes. Or...or we caught two of them. But the skulls are totally different." Dr. Medicci, the lead doctor, was rotating the 3-D image on screen to view it from different angles. "It's like two beings..."

"Are they connected? Symbiotic or something?" Savas' innards recoiled at the grotesque image on the screen. "It's a monstrosity."

"I can't tell if they're connected. The one skull looks similar to humanoid ones, but the forehead is different and the eye sockets are larger. It's longer, too... The other one looks animal-like." The doctor stood to position his widened eyes closer to the screen. "Wow..."

"Where's the shielding device? The weapons? She could awake any moment." *They have no idea how dangerous this thing is.*

"It's... impossible." Dr. Medicci flipped through the images, lining them up on the large screen. Without taking his eyes off the screen, he asked his colleagues, "Do you see any metal? Anything not a part of its body?" His hand controlling the computer trembled.

"What do you mean? It must have a shielding device. The reaper was shielding when I shot her. When I picked her up, nothing dropped, so the shielding device must still be in her possession." Savas mentally reviewed the abduction. The snow in the area was packed from the rover tracks and footsteps. Any dropped tech would have been obvious. She hadn't dropped anything.

The guard within the scanning room yelped. "It moved," the guard said, shuddering. "It's waking up."

Savas raced to the scanner, his rifle raised to his shoulder.

"Get it out and into the cell. Now." His heart thudded. He rechecked his gun. *We should simply shoot and dissect it.*

"Wait." Dr. Medicci ran over, holding a large syringe of silvery liquid. "Just as a backup…"

He plunged the syringe into what appeared to be the reaper's shoulder. It was hard to tell under all the fur, and simply getting near it made one feel nearly drunk. Dr. Medicci ran back, trembling. The guards rushed forward to move the alien.

"What will that do?" Savas narrowed his eyes at the doctor.

"I'm hoping it may protect us from their mind control. I mixed it up when I heard you had caught one and were bringing it here." Dr. Medicci's eyes flashed with excitement over experimenting on the reaper.

Savas nodded, trying to hide his doubt. *We've never dealt with anything like reapers before.* He grimaced as the team gingerly moved it into the cell. He glanced at the floor. Small holes had already been made for the darts.

"Are the darts in there?" Savas asked, impressed.

"Yes, but we're still working on the remote's programming. We need a few more minutes." The engineers scuttled out of the cell.

Savas stood, every muscle poised for immediate action. His breath shallowed as his index finger neared the trigger.

The thing was lowered onto the bench in the cell. The guards hurriedly backed out, grabbing for their guns.

The door clanked shut. There was no more noise except for the murmuring doctors who continued to scan the images, looking for the hidden tools. From their unhappy murmurs, they weren't having much luck.

"Where's my team?" Now that the reaper was contained in the cell, Savas needed to organize this room and the mess of citizens running through the halls.

"You mean Girak and Zach?" Prime Minister Pridbor asked.

Savas froze, then smiled.

"Of course." He stood straighter, not wanting Pridbor to know how lost he was with no men to command. "Though I also assumed I'd be in charge of defending the door. Excuse my judgment, sir, but Councilor Bergstrom seems a bit unsuitable for that task."

Prime Minister Pridbor sneered. "Yes, from the sounds of things, he is out of his league. You should take charge, but let's get you the other two trained people to assist."

Pridbor spoke to a guard, who left and returned moments later. "Zach will be here in a moment, sir," the guard informed him. "He still wants nothing to do with the Surface after the second expedition, but he knows this is an all-hands-needed situation. And Girak was just behind me..." The guard turned to look back into the hallway.

The Deplorable entered like he was coming into the dining hall for a casual meal, gun holstered, arms dangling loosely. Hatred roiled Savas' stomach.

Savas gave the guard a slight nod and barked, "Girak."

The man jumped slightly, tearing his gaze from the bundle in the cell, and Savas smirked.

"Yes, sir?"

"What did she say to you out there? The other reaper?"

Girak sniffed and Savas ground his teeth in frustration. *Has the damn fool been crying again?*

"We all heard or sensed her." Girak shrugged. "She simply wants her"—he pointed toward the cell—"back safely. She said she'll break in if we hurt her."

The prime minister frowned and shot Savas a concerned look, and the guards glanced nervously between Girak and their commander.

But Savas smiled. "And did you believe the reaper, Girak? That she comes in peace? Can bust in here? You believe all that?"

Girak remained silent but returned his commander's gaze.

"Well?" Savas glared at the redheaded jackass. How had they ever let him be an educator?

"Our weapons were useless against her, but she let us live. When Europeans first met the natives of other lands, their hatred of people that were different caused centuries of violence," Girak replied, daring to lecture him. "The reapers aren't human, but—"

"But *we're* the natives on this planet. I'm not letting us be devastated like they were, superior technology or not."

"We found technology?" The fool's eyes lit with excitement.

*That damned innocence.*

"They're working on it," Savas said.

One of the doctors stood up and threw his hands in the air. Girak observed the medical staff and raised an amused eyebrow. "Looks like it's going well." He returned his gaze to Savas. "You wanted me for?"

"I know she told you something, and I'm still your Commander. What. Did. She. Say?" he demanded.

The Deplorable's expression turned stony and he remained silent.

"Girak," Pridbor said, "may I remind you that you agreed that if we let you out of your module, you would obey your Commander?"

The bastard looked away and then said, "She told me she was sorry Stamf fell. She couldn't hold him while...while *we* fired on her. That's it."

"And you believed her?" Savas had fired on the reaper. *The coward's blaming me for Stamf's death?* Blood pounded in his head.

"I have no reason not to believe her." Girak glanced from the furry reaper to the guards. "I'm...undecided."

"Maybe you should go speak to Abdul and Stamf about that. Oh, I forgot. They were killed by the reapers. Dead, Girak. Like Josefina."

At the mention of his wife, the useless fool closed his eyes.

Fury over Girak's murderous neglect overcame him. *Why am I always stuck with the consequences of others' stupidity?* He'd sworn to protect them all, but Girak took Josefina and the council left him defending humanity with less than a dozen guns.

He shoved Girak against the wall. "Are you going to continue making choices that cost lives? Whose side are you on, anyway?"

Girak opened his eyes and glared. "Humanity's."

"Then go guard the entrance to this medical suite," Savas said, pointing to the door. "We need men with more clarity in here."

# Chapter 42

*nknown Location: Rana*

Unknown Location: Rana

Rana sensed the pain first. Her head throbbed, the air burnt her nose, and she was sweating. Something was horribly wrong. She opened her eyes to dim grayness and buzzing. *Falling stars! Where am I?*

Instinct told her not to move. As her eyes adjusted to the gray light, she became aware of the lack of movement on her chest. *Digga?*

No response.

Was the pup still there? She drew in a quick breath in panic but remained still, following her intuition. At the sound of her sharp breath, her surroundings burst to life.

Strange clicking and gruff yelling came from her side. A bright light suddenly shone on her from above.

The sudden brightness made no sense. *Someone's controlling the sun?* She tried to remember back. She and Balavati had been Calling when the Earth's children had shown up and...

Fear took over and she twisted her neck toward the unknown clicks and yells. She stared, confused at the sight. Everything appeared dull in the piercing, gray light.

Strange, thick lines surrounded her, separating her from the Earth's children. She attempted to wiggle, but something wrapped her in a death grip. One of the creatures pointed a stick at her and gave a cruel snarl.

*Crowned Ones, help.* Rana sent the Call in panic. This time, unlike her experience in the cave digger's cave, they heard her. They must have been searching.

A wave of wellbeing washed over her as they mind spoke. *Keep your shield up. Try to communicate. Don't scare them. What do they want?*

She hadn't put up her shield. Why hadn't she? She inhaled, preparing to expand her energy when she realized her body didn't want a shield despite it seeming the logical step to protect herself.

She was about to be hunted, yet for some reason, her intuition warned her not to create one. She paused. They could have shot her already yet hadn't. What should she do?

She gave them a weak smile.

They didn't respond.

She wished she could sit up, but she was trapped in this net thing.

*Digga?*

No response. Was the pup still tied to her chest, or had they removed her? *If they hurt her...*

Rana stopped herself. Anger would get herself hunted. She breathed deeply, trying to focus on the One In All. The energy here was sluggish, heavy, and fearful. That was a place to start. She had no idea how to start a conversation with children who wanted to hunt her. She couldn't fathom their conflicting and chaotic emotions. But she did know how to deal with energy.

If they were childlike, maybe she could teach them to trust her, like she'd taught Digga. She focused on everything she loved, on her appreciation of all beings. She filled the dank box that enclosed them all with love.

At first, nothing happened. Then a few of them relaxed, their fire sticks still raised but not gripped quite as tightly. She closed her eyes and asked her village to help her stay centered. She sensed them now, gathered at the Lion Circle. They responded with waves of love so uplifting that she literally began to rise off the hard thing she was lying on.

Again, her surroundings exploded with yells and clicks. She immediately dropped.

*What happened, Rana?*

*Not so much at once. It scares them.* These were indeed peculiar beings.

How could love be scary?

She'd have to strike a balance—generate enough love to allow them to relax and hopefully not hunt her, though not enough to scare them.

She related this to the Crowned Ones, who were equally perplexed but followed her lead. She tried again.

This time, it took longer for them to allow the love in and to settle down. After a while, only the one with the longest hunting stick remained tense and reactive as if he was impenetrable to love, walled off from it as if love were the enemy.

He still boiled with fury and fear, and when she met his icy gaze with love, his face tightened even more. *He enjoys hunting more than receiving love?* She never would have guessed such a creature existed.

Time passed. By now the sun must have set, and perhaps the moon as well. *How do they stay orientated when they can't see the sky?*

Fatigue crushed her spirit, her limbs had long ago cramped from lack of movement, and her throat burned from the hot, dry air. The children had shifted so that, while two always pointed their sticks in between the metal bars, the others had their sticks down. It was progress, but that one that was walled off from love still wanted her dead, his fury and disgust nearly smothering her. She had never experienced such a horrid feeling. Even though he was on the other side of the bars, his aimed fury caused physical pain.

Running this much energy without sustenance left her drained. When her stomach growled, all the hunting sticks swung in her direction. Did they fear she'd eat them? Out of tiredness, she temporarily lost her connection to the Crowned Ones. Fear overtook her and affected every being within the boxed space. They all grabbed their hunting sticks and stared at her as if she was a rabid beast.

She yearned for the refreshing coolness of air blessed by the sun and stars. Why had they chosen to live in boxes? Once, the side of the box that extended beyond her bars had opened, and she yearned to see the sky outside. But outside this box was another box.

They had themselves completely boxed in, blocking the beauty around them. So strange. Did they fear their connection to other life? Were they even aware of the possibilities of connection? Of true awareness?

Confused, exhausted, and weakened by the lack of food and water, she drifted in and out of sleep. *I can't do this forever. Please One In All, help me.* She feared she'd fall asleep, have a nightmare, and scare the children. Then they'd hunt her like Kahali...

She was jerked awake by one of the dark-haired children poking her with his hunting stick. His gaze met hers as she struggled to full alertness. He held out an object, as if offering it to her.

*I can't move.* She projected this thought and guessed by his sudden shocked face that he had perceived her mind talk. Did he understand?

The dark-haired one turned to the others and made harsh noises with his throat. Rana strained to understand what was happening. The guy nearest her was asking a question of the one that wanted to hunt her—The Walled One—as Rana had begun to think of the anger–filled creature.

The Walled One laughed, then came closer as if to threaten her. She forced herself to meet his gaze. His hatred pierced her like a dagger, and in response she contracted her energy into herself to avoid the pain. Wait, she had to stop this. She couldn't allow him to change who she was, to make her energy literally smaller.

Rana allowed the love of her village to pulse through her. The Walled One stopped advancing toward her as if hitting an invisible force. She resisted, giving him an amused smile. The Walled One really couldn't tolerate love. What was wrong with him? He turned toward the other dark-haired one next to her and grunted something.

The dark-haired one standing over her took the object he had been handing her, did something to the end of it, and then lowered it to her face.

Rana met his gaze. She fought her mind's impulse to put up her shield. She sensed he was trying to help, but she couldn't understand what he was planning. His mind was too clouded with fear to read.

He squeezed the object, and wetness squirted against Rana's mouth. Water. She grinned in relief, snorting the water from her nose. After freezing at her sudden facial change, he returned the smile. Slowly, he lowered the object again and squeezed.

This time she was ready and drank eagerly, nearly gagging on its bitterness. Still, she drank till the container was empty. The man backed away.

*Thank you,* she mind spoke to him.

He nodded his head. He had heard her! She had found the correct vibration and had connected. Now she'd be able to understand them.

"Is she telling you to do something? Don't let her control you." The Walled One came closer, hunting stick raised.

Despite the closeness of The Walled One, energy seeped back into her, either from her new-found hope or the bitter water. She considered struggling into a seated position, but the risk of upsetting the children's chaotic emotional systems was too great. She even ignored the hunting stick pointed at her. There was little she could do if they decided to kill her.

The Walled One barked some commands, and one of them scurried from the room. Then he turned to the water-bearer and tried to increase his fear.

*No, he's warning him about me. He thinks I'm a...* Rana struggled to understand the foreign concept. *One who kills? One who hunts? Reaper who kills humans? Is that what they call themselves? Humans?* She had found their frequency, and their thoughts were becoming clearer. *But we're not the hunters, they are.*

A new one with surprisingly bright hair entered. He looked at her, nodded, and then grunted to The Walled One...Commander Savas. She was getting better at this, deciphering their thoughts nearly as quickly as they thought them. It was simply a matter of recognizing their dense vibration.

The Walled One called himself Commander Savas. They treated him like he was more important than themselves—another oddness.

Next to Savas stood the bright-haired one. He was not familiar, so why had he nodded at her when he entered? He wasn't afraid like the others.

*Rana?*

Rana blinked at the bright-haired one. He had just thought her name, but thought it strongly enough to nearly be mind talk. He was all-around surprising—his hair and his ability to connect. *Pleasantly Surprising, that's what I'll call him.*

She shifted to mind talk and carefully attempted to communicate with only Pleasantly Surprising, not the commander. *Yes. How do you know my name?*

Pleasantly Surprising seemed to consider their brief exchange. An intense, internal conflict burned within him. A push/pull energy emanated from him as if he couldn't decide whether or not to trust her.

She smiled in reassurance.

But Commander Savas, having observed them, made a sudden loud noise and smacked Pleasantly Surprising's cheek with his hand.

*Oh my Oneness! They hit each other?*

Commander Savas sent Pleasantly Surprising to get something. Pleasantly Surprising, the only human to have communicated back with her, left the box, leaving her with The Walled One. Her heart fell. The moments passed as she avoided meeting Commander Savas' hateful gaze.

Pleasantly Surprising returned, looking from the flat object in his hand to Rana. Commander Savas raised his hunting stick again, pointing it at Rana's face. He grunted to Pleasantly Surprising, who took a metal object out of his loose clothing. An eating utensil? Thrusting the utensil toward the flat object, he speared something with it. He began lowering the speared food toward her face.

Immediately, Commander Savas barked something, and Pleasantly Surprising startled. *He's repulsed?*

Her whole body reflexively tightened. She had experienced a connection to Pleasantly Surprising as soon as he had mind talked her name. He seemed a bit connected to the One In All. If the kind Pleasantly Surprising was repulsed, what was he being told to do to her?

Pleasantly Surprising again stabbed the utensil near the flat object and then raised it with a chunk of uncooked flesh on the end of it. Grimacing, he lowered it toward Rana's face. The horrible smell of blood and death wafted over her. Completely entangled in the net, she could only press backward against the hard surface and twist her neck away from the bloody, dripping piece of flesh.

For some reason, Commander Savas laughed, but it rang of mockery, not joy.

*No. Please*, she begged as she attempted to curl into a fetal position.

"Sorry." Pleasantly Surprising immediately dropped the flesh back onto the flat object in his trembling hands.

Rana panted in relief. *Help me*, she pulsed only to him.

Unexpectedly, Commander Savas grabbed the tool from Pleasantly Surprising and shoved the repulsive bloody flesh at her, rubbing it all over her face. Bloody juices ran into her nostrils and between her forced-open lips. He shoved the bloody chunk into her mouth. He smiled in a most unnatural way, full of cruelty.

Rana struggled to get away and attempted to spit the foul blood from her mouth. Her stomach curdled. She couldn't breathe.

Pleasantly Surprising yelled at Commander Savas and pulled his arm away from her face.

She gasped for fresh air, but her lungs only filled with the rank smell of the box. She panted and spit as her stomach continued to roil.

Commander Savas laughed, then turned and smashed his fist into Pleasantly Surprising's face. Rana nearly lost consciousness herself at the smack of flesh pounding flesh. Pleasantly Surprising reeled backward, falling onto the bars that surrounded her. The room flooded with fear and rage.

Tears streamed down her face as she tried to connect to the Crowned Ones. But she couldn't. She was alone, adrift in a sea of these horrible humans. Her own fear and shock blocked her connection to them. She opened her eyes. Pleasantly Surprising's pained face was shoved against the outside of her bars, blood running down from his nose.

Savas said something about "carnivores" and "herbivores." The other humans holding hunting sticks laughed, but not Pleasantly Surprising.

His commander yelled at him, and the other humans in the box now pointed their hunting sticks at her and exuded fear. Rana froze, afraid to spit again. Savas released Pleasantly Surprising, who grabbed the bars to remain standing. His gaze flickered to hers and then away just as quickly. Then he straightened, nodded to his commander, and walked away from the barred area that entrapped her.

*Please don't leave me... I know you hear me.*

Pleasantly Surprising continued across the box and left through the small rectangular opening.

*Don't leave me here. Please.* Tears streamed down Rana's face as she cast her gaze among the sea of unfriendly faces. Then, at the edges of her awareness, there was something...a weak mumble. She zeroed her concentration in on the weak communication.

*Can you still hear my thoughts? From out here?*

It was Pleasantly Surprising!

*I hear you,* she responded.

He exuded surprise. *I will help you, but I can't do it alone. I'll need to get help.*

*He's going to hunt me.*

There was a pause, as if he hadn't understood or heard her. Rana's heart thudded. Had she lost him? Had someone else hurt him? She attempted to extend her awareness but couldn't connect. If only she was a Crowned One, she could have star beamed herself out of here. Her stomach lurched. Why hadn't they rescued her? Had something happened to her village?

Her heart raced as sweat poured from her body, soaking her furs. She ignored Commander Savas as he yelled at her and made the others laugh. None of them laughed in joy. What did laughter mean to this species?

A distant reply came...

*What?* She had to hear him. Desperation cast her awareness out further than ever before.

*I don't think he'll kill you. Not yet, at least. He'll be cruel...if you put up your shield, they'll kill you. No shield. I'll hurry.*

*How did you know my name?*

*Your friend, Kala-something.*

Kalakanya. Hope washed over her. *And you? Do you have a name?*

*Girak. Diggory Girak.*

# Chapter 43

*The Surface: Bleu Reinier*

Bleu jerked awake. His heartbeat pounded in his ears, and wooziness filled his head. Holding still, he took in the frigid air, the white frozen walls and ceiling, and the hard floor beneath him. He shoved off the creepy fur skin that covered him. Struggling to stand, he nearly tripped on Neviah, who lay next to him. *Where am I?* Murmuring came from behind him, and he groggily spun to face two seated creatures.

*Shast.* He'd been captured by reapers and was trapped inside a cramped building with them.

Though they sat cross-legged on woven mats, both were clearly taller than him and appeared too strong to take by himself. *Double shast.*

Dropping his hand to his thigh, he found his gun holster empty. Their long, human-like faces followed his movement, and their light brown skin emanated a golden glow as they smirked. They knew he was at their mercy. He had to be careful not to upset them, because if they killed him before he found the cure and escaped, Ayanna would die as well.

Could he outwit them? Unsure of their weaponry, he held still and studied them. Long, snow-white braids were wrapped in an elaborate fashion around their high brows, yet they looked too young for white hair. One was feminine-looking and curvy, while the other had a gray beard under his twitching mouth. They both wore loose, leather clothing covered with fur cloaks that could easily hide weapons. But creepiest of all were their horizontal pupils that zeroed in on him.

Mind-controlling reapers—that's why his head was pounding and wooziness threatened to topple him. Could he trust his senses? He had no idea how he'd gotten here. Hoping his movement wouldn't elicit an attack from them, he nudged Neviah with his boot.

"Neviah. Get up." He risked a quick glance away from the reapers to check his friend. Her chest rose and fell, and relief flooded him. *Alive.*

"Neviah." He nudged her again.

The reapers still grinned with not a care in the world. *As if they were not just attacking us.*

*We did not attack. She is okay.* The words washed over Bleu.

He stared up at them, trying to comprehend the likelihood that aliens would speak Standard language. Perhaps he was hallucinating?

Willing his voice to be authoritative, he demanded, "She *better* be okay. Where are we?" If he could keep them talking until Neviah gained consciousness, then maybe…

*You are in our village, Peleguin-Rookery-By-The Lake. We did not attack you. We only wanted to return the body of your den mate. And your friend beside you is okay.* The bearded one motioned toward Neviah.

Bleu glanced around the enclosed space, considering his options. Fear told him to grab Neviah and run. If he could trust his senses, they were in a small building made of ice with woven mats on the ground and covering the entrance.

The door wasn't blocked, but he doubted they'd let him leave, and he had no idea if it led outside or if a guard stood on the other side. *And how did he talk to me without moving his mouth?* Curiosity bested him.

"How do you do that? Your mouth didn't move." He stared hard at the reaper's mouth, determined not to be mind-tricked.

*It can.* The man playfully wiggled his lips and opened and closed his mouth. Then he became still. *We mind speak so you can understand us.*

"Huh?" Bleu asked, experimenting and plugging his ears. "Do it again."

*We don't have time for this, young one.* Despite his reproach, he smiled. *All species understand the language of the heart. Your den appears unaware of the natural order. We have work to do.* The two beings stood. *Will you join us?*

Bleu considered his options. They hadn't killed him when they'd had the opportunity to do so. Neviah and he had been unconscious. So, what game were they playing at? Could he assess them for weaknesses and then escape? Were they reading his thoughts now?

"Neviah, get up." He wasn't about to leave her here alone. Kneeling, he shook her shoulder. He got no response.

The feminine one approached and knelt on the other side of Neviah. As she reached out a tentative hand, Bleu shoved it away.

"Don't touch her." His own aggression surprised him. How had Neviah become unconscious in the first place? What had been done to them? The last thing he remembered was being trapped in that bubble thing and then... Blood pounded in his ears and the wooziness increased. He had no idea what had happened next.

*We put you both in that shield to prevent you from hurting any more of us. It was self-protection. You do not understand the destruction you cause. Your own leader shot your shield, causing a shock wave that knocked you both unconscious. When he left you, we brought you here. You are safe,* she said.

Bleu's mind spun as he attempted to decipher the truth when he couldn't trust his senses. Commander Savas wouldn't endanger his own life to save them, but these reapers used mind control.

*Mind control? We don't seek to control. Why would we want to do that?* she asked.

"You killed Abdul." The accusation spat from his lips.

*Are you speaking of the one Kalakanya said fell off the cliff?* the bearded one asked.

"What?" Bleu's heart leapt in his chest. "Who fell off what cliff?" He pressed his sweaty, trembling palms against his forehead. Cliff...cliff. Abdul had died in a cave.

The high plateau—Stamf and Girak had been up there. He stared at the two beings, terrified of the answer they'd give, but he had to ask. His stomach clenched as he forced out the words. "W—what cliff? Who died?"

The two reapers stared at him with—what, in their weird eyes? Sadness? Pity?

"Answer me." His whole body shook with anticipation.

*May I explain? Please, we mean no harm. I'm very sorry.*

"Explain what? Your eternal innocence?" Bleu couldn't catch his breath. Were Stamf and Girak okay?

The man moved closer to Bleu and sat next to him and Neviah. The reaper tried to lull him, and his body started to relax.

No. He couldn't let them control him. Bleu stiffened. He glanced from the sitting bearded one, to the woman, and to Neviah's curled up body. He put one hand protectively on Neviah's unconscious form.

The bearded one touched his own chest. *I am Gandhapalin. This is Desna.* He motioned with his hand toward the other reaper. *I know this is a lot to take in. One of your friends died, maybe after you were knocked unconscious. He was on top of a cliff. The cave diggers—*

Bleu shot him a blank look.

The man said, *The large, furred ones that were attacking you...*

"You *sent* them to attack us," Bleu accused.

Gandhapalin's eyes widened, and he sat back in silence. His gaze met Desna's, and Bleu sensed they were communicating.

Gandhapalin sighed. *We did not send them. We were trying to keep them away from you while keeping you from killing them. They are a proud species that does not consider the One In All. They never...* He paused as if reconsidering. *They have only once been cooperative.*

Desna nodded, tears in her eyes. Bleu sensed he had somehow hit a nerve. Both reapers sat in silence then clasped each other's hands as if uniting in will.

Bleu swallowed. *Is this when they kill us?*

They stared at him as if he was incomprehensible. Tears streamed down Desna's face. *You have our daughter, Rana. You stole her from us. She was the only one to ever get a cave digger to cooperate.*

"We...we...have...your...daughter?" he asked, his voice detached like in a dream.

*Your leader stole her and took her underground.* Gandhapalin said.

"Oh, shast." He gripped his head with both hands as if that would make the world make sense again. "He probably thinks having a hostage will keep them safe."

The reapers looked lost.

"Who...died?" As he struggled to get the words out, dread filled him. He needed a few more moments of believing his teammates were all still alive.

A chill spread over him as he waited, breathless for the answer. *I have to get Neviah and myself out of here. I have to get Neviah and myself out of here.* It became his chant, like when he had tried to reach Josefina in time. Except, this time, he tried to shield his thoughts from these beings. Was such a thing even possible?

Gandhapalin's eyes glazed for a moment as if he was elsewhere—the same expression Bleu's mom made when she got a premonition. *The one that died went by Stamf. I'm so sorry. Were you two close?*

Stamf was dead?

His face contorted as he fought to control his emotions. Eyes stinging, he turned away, pretending to check Neviah.

No, it couldn't be. He gasped for breath like an eyeless fish caught in a net. He couldn't stop shaking. *Stamf dead? No. No, No. No, Stamf, I can't do this without you...*

Hot tears spilled down his cheeks. He couldn't comprehend a world without Stamf. He remembered a game, years ago, when Stamf had been surrounded by a pride of snarling lions. He had blasted them until the game turned itself off, a signal that he had died. It was the only time Stamf had died in a game. But this wouldn't turn off and reset.

"What do you want from us?" He needed to focus on getting them both out of here safely.

Neviah murmured and sat up. Her eyes widened in terror as she lurched into a crouch beside him.

"They...caught us?" Wobbling, Neviah searched in vain for her weapons. *Stop. You are safe. We are here to help,* Desna said.

Neviah froze as if she had heard it, too. She turned to Bleu with one eyebrow raised.

"They speak with their minds." That idea was easier to accept than Stamf's death.

*Stamf, I need you, you old Loud Foot. This was to be our mission together.* He sniffed and turned from Neviah, swiping his cheeks dry.

Desna turned to Bleu. *I'm sorry about your friend, but we don't have much time. We need to get Rana back and prevent any more deaths.*

"Deaths?" Neviah asked. "Bleu, what happened?"

"Stamf," he whispered.

Neviah's eyes filled with tears. "They killed him?"

Bleu shook his head. He believed them. If he was being mind-controlled, he wouldn't be in this much pain, would he? Wouldn't they try to convince him everything was okay?

*He fell from the cliff.* Gandhapalin said. *We will all meet at the Lion's Circle and seek answers. Danger approaches, and we must act to prevent more violence.*

Bleu couldn't imagine how to accomplish anything without Stamf around.

Neviah's eyebrow appeared to be in a permanently raised position, her mouth an open O. She turned to Bleu, apparently expecting an explanation, but he only shrugged.

Taking a few deep ragged breaths, he wobbled into a standing position. The familiar thump of his dagger struck his hip. They hadn't stolen it. In an attempt to prevent their captors from reading his thoughts, he thought of Ayanna and how much she was counting on him.

Gandhapalin and Desna motioned for them to follow the reapers out the ice building's door. Desna held open the mat, giving them their first glimpse of the reaper village.

It was late afternoon. The sun hung low in the sky, an orange glowing orb that turned the clustered ice huts pinkish-red. Everything appeared alien and threatening, and soon, it'd be hidden in the blackness of a Surface night. He'd never been in darkness that couldn't be solved by the flick of a switch. Even on his solo mission, he'd had the light of the snow rover.

*This way.* Gandhapalin motioned for Bleu and Neviah to follow him. Desna waited as their rear guard in case they tried anything.

He shivered as the wind whistled around the huts and found every crevice in his outer gear. "Come on," he said, motioning to Neviah.

But as his body brushed hers in the doorway, he leaned close to her ear. "We have to get out of here."

Because if he remained a prisoner and didn't find the cure that his vision had suggested was up here, Ayanna would die.

# Chapter 44

Peleguin-Rookery-By-The-Lake: Kahali

Kahali only lasted an hour in the Lion Circle before swaying from exhaustion. It was pointless anyway. Rana was captured and terrified, and they were only sending her energy to help her think clearly and keep herself alive. He backed away and headed back toward the village, bitter and confused.

The orange sun sank beyond the hills. He, too, sank to the ground. To his knowledge, star beings had never faced such a situation. They did not hunt or fight unless attacked by a rabid predator. And somehow, the Crowned Ones did not consider the Earth children rabid, no matter what he, Eka, and Balavati said.

No one ever went against the community's general consensus, and he'd been powerless to convince that many. Didn't they understand Rana's life was at risk?

*Sitting here crying won't help.* He struggled upright, gritting his teeth against the sharp, stabbing pain in his shoulder. Too much movement today. He needed food, and then maybe he'd have the strength to think of something heroic. *Heroic.* The word made him laugh out loud with bitterness.

"What's so funny?" The whisper from behind him sounded a lot like Eka.

He spun. Mr. Perfect stood between him and the Lion Circle and studied him with a concerned frown.

Kahali shrugged. "Me. Them." He motioned toward the crowd gathered at the circle. "We're doing nothing, and they'll kill her."

"You never told me your idea. Back at the hut," Eka said. He hunched, his white stripe hanging limply over his pallid face, but his eyes burned with the same frustration as Kahali felt.

"Since no one else was doing anything, you and I find her ourselves." He sighed. "But they've already decided, so we're stuck."

Eka nodded. "Walk with me?" He hooked his arm in Kahali's and led him away from the circle.

"I need food. Go toward the gathering hall." He didn't know if he should be annoyed or relieved by Eka's behavior. Yes, he was helping him walk faster, but he was practically carrying him.

"Shhh. We can get you food, but I have another idea." Eka stopped pulling and looked back toward the crowd. "Block your thoughts now."

"What?" Kahali laughed but blocked his thoughts. The guy was acting too weird.

"Blocked?" Eka asked.

"Yes," he said, raising an eyebrow.

"Good. What if we don't go along with the consensus? What if...what if we rescue her anyway?"

Kahali's jaw dropped. He pulled his arm from Eka's and stiffened. What he proposed was horrific. Unimaginable. But so was letting Rana die. "That's never been done."

"So they won't expect it," Eka responded, and they stared at each other.

Two figures approached them from the direction of the circle.

"You were saying?" Kahali asked, nodding toward the two approaching figures. They must have sensed their plans. His heart sank, because he wanted this unimaginable thing. This way to save Rana.

The figures stepped into the moonlight. Tejas and Balavati. Kahali sagged against Eka in relief. Oh, the irony of him needing Eka to hold him up while they discussed Rana.

"I'm not letting you do anything wild without me," Tejas whispered.

"She's my best friend," Balavati said.

Kahali exchanged a glance with Eka. "Where's Daman?" Their other

339

friend would also want to be involved in a rescue.

"It's his night to cook. He's at the hall." Balavati seemed to know everything today. Thank the One In All she was helping them.

"He'll have to stay, then. They'll miss him if he leaves."

Eka gave him a concerned look. "Kahali, I need to know where things are in your village and have your permission to gather supplies. But, no offense, you're not in any shape for a rescue."

Kahali knew this. He also knew the rage that swelled up inside him. *Not now. Please, not now.*

He unclenched his fist and snorted. "I..." He squeezed his eyes shut with the effort to not scream. "I know." The declaration deflated him. He opened his eyes and stared at his boots.

Eka sighed. "I'm sorry. It's not fair. But I can do this for both of us, okay?"

Kahali studied him through narrow eyes. He found no pity or rivalry in Eka's sincere expression, only friendship. Falling stars, he meant it. "Okay. I'll cover for you."

"You mean, you'll cover for all of us." Balavati said. Hugging him, she whispered so that only he'd hear, "I'll make sure Rana knows you helped."

He nodded, too upset for words.

Balavati shoved her hand deep into her cloak pocket. "Will this feed you for now?" She pulled out some dried jerky. "If you eat it here, you can intercept anyone who might follow to see why we left. That work?"

He grimaced at the jerky, which had seen better days, and chuckled. "Yeah, if that jerky doesn't kill me first, I'll stall them. But hurry. The sooner you leave the better."

Balavati gave him a quick hug and they hurried away.

As the darkness swallowed their dark silhouettes, Kahali found himself in the odd situation of praying for Eka's success with Rana.

# Chapter 45

*orthern Haven: Atsushi Collins*

N Atsushi had tried everything to distract Ayanna, but she kept staring at the door of her module as if Bleu would miraculously burst through it at any moment.

Commander Savas had reported Stamf dead and Bleu and Neviah missing on the Surface, presumably dead. Ayanna refused to believe him. Given that Commander Savas and Girak had returned and they lacked Bleu's years of secretly researching survival, Atsushi agreed. Bleu would make it, and if they stayed together, hopefully Neviah would as well.

But Stamf's death had shocked the whole of Northern Haven. He had always seemed the golden guy, untouchable and perfect. Nothing made sense anymore. After being raised on fearful tales of the dangerous Undescended, they were now being attacked by aliens? It was enough to make him stare at the door like Ayanna.

"Want to play another game?" He waved his comm in the air, but she continued to remain transfixed on the closed door.

When Bleu had left, he and Ayanna had touched hands at that door, as if they were mirror images of each other. Atsushi sighed, wishing that if someone had to lose a sibling, he could volunteer Liam over Bleu.

"Ayanna?" he said, touching her arm. Her red swollen eyes remained fixed on the door and she sat too still, her fingers touching her chest where her special pendant had hung.

She'd been shaky ever since they had gotten word of Bleu being MIA, and if she had another episode, he was on his own. Her parents had been gone for hours, trying to encourage the Council to send out a search and rescue for Bleu and Neviah.

"He's really smart. He's going to be fine."

"The reapers are dangerous." Even her voice was shaking now.

He laughed. "So is Bleu. He's kind of terrifying when he's angry."

She turned and gave him a quizzical look. "Terrifying? Bleu?"

"Come on, you've seen him playing in the arena. He's super intense."

She gave a week smile and glanced over at the picture of the two of them when they were younger and dressed to enter the arena. "Yeah, you're right. He is a bit scary in there."

A thin, piercing wail erupted in the hallway, and they both stared at each other. It clicked off, and a voice over the Haven-wide intercom replaced it. "This is not a drill. An attack by the reapers is incoming. Children should proceed to the cafeteria where they will be taken to a secure area. All adults will arm themselves and meet near the door. Reapers appear as tall humanoids but they possess the ability to somehow influence the human brain. We do not know what they truly are. I repeat: An attack..." The entire message droned on, over and over.

"Where should we go?" Atsushi asked, heart racing. *Do we qualify as kids or adults?*

Her eyes shone with rage. "They attacked Bleu, so I'm killing me some reapers." She sprang up and searched the module for something weapon-like.

"Stop," he said, grasping her arm as she raced by. "Please. Bleu wouldn't want you risking yourself to avenge him."

"The hell he wouldn't." She shook herself free and ran into the kitchen, coming back with two small knives used for spreading protein butters on bread. "Here." She handed one of the ridiculous weapons to him as the hall beyond her module filled with shouting people.

He accepted it to get it out of her hands, not that it would be useful unless they encountered a ravenous alien that wanted protein toast. Her tremors were getting stronger, and he needed to get the other knife from her before she accidently hurt herself or him.

"Wait." He dashed into her room and brought back a blanket. Dr. Reinier had told them that wrapping it around her might stave off an episode. "Ayanna, you're shaking. If you have an episode, and a reaper shows up, you'll be defenseless. You agree, right?"

"I'm fine." She clutched the knife as if she could take on a whole reaper army single-handedly.

"Please, trust me?" He caught her gaze and held it. "You're shaking. If you want to fight reapers, you need to be…" He hesitated, *so* not wanting to insult her. "You need to be thinking clearly."

Her gaze narrowed, and for a moment she seemed a bigger threat than the reapers. "Fine, but I'm keeping this." She clutched the knife to her chest and glared at him.

"Okay." He tried to wrap the blanket around her shoulders. "Can you hold that *and* the blanket wrapped around you like your mom suggested?"

She spun on him and screamed in his face, "Stop telling me what the *shast* to do. I'm not sick."

He stepped back in surprise, then took a deep breath and tried again. "Ayanna…"

Tears filled his eyes. The hell of watching her change from the strongest person he knew to *this*…. It tore him to pieces, and he imagined it was even worse for her.

Keeping his voice as calm as possible, he said, "I didn't mean it that way. I just wasn't sure you could work the knife and hold the blanket."

She blinked and her rage evaporated. "I'm sorry," she whispered. "I can't stand being like this…"

"It's not you, it's the Sickness. I know that."

That earned him a weak smile and fueled his determination to get her to the safety of the cafeteria.

"Here." He tried again, and this time, she let him assist her with the blanket.

"Okay, let's get going." With his hand gently on her back, he led her toward the door, but when it opened, they both shrank back.

Mothers carried screaming toddlers through the halls while men yelled back and forth about whose module contained the most dangerous weapons. Sadly, no one had anything more lethal than their knives.

Ayanna shrank back into him. He needed to get her through this high stimulation mess as quickly as possible.

"Can you run?" he asked.

At her nod, they took off. As they rounded a corner, a huge crash exploded to their left. They both ducked into the opposite wall to avoid the shower of wood pieces and splinters. Were the reapers busting through the walls?

He and Ayanna bolted past, and when he glanced over his shoulder, he saw Sera's father was picking up debris from a smashed end table and handing out the wooden legs as clubs.

"It's not the reapers," Atsushi shouted to Ayanna.

They burst through the far end of the crowd, but as they neared the cafeteria door, wails of frightened kids and babies blasted them.

Ayanna skidded to a stop. "I can't do that," she warned, motioning with her chin to the cafeteria. "It's too much. I'll lose it and put everyone in danger."

"All right," he said, even though it wasn't. Panting, he considered their options. "We'll go as far back into the heart of Northern Haven as we can get and hide. Will that work?"

She nodded from under her blanket hood.

They proceeded down a side hall. Passing a mural with several laughing kids high-fiving each other, he pressed his palm to theirs and said, "Wish us luck, okay?"

Ayanna doubled over, snorting with laughter.

He cringed. What had he been thinking? Talking to murals in front of her? "Sorry, I'm a bit stressed."

"No, its fine." She waved her hand, making light of it and seeming more herself as she hurried along beside him. "Bleu and I talk to them all the time. I've just never seen anyone else do it."

"Really?" He grinned at the image of them doing the same thing. Especially Bleu. Talking to murals seemed way too playful for that guy.

"Well, let's hope our mural friends don't all get ruined in the attack. Come on."

They continued on until he found a storage room filled with root vegetables. He stepped in and looked around. Even if the reapers entered, he and Ayanna could still hide behind the crates. And if they were here for a few days, they'd have food.

"This looks good. What do you think?"

She entered, and her hunched shoulders dropped in relief. "Nice and quiet," she whispered, studying the crates. She looked up at him with a twinkle in her eyes. "And if we build a catapult, we can defend ourselves with rutabagas."

"No," he said, laughing. "Onions are round and easier to aim. Besides, if we get hungry, rutabagas will be tastier than raw onions."

"Better breath, too." She giggled.

"Right, breath is important." He turned aside to hide his blush. *Breath is important? What kind of response was that?* "Uhm, I'm going to shove things around a bit in case we need to hide."

At his mention of needing to hide, her shaking returned. "Are they heavy?" she asked, frowning at the crates. She wrapped her blanket even tighter, and he got the impression it was all she could manage to hold herself together.

He gave an experimental shove to one of the crates with his foot, testing its weight. "Nope, I got it."

Beyond their room, the hallways grew quiet as everyone reached either the distant cafeteria or the even more distant Surface door. He shifted and carried the foodstuffs, leaving the front crates in place. If the reapers entered, it wouldn't look like the dust had been disturbed.

Once everything was in place, he searched the room for anything that might be useful in case of attack. All he found was a broom, so he broke off the handle and swung it around to get the feel of it. Northern Haven never fell this quiet when the MLs were lit. The silence smothered him. They should be in the cafeteria, not out here by themselves. He swished the handle through the air harder, comforted by its whistle, but Ayanna only gave him a grim look.

"If they make it inside, we're screwed." she said. "A broom handle won't save us from creatures capable of interstellar travel."

He glanced at the shut door and whispered in the stifling silence, "I'll at least give them headache."

With a sad smile, she patted the crate next to her, and he joined her. Now, the only sound was their breath. He'd imagined taking Ayanna somewhere fun plenty of times, but sitting on onion crates and waiting for aliens to attack had never been on his list of ideal dates.

He fiddled with the old comm that Neviah had hacked so they could message each other. With her up on the Surface and maybe even dead, it was useless, but he couldn't help pulling it out of his pocket and stroking the keyboard. "I wish," he whispered, "we had some way of knowing what was happening out there."

"On the Surface, or down here?" she asked as she scooted closer.

"Both." Her delicate, fruity scent almost squashed his terror of only having a broom handle to protect them from aliens. *Almost.* "But I'd settle for either."

Soft footsteps outside made them both stiffen. *Get into the space,* he mouthed, and pointed to the hiding space he'd created.

The footsteps stopped outside their door. Were they human? As humanoids, would the reapers' footsteps sound different?

Ayanna slid into the hole, and he wanted nothing more than to follow, but the door began opening. He rushed it with his broom handle raised. The shadowy figure entered, and he swung the handle.

"Oof." The figure doubled over.

He readied to strike again when he noticed the red hair. "Educator Girak? Are you okay?" Why wasn't he protecting the door? Dropping the handle, he rushed forward and helped him up. "What the *shast* are you doing back here?"

His teacher regarded him with alarm. "I was looking for..." His face grew guarded. "Wait. Why are *you* back here?"

"Hiding with Ayanna." He motioned behind him to where Ayanna slowly crawled out. "The ruckus was too much. We had to get somewhere quiet, because of…" He gave their educator a knowing look.

Girak nodded and cast Ayanna a worried glance. "You okay, Ayanna? Your mother is frantic looking for you."

She nodded, the blanket hood wobbling over her head.

Girak frowned. "It could be even more dangerous being back here… alone." He studied Ayanna, and Atsushi got the distinct sense he was concerned more about Ayanna than the reapers.

He glared at his educator. "I promised I'd keep her safe."

Girak held up his palms to signify he'd meant no offense. "Okay," he said. Clearing his throat, he added, "I'm trying to completely prevent the attack. To keep everyone safe."

"But you're one of the few trained people." Atsushi studied him with his eyes narrowed. "Wouldn't the best way to prevent an attack be to defend the door?'

Girak sighed. "It's complicated."

Girak told them everything—how Stamf had died to save him; how he didn't blame the strange reapers for his death, and how Savas had captured one.

He glanced from Ayanna to Atsushi. "Do you see how this doesn't have to be war? They only want her back. We're all she has right now…"

Atsushi snorted. "Then she's in trouble. I see how it could be a misunderstanding, but…" He side-eyed his educator. Would Girak look or act differently if he were mind-controlled?

"They could have killed us all up there, yet they didn't," Girak said. "If they attack, it's only to save the one Savas caught. Her name is Rana."

At his side now, Ayanna inhaled sharply. "He brought her *inside*?" No one new had entered since Descension Day, and that was ages ago.

Girak nodded. "To torture her for information, and then probably they'll vivisect her," he said, shuddering. "He clearly stated she was only a specimen."

"Vivisect?" Atsushi asked.

"Cut her open while she's alive and experiment on her," Girak answered, grimacing.

"No..." Atsushi gagged.

"I know that intercom announcement probably made you think she's mind-controlling me, but she's not." Girak spoke like his usual impassioned self, like he'd been before Josefina had died. "I've talked to her. She only wants to get home."

He scowled at Girak. "Wait. She speaks Standard?"

"She can't," Ayanna interjected. "She's messing with you."

"She speaks with her mind, not her mouth." He grinned. "It's wild. Some sort of telepathy or something."

"Or something," Ayanna said, eyeing their educator.

"This doesn't have to be war," Girak pleaded. "They want her back, and we're all she has right now."

"I don't trust my own thinking anymore." Ayanna shook her head. "I'd like to help, but if my mom is with the others, then I trust her to know what's right."

"She's only heard what Commander Savas reported. I was up there, too, and they never attacked us. I never saw any weapons. They scared us, but they used their shields for defense, not offense."

"Really?" That was new information. Maybe Girak was onto something.

"Yes, really. The one on the Surface asked me to return Rana so that they don't have to enter Northern Haven to save her. And Rana asked for my help getting back to the Surface." He sighed. "Please, believe me. I can stop this." He gave then a pleading look and then said, "I can stop it, but I need help. I hate to endanger you, but if this turns into war, then none of us stand a chance. Their technology or whatever it is they use is *way* more advanced than anything we have."

If it came to war, Atsushi might protect Ayanna initially, but they'd lose all hope for a cure. And no one, including an alien, should be experimented on just for being different. What if the council had done that to him because of his genes?

But to do what Girak asked, he'd have to go against the council. Go against his whole community.

Girak raised both eyebrows. "So? Will you help me return Rana to the Surface and stop this?"

Atsushi held up his hands. "I just want to make sure I understand. You think Commander Savas misjudged them because they look different and talk differently?"

"Well, aliens *are* different." Girak said, chuckling. "But that doesn't mean they're bad, right? It's all a massive misunderstanding, and"—he wringed his hands—"I don't want anyone else to die because of it." As his gaze fell to his wedding-inked palm, he fisted his hand and whispered, "No more deaths."

Losing Josefina, Stamf, Abdul, and now possibly Bleu and Neviah...it was too much for him, too. "Right," Atsushi agreed, "no more deaths." He raised his chin to Girak. "Okay, if Ayanna's in, I'm in. But if she's not, I'm not leaving her back here alone."

Then he turned to Ayanna. "Your mom doesn't have all this information. She doesn't know what we do. And,"—he looked her in the eye—"I know your brain still works. You're still you. Should we hide, or should we save Girak's alien girl?"

Ayanna twisted the edge of her blanket. "If Bleu and Neviah are still alive, a war decreases their chances of survival. I'll help you...but when I meet this alien, if I think it's a bad idea to free her...well, then I may change my mind."

Girak let out a long exhalation. "Good enough." Some of the tension drained from his face.

"So, what's your plan?" Atsushi asked.

"Plan?" Girak's face froze, and then he sniffed and looked away. "What's my plan?"

*Shast.* His heart fell. The attack was imminent, and Girak didn't even have a plan. He and Ayanna exchanged worried looks.

"You have no idea how we can save her, do you?" Atsushi asked.

"No," Girak frowned and pulled at his beard. "No, I don't."

# Chapter 46

*orthern Haven: Atsushi Collins*

**N**Atsushi cracked open the door and checked the hallway. It was amazingly clear of reapers, parents, and the reek of onions.

"We need a plan," he whispered to Girak as he ducked back in and shut the door. "Where's Rana imprisoned?"

"She's in a guarded cell a few halls from the Surface door." Girak rubbed his temples, the only unbruised area of his face. "Everyone's defending the hall leading to the elevator shaft. We'll need to get them to leave that area, then free her and get her up the shaft to the Surface. Maybe a distraction?"

"Okay, a distraction..." he said.

Girak only frowned. The educator who planned complicated experiments for them apparently sucked at planning jailbreaks.

Atsushi's memories lit. "Wait. I've got it. Remember how I helped Neviah set up the Spring Reigns Festival? Remember the surprise fireworks?"

"I remember a few surprises that day," Ayanna said, smirking from her onion crate throne.

"Those fireworks would be hard to forget." Girak's face softened with nostalgia.

"Since Neviah had wanted to surprise even her dad, she had engineered a portable holograph machine programmed to create the fireworks." She'd also surprised him with the cherry blossom tree, her special gift to him. *She can't be dead.*

"You know how to use this portable machine?" Hope illuminated Girak's weary face. "And where to find it?"

"Yeah." He grinned. "If I set it up and hide it, it'd take them a while to find it, you know?" Maybe this could work.

"Brilliant! They'll think it's a reaper attack. Now, to get Rana out, we need to get past the guns." Girak's eyes narrowed, and he began pacing. "Oh!" He laughed at whatever he'd just plotted. "Yeah, that's devious enough to trick Savas." He chuckled again. "Can you two act?"

"I guess?" Ayanna pushed the blanket off her head to study Girak.

"Act?" Atsushi grimaced and then shrugged. "I suppose?" He was willing do anything to keep his friends safe. "This plan...you've already thought it the whole way through?"

Girak nodded. "Thank you for trusting me about Rana's innocence." His eyes glistened in appreciation, as if he were in danger of crying again. Instead he patted his pockets, pulled out his comm, and checked the time. "Can you set it to go off in half an hour and meet me right back here in fifteen minutes?"

"Of course. That's easy," Atsushi said, relieved not to have to comfort his educator again. He retrieved his broken broomstick in preparation for whatever they faced and smacked it reassuringly into his other palm. *Just in case.*

Girak raised an eyebrow. "We shouldn't have to actually hurt anyone," he said, and again consulted his comm. "If anyone stops us, you"—he looked at Ayanna—"pretend to have an episode. Atsushi and I will pretend we're helping you. That's our excuse for not being at the door with everyone else, okay?"

Ayanna blushed. "I never thought having the Sickness would be useful."

Girak gave her a sad nod. "Today, people's underestimation of our mental status may save Rana."

"*Our?*" she asked.

"Yes, you'll see. *Our.*" Girak smiled, and Atsushi pondered just what his educator's plan entailed.

Girak motioned for them to follow him into the hall. He whispered, "I'm also heading to the Gaming Arena. I'll check who's leading the crowd, and then I'll meet you back here."

*Why does it matter who's in charge?* But they were already speeding down the hall toward the Gaming Arena and had to remain quiet.

When they arrived, Girak stopped at the supply closets, while Atsushi led Ayanna toward the staff offices where Neviah stored her stuff. Skidding to a stop in front of Neviah's desk, he realized that without her comm, he'd need to break in.

The most illegal thing he'd ever done was to skip school to help Bleu and Ayanna. Smashing open Neviah's desk paled in comparison to the destruction a war would wreak, but she had trusted him with this secret.

He grimaced and turned to Ayanna. "This is for Bleu and Neviah, right?"

"Just smash it," she urged, glancing toward the distant shouts of the crowd. "And hurry!"

"Right," he whispered.

Wedging the jagged end of the broom handle between the drawers, he used his weight to leverage it and hefted. As the drawer popped open, his weapon splintered.

Dropping the broom handle, he grabbed the cords and holographic machine and blew the splinters off its delicate keyboard.

"Grab Neviah's tool bag…there," he whispered, pointing to the tools they might need.

Ayanna slung the bag over her shoulder. Together, they raced back through the hallways, dodging in and out of doorways to avoid the others while searching for a room to set their trap.

"This one's good," Ayanna whispered, motioning to him to follow. She pointed to a covered vent in the back wall and began searching through Neviah's tools for the right one to remove the vent covering. "Here," she said, handing it to him with one of her amazing smiles.

He climbed on the desk, opened the vent, and inserted Neviah's contraption. If the sound and lights came crashing out of the wall, maybe his fellow Northern Haveners would think, as he had previously, that the reapers were coming through the wall. It might make them hesitate to investigate and buy them more time to rescue Rana.

"You sure you know how to program it?" Ayanna whispered up to him.

"We only have six minutes."

"I got it." Sweat trickled down his spine as he initiated the program's countdown as Neviah had shown him, adding in several repeat performance loops for good measure. "Done," he exclaimed and hopped down. "You still okay? This isn't too much?"

She grinned and leaned closer. "This is the most fun I've had in weeks," she whispered, her breath warm on his face.

She was close enough to kiss, but that might ruin their budding friendship, so he only laughed. "Aww. What about all those games we played?" he teased over his shoulder as he took off for the meeting place.

"This is *way* more fun." With a burst of speed, she sped past him and burst into the storeroom and straight into a startled Girak.

"Whoa! Everything okay?" he asked, his eyes wide with alarm as he steadied himself.

"We...did it." Ayanna giggled as she caught her breath.

Girak gave her a concerned glance, clearly worried an episode was coming on. "Great, but are *you* okay?"

"She's fine," Atsushi reassured him, having become well acquainted with her warning signs. "You saw the crowd, and your plan still works?"

"Yes." Girak affectionately patted the long, rectangular bag hanging from his shoulder. But when the distant crowd roared, he cast a worried glance toward the open door.

"Are you going to share the plan?" Atsushi asked to squash his looming doubts. Surely, he could tell them now. They couldn't exactly assist the guy if they didn't know what they were supposed to do.

"Not yet. That way, if we get caught, you can blame everything on me. Tell them I made you do this, okay?" Girak had re-entered his responsible educator mode.

"I'd never blame—"

"Promise it," Girak commanded. "My reputation is already ruined, but you both have your whole lives before you."

"Not me," Ayanna said, scowling.

"Promise," Girak insisted.

"Fiiine," she said. "It's not like I have another option to help Bleu."

"I guess," Atsushi grumbled. He'd never blame Girak, so his super-secret plan had better be damn exceptional. "I wish you'd tell us. You *know* I can keep secrets." He gave his educator a purposeful look.

Girak ignored his plea. "Good. Don't lose me in the crowd. And, Ayanna, keep your head under that blanket. We don't want your mother to see you and get involved with this." Girak turned and sprinted toward the distant yelling.

They followed. When they reached the crowded hallways, Atsushi grasped Ayanna's wrist for fear of losing her in the crowd. He hoped she could still see Girak, because Atsushi was lost in the sea of sweaty, shoving bodies, guided only by Ayanna's grip.

She dragged him past Prime Minister Pridbor, who was handing out tools that might work as weapons against squirrels but certainly not against towering aliens. If they didn't return Rana and stop this attack, humanity was screwed.

Ayanna yanked him from the press and through a doorway. As soon as they were through, Girak slammed the door behind them. "We've got five minutes before they hear the fireworks and run off. No one's trained except Commander Savas, Zach, and myself, so I'm hoping they all rush en masse toward the sounds of attack."

"Or in the opposite direction," Atsushi murmured. At Girak's grimace, Atsushi shrugged. "Not everyone's brave."

"Let's hope that today they are. As far as they know, fighting together is their best chance of defending this place," Girak said as he pulled a large gun from his shoulder bag.

Atsushi gasped. "Have you lost your mind?" Had he made a terrible mistake in trusting Girak? Had Rana been controlling him all along?

"No way. You said no one would get hurt." Ayanna shook her head as she backed away.

"It's okay, they're the gaming guns," Girak said, smiling. "But like you mistook them for real, everyone else will, too."

Reality righted itself. Atsushi sagged in relief.

"Brilliant," he said, accepting the gun as Girak pulled two others from his bag.

"I have my moments." Girak gave a sad chuckle. "Here's the plan." As their educator explained, it became clear Josefina hadn't been the only devious one in their family.

"If you forget, or things change, I'll give commands." Girak checked the time on his comm. "Atsushi, go out there and get Prime Minister Pridbor. Tell him you were sent here as a messenger by Commander Savas. Pretend you need him to come in here, out of the noise, to hear the message. Only let him follow you in the room, okay? You have less than a minute."

Atsushi nodded and dashed out the door. The prime minister, finished with handing out his ridiculous weapons, now paced the length of the hall.

"Sir," Atsushi said, yanked on his arm.

"What?" Prime Minister Pridbor, eyes flashing with battle excitement, spun toward him.

"Commander Savas sent me." Atsushi grabbed his arm again, hoping the guy didn't club him with his squirrel-sized armament. "This way, quickly." He dragged him toward the door and pushed it open. "Hurry!"

As the prime minister fumed about the improprieties of being dragged, Atsushi hurried him through the door.

The prime minster yelled, "Atsushi, what's this about? Why didn't Comman—"

Girak slammed the door shut behind them, grabbed Pridbor's head in a neck lock, and held the muzzle of the gun to his head.

Atsushi stumbled backward into the closed door, shocked by the fury on Girak's face. *It's fake*, he reassured himself.

The prime minister's yelp was drowned out as the firecrackers went off. The panicked crowd roared and raced off toward the noise. Points to his fellow Northern Haveners for bravery.

Meanwhile, Atsushi was sneaking around and betraying them all. Sweat dripped down his back as Pridbor's eyes bulged at the gun to his head. How had Atsushi's day gone from finally being alone with Ayanna to taking the prime minister hostage?

"Rana needs us," Girak said as if answering his question.

With his expression a bit contorted for effect, their educator shoved the terrified man into the now empty hallway and toward where Rana must be imprisoned. Atsushi and Ayanna followed, doing their best to look dazed.

"Diggory? Are you mad?" Pridbor's eyes narrowed as he twisted to see the educator's face.

Girak dreamily responded, "I can't help it...she's mind controlling me. And my students." His face contorted between focused concentration and fake dazed mind-control. He truly looked crazed as he shoved Prime Minister Pridbor forward again.

Pridbor's eyes flashed with anger. "Atsushi, you're better than this."

The jerk sounded exactly like his father. Not trusting his voice, Atsushi kept his face as blank as possible while his insides roiled.

"Atsushi." Pridbor tried again, not even looking at Ayanna. Apparently, she wasn't even worth trying to communicate with.

All Atsushi wanted was to scream at the prime minister for being so hateful, but instead, he and Ayanna stumbled along in an apparent daze as the firecrackers popped and rumbled in the distance. This had to be a high stimulation nightmare for Ayanna.

*Please let her hold it together.* He didn't want to have to choose between her immediate safety and preventing a war.

*Hurry. Those explosions made Savas decide to hunt me!* The reaper's words blasted into Atsushi's mind with such force that this time he stumbled for real. An actual telepathic alien had just spoken to him, begging for help. He blinked and gasped, turning to Girak for guidance, but Girak only sped up.

*Girak, please!* Her plea again vibrated in his mind.

Rana's terror echoed within Atsushi's skull and twisted his intestines. He had to stop this. He strode toward the sealed door where an angry and armed Commander Savas readied himself to commit murder. If they didn't hurry, there'd be no one left to rescue.

# Chapter 47

*orthern Haven: Atsushi Collins*

As Atsushi scurried down the hall after Girak and Pridbor, his fear of facing Commander Savas grew. Atsushi had once seen Savas play in the Gaming Arena. He'd been brutal, decisive, and deadly, slaughtering an entire pride of holographic lions in under two minutes. Rana, an unarmed prisoner, didn't stand a chance. It was all he could do to not race down the bright hall to rescue her.

*Walk slow. Appear dazed,* he chided himself. They needed that ruse so that, if all else failed, perhaps the council might see them as victims and not kill Girak as a traitor.

Due to his own genetic status, he'd be fine as long as no one accidentally shot him. But a Deplorable and a girl with the Sickness would be considered acceptable casualties. No, somehow, he had to keep his friends safe.

They'd reached the solid metal door to the lab serving as a prison, and Atsushi tapped the entrance keypad. Locked. He stole a panicked glance at Girak.

Girak grasped Pridbor more tightly and droned, "Prime Minister, tell them to open up, or she will make me shoot you. I'm...so...sorry..." The guy could really act.

With a glare of utter contempt, Pridbor said, "Open up. It's Prime Minister Pridbor."

As boots sounded on the other side of the locked door, Atsushi brushed his fingers against Ayanna's hand. Their brief contact fueled his determination to be the first one through the door.

The click of locks being opened resounded, and Vincent, the agriculturist who was to be Bleu's future boss peered out warily, a handgun strapped clumsily on his thigh. "We heard gunshots, sir. Are you—"

Atsushi waved his gun in the confused guy's face. "Stay quiet and don't make me hurt you."

Vincent raised his hands, and Atsushi directed Vincent toward the humming medical equipment and tables.

As the other three entered behind him, Atsushi bent to remove Vincent's real gun but straightened as Vincent tensed to knee him in the face.

"Keep your hands up," he warned.

The room's opposite left corner held a barred cell. Inside lay the reaper, hairy and wrapped in netting. Commander Savas and another newly drafted guard had their guns trained on her.

"What is this?" Commander Savas glared over his shoulder at them. His icy blue gaze snagged on Girak and narrowed. The alien wasn't the only one Savas wanted to murder.

Atsushi had to get Savas' attention off Girak. "She's controlling us."

Savas ignored him and kept his glare locked on his nemesis.

"Sir, I...can...not...stop myself." Girak restrained the prime minister. "Let her go..."

"And of course, Diggory, your weak mind would be the easiest for her to control." Commander Savas assessed the situation, then spun away from Girak. "No problem. I was about to kill her anyway." He locked the sight of his gun back on Rana and curled his index finger around the trigger.

Rana's almost-human face drained of color as she mentally begged, *Please...don't.*

At Ayanna's gasp, Atsushi guessed everyone in the room had heard her. Whether she truly was human-like under those furs or the human-like face was an illusion, he connected with her terror.

"Stop," he shouted, willing Rana to understand, "or she'll make me kill Vincent."

*Me?* Rana asked, not exactly bolstering his claim.

*Shast.* Nothing like introducing yourself to an alien while holding the prime minister hostage.

"Savas," Girak said, "I can't stop myself." His arm wobbled, bumping the side of Prime Minister Pridbor's temple with the gun's nose. "Let her go…"

Commander Savas glared from Rana to Girak, eyes squinted in intense calculation. Poor Vincent didn't seem to enter the equation.

Atsushi's heart raced. With only a fake gun, he was too far away to stop Commander Savas if he tried to shoot Girak or Rana. Beside him, Ayanna had the same problem. The other armed guard cast Girak and him foul looks but remained still, awaiting Savas' orders.

"Well, we can't endanger the Prime Minister's life." Commander Savas turned to the armed guard. "Cover her while I put in the code to open the door."

He holstered his gun and sauntered near the door. Covering his hand, he entered a series of symbols into the keypad. The lock opened. He paused, then pulled the door outward and backed away, and turned, smiling toward Girak. "Come free her, Diggory. She's all yours."

This was too easy. He must be setting Girak up, but how?

"Atsushi," Girak said, "she says to remove Vincent's gun and keep your own gun on Prime Minister Pridbor. If anyone moves, shoot him."

Atsushi nodded. "Vincent, slowly hand me your gun."

"Right," Vincent argued, "so you can shoot me with it?"

"I already have a gun," Atsushi said, thumping his fake one against Vincent's chest. "So, *listen*, and she won't make me shoot you."

Vincent opened his mouth to argue again.

Ayanna strode up to Vincent. "Hey," she yelled, smacking his arm. "I'm the easiest for her to control, you know, having the Sickness and all. I have no qualms in killing you. Hand it over." She held out her hand. "*Now.*"

What was she doing?

Vincent swallowed, clicked on the safety, and handed her the gun.

"Good boy," Ayanna said, smirking. "Sit over there." She motioned to the far corner. "And if I hear a peep, it'll be your last."

Atsushi shivered at the coldness of her tone. Yes, she'd disarmed Vincent, but Commander Savas now gave her the same killer glare reserved for Girak and Rana. Atsushi should have handled that and kept Savas' focus on himself.

As Vincent backed away from Ayanna, Atsushi stepped forward and replaced Girak as Pridbor's captor. Ayanna, now holding two guns, put the real one down on a desk filled with equipment, and pointed her fake one toward Vincent.

Girak walked toward the cell door.

*No. It's a trick.* Rana's mind-scream caused Girak to freeze and Pridbor to step back into Atsushi's gun.

It had to be a trap. Savas would never just hand over his captive. Atsushi tightened his grip on Pridbor and stepped closer, pulling the Prime Minister alongside to get a better look. The net around Rana pinned her arms to her side, but no signs of trickery were apparent.

Commander Savas motioned to catch Atsushi's gaze and mouthed, "Fight her."

"Stop," Girak yelled, "or I'll shoot you."

Confused, Atsushi jerked around. The other still-armed guard had slipped into the small computer room attached to the prison area, and he reached toward the instrument panels.

"I don't want to hurt you," Girak warned.

The guard's face twitched, but his hand still hovered, frozen, over the panel.

With Girak distracted, Commander Savas again nodded to Atsushi. "I know this isn't you, kid," he whispered. "Fight her. You're stronger than those two..."

Atsushi tightened his jaw in fury, then panicked and realized he looked too normal.

Savas smiled. "See?" he whispered. "You can do it. Let the prime minister go and shoot Diggory."

Girak had walked over and was studying the control panel. Atsushi watched his educator as if considering Savas' words, but rage made his hands shake.

"Yes, fight her," Savas whispered.

Okay, so he looked like he was fighting off Rana. Atsushi tightened his grip on the prime minister and wished he could help Girak decipher the electronic board. Technology was his thing, not Girak's.

Girak must have had a similar thought, because he grabbed the guard's gun from the table and shot the connecting wires. A hiss came from the floor of Rana's cell.

Commander Savas chortled.

Rana screamed as tiny needles popped up and began flying into her body. She went limp.

"She's dying." Ayanna raced toward her.

"Careful," Atsushi warned, "there might be more traps."

But Ayanna rushed to the reaper's side and held her hand over her nose, checking for breath.

"Thank you, Diggory. That was brilliant. You saved us all." Commander Savas walked over to relieve Girak of his gun.

Atsushi's heart thumped wildly against his ribs. Their ruse of being mind-controlled would be shattered if Rana was dead.

With a wild look, Girak fired the guard's gun at the floor in front of Commander Savas. "What did you do to her?" he yelled.

"She's still breathing," Ayanna said.

Commander Savas froze, and his calculating gaze bounced from Rana's still body to Girak's face. "She's unconscious. Maybe in a coma. How do you feel, Diggory? Give me the gun before you do something stupid."

Atsushi's heart pounded a bassline in his chest. If Savas realized Rana hadn't been controlling them, Girak would be executed as a traitor. "She still wants us to—"

A percussive boom of fireworks cut off his words.

Vincent yelped. "The thing's moving, sir."

Rana stirred, rolling onto her side to face Girak. *They can clear most of this out of my system. Can you still get me out?*

Commander Savas cursed and lunged at the educator. Girak jumped backward, knocking over the guard and stumbling over his splayed limbs. The gun crashed from his hands.

"Stop," Atsushi yelled, but Pridbor's elbow smashed into his ribs. "Don't make me," Atsushi sputtered and slammed the side of the gun into Pridbor's cheek.

Pridbor froze, eyes wide.

"One...more...move..." Atsushi said, gasping from the pain in his side, "and you're dead."

Commander Savas loomed over Girak and raised his gun to fire directly at him. "This has been coming a long time, Diggory."

"Nooo," Atsushi yelled as something rushed behind him, but he couldn't take his eyes off Girak, helpless before Savas.

Hands up, Girak cast Atsushi an anguished look. "I'm sor—"

Savas crumpled onto Girak. Confused, Atsushi, blinked. Ayanna now stood where Commander Savas had, her fake gun held like a club.

"Ayanna..." Girak's lips formed her name like a prayer of gratitude.

"She's psychotic," Pridbor shouted.

"Shut up." Atsushi tightened his grip on the jerk and yanked him back from Ayanna and the fallen men.

Girak disentangled himself from the unconscious Savas, and the guard tensed to spring for his gun.

"Freeze, or I'll kill Pridbor," Atsushi threatened.

The guard growled and held up his hands in surrender.

"Ayanna?" Girak said, gasping from his brush with death.

Ayanna managed a weak smile, and Girak gave her a thumb up.

As he scooped up the gun, Vincent dashed to the table and grabbed his gun. He spun and took aim at Rana.

"Seriously, do you want the Prime Minister dead?" Atsushi shouted. How many times could he threaten it before they called his bluff? Surely, he'd given himself away by now?

Girak pointed the real gun at Vincent. Did he realize he held the real one? "Vincent," Girak said, taking a few steps toward the terrified agriculturalist. "Drop the gun, or she'll make me kill you all. She's *very angry*."

In reality, the bleary-eyed Rana appeared anything but mad as she struggled into a sitting position, net still around her. She peered at her heaving chest.

"But she'll kill us all. Fight her, Diggory. Atsushi, you don't need to do this. Put the gun down." Vincent sounded desperate, almost crazed, his gun shakily pointed at Rana.

"She just wants to go home," Atsushi explained. With Savas unconscious, could he convince the others to free her?

"She's controlling you," Vincent screamed, and he fired at Rana. As she collapsed, Vincent froze in horror of what he'd done.

Girak rushed him, knocking the gun from his hands, and smashed his fist into Vincent's jaw. The agriculturist collapsed on the ground, unconscious.

Shaking out his fist, Girak grabbed the gun and shoved it into a cabinet. Of the four hostiles, only the prime minister remained conscious and would know where to look for it.

"*Shast*." Atsushi stumbled closer to Rana, yanking his hostage with him. "Is she...?"

Girak raced through the cell door to where Rana lay face down on the floor. He hesitated, then grasped her furry shoulders and rolled her over. "Rana?"

Outside, the fireworks still blazed, and Dr. Reinier shouted for Ayanna over the sounds of the panicked crowd.

Was this all for nothing? Atsushi's entire awareness focused on Rana's chest. *Breathe. Please, breathe.* If she was dead, there would be no way to stop the reapers from invading.

"Rana?" Girak tried again, this time adding a little shake.

She shuddered with a cough. *It hit my furs, not me, and knocked me down. Can you get this off me?* Rana pointed with her chin to the net that still wrapped her arms to her sides.

Relieved, Atsushi bowed his head against the prime minister. They still had a chance.

"Oh, thank goodness," Girak said, nearly deflating with relief. "I thought we'd lost you."

Pridbor cursed under his breath, and Atsushi shot him a glare worthy of Ayanna. Wait. Why wasn't Ayanna also checking on Rana? Turning, he called to her, "Hey, you okay?"

Ayanna nodded, dropped her fake gun, and stared down at the crumpled Commander Savas.

"I don't think he's killable," Atsushi joked, attempting to reassure her.

"Ayanna," Girak called, "he's unconscious, not dead. Can you find a knife or scissors and help me?"

She nodded and hurried to the tables. After a quick rummage through the drawers turned up nothing, she ran back to Commander Savas.

"Careful," Atsushi said, "he might wake up."

With a determined grimace, she hurriedly rolled him over, withdrew his knife from its sheath, and joined Girak in the cell. Awkwardly, the two of them cut off the tight webbing.

"I heard her, Girak. She talks." Ayanna's smile was a bit…odd.

*No, not now,* Atsushi thought.

Girak returned the smile, his eyes brimming with tears. "Yes, she can. And you saved my life. Thank you. I had no idea you were that strong."

"Neither did I. I didn't even think. When he pointed that gun at you…" She spun to examine the unconscious commander. "I didn't kill him, did I?" Her eyes shone wild as her arms trembled.

Girak put an arm around her. "He'll be fine. Just a bad headache…"

As Ayanna's trembling grew stronger, Girak's comforting smile grew concerned. His gaze met Atsushi's.

*Shast, not now…please not now,* Atsushi pleaded.

But there was no help for those cursed with the Sickness.

# Chapter 48

*orthern Haven: Atsushi Collins*

Northern Haven: Atsushi Collins
Atsushi swallowed his rising panic as Ayanna hugged herself, shaking so hard that she fell to the floor of Rana's cell, overcome with another episode.

*No, not now. I can't help Ayanna now.*

Ayanna clawed her legs, her eyes becoming distant and unconnected to her surroundings, and Atsushi was stuck holding Pridbor hostage with the gaming gun.

"Girak, take him," Atsushi said, shoving the prime minister toward him. "I'll help her."

As Girak rose from the floor, she shrieked.

The door to the hallway flew open and her mother ran into the room. "Ayanna, are you okay?" Dr. Reinier flew to her daughter's side, oblivious to the chaos around her. Or that she had just entered the prison cell.

Ayanna was clearly not okay, and if she screamed again, they'd be discovered by the rest of the crowd. Plus, in Dr. Reinier's hurry to reach Ayanna, she had shoved the exiting Girak deeper into the cell, and Atsushi was still stuck outside, restraining Pridbor and unable to reach Ayanna. Atsushi's eyes stung as she convulsed and he could do nothing.

Dr. Reinier glared at Girak with fury. "What happened? Why is she not safe with the other kids?" Then she noticed Atsushi in the adjoining room, holding the gun to Prime Minister Pridbor's chest. "Atsushi, what are you doing? Are you all mad?"

From behind her, Girak motioned for Atsushi to continue acting dazed.

He frowned. How would that work with Dr. Reinier?

Girak gave him a sterner look. *Shast*, this was never going to work, but Girak *did* know her better. Atsushi softened his frown into a drunken-looking pout. Even so, he couldn't get himself to lie to Dr, Reinier, so he stared at the ground between them, wincing as Ayanna's body thudded against the hard floor.

"What is going on?" Dr. Reinier asked, scooping up Ayanna.

He remained silent, avoiding her gaze, drowning in the guilt of having failed in his promise to Bleu to keep Ayanna safe.

"It's the g—girl," Girak responded and pointed at Rana. "She's con—controlling us."

Ayanna had now crumpled into her mother's arms, shaking and moaning.

Dr. Reinier spun to glare at Rana, still sitting on the cot.

"Then shoot her." She reached for Girak's gun.

"Don't make me shoot him," Atsushi shouted as he shook the prime minister.

Dr. Reinier glared at him, assessed the damage in the two adjoining rooms, and then wilted. "Are those three alive?" She appeared torn between her medical duties and not wanting to release Ayanna.

"Yes, just unconscious," Girak said. "She doesn't want anyone to get hurt. She only wants to go home." His act was slipping, too. Dr. Reinier could pull truth from those around her.

She wrapped her arms around Ayanna, like Atsushi yearned to. Dr. Reinier sank to the stone floor, leaning against the thick metallic rods separating Rana's prison from the main room as she rocked her daughter.

In the distance, firecrackers still exploded. He exchanged a desperate look with Girak. He had heard the same thing.

*How much longer will it take them to figure out it's a hoax?* Were they avoiding the explosive sounds and didn't deserve his earlier points for bravery? He'd programmed several repeats, but they had to be nearly out of time on the firework program and hadn't even gotten Rana to the elevator yet.

Rana stood, swaying in place, and then took a few unsteady steps toward Ayanna. Dr. Reinier shrank back against the inside prison wall. "Get away from us!"

*I am not your enemy. What happened to her?* Rana sent.

From everyone's expressions, it was clear they'd all heard her.

Dr. Reinier grimaced in disbelief. "She speaks Standard?"

"Somehow, with her mind, yes," Girak responded. "They're not monsters. This has all been a misunderstanding—"

"She's controlling you two. Get away from us," Dr. Reinier commanded and pulled Ayanna to her chest.

This farce had too many limitations, and it wasn't working. "The expedition grabbed her against her will. She just wants to go back home," Atsushi said, hoping to appeal to her maternal instinct.

"Says the boy pointing a gun at his prime minister," Dr. Reinier retorted. "You're not exactly yourself, Atsushi."

"Cass, please," Girak pleaded. "I was out there with them. I saw everything."

Dr. Reinier's hand had flown to her mouth.

Atsushi followed her terrified gaze to Rana, who repeatedly put her palms together as if praying and then pulled them apart. Whenever her hands neared each other, a soft violet glow erupted and surrounded them.

"Whoa." Atsushi nearly released the prime minister in his shock.

With the pastel emanations coming from Rana's palms, the metallic room took on a soft lavender hue. Ayanna now shook so violently that her mother had to grab her before she slid off her lap to the floor.

"Rana?" Atsushi called. "What are you doing?"

"You're going to let her blow the whole place up, aren't you?" Pribor yelled.

"Doesn't look like a weapon to me," Atsushi said. "It's beautiful." Could she have nanotech in her hands, or was this advanced reaper science he couldn't grasp?

"Rana," he whispered, "she came here to rescue you. Don't hurt her."

Rana gave him an odd look and then turned to Girak. *May I assist her?*

Atsushi couldn't breathe. Was this really happening?

Girak cleared his throat. "She wants to help her."

"I heard, too," Dr. Reinier said. "But what? I mean...how..."

Hope surged in his chest. If Rana could help Ayanna, he'd carry the reaper home through the snowdrifts himself. "Yes, please. Help her," Atsushi begged.

Rana's focus remained on Dr. Reinier. She stopped in front of Ayanna, stumbled a bit as she knelt, and then tilted her head as if in a question. Dr. Reinier, her mouth agape, stared at Rana's lavender hands.

*May I?* Rana swayed slightly, still affected by whatever drugs had been in those needles.

"Cass," Girak whispered, "let her try..."

Pridbor grunted. "Her hands glow, and suddenly, everything you've studied about protecting your patients goes out the air vent?"

Dr. Reinier flashed him a look of such ferocity that it left no question where Ayanna'd got it. "She's *my* daughter, and *my* patient. And your council is debating killing everyone with the Sickness, so shut up!" Then she nodded to the reaper to proceed.

Rana learned forward and placed one palm to Ayanna's chest as her other palm cradled her trembling head. The violet light rippled like waves over Ayanna's body. After a few shudders she stopped shaking and sank into her mother's arms.

Dr. Reinier scrutinized every miniscule movement Rana made, but her shoulders had relaxed, too. After several huge breaths, Ayanna's eyes drifted open, and she gave a tired smile.

"Yes," Atsushi shouted, his heart soaring. She'd never come out of an episode that quickly.

Dr. Reinier widened her eyes, then whispered, "Girak, do you see what I'm seeing? Is this possible?" As Ayanna sat up and sighed, tears streamed down her mother's face.

"Rana, you're amazing." Atsushi had never believed in miracles, despite the myths. He sniffed and swiped his damp cheek against Pridbor's shoulder, making him cringe in revulsion.

Ayanna turned to her mother and said, "Mom, she's magical."

Even Prime Minister Pridbor stopped struggling and stood submissively after Rana's display.

*We must go.*

Girak nodded. "Whatever that was, thanks." Girak turned to Atsushi, and his eyes filled with horror. "At—" he yelled.

Prime Minister Pridbor's elbow smacked into his face. Atsushi staggered backward, stunned by the pain. Blinking, he regained sight to see crimson spraying from his nose. He made a gallant attempt to maintain his grip on his gun, but Pridbor pried it from his grasp.

Girak leapt over Ayanna and her mom but tripped on Rana's netting. He shook it off and lunged forward, reaching the door just as the prime minister slammed his heavy frame against it, closing it.

"Nooo," Atsushi screamed.

The barred door clicked into place. Ayanna, her mother, Girak, and Rana were all trapped on the wrong side.

Pridbor grinned. "Like to see you get *that* open. Only Commander Savas knows the code, and he's not of any use now. Even to a mind reader." He pointed to the still unconscious commander and shook his head, sneering.

Atsushi spun around the main room, arms flailing, looking for another option, but they were hopelessly trapped. Even though he was on the outside of the barred area, their escape was impossible. He had no way to open the lock.

# Chapter 49

*orthern Haven: Rana*

N Even though the Crowned Ones were sending her long-distance healing, she struggled to think clearly. The small spiky things that had flown into her were a strange weapon. They hadn't hurt much but had made her groggy and clumsy.

With the netting off, she took a moment to pull the sharp things from her furs. Biting her lip, she yanked the fourth one out. Sweat trickled down her back as she attempted to rise and check Digga. The pup hadn't moved since their capture, but at least no one had separated them.

Struggling to untie the clasps on her furs, she startled at a sudden yelp. Blood dripped from Atsushi's nose, and she was again trapped behind the bars. Except, this time, there were three others trapped inside with her.

She turned to Girak. *What now?*

His eyes were closed, and he shook his head. She wasn't sure if that was a communication, but hopelessness emanated from him. She needed help to find her way out of here, and the Crowned Ones hadn't completely cleared the effects of the spiky things.

"Help us," she screamed to Atsushi. He was injured, but he was the only one free.

Everyone turned in alarm to stare at the noise she had made. *Oh. They don't understand my speech...*

"Shut up, you vile thing! You can't control my mind. You're done for." The angry one—was his name Prig Boar?—glared at her like a hungry predator and then hurried toward the door.

She had to stop him. Girak had said no one could know of her escape, but how could she stop Prig Boar from in here? All the strange facts she had learned about these children flew through her mind. Earlier, the guards had responded to love. *Except for the Walled One, Savas.* Instinctively, she opened herself fully to the One In All, and sent a wave of love over the man.

He froze.

Rana smiled. Maybe escape was possible without any more violence. She created a ball of love energy and tossed it between the angry man and the door.

Prig Boar backed up and examined the orb between him and the exit. Then he stopped and extended his arm toward the hovering light. A mix of fear and curiosity bubbled from him.

Rana willed the orb to grow. She was vaguely aware of Atsushi approaching their barred room and that Girak handed him something. *Focus on the orb.*

Suddenly, Atsushi leapt, arms outstretched, like a soaring bird onto the back of the now-enchanted man. As he made contact, he quickly wrapped Prig Boar in the net and tumbled him to the floor.

Rana yelped and turned in fury toward the others. *Why are you always violent?*

Girak cringed at her mental scream. "I'm trying to get us out of here before the others rush in."

Rana glared. *My method worked and was not violent.*

Atsushi tied up the stunned man, who was still angry his hunting stick hadn't worked.

"We brought in fake guns. That wasn't violent." Girak exuded pride at this.

Rana had no idea what he meant by fake. She teemed with frustration. Why bring any hunting sticks even if they were "fake guns"?

Atsushi ran to the bars and grabbed them, looking at Girak.

"How do we open it? Can she?" Atsushi and the others all turned expectantly to her.

*I will not help you fight. I will not...* She had helped them hurt that man. Her stomach twisted. *Can he breathe?* They all turned toward her as her outstretched arm directed their attention to the torn clothing that Atsushi had shoved in Prig Boar's mouth.

The woman who had been hugging the young girl turned to Rana. "Yes, he can. If we didn't stop him, he would have gotten the others, and they'd kill you and Girak. We need to get this door open... Do you have any way to open it? We must hurry."

*How would I open it? Do you believe I can do whatever I want?* She stamped her foot in frustration, her exhaustion making her wobble. She now understood why Sohana had called them children.

Girak stepped forward, his face sorrowful. "Rana, I'm sorry. I thought you were distracting him to help us get out." The sadness and desperation coming off him was palpable. She sensed his sadness was related to something bigger than what had just occurred, but she didn't have the energy to figure it out.

She met his sorrowful gaze. *I cannot do whatever I want, but I may have an idea.*

Rana again began untying her furs. She sensed their stares, but her full attention was on uncovering Digga. *Please, let her be unharmed.* As she opened the skin carrier Desna had made, she gently cooed to the striped mound of sweaty fur. The crowd around her collectively sucked in air and leaned in closer.

There was no movement. Tears stung Rana's eyes, as she stroked her charge. "Digga... Digga, wake up." Her right hand flared golden as she caressed the pup's back.

Nothing.

Tears streamed down Rana's face. "Digga."

She'd risked her life meeting this lovable troublemaker, and Kalakanya had said that journey meant something. She *had* to be okay.

Frantic, Rana pulled the still pup completely free of her furs. She was still warm, but Rana worried that was due to her own body being overheated in this sweltering box. But Digga's body wasn't stiff...

"Oh my Oneness, you can't be dead. Please."

They all stood around her in a circle, spellbound by the motionless furred one. Digga sniffled, her mouth yawning open with a squeak. Her lethal, canine teeth snapped back together.

"Oh, Digga." Rana clasped her furry love to her chest. "What were you doing? Making up for all the lack of sleep before?" She laughed in relief.

"What is that?" Ayanna leaned closer.

"She has a pet," Atsushi said, grinning in wonder.

Rana looked up at Girak. *This is my idea.* She held up Digga's small, front paws. Five sharp claws protruded from each one. Digga could save them all.

The others were unimpressed. They looked from the claws to each other. Rana chuckled. These humans lacked experience with cave digger claws. *They slice through everything. I'll show you.*

She shifted in the crowded and barred box to the nearest metal rod. She whispered to Digga and held up the pup's paw. Digga scraped it as if uninterested. A huge gauge mark now covered the metal.

She scowled at the bars. How could she interest Digga in clawing with more force? She came up with nothing. Could she move her claws for her? Would Digga tolerate that? Was it worth the risk? The sharp claws could slice through her gloved fingers. She glanced at the unconscious men beginning to stir outside their enclosed space. There wasn't much time.

She turned to the others. *Do not make any sudden noises or movements.* They nodded.

Rana whispered to Digga and then firmly clasped her paw, holding the nails by their base. She paused, concerned the tactic might hurt the young pup. Given the violence she had already witnessed, she and Digga's only option was to escape or be killed. If this hurt Digga a little, it would hurt less than being hunted by the humans.

She sliced the longest claw against the bar at chest level. The bar separated where she had sliced but stayed in place. *Good work, Digga.*

Rana knelt and repeated the same motion lower on the bar. It clanged to the ground. One of the guards stirred. Atsushi cautiously approached, tied, and gagged the guard.

She turned to Ayanna, who now stood quietly beside her mother. The girl was petite enough to reach around Rana in this small room without brushing against Digga. *Can you hold the next bar and prevent its fall?*

"Yes." Ayanna approached, never taking her wide eyes off Digga.

Rana repeated the slicing movements on two more bars, then looked at Girak and decided to do another one. Finished, she tucked Digga back into her furs. As the others scrambled out of the hole, she passed Digga a piece of dried meat from the pouch attached to her belt.

*Quiet now, Digga.* She climbed through the bars and eyed Savas, but he remained still.

Now that she had to walk, her legs wobbled with each step, and her brain remained garbled from the needle weapons. She couldn't Call to reach the Crowned Ones.

*They must believe I'm sleeping like they told me to do. If only I could sleep...* Her eyelids weighed heavy, but danger still surrounded her.

Atsushi and Girak tied up the Walled One. His hate-filled eyes snapped open and shot daggers at Rana, making her stomach flip. She yearned to flee this box, but the idea of running was ludicrous. Her knees might buckle at any moment.

She shuddered as Girak picked up Savas' gun. *What are you doing?*

Girak's face was somber. "Planning ahead. I'm taking his real gun for up on the Surface."

Rana narrowed her eyes. *I will not help you kill.*

He shook his head. "I don't want to kill anyone. It's in case we meet any dangerous animals."

*Animals don't need to be hunted. No hunting sticks.* Rana shook her head vehemently, almost falling over again. Digga snarled.

"But the dangers..." Girak sighed. "Rana, we can't do what you reapers do. We need protection."

*No. Get me out, and I'll show you. And stop calling me reaper. You have horrid associations with that word. We're star beings, and I won't travel with weapons.*

Girak grimaced as his energy tangled within him. Rana strived to read his conflicted energy and thoughts, to understand what she was up against. He seemed caught between his experience of the world and wanting to believe hers was possible.

*Trust the One In All.*

"What?" His face contorted even more as if his conflicted energy had wrapped itself so tightly, it now twisted his facial muscles.

*The connecting love that unites the universe.*

Girak's eyebrows rose.

*We need to hurry. Trust me, no hunting sticks.*

Girak sighed, shook his head, and placed the hunting stick on the ground, well away from the tied men. "We need the fake ones to get you out. These," he said, holding up other weapons. "They don't shoot. They're for playing games."

*You play games with hunting sticks?* Rana could not understand these strange humans.

She consented only because her limbs trembled with weakness, and she feared wasting any more time and energy on communication. She stumbled after the others toward the box opening, grateful for the mother's supporting arm around her.

# Chapter 50

*orthern Haven: Rana*

Rana hoped that the box opening they were about to go through wasn't far from their den's exit, and a lovely, sparkling, ice-covered plain with peleguins calling overhead, and blissfully fresh air.

But Girak poked his head through it and then quickly pulled it in and turned to grimace at the others. Not a good sign.

"They must have found the hologram, because I can't hear it. Two men stand near the hall entrance to the elevators," he said. From behind them came muffled laughter. She turned to see Savas, gagged and tied, but now sitting and watching them like a hawk.

At his taunts, the others leaned toward each other and whispered plans. Then Ayanna's mother—Cass, apparently—passed Rana's arm to Ayanna and slipped out the door.

Rana wasn't sure why Cass had left, but her concern grew with every passing moment that she hadn't returned.

*Don't we have to hurry?*

An odd rhythmic knocking on the door drew their attention from her question. Girak opened it, and Cass stumbled in under the weight of a heavy sack on her shoulder. She began yanking out footwear and many layers of clothing.

Girak's eyes widened in delight. "You found Savas' outerwear?" He shot a worried look toward Savas, who observed all they did.

*Don't we have to hurry?* Rana asked again. Would those bindings hold Savas?

"We need proper clothing, or we'll die up there," Girak said as he quickly slipped on a second layer and boots, ending with the familiar orange pelt. He checked himself carefully and again conferred with the others.

Rana was too tired to follow the conversation. Head down, she swayed next to Ayanna, struggling to keep her eyelids open.

The mother hugged Ayanna and smiled at them. "I don't like this, but it will take all three of you to deal with the guards and help Rana. Returning her is our best chance of helping Bleu and Neviah." She glanced toward Savas.

"He knows you helped us," Ayanna warned her mother.

Cass nodded, and her face tightened. "SHAST founded Northern Haven to preserve humanity through science and technology. As head researcher on the Sickness, I observed as Rana healed you. It will be my word as a scientist and doctor against his as a commander." She spoke with confidence, but her energy was a tangled mess. "Take care of each other." Her gaze took in all of them.

She hugged Ayanna. "I love you."

Blinking back tears, Cass hurried from the room.

They faced the door, not moving. What were they waiting for? Loud, running footsteps came from down the hall, and then the mother yelled, sounding terrified.

Rana bolted fully upright and lurched toward the door.

Girak grabbed her arm. "No. She's pretending she saw something down the hall to get rid of the guards."

Did these humans constantly trick each other? They were all too natural at it. More running footsteps passed outside their doorway and disappeared down the corridor.

Silence followed. Girak opened the door, poked his head out, and then motioned for the others to follow him.

Running and shouting echoed off brightly colored walls of a tunnel so huge it'd make any cave digger jealous. Mini suns hung evenly spaced along the roof, never moving. Their orange light made her vision waver.

She shivered, and Digga mewed and squirmed, sensing her fear. *Quiet,*

*Digga. Just a little bit longer.* She yearned to stroke her soft head, but Ayanna still held one of her arms. She trailed the other arm against the wall, helping herself stay upright.

They approached a reflective wall with lines in its smoothness and small glowing squares clustered at chest level. Girak approached the glowing area and said something to the others. Atsushi pointed his pretend hunting stick at the wall as if it were to attack them, while Girak tapped the glowing spots.

Loud, hissing noises erupted from the wall, and Rana fell backward in a panic.

"It's okay. It's okay, don't be scared." Ayanna smiled at Rana and pulled her up onto her feet. "It's going to open, and once we make sure it's empty, we'll get inside and take you up there."

Ayanna pointed with her finger to the ceiling and pulled Rana back toward the reflective wall.

Girak motioned for them to move to the side so that only he and Atsushi were in front of the odd surface. It snapped open like an angry sideways mouth. Two orange-pelted men yelled out.

Rana couldn't understand what they said, but when Girak and Atsushi jumped in front of them, pointing the pretend guns, the men fell silent. Girak growled, and the two men slowly stepped out.

"Drop the weapons, and give us your clothing," Girak said.

The men's gazes found Rana, and they stepped back. Disgust and horror oozed from them, their energy thick and swampy.

Rana frowned. *My Oneness! They don't even know me.*

Girak pointed his pretend gun at the first man's chest. "Now."

The men dropped their weapons, and Atsushi kicked them away. Rana flinched at the hostility filling the air around her. Its corrosiveness threatened to consume her. The two guys stripped off their clothes until they were down to wearing only some cloth around their waist.

Girak grunted something to Atsushi, who tied and gagged the men and then forced them into a small box in the tunnel's side wall.

As Atsushi shut the box, Rana's heart fluttered with concern. *They will*

378

*be okay? Someone will get them out?*

"Ah, they're fine." Atsushi turned and grinned. "It's us I'd worry about."

They all rushed into the gaping mouth that had opened in the wall. Girak carried in the colorful, bulky clothing from the unfortunate guards. He turned and pushed the glowing lights on the inside of the box.

As the box closed, Rana's throat sank into her belly. She grasped her neck, heart racing. *What's happening?*

"It's okay. The box is going up." Girak pointed toward the roof. "We're taking you home, okay?"

Rana slowly nodded. Wooziness filled her head, and she stumbled against the wall. Ayanna helped her sit and then began listening to Girak's directions on how to dress. After he gave directions, both guys stared at the wall while Ayanna changed. What were they doing?

Moments passed, and the air grew damp and colder. She smiled and rested her head against the thrumming wall. Everything vibrated or hummed in the human den, none of it harmoniously. Despite being bone tired, the strangeness of it kept her awake. Barely.

"Educator Girak? A little help here..." Ayanna stood, arms outstretched before her, covered in thick clothing that was way too big.

"Hmm." Girak grimaced and shook his head. "Tragic waste, but you can't go out like that." He pulled out an odd tool, somehow transformed its shape, and then cut off the extra pant length. He shoved some of the extra material into the toes of the too large boots. After she pulled the boots back on, Girak instructed her to tuck the torn pants into the boots.

*So hot...*Rana had been sweating profusely in these hot boxes and was soaked. Using her remaining strength to unbutton her furs, she brought up as much energy from the Earth as she could to dry her skin, Digga, and her furs. The others stared as her sweat steamed off her, filling the box with Digga's musky scent. She smiled weakly. Dry, she closed up her furs and slowly drifted into unconsciousness.

# Chapter 51

Peleguin-Rookery-By-The-Lake: Bleu Reinier

Bleu and Neviah followed the two reapers out into the biting, cold wind. He searched the moonlit village for an escape, but ice houses surrounded their path, the doorways filled with reapers who watched them with unreadable expressions. He shivered but not from the cold.

Taking Neviah's gloved hand, he pulled her closer. "We can't let them separate us, okay?"

She nodded, her wide, brown eyes glistening in the starlight.

Bleu returned to scanning their surroundings. Many of the reapers were injured or bleeding. Moans drifted from several of the ice huts, and the beings in the doorways would glare at him before turning back inside toward the groans. His chest tightened as awareness thundered upon him. He had done this. He had shot them.

He sought Neviah's face, hoping to catch her reaction, but she had stopped in her tracks. She stared open-mouthed at a reaper's glowing hands. As they touched another's bleeding leg, the wound knit closed.

Gandhapalin tapped Bleu on the shoulder, and he startled backward. No reaper would touch him. They did enough with their minds. What could they do with their hands aglow?

*Sorry to scare you, but we must keep moving,* Gandhapalin sent.

Bleu grunted in agreement. Really, what choice did he have?

"Come on." he said, gently tugging Neviah away from watching the reapers healing their injured. Before escaping, he should steal whatever healing tech they had to see if it could help Ayanna.

As he walked past more injured, the thump, thump, thump of the dagger in his thigh pocket drummed out his guilt. Half an hour ago, it had been a reassurance, a chance to fight and flee. Now, his plan to stab them and escape sickened him. *What have I become?*

He didn't trust the reapers. He had no reason to believe them. But what would Ayanna think of him if she knew he was now a killer? He walked in a numb daze, vaguely aware of Gandhapalin and Desna pausing for him to keep up.

They were almost to the Lion's Circle, whatever it was. Ahead, a crowd of beings had gathered in a circle and... *Are they singing?*

He turned, and Neviah's eyebrows rose. A slight smile crept across her face.

"Bleu, they're communicating. Listen to the tones."

"Yeah, they're going to sing us to death." Bleu wasn't sure whether he was joking. Surely, what he'd done to them was punishable by death?

Ahead of them, reapers—maybe forty?—chanted with their unearthly voices that vibrated every cell of his being. They stood evenly spaced among large boulders, and the air glowed as if an electric cloud surrounded them. The far edge of the rock circle lay in a partially frozen lake, and something large swam just below the surface of the dark water. A chill rose up his spine.

A lithe reaper stepped from the circled group, nodded, and pulled Neviah into the circle. Bleu, still holding her hand, followed.

It was like walking into an invisible tornado of energy rushing in a circular motion. He struggled to stand upright and crashed onto the reaper next to him. Both he and Neviah crumpled to their knees. Neviah shrieked, and Bleu grunted as he tried to rise. But gravity seemed to be shifting, and his body no longer responded normally. He couldn't breathe.

The beings next to him attempted to pull him up as the horizon shifted and he fell onto his side. Nothing made sense. Everything buzzed and swirled around him. He blacked out.

He awoke to the same buzzing and singing noises, but now they were distant. He blinked slowly, willing his eyes to focus. A feminine-looking reaper leaned over him, and above her was the roof of an ice hut. She wasn't Desna. Despite having white hair, this one was much younger. And attractive.

Warmth flooded his chest as she touched it, and a coziness spread over him that brought memories of being rocked by his mother. He shook his head, fighting the urge to relax, to be lulled. He had to get up and find Neviah, but his mind was sluggish. He sucked in a slow jagged breath.

*Better? Can you sit up?* She peered deeply into his eyes, and another wave of lightheadedness washed over him.

This particular reaper made him dizzier than the other two combined.

Her eyes widened as if she had heard that thought, and then she visually scanned his whole body. *Are you okay? Your body? We didn't expect the Circle to affect you like that.*

He nodded slowly and cleared his throat. The odd sensation of floating above his body overcame him. "Where...where's Neviah? My friend?" His throat was numb, and his voice cracked.

*Right there.*

Despite the night's darkness, Bleu followed her pointed hand to where Neviah sat a few meters away, sipping a steamy liquid from a bowl. Her expression was trancelike, focused solely on her drink. She didn't notice that they had mentioned her name.

Bleu struggled into a sitting position. "What are you going to do with us?"

*Do?* Am amused smile flickered across her face.

"I shot a bunch of your...your..." He didn't know how to refer to them.

*We are star beings.*

Bleu stared. Stamf had been right when he'd joked about the aliens taking over the surface. Grief slammed into him again. He looked away, his eyes stinging.

*What does your species want? We do not understand why you are determined to fight us. Explain yourself.*

Bleu turned back. Anger flashed in the star being's green eyes. Then it evaporated as they stared at each other.

"Explain ourselves? We simply came outside, and you lulled and killed Abdul and then attacked us again outside our door."

Her jade eyes narrowed. *We do not control minds, and we never attack.*

"Yeah, and I've never shot a star being."

He regretted it as soon as it left his mouth. All those moaning injured star beings had been shot by him and Savas. *What's wrong with me?* What *did* he want other than to find a cure for Ayanna... He looked up and blushed. She had been following his thoughts.

She studied him intently, head cocked.

Bleu felt naked, incapable of hiding secrets from this being, like a captured protozoan observed under a light scope. Yet from her furrowed brow, he knew she still couldn't fathom him.

She sighed and placed her hands in a strange arrangement in her lap. Bleu tensed. What was she doing now?

She looked at his face, then down at her hands. *This is a hand position to help me focus. I take your concerns very seriously, and I want to make sure we understand each other.* She held her hands up and displayed her interconnecting thumbs and fingertips. He nodded.

*Let's start over. I am Kalakanya. What is your name?*

"Kala what?"

"Ka-la-*kan*-ya."

She had a voice. He stared at her mouth, grinning like a fool. She laughed, her whole frame shaking.

He leaned closer, fascinated. "You can speak with your mouth?"

*Of course.* She tapped her lips with a finger, her eyes full of mirth. *But you wouldn't understand our language. I'm using mind speak because all creatures understand it.*

He stiffened. "We're lowly *creatures* to you?"

She frowned. *No creatures are lowly. We are creatures, too.*

"Oh." Bleu looked away from those haunting eyes. She looked his age, but her eyes...

His thoughts got tumbled for a moment. Again, she watched him, head tilted as she pushed a white strand that had escaped from the long, spiraled braid behind her ear.

"My name is Bleu."

"Bl-?"

"Bl-eu." He enunciated the sounds clearly.

"Bleu." She smiled. *Do you know we met before? I was one of the three star beings returning Abdul's body. I put up symbols of peace and faith, but you still hunted us. Now you act friendly. I do not understand why you would hunt us without knowing about us. Why did you do that?*

Bleu stared. *We've met before.* "You. You were the—there..." He closed his mouth. *What is it about her? It's like...* Again, he had the uncanny sensation she was following his thoughts.

He cleared his throat. "We thought it was you hunting us."

Kalakanya stared at him open-mouthed. *Why? We never hunt.*

"You must. You need to eat, don't you? I don't see any crops growing around here." He swept his arm around them. Surely, she was joking.

*No. I eat very little. But our children eat meat. We Call furred ones to the Lion's Circle. They volunteer. They enter the Circle and lie down and their spirit leaves. It is painless and nonviolent.*

Bleu jumped to his feet, his arms thrown out in front of him. "That's what you were trying to do to Neviah and me?" Ripples of horror cascaded through his body.

Neviah had turned at her name and wandered toward them.

*Oh my Oneness! Never. How could you imagine such a thing?* Kalakanya held her hand to her mouth, frozen.

They stared at each other. Bleu's heart pounded and his muscles tensed, ready to fend off this powerful alien.

Neviah began circling him. "Bleu? What did I miss? Bleu? Bleu!"

"Get away from her," he shouted to Neviah and pulled her behind him, never taking his eyes off Kalakanya.

They'd almost been lunch for the alien kids. Glaring at the alien, he maneuvered his hand down to his pocket. In a flash, he held the dagger to Kalakanya's heart. At least, where he figured her heart was. The idea of stabbing her sickened him, but he hadn't come this far to be eaten.

Kalakanya stared at his dagger and gasped. *You're Cassandra's son?*

# Chapter 52

Peleguin-Rookery-By-The Lake: Bleu Reinier

Peleu literally rocked backward with the shock of hearing his mother's name from this star being. He hunched, his knife again dangerously close to Kalakanya's chest.

She didn't flinch, her intense jade eyes continuing to search his face. She was messing with him. How did she know his mother's name?

*Bleu, I would never hurt you or your friend. We are not violent. I know your mother. I gave you that dagger. I didn't... didn't recognize...you...*

Bleu sensed he wasn't the only one reeling from this revelation, but he continued holding the knife poised to kill. He glanced down at the gifted dagger.

She had said, *Keep it with you always.* He had trusted that luminous woman...been in awe of her. Had she *caused* Ayanna's Sickness? She appeared the same day. She controlled minds. Were these beings the cause of the Sickness? *How deeply would I need to thrust it to kill her?*

"Bleu," Neviah yelled and grasped his forearm. "Stop it."

He blinked. His fury at Ayanna's situation had almost driven him to kill again. "How do you know my mother? She's never left Northern Haven."

"Bleu, we can't fight our way out of here. There are too many of them." Neviah tugged at his arm that didn't hold the dagger. "Bleu, stop. They could have killed us before, but they didn't."

He didn't waver in his stance. "What about Stamf and Abdul?"

*Bleu, you misunderstand me. We wanted you to join us in the circle to see what our community is like. To create peace. We were all in it. When we Call*

386

*the furred ones for food, they are not controlled by us. They come willingly. They know what they are doing when they come. It's reciprocal; we help them also. We do healings, we nurse orphans, and we pull up seaweed during the winter to feed the salt deer. We work together with all. We would never trick you like that.* She hadn't moved a muscle to protect herself and instead seemed to reach out with her warm gaze, tugging at his heart.

He glared into her green eyes, terrified of being controlled, yet a strange knowing welled up from deep within him that she had spoken truth. His heart still raced, but he took a step backward and lowered the dagger a bit. Extending his left arm, he kept Neviah behind him. Out of Kalakanya's reach, just in case.

Neviah batted away his arm. "Thanks, but I can take care of myself."

"I know, it's just…" Bleu's mind still reeled from learning Kalakanya had given him his dagger. He lowered it.

*Thank you,* Kalakanya sent to both of them, though her gaze remained on the dagger. *What would prove to you that you are safe?*

"Allow both of us to leave. Now," he demanded.

*That would be ignoring the dangerous situation we are all in. You believe we are the enemy. We have done everything in an attempt to help.*

"How did killing Abdul help us?" His hand tightened around the dagger's hilt. "Or killing Stamf?" His voice faltered on his friend's name.

*We haven't killed anyone. When you attacked Kahali in the ice cave, your weapons caused the cave-in that killed your friend. We found his body and returned it to you. Kahali had no weapons and would never have hurt any of you.*

He grunted in indignation. "There was a bright flash from a weapon. I *saw* it." No way could she argue that.

*Bleu, that was us beaming in to help Kahali after you hunted him. We get our star being name from the bright star of light that flashes when we appear and disappear. We never attack. It is not our nature.*

His fury wavered. Did she speak the truth? Her version differed greatly from what Commander Savas and Stamf had told them, and from what he had seen on their cameras.

But it *could* be true. Had Stamf made a mistake? And he knew nothing about how Stamf himself had died other than a cliff was involved, and he didn't really want more horrid details now.

Was she mind-controlling him? He had witnessed how the second expedition had reacted as if in a trance. If she wasn't, and he chose to believe her, then everything he had once been told and believed was wrong.

Pressure pounded behind his eyeballs as the two realities tore at each other inside his head. His decision would affect many lives...Ayanna's... his mother's...all of Northern Haven.

He massaged his brow. How does one recognize truth? He turned to Neviah, who was chewing her lip as she scrutinized everything within eyesight in the ice building. "Neviah? What do you think?"

She flipped off her headpiece, tucked her hair behind her ear, and leaned over to study a small carved piece of wood. Straightening up, she motioned around them. "Nothing here seems threatening. No weapons, no tech, no war or hunting trophies." She shrugged. "It used to be problematic enough when two cultures met, and these aren't even humans."

She met Kalakanya's gaze and blushed. "Sorry, was it star beings?"

Kalakanya nodded.

Neviah had a good point, but after everything that had happened, how could she trust them so easily?

"What do you all want?" Bleu pictured his mind closed off from hers, hoping he could block her.

*We were seeking the children of the Earth. There was a prophecy...we want to help you survive.* Kalakanya became luminous, glowing, like when they had first met in Bleu's vision.

He took a step back. "What are you doing? You're glowing..." His voice betrayed his awe. She was radiant. Beautiful.

"Do you think she's radioactive?" Neviah began searching in her bag for equipment. She pulled out one of her many strange personally designed devices and pointed it at Kalakanya.

*You are both still scared. I am connecting with the One In All and sending love. If you are not coated in fear, you will experience everything more clearly.*

*Your thoughts are becoming less clouded, right?*

"She's not radioactive..." Neviah's device began smoking. "But she's frying my equipment." She dropped the hot metal on the floor, shaking out her hands from the heat. "How did you do that?"

Bleu closed his eyes and opened them. She was still glowing. *If I still hear her thoughts, I must not be blocking her.*

*No, you are not.* Kalakanya grinned. *If you block me, we cannot communicate. It is our link. Do you feel better?*

He was treading on dangerous ground. Trusting these beings could be lethal. Yet he had such a strong sense that she wouldn't harm them.

"Okay, I might believe you. Maybe you meant us no harm. If so, I..." Bleu looked down at the matted flooring.

His mind returned to the battle. He was rolling and diving, shooting star beings left and right, trying to get to Neviah, then trying to get them both back to the rover. His breath caught in his chest. His eyes stung. He had killed too many. He had *killed*. He closed his eyes, determined not to shed a tear before this powerful being.

Warmth flowed onto his arm. His eyes shot open to find Kalakanya touching his forearm. He stumbled away from her touch, and the electric flow between them stopped.

"Don't you have any boundaries?" Neviah said, glaring at where Kalakanya's hand had touched his arm. "Stop doing that to him."

Kalakanya gasped. *I'm sorry, I was trying to help, and instead, I've upset you again.* She looked from Neviah to him. *I'd never hurt you.*

He met Neviah's concerned gaze. "It's okay, she didn't hurt me." Turning to address Kalakanya, his bloodguilt overwhelmed him. "I'm not a violent person. Well, not normally." He looked away.

If only he could undo all those deaths.

*You allowed fear to overcome your heart. Do not shame yourself for what you did not understand in the past.* She smiled. *But to prevent more deaths, we need both your help. I sense worse approaching from others in your den. Will you help us avert more tragedy?*

"Of course," Neviah said.

He nodded, his throat wooden.

*Bleu, we will forgive, but you must also forgive yourself. Awareness makes you a different person. Live your new life; don't relive the old one.*

He could only nod, his breath and voice still caught in his chest. He couldn't imagine how he could ever forgive himself for ending so many lives. Ayanna would be furious at him, and his parents would be so disappointed in what he'd become.

Kalakanya raised her palm. *May I?* she asked, her hand hovering near his chest. She waited.

He nodded.

She gently touched his breastbone, and his chest relaxed. His eyes welled up and a few silent tears ran down his cheeks. His breath flowed more fully. He cleared his throat; it worked now. She removed her hand and took a step backward.

Immediately, a sense of loneliness, of separation from all other beings returned. Was this new, or was this his normal state of awareness? He swiped away the tears and gave Kalakanya a slight nod of gratitude.

*Do either of you know what your humans will be planning?*

Bleu and Neviah looked at each other, then shook their heads.

"They'll attack," Neviah guessed, "and Commander Savas will be brutal. I wonder if we still have bombs?"

At that, Bleu's stomach churned. "He'll try to destroy you all. He has no heart."

*Every being has a heart. What if we all go and explain the misunderstanding?*

Neviah raised her eyebrows and stifled a laugh. She glanced at Bleu, then said, "Kalakanya, we want to understand you. We're willing to listen, unlike Commander Savas and the council. And now that we understand, if we go back, they'll believe you mind-controlled us, and they will still want to kill you."

*There is always a way, even if it is hidden from us.* Kalakanya motioned for them to follow. *Come. You will meet others, so you may better understand us. I must gather the Crowned Ones and decipher this incoming threat.*

# Chapter 53

*orthern Haven's Elevator: Atsushi Collins*

Atsushi grimaced and stepped away from Rana toward the elevator wall. "Is she, you know, dead?" He'd just watched Rana say something about being too hot, start steaming, and then go limp. Standing next to her, he tapped her leg with his boot. Nothing.

Girak knelt beside her and studied her face for signs of breathing. "Rana?" He gingerly tapped one finger on her shoulder as if expecting her to be ablaze. "Rana?"

"Is she hot? Spontaneous boiling doesn't seem like a good way to go." Atsushi backed up another step. Would she now completely self-destruct?

Girak shook his head. "No, she's not even feverish. Weird…" He shook her shoulder. "Rana."

A small growl erupted from her chest, and Girak flew backward, landing with a thud on his buttocks.

Ayanna giggled. "It's the animal."

"Great time to die," Atsushi complained. "What do we do now?" The elevator paused in its ascent as if it too were reconsidering their foolish plan.

"She's not dead. She's still warm." Girak squinted at Rana, his fingers tapping his fake gun.

"Of course, she's warm; she just steamed herself to death." Atsushi's mind raced. They were en route to the Surface, where they still had to sneak past guards to save an already dead alien. What was the point?

"Girak? Maybe we should pretend that when she died, we got our minds

391

back. You know, go down and turn ourselves in?" Was it cowardly to go back if she was already dead?

Girak paced the small elevator. The animal growled every time his footsteps neared Rana's crumpled figure. It became an eerie rhythm—thump, thump, thump, thump, growl, and repeat. The elevator's grinding, which had completely stopped, restarted as it surged upward.

"*Shast* it!" Girak spun back toward Rana, a determined look in his eye. He knelt and used his gun's butt to tap her leg. "Hey, Rana. Get up."

She stirred, her head lolling from her chest to rest against the wall. The growling increased, and a sharp claw appeared, ripping its way through the furs on her chest. A small nose popped out, and Girak jumped back. The animal's musky scent filled the elevator.

Atsushi chuckled. "The beast lives."

Ayanna joined his laughter as the animal's small nose wiggled in the cold air.

"Hmm," Girak grunted. "She's alive, so going back is out." He stood and turned in circles, examining the elevator walls.

"What are you looking for?" Atsushi's heart beat faster the closer they rose to the Surface. Girak had to have a plan. *Then again, he's spinning in circles...*

Girak stopped spinning and pressed on the walls as if testing their strength. "We need a way to move her. I can't carry her with that thing ready to bite my head off. If one of these panels came off, it could be like a stretcher..." He attempted to pry a panel off with an ice pick from his pack. It didn't budge. "There must be a way..."

Atsushi and Ayanna exchanged looks, then both shrugged. He had no idea what to do up on the Surface.

Girak cleared his throat. "Well, if we travel away from the door and hide for a bit, I'm sure they'll show up for her. They talk with their minds, so it shouldn't be hard for Rana to call them."

"But she's unconscious," Atsushi said, waving his arm toward the crumpled reaper.

Rana opened her eyes. She looked way too relaxed for their predicament—probably still drugged. Her gloved hand made a jerk toward the animal's protruding nose. The threatening growls turned to a whimper, then stopped as the striped snout withdrew back inside.

"Rana," Girak called, but she had passed out again. He groaned in exasperation and then looked up with renewed confidence. "Her friends will find us. Kala told me to get her out. They'll be waiting to help us. Trust me, they're good."

"It's their choice in pets that worries me." Atsushi stared at the empty hole in Rana's fur coat.

Girak chuckled. "We'll be there in a moment. Get your gear ready."

Atsushi flipped up the soft, helmet-like coverings that allowed them to have warmed air while keeping their faces from freezing. They had three fake guns and an unconscious girl with a growling chest. This would be the world's shortest rescue attempt.

The elevator grumbled and shook to a halt as if it had died. He hoped that wasn't a sign.

Girak checked both of their soft helmets and radio settings. "We don't want the others to hear us too easily, so I'm linking the three of us on an alternative channel."

"Your plan?" Atsushi's voice sounded strange in his own ears.

"It depends a bit on what we face. Follow my lead."

Not exactly reassuring words. He exchanged a worried glance with Ayanna through his visor.

The door lurched open.

"It's nighttime." The others could clearly see that for themselves, but despite the time, Atsushi had assumed they would arrive to a daylit Surface. He stood at the entrance, open-mouthed at the endless pit of darkness. The vast space yawned before him, ready to engulf any who dared cross the elevator's threshold. A cold sweat trickled down his neck.

Girak put a finger to where his lips would be and stepped just outside the door. Atsushi and Ayanna scrunched closer to each other inside the elevator, craning their necks to peer at the wondrous sky.

Girak dashed out and glanced in all directions. Then he ran back, grabbed Rana's arms, and began pulling her out, as the door began closing. Atsushi helped him get Rana's legs out of the way just in time.

"Where are they?" He scanned the blackness. "Aren't they guarding the door?"

Girak motioned for silence and pointed up to the sky. "I think it's only Zach and a lit drone to make it look like more than one person. At least, that was their plan earlier."

Atsushi followed his gaze up to the cliff over the door. Lights bounced around at the top of the cliff.

"Didn't he hear us?" Ayanna whispered. "The door's loud."

"He can't see under this ledge. If we don't move out more, he won't see us." Girak strapped on his fake gaming rifle.

"But the control room must have told him about us," Ayanna persisted.

"We were in the control room, remember?" Girak adjusted his headpiece. "Until the crowd goes in there, they're all tied up."

"But we can't move," Atsushi said.

Girak smiled. "I have a plan. If they are still tied up, it'll work. If not... well, you'd better be ready to run. Zach has training on real firearms, but it's dark. If we can reach those shadows from the cliff walls there"—he pointed to a darkened area about thirty meters away—"we should be good. You see it? If he doesn't fall for this, we have to run with her to that area. He can't see us from there in this darkness."

"What are you going to do?" Atsushi sucked in a deep breath of the cold but oddly fragrant air. It was strangely invigorating.

"Act like the sucker everyone thinks I am." Girak grimaced and ran out from beneath the ledge.

Atsushi caught his breath.

"Guys! Zach, can you hear me?" Girak loosened his headpiece, yelling and waving at the lights on the cliff.

Atsushi watched with growing horror as the lights above stopped bouncing around and all focused on his educator.

"Girak? Is that you?" Zach yelled.

"Yes. Were they able to contact you yet? The Control Room? We're having trouble with all our equipment," Girak yelled and tapped his headpiece as if the radio didn't work.

Atsushi grabbed Rana's arms, ready to run. The lights on the clifftop turned toward each other in an unheard conversation. Maybe they had two men stationed up there. *Please...let this work.*

"No, we can't reach them. Is everything okay?" Zach called down.

"We're making an exchange. I'm to return the one we caught, and they are going to return Bleu and Neviah."

Ayanna whimpered at Bleu's name. Atsushi yearned to offer comfort, but he couldn't risk letting go of Rana.

"Thank goodness they're okay. You're doing that alone?" Zach asked, incredulous.

"Well, they sent some others to help me carry her. They'll go back inside to be safe, and then I'm to wait over there with her." Girak turned to Ayanna and him and motioned for them to get ready to run.

There was a pause while men on top of the cliff, or maybe just Zach, considered his tale.

Atsushi and Ayanna stared at each other. Girak was going to take on all the risk and blame. He was going to be shut outside alone with a body too large for him to carry and no weapons. All this to save Rana, prevent a war, and get them back inside, where it was safe. Was he brave or suicidal?

"No," Atsushi whispered.

"Sounds dangerous, Girak. You volunteer?" Zach gave a nervous laugh.

"Of course not, would you? It's an order, and I'm a Deplorable. We're going over. Cover us." Before waiting for a response, Girak motioned and the three of them began carrying Rana toward the shadows as quickly as possible.

They got twenty meters before Zach's yelling broke out from the cliff top.

"Diggory! Digg-orrrrrry!" Commander Savas roared over the radio.

Zach yelled down, "Traitors!"

He opened fire on them, the bullets shooting up snow and ice as they struck the frozen ground nearest Girak.

"Ayanna, run." Girak shooed her away from Rana and toward the shadows.

They were almost there. She sprinted forward, falling into the shadows.

Atsushi tripped as a bullet caught the top of his helmet. Cold air rushed in, causing him to gasp and cough. Girak's eyes widened in questioning horror.

"O—kay." Atsushi panted, doing his best to continue toward the shadows. Only a few more meters...

Ayanna screeched at Zach to stop firing, her arms outstretched toward Atsushi and Girak as if she could pull them into the shadows.

Time slowed. Every crunch of his boots and every sharp stab of cold air in his lungs punctuated the seconds. Commander Savas again blasted Girak over the radio. When would the killing bullet hit? If it hit his head, would he feel anything? Or would he simply drop?

He tripped on an ice chunk. He had nearly made it to the shadows. Girak, unable to stop running in time, plowed over him, sending Rana flying over Atsushi's head.

The bullets stopped. He struggled to get up.

"Why'd they stop?" Atsushi yelled to Girak.

Girak jumped up and reached for Rana's arms again.

"We don't want to hit the children, Diggory. Turn yourself in. This is your last chance." Commander Savas' snarling voice rang triumphant.

Girak turned toward him. "Go. Take her and run for the shadows."

"No," Atsushi protested, panting. "They'll shoot you."

Girak straightened and turned to face the door.

Atsushi motioned for Ayanna to drag Rana to the shadows as he grabbed his educator's arm and faced the guns with him. He was the same height as Girak, and in the expedition clothing and darkness, Atsushi hoped they were identical. He was betting both their lives on Northern Haven's reluctance to kill him and lose his genes.

"Atsushi, don't..." Girak whispered over his radio.

Atsushi ignored him and stood his ground. *Please don't be able to tell us apart. Please let my genes save us both.*

# Chapter 54

Northern Haven's Door: Atsushi Collins

Atsushi and Girak stood side-by-side in the icy darkness. The continued silence and lack of bullets from the plateau above them lent Atsushi hope that Zach couldn't tell him from Girak and didn't want to shoot a teen. Especially a teen born of the last frozen embryo from the Surface. Never before had he been grateful to be a freezer baby.

Atsushi counted the seconds, trying not to cough from the frigid air leaking into his headpiece. Beside him, Girak growled his disapproval of his risk.

Behind them, Ayanna's boots crunched on the ice as she walked farther and farther away. Atsushi panted, expecting each pounding of his heart to be his last.

Glancing back, he couldn't even see Ayanna. She had already pulled Rana into the relative safety of the shadows. If he couldn't see them, Zach surely wouldn't see them. Ayanna was safe. He tapped Girak's hand. "Now."

As one, they spun and ran the last few meters to the black oblivion. Atsushi fell headfirst into the darkest shadow, shaking uncontrollably. The bitter air constricted and burnt his lungs. He coughed so badly that he ripped off the headpiece and threw up, coughing. As he struggled to catch his breath, a frigid wind kicked up, and the air moved through his hair like ghostly fingers. Even the air itself was alive up here.

"Let's switch headpieces for a bit. I'm more used to it out here." Girak removed his own headpiece and handed it to Atsushi.

Too light-headed to argue, he accepted the exchange.

Still gasping too much to speak, he nodded his gratitude. With the intact air warmer, his coughing slowed and his breathing normalized.

The radio crackled. "You fool," Savas said. "You can't run, there's nowhere to go." The jerk's contempt nearly made Atsushi vomit again.

Girak said, "I'm preventing a war. We got the last of the expedition clothing. Make some tea. It'll take hours for Zach to climb down and re-enter. When I have proof that you're wrong about them, I'll turn my radio back on." He clicked off his radio and camera and coughed from the leak in his headpiece.

Atsushi chuckled in admiration. No one ever spoke to Commander Savas like that.

Girak pointed to the door. "You both should go back," he said, racked by another cough. "There's no reason for us all to risk this. Go back and blame Rana and me."

"I'm not leaving you out here alone. You're stuck with me," he said. He clicked off his radio and Savas' cursing. Ayanna did the same.

"Are you sure?" Girak's voice trembled with gratitude.

"Ah, yeah. She saved my life," Ayanna said.

"We owe her," Atsushi added, still processing the fact that Ayanna seemed totally fine. No one ever survived the Sickness.

Girak nodded and coughed again. "Then we'd better move."

As Atsushi turned to help carry Rana, her eyes fluttered open, and she sniffed.

*Real air.* She inhaled deeply and gave him a weak smile.

"Freakin' freezing air," Atsushi responded as he searched Rana's face for signs of discomfort. "How arctic was your home planet?"

She scrunched her face. *I was born here.*

Was she older than him? How long ago had they arrived?

"We need to hurry. Rana, if you lean on me, can you stand?" Girak offered his gloved hand to her.

She wobbled up and smiled in delight at the frozen deathscape around them. *Thank you.* Her eyes glistened with tears as she gave them a small bow. *Thank you for returning me.*

"Don't thank us until we're safe. Can you contact your people...uh, I mean, the other star beings?" He studied her for signs that his awkward wording had offended her, but he still wasn't clear if what he saw was really her or a mind projection like the Council had warned of.

Rana closed her eyes and held very still, and they all waited. Then she exhaled in a frustrated hiss. *I can't Call. I can't reach them.*

"Why not?" His heart fell. "You can talk to us. Shouldn't it be easier to talk to them? Don't you have a radio or something? A location beacon?"

If Commander Savas caught them, he'd kill Girak. He couldn't allow that. *Shast.* How had he not seen it sooner? Girak was dead either way—he couldn't live up here or return. Atsushi stared through the darkness toward the distant door, their only lifeline to survival. "Girak—"

*I'm not clear from those things that hit me.* Tears streamed down Rana's face. *I need a clear mind to function properly.*

"It's okay, but we need to move. Can you walk?" Girak gave her arm a gentle tug. "Don't worry, Atsushi, we'll be fine."

Rana schlepped forward. *I'm sorry. They will catch us now.*

"Not if I can help it. Which way?" Girak asked.

Rana pointed, and he helped her hobble off into the depths of the frigid wilderness. Atsushi and Ayanna followed them along the dark base of the cliffs that lined the Valley of Ice.

Atsushi stopped. "Ayanna, your pack."

Her clothing was so oversized that her pack had slipped right off her shoulders. She stooped and picked it up.

"It's *so* heavy. Do we really need it?" She scowled at it and then shoved it onto her shoulders again.

Atsushi shrugged and caught up with Girak. "What's in our packs?"

"Hopefully, all the original safety and food rations. Now that you mention it, grab out a food container for Rana." Then he said to Rana, "You must be starving. Did they ever give you any decent food?"

*I would love some.* Her telepathic voice brightened at the possibility of food.

*This* he could relate to.

Girak told them how to open the food while continuing their brisk trek. Atsushi popped open the lid and stared at the glutenous, cold stew.

Rana accepted it with her free arm. Sniffing it, her nose wrinkled. *Thanks?*

"It's all we have. At least it's not raw this time." Girak cast a longing look at the dark, lumpy liquid.

Rana tilted the can into her opened mouth. Her face screwed up into a horrible grimace. She looked like she would vomit, but she gagged it down. *I'm going to need to teach you about real food.*

He laughed, suddenly very aware of his pinched, empty stomach. "I'll happily accept that lesson."

They walked on in silence except for Girak's periodic coughing and Rana's smacking and gagging as she struggled to eat. The whole time, Rana's appearance stayed the same—somewhat human but not quite.

"I don't want to offend you," he said, "but the expedition claimed you could make yourselves look different by affecting our minds. Is that true?"

"I never said that," Girak interjected. "Savas spread that rumor."

Rana's face scrunched up in confusion. Or maybe offense? Had he just said something thoughtless to her like when people asked him inappropriate questions about Japan?

*This,* she said, pointing to her face, *is me.*

"Of course it is," Girak said and then muttered something under his breath about Savas.

"Okay." Atsushi gave her a friendly smile, hoping she didn't think less of him. "I thought it didn't make sense, but then I wondered if maybe you had changed the way we see you to make us feel more comfortable?"

"If I could change and wanted to make you comfortable, I'd become a warm fire," she said with a grin.

"Right." He grinned back.

So, star beings had a sense of humor, and they liked good food. That was good, because if the three of them couldn't go home, they might end up begging to live on their ship.

After about half an hour, Girak stopped in his tracks and turned to him.

"Can you help Rana for"—a series of coughs racked him—"a bit?"

"Of course." Atsushi put his arm around Rana's waist and then tensed as his hand neared the last known location of her strange animal. "Will your pet bite me?"

*Pet?* Rana gagged down another lump of the stew.

"The animal in your coat. A pet is an animal that you own. You teach it tricks, and it keeps you company, and it's usually cuddly."

Rana laughed so hard she nearly choked on the stew. *Digga? She's not a pet. She's a young cave digger, the most dangerous wild animal around. She doesn't usually bite. I'm still working out how to get along with her peaceably.*

Atsushi froze. Was this another joke? His wide eyes focused on the rip in her furs.

*You are safe. How do you say your name? At-slushi?*

He laughed. "Atsushi."

"At—" She tried in her strange voice as she handed him back the empty food container.

"A-tsoo-shee." He unzipped the most accessible pocket of his pack and shoved the container inside.

Beside him, Girak wheezed. He frowned at Girak, but the educator waved off his concern.

"Atsushi." *Its vibration suits you well. What does this name mean?*

He shrugged. "There's no other Japanese to ask. The records say it means either 'compassionate warrior' or 'warm,' but I'm not much of a warrior, and I'm definitely not warm right now," he said, laughing.

*You are compassionate, or you wouldn't be helping me. What is this Japanese?*

"That's what I am, why I look different from them." He motioned to Girak and Ayanna.

*Different?* Rana considered this a long time, looking from him to the others.

He grinned. "You don't see a difference in us?"

She considered them all again and then gave him an apologetic shake of her head. *No. I mean, you all look different from each other. I can see what might be male and female and age differences, but I don't see this Japanese thing that makes you different. All three of you have different eye colors and skin tones.*

"It's not a single thing…" He bit back his amusement. It'd be such a relief if he could simply point to something specific about him that made him Japanese. He shrugged. "I can't define it. That's the tricky part. Do star beings have different skin tones and looks?"

Rana's brow furrowed. *Everyone's skin is a little different. We don't usually care much about looks…*

"Not even if you have a crush on someone?" Ayanna asked.

*Well…*Rana bit her lip and looked away. *I mean, it helps, but it's not what's important. We don't classify each other by our looks. But sometimes, different villages do their hair a little differently.*

"I guess a hair style could be Japanese, but not really. Not anymore…" Atsushi shrugged. "It doesn't matter." It did, of course. It mattered dearly to him, but right now, he couldn't explain it to himself, let alone an alien. "You sure we're going in the right direction?"

She nodded, then gave him a huge smile. *Whatever it means to be Japanese, I'm glad you're the way you are.*

"Right." His chest warmed at that. Why was it easier to talk to her about this than his classmates? He looked away from Rana to hide his happiness at her words. He noticed Ayanna watching him. "What?"

Her grin lit up the night. "I'm glad you're the way you are, too."

Something emboldened him. Maybe it was a side-effect of taking the prime minister hostage and then fleeing your only home with an alien? The words flowed from his lips before he could question them. "Yeah, I'm pretty cool." He laughed and looked away, feeling shy that he meant it.

They continued hiking across the flat icy tundra. To their left and right rose ominous, ice-covered cliffs that glowed under the pale moonlight. In the distance, the end of the deep valley widened into endless black horizon.

"Rana? Can you contact the others yet?" Girak stopped and scanned the horizon. "Commander Savas will be after us soon."

Rana immediately stopped walking, making Atsushi stumble. She took a few deep breaths and shifted as if trying to straighten while still leaning on Atsushi for support. Her eyes closed.

They waited, totally exposed in the open space. Only the endlessly circulating air and Girak's wheezing surrounded them.

What he would give right now for the security of four walls, a ceiling, and some heat.

Rana mumbled something in her eerie language. More silence followed.

Then her chin dropped so that her furred hood blocked her face from sight. *Sorry, I cannot contact them. And the Crowned Ones will not be able to locate us if I cannot Call. Well, Kalakanya could, if she tried...but she probably assumes I'm still a prisoner. She won't check my location.*

"We're on our own?" Hopelessness tugged Atsushi toward the safety of Northern Haven. He and Ayanna had no training, no skills. Even the failed expedition teams had equipment and Commander Savas protecting them. Atsushi and his friends had none of that. Instead, they had Savas hunting them.

# Chapter 55

*The Valley of Ice: Atsushi Collins*

Atsushi trudged alongside the others through the endless valley, wondering how long they had until Commander Savas found them. He'd catch them easily with a snowmobile. Atsushi had expected Rana's friends to be waiting to rescue her. To save them.

Instead, the star beings were nowhere in sight, and he and his friends were screwed. "We're completely on our own?" he asked. "You sure? We humans can't survive long up here."

*Yes, we are alone. But the One In All is always with us.*

"Huh?" *What gobbly-gook was that? They have a big mother ship or something?*

Rana furrowed her brow and tilted her head as if evaluating his sanity. *The One In All is the life force, the love that binds all.*

It was probably rude, but he couldn't keep his face from screwing up. *Whatever was she talking about?* "Sorry, Rana, maybe that's lost in translation, but love can't save us from Commander Savas."

*He is scared of Love. It may save us.*

Behind them, Girak snorted in laughter.

"Okay." Atsushi took a deep breath and tried again. "There must be *something* we can do. You live out here. How do we evade them? Maybe hide somehow until you're able to Call them?" He turned, scanning the endless black horizon.

*We never need to hide from each other.*

"You must have some sort of enemies. How do you protect yourselves?"

Girak fiddled with his useless gun.

Rana stared at him blankly. *We talk to the furred ones. Or put up shields.*

"Rana, we need to hide." Ayanna stepped in front of Rana. "Quickly. You must have ideas. Can you use your powers to dig a cave?"

*Powers?* Rana scowled. *I can't even Call. I'd never be able to shield. Those pointy things that got me...they messed me up. I still can't even think right.*

This was so not good. Atsushi's muscles were taut from the cold and the anticipation that at any moment gunfire would rain down upon them. "Wait." He pointed to where Digga nestled against Rana's chest. "Can she do anything?"

*She eats, sleeps, and digs.* Rana stopped to check Digga, and again, Atsushi stumbled. *Sorry, Atsushi. I'm used to others reading me as we—*

"A trench. Can she dig a trench?" Ayanna excitedly pantomimed the size and shape of a trench.

*Maybe? How would that help?*

"Well..." Ayanna glanced at him, but he had no idea where she was going with this. "My brother, Bleu, had studied how we could live on the Surface."

"What?" Girak spun to stare at them. "I taught science. Why did you never ask me anything?"

Atsushi shrugged, unsure whether to be annoyed or honored that Girak assumed they'd share their scheme with him.

"How many kids were planning this?" Girak asked, intrigued.

"Just me and Bleu. And well, Atsushi *overheard* us."

Atsushi turned crimson, but the twinkle in her eyes showed only humor, not anger.

Ayanna waggled her hands in impatience. "That's not the important part. Bleu researched how people used to survive in places like Antarctica. Sometimes, they would dig a trench, put their gear in it, and then cover it to make a roof. Then they took their gear out and the little snow house would hold in their body heat. Maybe if we made a bigger one, we could hide. They'd never expect that, and if we hid our tracks to it..."

"I had no idea..." Girak rubbed his headpiece in bafflement.

"Rana, can Digga do that?" Atsushi's own headpiece said it had already been two hours, which meant Savas and Zach would be already hunting for them.

"Check your packs. We should have small ice picks for climbing and stuff. If we all work together…." Girak had collected his wits.

Everyone rummaged through their packs while Rana explored and found a somewhat hidden dip near the base of the rising cliffs. *This spot may work. But if those rocks are huge under the ice…*

"Didn't you say her claws could go through anything?" Atsushi shifted from leg to leg as the sky lightened.

*Yeah…* Rana knelt and whispered to Digga in her singsong language, and then set her on the ground. The pup stared at her expectantly with its big brown eyes. Atsushi's gaze dropped to the sharp fangs protruding below the upper jaw, and the long, lethal claws that had easily sliced through metal.

Not a pet.

*Dig*, Rana requested.

The furry creature snorted and wriggled in excitement as it plowed into the ice. The pup was unbelievably fast, spinning ice and rock up between her hind legs with such a flurry that they had to step back. Rana kept redirecting her, and soon, they had a trench large enough for the four of them and Digga.

Girak, using the flat edge of an ice pick, swept away their tracks. Ayanna instructed them to put all their gear in the trench, as spread out as possible so its bulk would equal the size of their bodies. Then they covered it up while Rana fed Digga to prevent the enthusiastic pup from digging it back up. But the icy snow wouldn't pack together.

Rana grimaced at their crunchy mound. *We need fresh, wet snow, or it will collapse when you pull your gear out.*

"Wet?" Atsushi asked, rummaging through his gear. "I've got water. We all should. How quickly will it freeze?"

Rana blew out a long breath and watched it condense and plume about her. *We had better hurry.*

Atsushi and Girak sprinkled the contents of their water bottles onto the mound.

"No," Ayanna argued. "We'll need the water to drink."

"If her friends don't find us, we won't last that long." As soon as he said it, he realized his mistake. From Ayanna's expression, he assumed she was calculating Bleu and Neviah's chances and not liking the odds. "They'll be okay," he reassured her, though his tone rang hollow.

Her expression hardened, but she joined them in trying to ice the mound. For once, the bitter cold was on their side. It froze almost immediately.

"I'm making this our entrance." He opened up a small hole at the end against the cliff to avoid detection.

"Hurry and pull everything out," Ayanna said, "Put your gear back together in the pack so it doesn't take up much room. We'll take it in if it fits." She eyed the pile of gear and frowned. "Or we can cover it with snow outside."

"Bleu knew all of this and never mentioned it?" Girak said in awe.

"He's been obsessed with the Surface his whole life. He always jokes..." Ayanna released a strangled sob. "He joked..." She burst into tears.

Atsushi froze, unsure of how to respond. Did she want a hug? Bleu would have hugged her, but he didn't want to be like a brother to her. Cautiously, he walked over, and she flung her arms around him.

She sobbed into his shoulder as he folded his arms around her. Despite all her layers, her fruity scent mixed with the tanginess of the Surface air, and he nestled his nose onto her hood.

"It'll be okay. Look how much he knows. And if I know Neviah, she's probably got a backpack full of miraculous gadgets." It sounded pathetic, given all the others that had died on the Surface. There had to be something better he could say. "If they met Rana's friends and they're with them..." He peered over Ayanna's hood at Rana.

Rana nodded. *If they found them, they will be safe.*

Ayanna raised her head from his chest and looked at Girak.

Girak sighed. "I don't know. I was climbing in another location, and Commander Savas didn't exactly fill me in. Someone said they were taken, and that must mean Rana's friends, right?"

407

Ayanna nodded, pulled away from Atsushi, and sniffed. She had *hugged* him. *Him.* Hugged *him.*

He resisted whooping in joy. No need making Ayanna think he was insensitive about her brother. Despite the odds against Bleu and Neviah, Atsushi couldn't believe they were dead. They *had* to be fine, because he'd met the living cure for Ayanna. If they all survived, maybe they'd have a real date without onions and hostages.

They only needed to survive this.

Suddenly, Rana stiffened. *What's that?* She tilted her head.

They all froze, listening.

A moment later, the distant crunching of snow and shouting reached them. Atsushi's gut leapt into his throat. "Snowmobiles. They're coming."

# Chapter 56

The Valley of Ice: Atsushi Collins

The approaching crunch of snowmobile skis speeding across the crusty snowscape made Atsushi's neck hairs raise. They were out of time. If it wasn't for the darkness, they might already have been spotted. Distant pinpricks of the snowmobiles' headlights grew larger in the gloom.

"Get the gear out and behind the rocks so we fit," Atsushi said, exchanging a glance with Girak.

That look told him everything he didn't want to know. His educator believed he was about to die at the hands of the man who hated him.

Girak crawled inside and yanked out the gear and tossed it to him. He hid it behind the rocks, and Ayanna checked it to make sure nothing peeked out. Rana attempted to coax Digga back into her carrier.

"This is never going to work," Ayanna bemoaned. "They'll find us…our tracks…"

Girak rushed around, swiping tracks as he ran. "Get in. It's our best chance."

Atsushi rushed Ayanna into the trench first. Girak and Rana hustled in next, and they waited.

The two men on snowmobiles yelled back and forth, cursing the darkness created by the cliffs surrounding the Valley of Ice. One was definitely Savas. They drew nearer.

*I have an idea.* Rana placed Digga on the ground near the hole. She communed with the animal, and then the little thing loped off.

"Digga should hide with us," Ayanna whispered. The snowmobiles would soon reach them.

Rana shook her head. *If they find us, she and I are as good as dead. She's going to help.*

"They have heat sensitive trackers," Girak hissed. "They'll sense her. They might even sense us under this snow."

"Oh, no." Ayanna covered her mouth. "He'll shoot her," she whispered through her fingers.

Beside him, Rana stiffened and lowered her head to her chest. The snowmobile sound was too close and slowing. *I told Digga to lead them away and then dig a hole and hide. She'll find us later. Cave diggers have excellent noses.*

"They're right outside," Atsushi whispered. "Didn't they hear you mentally say that?"

*No. I was careful to send it only to you three.* She began whispering to herself again in her strange singsong language.

The snowmobiles stopped, engines idling. Commander Savas and another man conferred. Had they noticed their tracks? With nowhere to run and no weapons, Atsushi's heart thudded so loudly he feared Commander Savas would hear it through the snow.

Footsteps crunched nearer their hole. Then a growl erupted and the clicking of claws racing across the ice. The footsteps stopped advancing.

"What the *Shast* is that?" The other man yelped.

"Must be what our heat sensor picked up. Where the hell are they? They couldn't have disappeared," Commander Savas said.

"Maybe the reapers got them?" That was Zach, the only other person with weapon training.

*Shast,* they were screwed.

"There's no blood." Commander Savas sounded disappointed.

"As soon as the sun's up, they'll be easy to find." Zach coughed. "Want me to double back and check again?"

"Yes. And if you see that varmint, shoot it. I'd like a closer look." Savas laughed, adding, "And maybe a taste."

Rana gasped, and Atsushi leaned into her shoulder in support. But remembering she wasn't human, he pulled back, hoping he hadn't offended her.

"Probably diseased." Zach chuckled, and then one snowmobile drove off.

The second snowmobile continued to idle nearby. Then it, too, took off.

Girak had a sliver of a view through the ice. "They split up," he whispered. "They both went out of the Valley of Ice toward the open ice plains. Zach went right after Digga, and Savas went left."

The crunch of the hard snow beneath the snowmobiles' skis faded until only their own heavy breathing was left. Girak climbed out and squatted behind the boulders, searching the dark horizon up and down the valley, then motioned for them to exit.

As the girls crawled out, Girak studied Ayanna. She hugged herself, trembling.

Atsushi stepped toward her, but Girak shook his head. He paused impatiently, wondering if his educator knew this was a sign of a brewing episode.

"Ayanna, you okay?" Girak asked.

Ayanna's eyes were wider than normal, her breathing shallow.

Rana climbed out of the trench and cocked her head. *This is panic, not the illness you had. Breathe.* She grasped both of Ayanna's hands and breathed in and out with exaggeration.

Ayanna copied her, and slowly, she returned to normal.

Atsushi's shoulders sagged in relief.

Girak leaned in toward him. "Glad I was right about that. I think Rana's glowing hands may hold the cure we were looking for."

"I sure hope so. What now?" Grinning, Atsushi brushed the snow from his parka.

*Don't.* Rana pointed at the snow he'd brushed off his coat. *Your clothing is too bright, and the sun will be up soon.* She pointed down the Valley of Ice to where the sky had turned light gray. *The snow will help you camouflage.*

"Rana, do you know which way it is to your... your home?" Girak's

411

breathing with the broken headpiece was better, his coughs less frequent.

She pivoted to scan the horizon and nearly toppled over. Atsushi caught her arm.

*Thanks. Those pointy things are still in my system. We need to go that way.* She pointed toward the far side of the valley and up over the mountain edge toward the rising sun.

"Okay. They are already out of the valley, searching beyond it. We need to make it through before they return this way." Girak glanced around uneasily. "But we should eat while we walk. You shouldn't go long in this cold without eating."

They dug out rations and hustled as best they could in the direction Rana had designated. Eating with the headpiece required a special kind of grace. Atsushi had to get the food up under his headpiece to his mouth. It was complicated, but the scientists probably never expected the expedition to eat on the run.

Each bite helped settle his internal shakiness from being Zach's target. Atsushi wasn't chummy with Zach, but the guy certainly knew him. As he trudged along, the bullet's whizz as it nearly killed him kept repeating in his mind.

"Atsushi, look." Ayanna tapped his arm and pulled him from his reverie.

A golden glow had broken the horizon as they left the enclosed valley behind. Shining beams of sunlight skittered across the snow. He squinted and hoped its dazzling beauty wasn't the last thing he ever saw. His eyes stung. Even when he closed them, the brilliant light shone through his eyelids.

"How will we see them coming? Is it like this all day?" He hoped not.

Rana made a harrumph that was probably laughter, but the sun's brightness failed to amuse him. The light stabbed his skull and made him clench his teeth.

Girak patted his back. "Close your eyes if you need to until they get more used to the brightness. The ground here is pretty flat, so you probably won't trip, and we'll hear the snowmobiles crunching the snow. In a few hours, your eyes will be more adjusted. I hope. We didn't get the goggles, so we'll have to deal with it."

*I'll be your eyes.* Rana walked more steadily now and barely leaned on him. Perhaps the drugs were finally working their way out.

They walked for eons, and Atsushi struggled to grasp how expansive the world was outside their tunnels. Everything resembled the old, tinted photographs he and Neviah had explored—layered blues, grays, and white with the occasional splash of rusty-yellow ice. Despite that, he never tired of it.

He especially liked the cloud shadows. Who knew clouds would have shadows? They caused ripples of gray to run along the white landscape, giving it a surreal quality, as if the ground was covered with waves.

He paused, panting as the long, gradual hill grew steep and rocky near the top.

*My village is beyond this. Not far,* she encouraged.

"Why do I get the sense *not far* to you might mean a two days' walk?" he joked.

The grin she flashed him in response wasn't exactly encouraging.

He wasn't the only exhausted one. Girak huffed, and his usually ruddy face was crimson under his headpiece. Ayanna looked as if a good breeze would knock her over.

*Do you hear that?*

Everyone paused and shook their heads. Her hearing was more acute than theirs. She motioned for them to continue on but to stay quiet.

Ayanna widened her eyes. "Is it bad?" she whispered.

*Depends. It's peleguins. They don't usually come this far from the shore.*

"That's supposed to clarify things?" Atsushi grumbled.

Rana chuckled. *You'll see in a moment.*

As their group crested the hill, a strange gurgling noise rose to meet them. They crawled up behind large boulders and peered over the top.

"What are those?" Ayanna whispered. Below them lay a field of moving gray that shifted and transformed.

*Feathered ones. They can fly but prefer to walk and swim.*

"There's thousands of them," Atsushi said, his stomach flip-flopping.

"Will they attack us?" Girak riffled through his pack, checking and rechecking its contents, presumably for a weapon to fight peleguins. As if they'd be that lucky.

*It's their breeding season. They gather once a year and will leave us alone if we keep our distance, but we need to travel through them.*

"Sounds like you do this a lot. What's the trick?" Atsushi waited for the mystical answer.

*Shields. We walk through with shields. But I still can't do one...*

His expectant smile collapsed. *Shast.*

"Maybe if we walk slowly?" Girak asked without taking his eyes off the birds.

Rana heaved a great sigh. *They're not friendly during breeding season. They will attack us with their beaks and talons. And there are a lot of them...*

A horrible crunching snow sound began behind them, and Atsushi spun. A snowmobile. They would be forced into the mass of birds. Or maybe they would be lucky? Maybe they hadn't been seen? He pulled Ayanna to the ground, but the snowmobile's driver began yelling. The birds, sensing the rapidly approaching machinery, erupted into a squawking maelstrom. As one, they rose into the air and dove at them.

"Ahhhhh!" Atsushi screamed, throwing up his arms, but the birds engulfed them in wings and beaks.

*Run. Follow me.* Rana bolted forward, dragging Girak behind her. Atsushi grabbed Ayanna's arm, and they pushed ahead, desperate not to be separated from the others.

But they couldn't move. Beaks and wings were everywhere. Atsushi's head jerked as a beak punctured his headpiece. Frigid air rushed in. Coughing and tripping, he pulled Ayanna down with him.

The birds again rose as one, swirling and diving but now stopping just short of them.

Ayanna yanked Atsushi up and pointed ahead through the birds' strange fury. "What's that?"

A huge, furry beast—a lion?—raced toward Rana, lashing upward with massive, clawed paws at the birds as it forced its way closer. It would reach her and Girak within seconds.

"Watch out," Atsushi shouted.

Girak had already turned to face the huge lion. It stopped a few feet in front of them, still lunging into the air at the lowest screaming birds. It paused, looked at Rana and the others, and then turned toward them, a vicious snarl on its massive muzzle. They were larger, more satisfying prey than birds.

Atsushi's heart thumped wildly as he raced forward, smacking peleguins out of his way. "Ayanna, grab the ice pick from my pack."

His friends would not be its next meal.

# Chapter 57

P eleguin-Rookery-By-The-Lake: *Bleu Reinier*
Bleu shivered as the biting wind blew tiny snow crystals across his cheeks. He flipped up his headpiece. He and Neviah shuffled at the edge of a field where Kalakanya had left them, not quite sure what she expected them to do here. Perhaps babysit? Around them played a crowd of rowdy, young star beings. Unlike the mostly white-haired adults, they had all colors of hair—black, brown, chestnut, or amber.

They'd arrived with hooded fur coats but rapidly shed them as they ran around, chasing each other. At this point, most only wore long leather or woven tops over leather leggings and leather boots.

As a tall girl arrived with a much younger boy, they all stopped chasing each other. The new arrivals appeared to signal that now something would begin.

*Wanna play?* The tall girl hesitantly approached them, holding out a misshapen ball-like object. It was sewn of skins and stuffed with what might have been dried grasses. Some stuffing protruded through the seams. Bleu guessed they were about to learn a popular sport. Blob ball?

He smiled, looked at Neviah, and stepped forward. "Okay. What are the teams?"

*Teams?*

"Sides—you know, who plays against whom?" He waited expectantly.

The young star beings raised eyebrows and huddled together, murmuring in their strange rhythmic language.

"What did I say?" Bleu turned to Neviah for answers, his palms up.

She shrugged.

The girl approached again, this time with the whole gang behind her. She waved her arm, motioning to all the others. *We are one. We do not play against each other. We have fun.*

Bleu stared, open-mouthed. *They're going to lecture me?*

He could almost hear Stamf laughing at him. What he would give to have Stamf tease him again.

Shoving his grief away, he attempted a carefree smile. "We play games with teams, that's all. We aren't against each other."

Yet as he said it, he wondered if this was true. Were they always fighting, even in play? That possibility made his mind whirl as he sought an exception to it. He couldn't find one.

The children were still watching him with upturned, inquisitive faces.

Neviah stepped forward and smiled. "What if we observe for a while to see how it's played?" She motioned for them to start.

The kids nodded and skipped a short distance away. One ran across the field and drew a line in the snow with his foot. The tallest girl tossed the ball-like blob ahead of them all by a few meters. They all encircled the ball, joined hands, and stared at it.

"Well, this is exciting," Bleu muttered.

Neviah hit his arm and stifled a giggle.

The young star beings continued staring at the ball. Even the youngest seemed fascinated.

"Maybe they're messing with us? Like, it's a joke?" Bleu asked, swinging his arms for warmth.

"I don't think so. How old do you think they are?" Neviah pointed to the shorter one. "That one's so small. He's only, like, five?"

The boy in question stood, eyes squinted at the ball, tussled, black hair tumbling down his small shoulders.

"Who knows? He could be a week or twenty years." He shook his head. "The only thing I'm sure of is that they don't know how to have fun."

As if on cue, the blob ball quivered and shot up in the air. The kids grinned and began walking toward the line, the ball hovering unsteadily above their circle. Then one of them slipped on the ice, and several others tumbled to the ground. The ball fell and hit the small boy on the head. They all roared with laughter.

*Want to join now?*

Neviah and Bleu had backed up and stared wide-eyed at the ball. The kids laughed at their surprise.

He came back to his senses. "Uh, how did you do that?" He walked toward the blob ball to examine it.

The smallest boy grabbed it, holding it to his chest. Bleu stopped, unwilling to frighten the tyke.

*We work together. It's the best way to learn. And it's funny when it doesn't work. Yesterday, it shot way off, and we all had to go find it.*

The others nodded and grinned.

"Uh, I'll just watch. Thanks." Bleu walked back to Neviah, silently mouthing, "What the *shast?*"

Neviah giggled. The kids went back to playing.

Their joyous laughter was cut off by the sound of crunching snow. They all turned to see a single metal vehicle racing toward them.

"It's a snowmobile," Neviah announced, waving and running toward the one familiar object.

The driver raised a rifle.

Bleu yelled, "Neviah, stop!"

A shot rang out, and the tall star being girl fell into a heap. The snowmobile driver shifted the barrel of his rifle toward the small boy, and Bleu dove in front of him. As he crashed to the ground in front of the boy, bright lights appeared around him. Such brilliance. His awe was smothered by a sudden searing pain in his chest. His next breath was impossible.

Distant screams and shouts surrounded him. He struggled to keep his eyes open, but he couldn't focus. Hot blood spread over his chest. His breath came in gasps, each causing another knife-sharp stab. *I can't die... Ayanna needs me.*

He sucked in another racking breath. His blurry vision began to spin, to float.

A shadow appeared above him, and then a man said something undecipherable and cut open Bleu's parka. The movement was unbearable, and he passed out.

*Whiteness.* He floated in pearly-white light, the pain gone.

*I'm dead.*

*No. You will live. Rest.* The man removed his hand from Bleu's chest, and the white light disappeared, to be replaced by the crisp blue sky. *Do not move. Rest.*

But as much as he wanted to rest, a vision pulled at him. *Not now...*

Unlike in his past vision, in this one he floated above his injured body, pulled toward a Crowned One. Kalakanya's hands clasped something to her heart, and her intense emotions crashed over him like waves. She shifted and shimmered as if she were two different beings.

The shifting Kalakanya seemed of vital importance to him, but the meaning of her twofold appearance evaded him, like a floating dust mote that flew away each time his fingers tried to close around it. Again and again he tried to grasp it.

And then it was gone. He had no idea what had pulled him or why. He fell back into his body with a painful jolt.

"Bleu?" The older star being touched his arm. *Are you okay?*

Bleu stared up at him, unable to answer.

*You appear unable to rest. Do you have the strength to listen? Kalakanya would like a word with you. Are you up to it?*

Bleu attempted to nod, but the slight movement of his chin sent renewed pain throughout his body. He gasped, unable to stop himself.

Kalakanya stepped forward and knelt close, her eyes moist as she met his gaze. She turned and rapidly spoke in her strange, musical language.

*Can you breathe okay? I have asked them to get you herbs for the pain, but they may make you groggy. Are you okay with that? I do not want you to misunderstand us again.*

Bleu completed the most miniscule nod in the history of mankind.

*May I?* She must have sensed his desperation, because she placed her right palm over his chest, and his pain lessened. He took a deeper breath and sent a mental thanks.

*We thank you. Within one day, you have gone from trying to kill as many of us as possible to risking your own life for one of our children. You give me much hope for your humans. You saved Shams' life, and this saved yours.* She held up the blue pendant necklace that Ayanna had given him before leaving on his first mission. *It cracked, but you're alive.*

Bleu eyed the new lines marking the blue stone like lightning bolts. So close to death. *Bleu saved by a blue stone.* A weak smile played on his face.

*What?* Kalakanya's eyes widened.

What had he said? "Bleu saved," he said, gasping, "by a blue stone."

*Those two words sound different. But they both mean the color? Like the sky?*

"Yes." It was barely audible. *What's wrong?*

His foggy brain was missing something. He remembered that odd vision he had experienced a moment ago. It was disorienting, like hearing a distant drum, knowing it was a drum, but not being able to tell it was a drum. It made no sense.

Her eyes turned a darker green under her squinted lids. *Are you sure you don't know what your humans are planning?*

"No..." Why was she acting so mysterious?

*The Prophecy of the Three Blues...*

She looked from the pendant to Bleu to the bright sky. A series of emotions sprinted across her face, only to disappear before he could identify them.

*How did you get this?* Her gaze returned to him as she held up the lapis pendant. *Is it really yours?* Her tone was almost accusatory.

"It's..." He panted shallowly from the pain, unable to speak.

Kalakanya placed her palm on his chest, and the pain began receding. *Think it clearly, don't use your mouth. I'll get it.*

*It's been in my mother's family for generations. Why?* It was hard to focus with her healing him.

Kalakanya's face settled into a tense smile. She was hiding something big that involved him—he was sure of it.

"Why?" he repeated. Didn't she appreciate how hard it was for him to speak? *Answer me.*

She shook her head. *Nothing to worry about.* She pressed the blue stone to her lips and whispered something onto it. *This is entrusted, so protect it, okay?*

She folded Bleu's fingers around the warm pendant. *I must go. Bahujnana here*—she motioned to the older star being guy—*will have that healed in no time.* She rose and hurried away before he could ask her another question.

But as she'd risen, he had noticed her long, slender hands had trembled.

# Chapter 58

*eleguin-Rookery-By-The-Lake: Kahali*

Kahali glowered down at his empty coat sleeve, blowing in the wind. *Earth children! If I ever get my hands on them... Hands?* He instantly regretted this thought as his fury bubbled up. He didn't want to be ruled by anger. He'd never Crown and re-grow his arm with such a mindset.

Sohana threw her arm around him in a playful sibling way. "I refuse to let you drown in anger. We're in this together."

"But that's the problem. We're *all* in danger—our whole village. We're under attack." He shivered and pressed his arm into his chest, and for the thousandth time, he wished he could simply cross his arms for comfort.

Nothing was normal anymore. Crowned Ones stood scattered around the perimeter, guarding the community. The children's fears had gotten the best of them also. They gathered in small groups, whispering. No contagious laughter and buoyant balls drifted between them now.

"Look around, Sohana. It's not just me they've changed." Kahali gestured with his arm, drawing his sister's attention to the clustered children.

"We need to learn how to deal with this new situation. It will take some adjusting, that's all." Sohana remained annoyingly calm.

He grunted his disagreement. Then, eyeing the huts, he asked, "Where are they keeping the one that killed Ameya?"

"Why? Are you having thoughts of revenge?" Sohana smiled as if such a thing were ridiculous, but her gaze betrayed her concern.

He snorted. "I want them to leave and take their thoughtless violence

422

with them."

Sohana sighed. "Not going to happen."

"Maybe they'll get blown away by the spring winds? They're kind of small..." A grin burst across his face. It had been a long time since that happened. *Maybe I'm not a lost cause...*

Suddenly, a wave of emotions hit him, and his vision darkened. He floated bodiless in a strange, gloomy place with the same heavy energy he had experienced right before the Earth's children had shown up and hunted him. He recognized he was experiencing some sort of soul travelling, but he'd never been particularly good at that skill and he'd never before seen a place as dark and dense as this. Sweat covered his body as he held his breath, hoping he couldn't be seen.

In the enclosed box lit with only wavering light, two Earth children talked over a machine. At first, he couldn't grasp the meaning of their speech, but then he remembered the vibration he had Called them with. Making sure he didn't Call, he listened to that vibration, and their words took form.

"Do you think humanity's a lost cause?" one man asked the other.

"Not if this works. It'll blow them and their damn shields to the end of the universe."

"Yes, but it will trap us down here for centuries. We may die out."

Images of mass death and destruction of all above-ground life flooded from the man's mind to Kahali's. The very Earth itself turned poisonous against her many dependent life forms.

"Better to take our chances down here than to be slaughtered up there by those reapers."

"I know that's what the council decided. I'm not thrilled with either of our options."

"Well, at least Commander Savas radioed back their location before he got captured. Sad we can't rescue him first. But now, we know exactly where to hit them."

The other man nodded and continued to tap square little things and stare at flat pictures on the wall.

Just as suddenly as Kahali had left his body, he slammed back into it and fell back against Sohana. They both tumbled to the ground.

"What just happened?" his sister shouted, panicking.

"We need to find the Luminaries. Now." His mind warped at the calculated hatred he'd witnessed. He jumped up and wobbled from the horrible vision.

"What happened? Where did you go?" Sohana grabbed Kahali's shoulders, sending comforting energy to him.

He shrugged her away. There was no time for that.

"Come on. I'll tell you on the way." He raced off to find the Luminaries, Kalakanya, or anyone with the power to stop this coming horror.

The Crowned Ones, hearing his mind speak question about location, turned from their posts and pointed. He nodded and led Sohana in that direction. Racing through the paths, he slipped on the slush and slid into huts and trees. Every heartbeat was a moment less he had to save the Earth.

"Kalakanya," he shouted across the path.

The usually calm woman was gesticulating to several other Crowned Ones who had their backs to him. They spun to see who was causing such a frantic interruption.

He slid into the group, just stopping short of knocking Luminary Vadin, his father, over.

"I...I know what they're planning." Kahali gasped.

"How?" Kalakanya and the two Luminaries studied him. He hadn't exactly been reasonable of late.

"Son." Vadin, rested his hand on Kahali's good shoulder. "Are you all right?"

Kahali ignored him. There was no time to worry about his feelings. This was life or death. "I don't know how I know. I was talking to Sohana, and then I somehow soul travelled to their den and saw what they are planning. It's horrible."

"Did they see you?" his father asked.

"No. I don't think I was actually there—only seeing them and hearing

424

them." He shrugged. "I don't know."

"Why is he able to see when we are not? Is this trickery?" Luminary Samasti asked. Both Luminaries turned to Kalakanya.

"Maybe they are at such a...different mental wavelength that we are having trouble reading them. But Kahali has been caught up in anger and fear, and that's their wavelength..." She gave him an apologetic smile.

"You mean, I've been lowered to their level of brute violence?" Kahali's hand fisted at his side.

"No," she reassured him. "What did you see? It may save us. Perhaps it's a gift."

He snorted. Only the Crowned Ones could see this as a gift. He fought down his new best friend, Fury, and answered, "They're sending a thing through the air that will blow up our whole village and everything around it. All life and elements will be poisoned."

Kalakanya paled. "I know what this is. We must act immediately."

She exchanged a brief look with the Luminaries, who nodded solemnly. She turned and ran to Bahujnana's home. Kahali raced after her. He had seen the horror and couldn't sit and wait for her to fix it.

Kalakanya ignored the usual greeting and burst through the mat door, and he followed a step behind.

*Bleu, are you able to walk? He fixed you up?* Kalakanya asked one of the horrid Earth children.

Kahali gasped in horror. He had forgotten about the two they had rescued. Their village was being overrun with them.

The one called Bleu nodded. "Much better. I'm standing..." He held out his hands like standing was a big accomplishment. Then he noticed Kahali's snarl and stepped backward toward his friend.

*Kahali, this is Bleu. He saved Sham's life in the attack. You can trust him. And this* –she motioned to the woman—*is Neviah. You can trust her as well.*

Kalakanya had mind talked to include them.

Neviah sat very still, but Bleu, despite his injuries, looked ready to spring. Kahali and Bleu eyed each other from opposite sides of the Crowned One.

*Didn't he just kill five of us?* Kahali sucked in a tremulous breath. *Has he*

425

*even had time to apologize to the families?*

Bleu's face paled.

*Stop that. He didn't have time to apologize, because he jumped in front of a hunting stick for Shams. He's had quite the day.* Kalakanya had the gall to give the disgusting creature an approving nod. *A day of awakening.*

Kahali took in Bleu's ashamed face and blood-stained clothing. The blood was clearly from his own wound. *Fine.* But he would never trust the freak, even if Kalakanya vouched for him.

Bleu gave a strained smile, keeping his hand near his hip. Kahali narrowed his eyes. Why did he hold his hand like that?

*Bleu, you can trust Kahali, right?* She raised her eyebrows at Kahali as if he were the problem.

Kahali nodded, though he never broke eye contact with Bleu. Bleu nodded, but his hand remained in that odd position near his hip.

*Good. Now, we need to go into your den immediately. They have a nuclear missile aimed at our village that we need to deactivate.*

Bleu and Neviah both gasped in horror remarkably similar to his own when he'd experienced his vision. So, humans *could* know certain things were simply wrong. Interesting.

"How will we get there?" Bleu asked. "We won't have enough time even on the snowmobile."

Kahali snickered at the crudeness of their language. The human's thoughts and energy were as readable as the direction of the wind. *It's amazing that such simple beings are so dangerous.*

Kalakanya cast him a warning look, and then addressed Bleu's ridiculous concern. *Remember I told you we star beings get our name from the bright star of light that precedes us when we appear?* she explained.

"You can just appear inside? Like that?" Bleu snapped his fingers.

*Yes. But you must stand close and hold on.*

*Or not,* mused Kahali. Maybe the killer could let go and get lost along the way? No, that was a horrid thought, but Kalakanya trusted these creatures way too much.

"What about me?" Neviah asked, jumping up. "What should I do?"

Kalakanya considered her. *Can you stay here to answer any questions we may have about your people?*

"Of course," Neviah said, but her dark eyes narrowed. "Bleu, you know there won't be any going back from this. It'll be seen as choosing them over our own."

"I'm choosing peace. I'm choosing the planet, so we all have a place to live." Bleu looked oddly sincere.

How could he hunt innocents and then claim to choose peace?

She nodded in acceptance as if this contradictory behavior was common among them. "But no one at Northern Haven will see it that way."

Bleu's expression fell. "Not even you?"

She shrugged. "I understand, but it still feels like you're rushing into this and choosing her." Neviah's glance flickered down to Kalakanya's boots. "I mean, them."

The guy looked utterly confused. Any fool could tell Neviah liked him, but apparently, his awareness was the lowest of the low.

"I'm rushing to a decision because *she* has the power to stop this." Bleu turned back to Kalakanya and missed the hurt in Neviah's eyes. "We leave now?"

*Yes,* Kalakanya replied.

"I'm coming, too." He couldn't let Kalakanya do this alone with this creature. What if Bleu turned against her when they got within his lair?

*No, Kahali. You have been a great help. We shall return soon.*

"But—" He pointed at the small weapon Bleu still wore.

Kalakanya, seemingly oblivious, stepped closer to Bleu, and they clasped hands.

As they started to dematerialize, Kahali rushed forward and grabbed Kalakanya's arm. The three winked out of being.

# Chapter 59

*eleguin Rookery: Rana*

P    Rana struggled not to lose her grip on Girak as they both fended off the furious peleguins. Her heart soared every time Sukti's familiar white form leaped to scatter the feathered ones.

Her new friends, however, were clearly threatened by the lioness' proximity. Atsushi pulled out an ice pick, and Girak thrust his backpack between himself and Rana and the lion as if that would protect them.

Rana laughed. *It's okay. She's a friend.*

"Hmm." Girak grunted noncommittally, struggling to assist Rana and keep up with the giant feline.

"Again, questioning the whole friend thing," Atsushi whispered to Ayanna, not grasping the acuity of Rana's hearing.

Rana glanced behind to see if they were being followed, but everything was a flying fury of feathers. Through the squawking chaos surged the search-and-kill energy of their hunter.

Her heart fell. She knew this area; after this field were a few copses of trees but no adequate cover for hiding. Sukti could get them through the peleguins, but beyond that, they had no defense against his hunting stick.

Even Sukti would be powerless against the weapon. She was only one year old. Lion Masters like Sukti's parents could outmaneuver a Crowned One—that's why they were Masters and taught star beings. But Sukti, despite her size, was still young. Desperation clawed at Rana's heart. She had told Girak she would keep them safe, but this was beyond her.

*Can that thing climb rocks?*

428

"The snowmobile can't, but he can get off it and chase us," Girak shouted over the din of the feathered ones.

*But that would give us a better chance, right?*

"Yes, except he won't need to chase us. That gun shoots long distance. As soon as he gets a clear shot—if these birds stop flying—we'll be in trouble. They'll try to shoot you and me first, not the kids. Or maybe this friend of yours." Girak's normally pale face was red with exertion, his blue eyes determined.

Gratitude for her new friends washed over her. As violent as the other humans had been, these three were risking their lives for her.

They neared the other side of the impromptu breeding ground. Soon, the peleguins would stop attacking, making them clearly visible to the violent human. The rocky hill offered their only chance for concealment. The incline, just past the first few trees, led straight up and eastward and was the quickest way home if one didn't mind the steep climb.

*Sukti, he has a hunting stick. Don't let him see you.* Rana sent visual images of how the humans hunted.

The lioness growled.

At her rumble, Girak froze. The remaining birds, seeing them separated from the big cat dove at them viciously. A beak pierced through her hood and speared her ear. Blood trickled down her jaw.

*Keep moving. She won't hurt you, but these peleguins will.* She batted the riled bird off her head.

They broke through the last few peleguins, and Rana turned. The agitated flock swarmed in the air, thrashing their gray wings against a blue, cloudless sky. Their squawks were deafening. Directly behind them across the field, she spied the human on his snowmobile.

His chin rose as he spotted them. The snowmobile sped into the field, knocking aside peleguins before they could get fully airborne.

*Run.*

The sickening thwack of peleguin bodies against the rushing snowmobile filled the valley. They'd reached the first set of trees when Sukti paused and leapt up into its branches.

*What are you doing? He'll hunt you.* Rana feared she knew exactly what Sukti was doing.

Rana received a mental image of the two of them when Sukti was a small cub, rolling on the ground, taking long strolls together, and sharing food. Sukti's memories. Love pulsed between them.

*Go on,* Sukti mind spoke. *This is my choice.*

"No!" Tears filled Rana's eyes as Girak pulled her past the tree.

"Rana, he'll be here soon. She's...she's going to stop him?" Girak panted, his face dangerously red.

Rana couldn't answer. It took all her power to desert her friend in the tree, her white tail lashing against the dark bark.

*She's not even camouflaged. One In All, please keep her safe.*

They sprinted toward the rocky outcrops that offered the only shelter. Each foothold was tenuous in the slippery steepness. Girak climbed behind Rana, supporting most of her weight. She wished she had long claws like Digga to assist her. Was her pup okay, or was she going to lose all her furred friends?

She glanced back as the snowmobile approached the tree where Sukti crouched on a branch. The man paused his snowmobile and raised his gun toward them. He had stopped too far from the tree for Sukti to help them.

*Get down,* Rana mentally screamed.

She scurried behind the nearest boulder, keenly aware that her slowness blocked Girak's safety. Ayanna and Atsushi reached the rock's shelter as a sharp *twang* hit the ground.

Sukti's roar bounced off the rock face, and she leapt from the tree, landing just shy of the human. The human reeled backward in fear but kept his hunting stick to his shoulder.

Rana threw her arms up, willing a shield to rise around Sukti.

Nothing happened. Rana tried again, tears running down her face.

Sukti remained exposed.

The man faced the snarling, tail lashing mass of graceful fury.

"Noooooo." Rana screamed as if the vibration of her voice could knock

430

the hunter over. Her own powerlessness tore her heart to pieces.

Sukti launched straight at the hunter as his hunting stick reverberated the air. Her body crumpled in midair.

"No! Sukti," Rana screamed and leapt up.

Girak yanked her down behind the boulder. "We can't help her," he managed, his voice choked with tears. "She did that to save you, so don't give him our location."

Rana was too numb to rise again. This couldn't be real. Sukti hunted? Could a lioness survive such a blast?

She was vaguely aware of Girak's arm holding her head down. The dreaded blast of the hunting stick bounced off the boulder. Icy rocks shattered, covering them in debris. She muffled her choking coughs.

He knew where they were. There was no way to climb farther without exposing themselves. They were trapped. Sukti had died for nothing. They would all still die despite her sacrifice. Silent tears tumbled from Rana's eyes. It was all too much.

"Please tell me you can call for help," Girak mumbled into her shoulder, trying to keep them both out of range of the dangerous weapon.

Rana closed her eyes and tried to focus. Nothing. Her focus was nonexistent. They were all going to die. She wasn't afraid of dying, but she didn't want to. Not yet.

And she feared the pain.

What would Kahali do if he lost her on top of losing his arm? And Eka. Why had she yelled at him without explaining? She couldn't even Call to him and apologize.

*I can't Call.* Rana sent it to all three of them. *I'm sorry.*

"He'll need to reload soon. We could make a run for it to the next set of boulders." Girak craned his neck and estimated their chances to make the next rock outcropping.

Atsushi and Ayanna stared wide-eyed at the distance to the next rocks.

"You can do it. You're both fast," Girak reassured them.

*Leave me, Girak. You will never make it if you help me. They will need you to get them home.*

431

Girak was silent. Rana could hear him shuffling around with something behind her.

"Do you know how to hunt, Rana?"

*What? Of course not! We don't hunt.*

Another piece of their rock exploded.

"Time to learn, then." Girak pulled out the long rifle that he had strapped to his back.

*No, I will not kill.* Even in mind speak, her voice was a desperate sob.

Girak chuckled behind her. "It's not real, remember? But you could hit him over the head with it to knock him out and not kill him. And I can throw rocks."

Another shot hit the boulder near Girak, shattering the edge of it.

Atsushi scoffed. "That's your plan?"

"Rana, your friends will be looking for you, right?" The desperation in his eyes pained her.

*I think so. But they can't locate me if I can't Call.*

"I know, I understand. But it's you and me he wants. Not the kids. If you two"—Girak indicated Atsushi and Ayanna—"keep running up to the next boulder every time he reloads, you might make it far enough to be found by the star beings. They will help you. He doesn't know exactly where we are. We'll stay back and try to slow him down. I'm not leaving you, Rana, so don't even mention it again."

The hunting stick stopped.

Girak shifted quickly to peer out.

"Now!" He shoved Atsushi and Ayanna out of the boulder's shadow.

Rana's heart raced as she stared at their pounding boots on the icy rocks.

The hunting stick sounded and hit a rock to their left. Swerving, the kids ran on and dove behind the higher rocks.

*They made it.*

"Yes. Now let's get him up here." Girak had picked up a few rock shards. He lobbed one behind the boulders below them.

The hunting stick went wild.

Girak was trying to confuse their hunter about which rocks they were

432

behind. If the hunter had to search as he climbed, he would be easier to surprise. She admired Girak's smarts, if not his willingness to club the ascending guy over the head.

Would she be able to do it to keep the others safe? Her throat tightened, and she swallowed hard. Maybe Girak would take care of him. *But I'm in front of him. It'll have to be me...*

Rocks rattled and tumbled down the hill as their hunter approached. He was not coming straight up as they had, but at an angle directly toward them.

Her heart raced. *At this angle, he'll see us before we can reach him.*

"I know." Girak's whisper held the desperation of defeat.

# Chapter 60

*eleguin Rookery: Rana*

P Rana and Girak huddled behind the boulder as the hunter's footsteps drew closer, but as the rocks he displaced rattled downhill, she couldn't calculate his position.

*Where is he?*

A rock to their left exploded. "Gotch ya."

She spun. From a position parallel to theirs on the slope, the hunter pointed his weapon directly at her. Shoving Girak sideways, she dove around the boulder as the rock near her head disintegrated.

He had them trapped. If they ran to another boulder, he'd have a clear shot. His heavy breathing drew closer. Shuffling footsteps from farther up the mountainside raised her hopes that Atsushi and Ayanna were still scrambling up the mountain face. Maybe they would live...

The hunter rounded their boulder.

As they circled it to avoid him, he caught up. Girak raised his hands, pleading with him. "Zach, don't do this...please."

Zach maintained his mask of hatred. "You've betrayed all of us."

He shifted his aim from Girak to her. So, she was to be first.

She tried again to shield but failed. "I'm sorry," she murmured to Girak, to her family, to her friends. This was it. Her life was over.

Except she would not die in fear. She'd never Crown, but her last act would still be one of love. She met her hunter's gaze, her compassion for whatever had messed him up this much facing off against his raw hatred.

A shimmering light appeared around the human. Zach fired, and the explosion was contained in the shimmering air in front of her.

"You saved us." Girak grinned and pointed at the shield surrounding the hunter.

*Not me.* She glanced around them, then looked higher up the rocky slope until her heart leapt like a salt deer.

Eka waved to her from his high perch. Then Balavati and Tejas peered out from behind another boulder. Rana's grin grew.

"Is he the only dangerous one?" Balavati pointed at the shield-encased Zach.

"Yes," Rana yelled back.

Reassured, her friends clambered down. Eka focused on the shield, Tejas held a hand protectively on his cloak where he probably still housed birds, and Balavati scrambled to reach Rana.

As Balavati slipped down the last few lengths to Rana, she pulled up short at Girak's nearness. Girak smiled in welcome, and Balavati gave her such an enthusiastic hug that she nearly fell over.

Balavati steadied her. "Are you okay? You have blood on your face."

"It's from a peleguin attack, and the other humans hit me with a bunch of strange little weapons. I'm a bit off balance, but I'll be okay."

Balavati looked her up and down and then carefully hugged her again. "I'm sorry. I thought you were right behind me. I had no idea he stole you."

"It's okay. I didn't know, either, until I woke up there." Rana half-laughed, half-cried into Balavati's curls as Eka and Tejas climbed down to join them.

Far below, the peleguins restarted their normal cacophony as if welcoming her home.

Eka, still shielding Zach, shot her a tentative smile. *Sorry about being a saphead before. Balavati set me straight. Talk later?*

Rana nodded, distracted by the white streak in his hair. Was he Crowning right now? "Your hair...?"

"Yeah, that." He chuckled as he continued to make the shield smaller and smaller, forcing Zach to point his hunting stick toward the sky. "That would be a sign of my desperation to reach you."

"What?" Rana looked from Eka to Tejas to Balavati. Was he joking?

"I'll explain that later, too." Eka nodded toward Zach. "When we're safe."

Tejas snickered. "That'll be an interesting conversation, considering the Crowned Ones couldn't fully explain it." Then, looking grim, he thrust his hand through the shield and yanked the hunting stick out of Zach's trembling hands.

"Stop!" Girak lunged toward Tejas, but Balavati encased him in a shield.

Girak froze, wide-eyed. "The rifle," he said, pointing. "Don't hold it like that."

Tejas extended his arm as if the hunting stick might bite. "Rana? What's he saying?"

*Careful. He's saying you're going to hurt yourself,* she said in mind speak for everyone's sake. Then she explained the human frequency, so her friends could understand each other. *Try asking Girak how to hold it safely,* she said to Tejas.

*What should I do to be safe?* Tejas attempted, slightly off vibration until the last word.

Girak's brow furrowed, not understanding him. "If you must hold it, let me unload it first, okay?" He extended his hand, offering to fix the weapon.

"That one's safe?" Tejas nodded toward Girak.

*Yes. Balavati, you can let him out.* Rana flashed Girak an apologetic smile. *This is Girak. He saved my life. He won't hurt us, but he also won't understand you unless you use mind talk.*

Balavati dropped the shield, and Girak nodded in gratitude.

*You sure, Rana?* Tejas' fingers tightened on the weapon as he eyed Girak suspiciously.

*You can trust him.*

With a frown, Tejas handed him the hunting stick.

Girak removed several small things from it and pocketed them. "Now, you won't accidentally shoot anyone. But it's always good to keep this end pointed down, okay?" He handed the hunting stick back to Tejas.

*No. It's death. Rana says you're trustworthy, so you hold it.* Tejas turned his broad shoulders and glared down at the hunter, daring him to try something.

Zach, eyes wide, didn't move a muscle. "Girak?" he begged.

Girak scoffed. "Oh, now you acknowledge me? You nearly blew my head off five minutes ago."

*Don't try anything,* Tejas mind spoke to Zach, *or I'll be forced to restrain you.* He then nodded to Eka, who dropped the shield.

The terrified human attempted to dart downhill, but Tejas grabbed his arm and yanked him back to his side. *Do you not understand, or do you want me to hold you close?*

"I wouldn't hold him that close until you pat him down," Girak warned. "He might have a smaller gun or a knife on him."

"Traitor," Zach muttered under his breath.

Tejas' lip curled in disgust, but he patted him down and removed a dagger.

Pebbles scuttled down the hillside, and they all jumped. Eka and Balavati spun to deal with the approaching threat—Ayanna and Atsushi.

*Wait. Those two are also friends.*

The two younger humans slid down the rocky, frozen slope. Ayanna's huge boots made her as clumsy as a newborn salt deer. Laughing and clutching each other for balance, the two finally reached them.

Rana had totally forgotten about them. So much was happening that her brain was mush. She couldn't Call. She couldn't shield. *Shield?* "Sukti!"

"What?" Balavati turned about, confused. "Where?"

The earlier horrors descended upon Rana like a wave. *Can you check on...?* Her gaze travelled down the mountain to the first copse of trees.

Eka's face darkened. *What? Who got hurt?*

Rana closed her stinging eyes. She took a deep shuddering breath, trying to find her voice. *Sukti...*

"He shot her." Ayanna glared daggers at Zach.

"Falling stars!" Balavati raced down the hill.

Rana wished she had the strength to run beside her. Sukti had always been the strongest cub in her litter. A cruel hope tugged at her heart.

Rana glowered at the horrid Zach, still trapped under Tejas' arm to

437

prevent escape. Now, she understood how Kahali had been filled with rage.

The peleguins' sonorous voices filled the valley, but their calls were drowned by the pounding of her heart as Balavati hare-footed it down the rocky slope. She slipped to the bottom and ran toward the copse of trees. She bent to examine Sukti.

Rana inhaled sharply, her breath rattling its way in as she awaited Balavati's verdict.

*She's still breathing. I'll heal. Someone Call the Crowned Ones and Master Sandor.*

*Alive.* Rana's knees wobbled under her. Eka caught her arm.

She turned to him and buried her head in his shoulder. "I...I thought she was..."

"I know...let me Call for help." With his arms around her, he Called.

A moment later, Lion Master Sandor star beamed in with Luminary Samasti, immediately forming shields around themselves. As Sandor's tail twitched in agitation, his sharp blue gaze scanned the rocky slope for Sukti.

"Down there." Eka pointed, and Sandor raced down the hill. Luminary Samasti remained on the hillside, assessing Tejas' grip on Zach and the hunting stick held by Girak.

"*Another* white lion?" Girak asked, watching Sandor. "Do you breed them?"

Luminary Samasti frowned. *They are our teachers, not livestock. They came to us eons ago and taught us our role in balancing the remaining life on this planet. It had been left in a state of chaos by...others.* She gave him a slightly accusatory look.

"Oh," Girak said, grimacing. "Yeah, we did kind of mess things up before the Great Change."

*Indeed.* Luminary Samasti turned to Rana and smiled warmly. *I'm relieved to see you well. This*—she raised an eyebrow at her star being and human friends—*will need to be explained later.*

Rana nodded, appreciative that the Crowned One was continuing to use mind talk to include the humans. Oneness knew what their fearful minds might concoct as dangerous if the star beings all began speaking normally.

"Rana, there were two snowmobiles." Girak was ashen. "We need to move. I'm sorry, but if Commander Savas finds us—"

*We've caught him.* Luminary Samasti grimaced. *He attacked our village. You must all come back immediately.* She eyed Girak, Ayanna, and Atsushi. *You will vouch for these, Rana?*

*Yes, except him.* Rana pointed at Zach, who wilted under her decree. *He's the one who shot Sukti.*

*You removed his weapons?* Samasti queried.

Tejas nodded. *I have his knife, and Girak took his hunting stick.*

She nodded at the knife, but then frowned at Girak. *That hunting stick is not allowed in our village. Leave it here.*

"Like on the ground?" Girak looked horrified. "What if one of your children find it?"

*None of our children would go near a weapon of death. We'll return and deal with it later.* She waited while Girak placed it on the ground. *We believe another attack may be coming, and we need to get out of the open. I will beam us all back.*

Atsushi straightened, his eyes wide in a not-so-silent question to Rana. Rana chuckled. *Yes, all of us. You'll get to beam, too.*

Below them, more Crowned Ones and Lion Masters had appeared and surrounded Sukti in a healing circle. Rana glanced down there.

*Don't worry, she'll make it,* Luminary Samasti said. *Her energy is still strong.*

Rana nodded and sagged in relief. Sukti would live.

Luminary Samasti extended her arms and addressed the humans. *Simply grasp my arms with one of your hands and hold on.*

As Rana did so, Eka stepped up beside her. He put one hand on Samasti's shoulder and his other hand brushed hers in question.

*I thought I'd lost you. Can we maybe start over?*

Oneness, his grin got her every time. *I'll consider it,* she sent and folded her hand around his as they disappeared in a flash of light.

# Chapter 61

Northern Haven: Bleu Reinier

Extreme light blasted through Bleu's clenched eyelids as the earth disappeared below them. He was weightless, bodiless, and free. Then he lurched forward as his legs reappeared beneath him, collapsing on the stone floor. Heavy. Woozy. Disoriented.

*Bleu, get up. Where are we?* Kalakanya yanked him upward.

Blood rushed through his ears. He blinked, trying to focus. "What? I mean, where?"

*We're in your den. How do we get to the weapons area? Bleu, focus... What?*

Bleu pointed over her shoulder at a man standing in the hallway immediately behind her, but raising his arm caused him to stumble backward. He hadn't yet gotten used to being materialized. His body felt foreign, almost alien. Kalakanya spun, throwing up a shield in the same instant. The man fell backward.

Judging by the garbled sounds, it wasn't a man at all, but a star being. How had another one gotten in?

Bleu panicked. Had he been falsely tricked into trusting her? Was this an invasion putting Ayanna in even more danger?

He strained to see the face beyond the shadows. *Shast.* The angry star being he had just met, the one that he didn't trust, glared back at him.

The star beings quietly argued, and then Kalakanya turned back to Bleu, her shield gone.

*Kahali brought himself along by holding my arm. He will have to stay with us, as we don't have time to take him back. How do we get to the weapons room?*

Before Bleu could figure out their location, running footsteps and shouts of "The energy surge came from this way" echoed along the corridor toward them. He glanced around wildly, looking for the symbol to denote which particular hallway and floor they were occupying. His eye fell on the small orange sign: Floor 1, Corridor East 17A. His mind raced through the limited options.

He wasn't exactly sure where the weapons room was located, but the upper floors housed the important stuff. They may be on the right floor, but he had no idea other than that. And they needed to hide.

Quickly.

He pulled Kalakanya and Kahali into an empty room and quietly shut it as angry voices flooded the hallway. He wasn't sure whether he was more threatened by the humans or the look in Kahali's eyes. At every mechanical hum or click, Kahali tensed like a cornered animal ready to attack. The guy was terrified, and given his missing arm, he had good reason to be.

"It'll be okay," Bleu whispered.

Kahali raised an eyebrow. The corner of his mouth curled up slightly. *For you, sure.*

That stung. He'd tried to help.

Kalakanya grabbed Bleu's hand and squeezed it. *Focus. Which way?* she asked.

"I think we're on the right floor, but I don't know which direction." he said, trying to get his bearings.

She squinted at him in the darkness as if trying to read him. *Floors? Like levels? Like a repeating pattern of these tunnels on top of each other?*

"Yes." He imagined how bizarre that must seem to them.

*Let me scan for different energies. Kahali? You stay put, okay?*

Kahali met her commanding look, nodded reluctantly, and stood in place, continuing to twitch at every unexpected sound. He resembled Ayanna when she was about to have an episode.

Bleu took a step closer to say something but was met with a nasty glare.

"Fine, be miserable," he murmured.

Kalakanya, intent on her task, had closed her eyes. Waves of heat throbbed off her body, causing Bleu's body to gently rock as the shimmery waves passed through him.

Kahali, watching him intently, smirked. *Never felt peace before?*

The guy was making fun of him, but all Bleu could do was roll his eyes and smile.

Kahali continued to glare. It kind of killed the peace feeling.

She opened her eyes. *I know where we need to go.*

Was there anything she couldn't do? He grinned. "Well, then this should be easy. We simply need to get past the screaming crowds ready to shoot us. Can we use one of your glowing bubbles?" With his index fingers, he drew a dome over his head and around him.

Both star beings' eyebrows reacted equally but oppositely. Kahali's sank into a sneer while Kalakanya's rose in shock.

Okay, obviously he had said the wrong thing.

*You brought him why, exactly?* Kahali grimaced at him like he was a fool.

*Bleu, I can probably get us to the room with the shield, but I cannot both focus it and do what needs to be done. When we get to the room, you and Kahali will need to cooperate. I assume it will be guarded by hunters?*

Bleu nodded. "Definitely. And if they expect us, there may be traps, not just, uh…hunters."

For the briefest of moments, her gaze darkened, then cleared. *Kahali? Have you recovered enough to hold a strong shield? Perhaps it's good you came. We have no room for failure.*

Light immediately burst from Kahali. Bleu lurched backward as it passed through his body and enclosed the three of them.

*I see.* Kalakanya looked thoughtful. *Bleu, you will need to trust us and not jump every time the energy moves. It will not affect you, because you wish us no harm. It will pass through you, and you may pass through it. We will not hurt you. Okay?* She looked at Kahali, not him, as she said the last sentence.

Bleu nodded.

Kahali met Kalakanya's gaze with a ferocity of a lion. *I will not allow us to be harmed, Kalakanya.*

Bleu wondered whether he was included in the "us." The door blasted open from the hallway.

Kahali's shield flickered. Kalakanya turned, yelled something to Kahali, grabbed both of them and surrounded them all in her own shield. It happened so fluidly that Bleu was again awed by the energy dancing off her.

Her shield pushed the crowd back into the corridor. Bleu cringed as familiar faces screamed in terror. Then their fear morphed to horror as they recognized him as one of the intruders.

"It's okay," he yelled, wincing at his pathetic reassurance.

Kalakanya used her shield to force their way into the hallway, and then he led them at a run through the maze of corridors. Each time Kalakanya's shield bounced the armed citizens aside, she'd mentally apologize, but the Northern Haveners became even more panicked at her mind talk.

Nothing looked familiar. Even during his expedition training, he had never been allowed on the first floor. Strange labs and medical equipment could be seen through the door windows, and there were no murals. Just gray walls.

They approached a hallway with warning signs. Kalakanya paused. *Bleu, any traps?* She nodded toward the brightly lit hall.

Trying to focus, he ignored his friends' shouts that he was being brainwashed and going to get them all killed. *What if I'm wrong?*

Kahali shook him. *Look at me. You know we have to stop this!*

Bleu met his gaze. With all his shields and powers, the star being was terrified of humans. Star beings weren't the threat—the humans were.

Snapping into focus, Bleu scanned the walls for hidden weapons but found none. At the end of the hall stood a large door with a reinforced window. Through it, several armed men observed them. Their shield continued to be blasted from the other direction by the crowd.

*Hurry. We're almost out of time. The safe time threads are disappearing,* Kalakanya warned.

"I don't see anything." He spun in circles while Kahali cringed at each impact on their shield.

"Bleu, watch out!" his mother screamed.

He turned toward her as two men lunged out of the crowd and threw metal canisters toward their feet. Green, toxic fumes erupted, and the crowd ran. His mother reached for him but was also forced to retreat, coughing. Every fiber of his being yearned to assist his mother, but he had to stop the missile. He had to save them all.

"It's poison." He spun toward Kalakanya, hoping the shield would keep it at bay.

For the moment, it seemed to be working. He pulled back on his expedition headpiece which had been flopped back like a hood, hoping the air warmer might provide some protection.

Kalakanya's nostrils flared, her face a mask of disgust. She motioned for them to continue, and they ran down the hall, away from the billowing green cloud and stray bullets.

It was a hopeless act. The door would be locked, and he doubted any of the star beings' tricks would help with that. He pressed the button to open it, but the door remained closed. He attempted to pry it open with his fingers to no avail.

Kalakanya seemed at a loss.

"It's a door. It slides open, but it's locked." His heart beat out the seconds until the missile was fired and any chance of safely traveling the other Havens evaporated. "There's no way in."

*Let me try.* Her hands glowed as she touched them to the security device, which began to sizzle and smoke.

Bleu turned to check Angry Alien Guy, but he was gone. "Kahali?"

The young star being hadn't run with them down the hall.

"Kahali," Bleu shouted.

Kahali had fallen to his knees beyond Kalakanya's shield, coughing uncontrollably from the green gas.

# Chapter 62

*orthern Haven: Bleu Reinier*

Holding his breath, Bleu dashed out from the safety of the shield toward the fallen star being. Eyes burning from the green gas, he fumbled to pull Kahali into a standing position, but Kahali in his panic thrashed about as if Bleu were one of the attacking humans.

"Kahali, it's me," he shouted. Bleu ended up grabbing his torso and half carrying him back toward Kalakanya's shield.

Gunfire ricocheted around them, and Kahali coughed uncontrollably, making progress slow. But now the shooters fired from the other side of the green cloud and couldn't see them.

Burning pain ripped across Bleu's leg as he stumbled back within her shield. He dropped Kahali to the floor and yanked off his now gas-filled headpiece. Coughing, he threw his headpiece beyond the shield as he sucked in clean air.

His left thigh dripped blood. He was lucky—the bullet had only grazed him. He pulled Kahali closer to Kalakanya, who was still examining the locked door.

"What happened?" Bleu coughed.

*I got*—Kahali sputtered and coughed—*dizzy.* He gazed at Bleu in exhausted wonder. *You came back.*

Bleu nodded, his gaze darting to the edge of the shield. A small amount of the gas seeped through. Despite his weakened state, Kahali attempted to throw up his shield as well, but all he managed was a spark. That couldn't be a good sign.

Beside him, Kalakanya's hands glowed as she fiddled with the door. Kahali began coughing again.

"Should I do something? Are you going to be all right?" Could his new friends be killed by gas that was poisonous to humans?

Kahali gave a weak grin. *With this sort of welcome, I bet you don't get many visitors.*

The blunt truth of it made him smile grimly. "No, we don't. You're our first and probably our last."

Kalakanya groaned in frustration. *This isn't working. Bleu, can you open this, or should I star beam us through?*

He backed up and ran, throwing his weight against the door. He fell to the ground, groaning.

*Brilliant.* Kahali shook his head and coughed again. *A simple no-can-do would have sufficed.*

Truth be told, it hadn't been his brightest move.

*I can beam us through, but we will be unshielded for a brief moment as we rematerialize.* She frowned. *They might kill us before we have a chance to stop them.*

If they didn't stop the missile, he'd never find the cure, Ayanna and the others would die, and the star beings would be wiped off the Surface.

He stood and positioned himself between her and the door. "You have the best chance of stopping them, so beam us through with me between you and them. I'll buy you a moment to shield. I'm more disposable." He gave his best smile. "Just…if I die, find a way to help my sister, Ayanna, okay?"

Her troubled gaze met his, and then it fell to his chest, where the pendant lay under his clothing. *You're not disposable, Bleu, but we're out of good options. If the worst happens, I'll certainly help Ayanna, but try not dying. Okay?*

She pointed toward the window. *Notice their placement in the room. Our only advantage is that we may surprise them. Kahali, shield if you can, otherwise incapacitate them. Bleu, help me stop the machine.* She touched them both. *Now.*

They dissolved into blackness, and a moment later, they appeared on the other side, knocking over the one unfortunate man who had approached the door. The starlight must have zapped him or something, because he lay unconscious. The others had fallen back, probably believing her star beaming was a weapon.

Her shield burst forth, and she addressed them all, a force of reckoning. *How dare you threaten all life?*

The men rocked back at her accusation but kept their weapons trained on her. Apparently, he wasn't a threat.

He pulled the coughing Kahali closer while Kalakanya examined the room's chaotic activity. Her eyes narrowed at two men typing furiously on a keyboard.

"Stop them. They're firing it," Bleu shouted.

Kalakanya glanced at Kahali as he coughed. She had said earlier that she needed his help, but he had his hands full with breathing. Bleu and Kalakanya stared at each other a moment.

*I can't make a shield,* Bleu attempted to telepathically send, not wanting his fellow humans to hear their weakness.

Kalakanya's eyes glistened with tears. Bleu sensed her fear; he wanted to fix this. The pain of powerlessness echoed deep in his soul. Her entire village and Neviah were about to be destroyed. No. The whole Surface for kilometers around was about to be devastated.

Kalakanya huffed and brusquely stepped to her left, grabbing the gun right out of the man's hands. He stood still, shocked that she could pass through her own shield. A bullet hit her shoulder, making her rock back into her shield. She grimaced, turned, and handed Bleu the gun.

*They do not understand that they will die also. Stop them at any cost, but only do what is necessary. Do you understand me?*

"I don't want to kill anyone else," he whispered. He had injured and killed all those star beings, and he ached to toss the gun away. These were his fellow endangered humans.

Deep sadness filled her face. *I can't do this without you, and if we don't stop it, more will die.*

He nodded and swallowed down the bile rising in his throat. He had one gun, three men outside the shield aiming at them, another two men at the control panel, and the three of them to protect. He wished he had star being powers, just for five minutes. It could save everyone he cared about.

Behind him, Kahali, still coughing, struggled to his feet. He teetered into a stand, holding onto the wall for balance.

*Get ready*, she sent.

*Now!* Kalakanya lunged toward the computers, hands outstretched. Her shield traveled with her.

Bleu shot the armed man closest to Kalakanya in the shoulder and then smashed his gun into the face of the man next to him. The guy fired his gun at the wall as he fell over.

Kahali had sparked a shield, blocking some bullets, but it immediately fizzled out. Kahali muttered something, and Bleu wondered if star beings cursed.

Bleu turned, ignoring the burning pain in his thigh, as a bullet ripped the sleeve of his parka but missed his side. He shot that guy in the arm and then rushed him, knocking him to the ground. He'd disarmed them all. As he kicked the guy's dropped gun away, an explosive gunshot sounded behind him.

Another gun?

Heart racing, he spun, expecting to see Kalakanya dead. Instead, Kahali roared, blood gushing from his leg as he charged the guy who had been unconscious.

The star being bowled the guard over, and they wrestled for the gun. Kahali had no idea how to handle the weapon.

As Bleu dodged them to reach the control panel, he shouted, "Avoid the end with the hole."

Kahali grunted in acknowledgement as he attempted to wrench the gun from the guy's hands.

As Bleu turned, a bullet whizzed past his head. "Keep it pointed at the ground!" he yelled back to Kahali.

He raced toward the control panel, expecting Kalakanya to be as clueless about the missile as Kahali had been about the gun.

Kalakanya admonished Prime Minister Pridbor and the tech man. *You know nothing. The only danger on the Surface is your own fear.*

They stood in front of the panel, unarmed.

"Why are you talking? Make them stop it," Bleu shouted.

Prime Minister Pridbor's thin lips curled into a sneer. "Today, you all die."

*Today, you realize your ignorance. Bleu... Kahali... It has been fired.*

"What?" Bleu fell to his knees, overwhelmed with horror.

A strange, distant expression covered Kalakanya's face. *It's all up to you now.*

For a terrible second, Bleu thought she was speaking to him, but her eyes were seeing something unseen. Despite the chaos and danger around her, she had connected to the other Crowned Ones. Somehow, he just knew.

How long until the Surface was irretrievably destroyed? Minutes? Seconds? Bleu couldn't breathe. He looked about for something, *anything* that he could do.

When Pridbor slyly shifted toward a dropped gun, Bleu smacked him away and gathered the scattered guns. He emptied their bullets into his pockets.

All he could fathom was that he needed to ensure Kalakanya's and Kahali's safety as they'd be the last living star beings.

Kahali rushed to him, falling next to him on the floor, tears falling shamelessly down his face. *Join us!*

"What?" Bleu held up his palms in confusion.

Kahali grasped both of Bleu's hands in his one, with that same faraway look in his eyes that Kalakanya had.

*He's mad with grief.* Bleu watched him with growing alarm until a jolt of electricity shot through his and Kahali's linked hands. Suddenly, he was both back on the Surface at that terrible Lion Circle and at the same time also in the missile room. No, his body was in the missile room, yet somehow, he floated hand in-hand with Kalakanya and Kahali over the Lion Circle.

*Soul traveling,* Kalakanya informed.

Awestruck, he didn't question it. They drifted higher, revealing star being colonies all over the icy continent. Energy surged through his body with such an intensity that it threatened to explode his being. The overwhelming sensation mimicked last time he and Neviah had entered the Lion Circle, only this time, he didn't black out.

Village upon village upon village dotted the Surface. He hadn't imagined that. Each one had its own Lion Circle, where huge lightning bolts of energy were being created by the Crowned Ones and were sent streaming upward. The giant arcs of light coalesced to form huge, luminous streams of pastel-colored light surging through the sky. The rivers of light met with explosive force and spread out in the shape of a giant, pulsating shield. The targeted village and surrounding icy fields were domed by the massive radiant barrier. The resplendent vault pulsed gently up and down, a heart refusing to yield.

It overwhelmed his senses. He both observed the surging light and also was the surging light. It was no longer possible to tell where his body was, where his body began and ended. His very atoms were about to dissipate to nothingness. Then, his mind snapped back.

*It will still explode and poison the air above. It will still be fatal.* Bleu feared they didn't understand the devastating power that had been unleashed on them. *This is not a bullet.*

A streaming metallic object arced over the sky and plummet toward the oscillating shield.

*No,* he mentally screamed in warning.

Suddenly, a sonic growl sprang from the Surface, primal and terrifying.

Bleu strained to see. He seemed to float lower. A spiral of white lions had gathered at the intended impact site. Their fierce sonic roar intersected the shield just as it pulsed upward. The combined thrust met the incoming missile. The missile slowed, shifted, and was turned by the onslaught of roaring waves. It soared up into the atmosphere.

*They're sending it to space.* It was that knowing again. The missile was swallowed by the high clouds. All was still.

Then, oddly, the clear voice of a girl star being far below teased his fellow human.

*And that, Atsushi, is why they are Lion Masters, not pets.*

# Chapter 63

**N**orthern Haven: Bleu Reinier
Bleu crashed into his body like a helicopter plunging into a jagged ravine, jolted and constricted by his own skin. Had his body always been this small? He blinked up at the two wondrous star beings. Both had tear-streaked faces: fierce, radiant eyes, and triumphant smiles.

Forgetting they were aliens, he grabbed them in a fierce bear hug. "You saved everyone."

Kahali jerked away and studied him with narrow eyes, rubbing his arm stump. Kalakanya, laughing, pulled Angry Alien Guy back into their triangle. *Come on. We did just prevent a catastrophe.*

*Ughh.* Kahali pulled away and shook his shoulders as if shaking off Bleu's human germs.

Bleu found that hysterically funny. He laughed until he couldn't remember what had amused him. Then he giggled at his inability to remember the joke.

*Kahali, help Bleu energetically ground. I'll take care of these others.* She gave her fellow star being a stern "be nice" look and paced over to the injured humans.

As she began healing, Bleu's stomach began to hurt. He couldn't stop laughing. "Wh—...what's wrong...with me?" His guffawing continued. Then he noticed how itchy he was and started scratching himself every-where.

Kahali watched, an amused smirk on his face. *You absorbed too much energy. You're intoxicated. It happens to some very young children when they first attend ceremonies. You're the equivalent of...maybe a baby.*

"No, I'm fine." Bleu used all his willpower to resist scratching. He stood up, willing his hands to stay at his sides as he walked toward Kalakanya. "Can I hel—"

He tripped over a chair and collapsed. This set off his laughter again even though his cheek muscles were sore.

*Bleu, listen to him. I need to concentrate.* She hadn't even glanced up from the wound she was healing.

As the defeated and scared Northern Haveners allowed her to work, bruises faded and cuts disappeared. Beyond the locked door came shouts of those that had been chasing them through the halls, trying to get through the gas. *Too late, buddies,* Bleu thought, chuckling to himself.

Sitting, legs splayed out, Bleu gave in to scratching his hair with both hands. It was so satisfying that a grunt of pleasure escaped his throat. He glanced up at Kahali, who limped toward him as his pants reddened from his thigh wound.

"I can just scratch while you heal that," Bleu offered.

*Not yet. You need grounding before you hurt yourself or someone else. Hold still.*

Unable to stop himself, Bleu sprang up, itching as he stared at Kalakanya. She was lovely: her radiant face, glowing hands, sparkling green eyes...

*Bleu, give it up. It's awkward enough to witness this in a young kid, but in a full-grown adult...ughh.* Kahali threw his hand upward in exasperation. *It's painful. Sit down before I make you.*

"Fine." He was sick of this pompous star being. He plopped down and scratched both ears.

Kahali winced as he knelt next to him and placed his palm on Bleu's legs and feet, then his spine. The itching lessened and then faded completely. He became heavy-limbed as if a hole had opened in him and every bit of strength had seeped out. His eyelids were hard to hold up.

"Ka...hol...lee...Wha...?"

He fell over, awake but too tired to move. His eyelids drifted down, leaving him alert but unable to see and paralyzed with exhaustion. In rebellion, his heart fluttered against the stillness. He tried to force his eyes open, but all he could see was a thin line of light barred by his lashes. Too much work. He settled for remaining conscious and in darkness.

Kahali said something in their native tongue.

*Speak with mind speak, or they'll think we're plotting against them,* Kalakanya sent.

Kahali gave an annoyed sigh, and then sent, *We shouldn't have included him in rerouting the weapon from our village. He's too weak for that.*

Kahali's mental tone evoked a flash of fury in Bleu, but he couldn't even move his fingers to make a fist.

Kalakanya chuckled. *Trust me, he's not weak. Remember Sohana's Prophecy of the Three Blues? It's him...*

*Three Bleus? Oneness! There are two more of him?*

Kalakanya laughed, and at the strange sound, Bleu managed to pry his eyes open.

*Bleu,* she held up one finger, *came up to the Surface and was under the blue sky,* she held up a second finger, *and made the decision to save Shams, when he was saved by a blue stone pendant.* She held up her third finger. *I can't give you the full significance yet, but the Prophecy is unfolding. I knew it as soon as I saw that ancient pendant.*

Bleu's heart beat faster. His pendant? A prophecy? He must be really drunk on whatever energy he'd experienced.

*But that was when I had my vision and knew to come here. We've solved the great danger. It's done.* Kahali stood and moved out of sight. *I'll heal this one. That okay with you, human?*

The man must have nodded, because Kahali didn't move on to another man.

*It may be over, but I got this message before Sohana. Remember me saying that at the Spiral Ceremony?* As she spoke, her glowing hands touched the guard's face. His massive bruise faded to nothing.

*Yes. The One In All sent it twice because of its great importance?*

*Sohana's message was for the community. I believe we've prevented that one.*

454

*But it was also sent to me, personally. It's never before happened that way...* She glanced in Bleu's direction, but when their gazes met, she looked away.

Bleu yearned to ask questions. This was, after all, about him. But he couldn't fight the exhaustion any longer. His mind crashed into the darkness of unconsciousness.

* * *

Bleu awoke to a yelling crowd. His blurry vision spun, but at least he sat comfortably propped up between two large, warm animals. No, that couldn't be right.

He blinked in confusion as the angry, human voices became clearer. The spinning stopped, and he realized Kalakanya and Kahali supported him between their fur-clad shoulders while a luminous globe of light encircled them.

They had never made it out of the weapons room. The crowd must have burst into the weapons room just as the star beings had finished healing the men and destroying the guns. Broken weapons lay in a pile, and the previously injured men, now sullen but restored to health, stood beside the yelling crowd.

His two new friends patiently listened to the furious onlookers.

"What the—" Bleu jerked upright.

"Bleu, are you okay?" his mother cried out.

Her dark face was tear-streaked and lined with worry. Tadwell stood next to her. They were the only ones not yelling at the star beings.

Bleu managed a dazed smile and slight nod, though that sent the room spinning again. Both parents sagged with relief. Then Tadwell whispered something to Cass and ducked out of the room.

His mom ran up to him and knelt beside him, putting her palm to his cheek as if making sure he was real. "You're okay? The gas didn't make you sick?"

"No, I only got a whiff, thanks to her shield." *Wait.* He raised an eyebrow at his mom's ability to enter their shield and approach the star beings.

"How did you—"

His mother said to the star beings, "Have you seen Ayanna? Atsushi and Girak? Your friend, Rana? Did they safely find you?" She pressed her hand to her mouth as if her entire existence hung on their answer.

Bleu grabbed his mother's arm. "Ayanna? What do you mean? She's not home?" His breathing sped up, and the dizziness started again. "Mom, where is she?"

"She left with the other three." A huge grin blossomed on her face. "Rana healed her."

"What? Healed? Rana?" His heart raced as if it would burst through his chest. His mother wasn't making any sense.

The crowd now pounded on the shield, trying to get through as Cassandra had, but to no avail.

Kalakanya leaned over and rested her hand on his forearm. *Bleu, you are still being affected by the energy. Breathe.* A beautiful peace flowed from her hands to his arm as she privately mind spoke to those in the shield. *Ayanna and the others are all safe at our village, waiting for you. She's well, though she wanted to tell you herself.*

Bleu had to open his mouth and try several times before any word came out. "Cured? Like, for good?"

He searched Kalakanya's face for confirmation that his wildest dream had come true. That Ayanna would live...

*Yes.* Her warm smile literally glowed with joy, and then she leaned over and gave him a quick hug. *Our healer believes it may be permanent, but it's too soon to tell for sure. The other Crowned Ones have been updating me while the crowd yells.* She narrowed her gaze at the gathered mob. *How much longer do you think they'll keep this up?*

He shrugged. "Healed..." He pulled his mom in for a triumphant hug. "Ayanna's healed of the Sickness!"

The crowd went silent, all eyes riveted on him.

"What is this lie they've told you?" Prime Minister Pridbor limped forward and pointed his claw-like hands at Kalakanya. "They tricked Ayanna into leaving with one of them. She could be dead by now."

*Really?* Kalakanya smiled as she addressed them all. *Kahali, would you be comfortable holding this shield for a moment?*

Kahali narrowed his gaze at the crowd but nodded. The crowd had moved back at Kalakanya's mind talk. They shook their heads and poked fingers in their ears.

In a flash, she was gone. People screamed and yelled. One woman fainted and had to be carried away. Another flash of starred light appeared and faded, revealing Kalakanya and Ayanna.

After a stunned moment, Bleu and his mother pounced on her, hugging, jumping, and laughing. The crowd stood transfixed. Prime Minister Pridbor sputtered.

Bleu tightly hugged his sister and pinched his own arm behind her back. *Not a dream.* His heart surged in delight.

"How did you end up on the Surface with Atsushi and Girak?" He couldn't believe it. It was almost as bizarre as knowing she was cured. He took a step back and studied her face with a hand on each of her shoulders. "Say it. Tell me."

Ayanna grinned. "I'm fine! No symptoms. Rana was amazing, and then when we got to the village, some other star beings did more treatments... they're all so nice." She couldn't stop grinning. "And I hear you"—she punched his upper arm—"saved us all here."

"Not me. These two saved us." He motioned toward Kalakanya and Kahali.

Kahali raised an eyebrow at the compliment and stiffened as Ayanna ran at him.

"Thank you for keeping him safe. Thank you both." She threw her arms around him.

*They all love you now, Kahali.* Kalakanya cracked up at Ayanna's repeat of Bleu's bear hug.

"Ayanna, he doesn't like hugs." Bleu pulled his sister away and whispered an apology to the star being as his shoulders shook in revulsion.

Kalakanya turned to Bleu. *Girak and Atsushi are also well. Atsushi asked me to pass you a message. He said he kept his side of the bargain, and he expects you to keep yours.*

Bleu chuckled. "He and I will need to discuss that. A Surface trip isn't exactly my definition of keeping Ayanna safe." He pulled his little sister into another hug.

"What...bargain?" Ayanna's voice was muffled in Bleu's shoulder.

"Ah, nothing. Ask him." Bleu chuckled. Atsushi would never have the guts to ask her on a date.

Over his sister's shoulder, the crowd was silent as if they were acting out a play.

He released Ayanna and faced them. "It's all been a misunderstanding. They're not the enemy."

Prime Minister Pridbor glared at him. "You know *nothing* of governing. We can't have killer aliens barging in here whenever they like. We have borders. They are invaders, not diplomats."

"And you were diplomatic when you tried to nuke them? Come on, get real. What we need is a meeting and communication." He shifted his gaze to include the crowd. "We need their help."

"Do we?" Prime Minister Pridbor sniffed haughtily. "Why?"

"They can heal the Sickness, for starters." Bleu gave him a smug grin.

The crowd murmured.

*Bleu. Give them time to take it all in. We are a lot to handle in one day.* He sensed this was a private message to only him as no one else responded to Kalakanya's words.

His mother stood and faced the crowd. "You should all go home," she said in her official doctor voice. "The council will need to meet, right, Prime Minister? Then we could plan a meeting with the star beings in the near future."

She turned to Kalakanya. "If you would have me, I would love to witness more of your healing work. Would you be willing to heal more of our children?"

*Of course,* Kalakanya said. *However, it might be best if they came to us, since your leaders don't want us visiting.*

"Maybe you could beam one of my sickest patients there? I could report back to the council at the meeting."

Kalakanya nodded. *But first, before I leave, I'm checking for any remaining nuclear weapons. No species should ever possess such destructive power. I cannot allow your fears to put the whole planet in danger. I mean no disrespect, but your intelligence and technology have progressed faster than your wisdom.*

Prime Minister Pridbor began yelling again. Kalakanya nodded to Kahali, who nodded back. She beamed out.

The crowd went wild—some horrified that such weapons had been deployed, while others arguing that it was a necessary evil. Bleu, his mother, and Ayanna simply smiled, still disbelieving they were all together and well.

Tadwell, who had left, re-entered the room and said, "I have brought all the families of those affected by Sickness."

A roar went up from the hallway. The council must have allowed everyone access to the restricted floors to defend them from the star beings.

Tadwell said, "We all demand the council establish diplomatic relations. We want our children healed."

Another roar occurred, louder than the first.

Prime Minister Pridbor smiled. "Of course, we will consider diplomatic relations, but they must first stop their invasion. They cannot burst in here whenever they feel like it."

Kalakanya beamed in at that exact moment. Bleu chuckled at her timing.

"See? This behavior is totally unacceptable." Prime Minister Pridbor had the crowd in the palm of his hands.

They roared in outrage at her. Had they forgotten about the people with the Sickness that easily?

Kalakanya's gaze grew stormy as she eyed her accuser, but her poise revealed no fear, only an iron will. Again, he was struck by how well she handled everything.

*We will not enter again unless you threaten us or the Surface. You will find your atomic weapons are now useless. I am sorry for any problems this may cause, but I assure you the problems inherent in deploying them would be much worse. Already, the one you released will take weeks of work to clear from the atmosphere.*

Then she turned to Bleu's mother, and her demeanor softened. *I'd be delighted to show you our village and healing techniques. You have my eternal gratitude for assisting in Rana's return home. It is a gift to finally see you in person.*

His mother's eyes widened in surprise, and she paled slightly, but the corners of her mouth tugged upward. "Ahh. I thought there was something familiar about you. You look different in physical form. I...I always believed you were an angel."

*Not yet,* Kalakanya replied, laughing.

She turned back to the Prime Minister. *Do we have a deal? We will show your doctor our medical treatments and won't return uninvited unless you attack. Also, you will not punish any of your humans who helped us.*

"You keep adding conditions." Prime Minister Pridbor jeered.

She nodded in agreement. *And I'll also add in the safe return of your Commander Savas and Zach once they have completed their rehabilitation.*

Prime Minister Pridbor's eyes narrowed. "Fine. But they better be in good shape—no messing with their minds."

*I assure you they'll be better than ever.* Kalakanya flashed a mischievous grin that startled Bleu. *Go get your patients ready, Cassandra. Since I can't come back, could you meet me at the Surface near the door?*

"Do we have any extra expedition clothing, Prime Minister?" Bleu asked. His mother and her patients couldn't go up unprepared.

Prime Minister Pridbor appeared mortified to be asked this in front of what he clearly considered the enemy.

*I have an idea, Bleu. You and I will come with extra furs that you can carry in and your mother and her patients can wear. That way, we will not further inconvenience your people.*

He nodded, though he was pretty sure she had said it for Prime Minister Pridbor, not him. She grasped his hands, and in a sickening flash, they exploded into nothingness.

# Chapter 64

On the Surface: Commander Kern Savas

Savas awoke on a dead animal skin with a throbbing headache. No, correction—his whole body ached, and he was freezing. He sprang up to find himself surrounded by white-haired freaks. His hand dropped to his thigh for his gun, finding only strange leather pants. His other hand flew to his chest to find his compass gone as well.

"What did you do to me?" he asked, fuming.

*We removed your weapons and machinery and gave you weather-suitable clothing that will not hide weaponry.* The speaker, a super-tall creep with huge dark eyes, freaky pupils, and medium-brown skin, wore similar clothing. *I am Luminary Vadin, and I speak on behalf of our village, which you dared enter with your hunting stick.* His face tightened. *You killed Ameya, who was only twelve springs. What do you say for yourself?*

"What is this? Some sort of trial?" he shot back. "You attacked first, killing one person on my first team, and then killing three on my second. And three others are missing." He really hoped Atsushi and Neviah were somehow alive.

*You are mistaken. We do not kill. Ever.*

"Right. Of course not. I can see the halos round your heads," he said.

Confused, they considered each other's heads. *You must sit with us in this circle for a full sun. Then, you will live with Ameya's family until you have learned from your error. It is never right to kill another.*

*What the shast?* Savas' jaw dropped open. "Northern Haven will never accept this. They'll come for me."

Vadin seemed unmoved. *We have informed them that you will be staying with us for a while. They did not disagree.*

Savas snorted. Like Northern Haven had the manpower to disagree. But they did have nuclear weaponry that should be active now. He'd sent the coordinates as soon as he'd found the village. He should have turned around then, but he'd seen the two orange parkas surrounded by reapers. He'd hoped to save whoever it was—Atsushi and Ayanna, or Bleu and Neviah—before the nuke hit.

Why hadn't they already bombed the hell out of this place? By any rights, he should be dead, but if he was about to be atomized, he could at least be wearing his compass. It was only fitting.

"I need my compass back."

Vadin furrowed his brow in confusion.

Savas added, "The metallic object that was around my neck? It's not a weapon. I need it back now." He really did need it. Its absence left him naked and lost much more than the circle of reapers surrounding him.

*That is a directional device, correct?*

"Yes."

*You may need it underground in your tunnels, but we will make sure you do not get lost up here. You will always be accompanied by several Crowned Ones to assure everyone's safety, including your own.*

"I want it back." He considered his next words carefully. It gave them information about him that they could use against him, but he *needed* it. "It has sentimental value."

*You value an object, but carelessly take the life of a child you've never met?* Vadin's whole face tightened in disgust. Now, their cracks were beginning to show.

"Like that bitch of yours who took my son's life? Yes, I do," he said. "If you want my cooperation, give it back to me. Now." He thrust out his hand, palm up.

They were hard to read, sitting there placidly, but his response had stirred something in them. Surprise, perhaps? Did they not know the woman reaper had killed Stamf?

*I see in your mind that you are confused. The one in the cave-in, Abdul, died from the cave-in itself. Stamf fell after being attacked by cave-diggers—*

"I was there." His outstretched hand curled into a fist. "That bitch trapped him in a bubble of light and dropped him. She killed him."

Vadin's face went blank, as if he were somewhere else, and he blinked several times. *She reports trying to save him from falling when a human shot at her with a hunting stick. She could only shield one being at a time. She shielded herself, because if she died, Stamf would as well. She had hoped to still have time to then stop his fall, but she was unable.*

Savas stared. That couldn't be. Right? They were messing with his mind. That couldn't be the truth. He had played no role in Stamf's death. He had to resist their mind control.

Trembling, he swallowed and forced his voice to utter the truth. "You killed him."

Vadin shook his head. The jerk actually appeared upset. *No. I'm sorry for your loss, but she tried to save Stamf. Bleu said you thought the cave-diggers were under our control, but they were not. I know nothing of the other two human deaths.*

"Bleu? How did you talk to him?" Were Bleu and Neviah the two parka-wearers he'd tried to rescue? He'd only believed real humans wore those parkas because one had waved at him.

*Bleu and Neviah are alive and well. We brought them here after you left them unconscious on the ice.*

That changed things. He straightened his posture. "I want to see them. Now."

*No. You are in a healing ceremony.*

"I don't want your damn ceremony. I want to talk to my people and confirm they are okay." He hadn't lost them. Two more humans lived, and Neviah could still help him pilot the team to the other havens. *The other havens.* He attempted to snap his mind shut. He couldn't risk the other havens' safety.

*You will see them in a few days. Now, you need to focus on yourself and your decisions.*

Vadin appeared to be waiting for something. Did the fool actually expect an apology for his defense of Northern Haven?

"I'm not going to let you mind control me, you damn reaper. It won't work." He eyed the door; he'd never make it before they stopped him. Maybe he could escape when they transported him to the family's hut.

Vadin smiled, but there was concern in his eyes. Hell, he'd probably heard his thoughts of escape. *We have no interest in controlling you, only in preventing you from hurting yourself or others.*

"Sounds the same to me." That decided it. He could play this game. He'd done it before. Not with aliens, but they didn't know who they were dealing with. He'd bide his time and figure *them* out. Gather intel. He'd do whatever it took to protect humanity.

*...and we will save humanity by any means.* His mother's pledge echoed in his head. He had to find his clothes. His compass.

Because the animals at the top of the cliff hadn't killed Stamf. That bitch of a reaper had when she purposely dropped him.

*We are not your enemy, Savas. If you can't take in our thoughts, let me show you...* Vadin approached.

Vadin attempted to touch his forehead, but he slapped the reaper's long hand away.

Vadin frowned. *I do not need to actually touch you. Pay attention.* He touched his own forehead with his long index finger and then pointed it at Savas' forehead.

As that finger aimed at his forehead, his mind exploded with images. The deluge of information made him fall to his knees.

"Nooo." He moaned. "It can't be..." But the images of the reapers' past seemed so real. *It's mind control*, he mentally screamed as the terrible images deluged his consciousness.

Yet if it was, why would they share this damning information?

He had to warn the others, but he couldn't stand, and he was surrounded.

# Chapter 65

Peleguin-Rookery-By-The-Lake: *Kahali*

As Kahali inhaled his first breath of blessedly cold air, he swore never to enter the human den again. Due to the injuries they'd received in the horrible, dank lair, Kalakanya had star beamed them all—Ayanna, Bleu, himself—directly to Bahujnana's ice hut.

"Sorry to barge in, Bahujnana," Kalakanya apologized, "but these two"—she motioned to Bleu and Kahali—"need some checking. Me, too, but first, I'll take Ayanna back to the guest hut, where she can rest."

*No problem.* Bahujnana grinned at Kahali and Bleu. *Boys, you do know you can visit me without collecting injuries, right?*

Kahali grunted. *The humans are determined to kill me.*

"That's because they don't know you," Bleu said. "You terrify them with your power."

Kahali rolled his eyes. *Flattery will get you nowhere with me. Besides, you're human, and humans don't do it for me.* He grinned as Bleu processed his words.

Bleu blushed and then chuckled. "I meant it. You can do stuff we wouldn't dream of."

*Your dreams must be squalid. I can barely stand.* He limped toward Bahujnana and plopped down on a fur. *Where's Rana? Is she okay? I thought she'd be here.*

*She'll be fine, and she asked about you as well.* Bahujnana gave him a knowing smile then turned and nodded farewell as Kalakanya and Ayanna left.

465

Turning back to Kahali, he added, *Rana's maha helped her to the bath house, but she'll be back soon.*

"Don't let me pass out and miss her, okay?" he said, because Bleu didn't need to know how weak he really was.

"You have my word." As the healer examined him, he muttered about humans and their penchant for violence in their native tongue, and then handed Kahali a cup of tea. *This will clear those toxins you inhaled. I'm sorry, I have nothing pleasant to wash it down with. All these injuries have depleted my stores.* Tsking, he turned to Bleu and began checking his gunshot wounds from two days ago and today.

Kahali, awash in the safe familiarity of Peleguin Rookery, sipped the acidic brew. The wood smoke and herbal tinctures combined with distant peleguin squawks, laughter of children, and someone's joyful song lulled him. Feminine voices drifted in from the pathways.

"Rana!" He bolted upright, sloshing his tea. Her voice was headed this way. Gulping down the remainder of his brew, he half-ran, half-stumbled across the hut as she entered.

"Kahali!" She grabbed his cloak and pulled him into a tight embrace.

Oneness, it was good to feel her warmth against his chest, to feel her breath on his neck, to truly know she lived. "Balavati and Eka found you? You're okay? What happened?"

Clinging to him, she laughed. "Are you going to let me answer or keep tossing me questions?"

Everything disappeared except her laughter against his cheek and their bodies pressed together, until she tensed in alarm. "Who's this?" she asked, pointing over his shoulder.

He turned. Bleu, being examined by Bahujnana, smiled like a fool at them. "Oh, that's Bleu. He helped Kalakanya and me when we tried to stop the sky poison weapon."

Rana gave the human their traditional bow. *I'm Rana. Thanks for taking care of my best friend here.* She patted Kahali on the chest. Her natural switch to mind talk for Bleu's sake made Kahali uneasy. She'd just been stolen by these humans.

Bleu's grin widened. "We took care of each other." He cocked his head. "Are you the one who helped Ayanna?"

Rana nodded. *We helped each other.*

"Then I owe you everything. You saved her life." He motioned toward his face. "We don't look that much alike, but she's my little sister."

*You smile alike,* Rana noted and then gave Kahali a smile that made him want Bleu and Bahujnana to get lost. *We're so connected, that even when we're apart we end up with siblings, eh?*

Kahali nodded. *Intertwined. Seems like you're stuck with me.*

Bahujnana cleared his throat a bit more loudly than necessary. *Bleu, I think your leg is fine. Maybe I could point out some features of our village and we could give these two a moment of privacy?* And with a parting nod, he led Bleu out.

"Ooh, we get privacy." Rana laughed. She stood so close he could have just tipped forward and lowered his lips to hers.

"Rana," he began.

"You're not going to apologize for me being stolen instead of you, like Balavati did, are you?" Her playful grin melted him.

He shook his head slowly. "I wanted to apologize, but not for that."

"Huh?" Her eyebrow arched, accentuating those deep-blue eyes he'd feared he'd never see again.

Falling stars, he wanted to kiss her. "I'm sorry, I've been misleading. I joke and flirt with everyone else, because I'm awful at being serious. A bad joke can be waved off, but if someone says something serious, and it's not accepted..."

"Kahali," she whispered, "have I ever rejected you?"

He bit his inner cheek to avoid cracking a joke. "No..." When had it become so hard to talk to her? "What I'm trying to say is that I love you."

Her eyes widened, and her gaze drifted to his mouth. She smiled, her face mirroring back his own feelings. "I don't know what to say."

"Hmm. Personally, I recommend telling me how you feel about me. Or"—his grin widened—"maybe showing me?"

"You know how I feel, Kahali. I've always loved you. First as a friend,

467

and now as…" She bit her lip. "This isn't good."

His heart lurched. "No, it's better if you bite *my* lip." He laughed, but she didn't. "Sorry, no more jokes. What's not good?"

She frowned. "We need to go get Eka."

"I'm pretty sure we don't. This is between you and me." He grasped her hand, his breath caught in his chest.

"But it's not."

He sighed. "You just met him. Did he even tell you it was my idea that they go find you?" He was being a jerk.

Tears welled in her eyes, and he swallowed the lump in his throat as he struggled to gain control over himself. But he had loved her forever. Eka was a shooting star; his interest in her would burn out in a flash.

"He did." She glared at him and dropped his hand. "So, either you come with me and we all talk, or you and I drop this conversation like it never happened."

"But why? I can tell you feel the same way." A horrible thought gripped him. "Is this because of my arm?"

"What?" She grimaced. "Of course not. How could you even think that?" She sighed. "Look, I've had a bad few suns, and I'm only going to have the energy to do this once. I want all three of us to understand each other. Please?"

This was not the way he'd imagined this playing out. Maybe he should have stuck to jokes. "Okay, if it's what you want."

"Thank you. It's not what I want, but it's the best I can do."

With no idea what that meant, he followed her out into the bright pathways between huts. To his disgust, he realized she knew exactly where they had to go to find Eka.

# Chapter 66

Peleguin-Rookery-By-The-Lake: Rana

Rana's heart thudded against her chest as she and Kahali strode to get Eka. She was about to make either the best or the worst decision of her life.

"Eka," she called across the field to where he and Tejas were searching out food for the baby birds.

At the sound of her voice, Eka spun, his long mane of hair flowing around him, his face lighting at her call. However, when he noticed Kahali beside her, his smile faltered. Oneness, this was going to be horrid.

"Can you join us for a moment?" she asked.

"Just me?" Eka looked from her to Tejas.

"Go ahead, lover boy. I can feed the children myself." Tejas fake-pouted.

Eka snorted, shook his head at Tejas, and jogged over to Rana and Kahali, his face growing more concerned the closer he got. "Everything okay?"

"Yes." She attempted a smile. "No. Maybe?"

"That's the way to clarify things," Kahali murmured beside her.

She shot him a dark look, but he was grinning. So, he was back to joking? Maybe that would make this easier.

"Any sign of Digga?" Eka asked as they walked. She loved how he always thought of her fur baby.

"No." She stroked the empty carrier still strapped to her chest. "It was early last night that she helped distract the humans. She should have been back by now."

"Well, you know how she is," Eka reassured her. "She's probably

469

distracted with digging tunnels somewhere and won't remember to return until she's good and hungry."

Sighing, she said, "I hope that's it."

She led them to the Nest on the outskirts of the village, the closest relatively private place that Kahali could reach in his current state.

Kahali tapped her arm. "We're doing this on *our* rock?"

Her heart jumped. "Is that okay? Since we're all exhausted, I thought the closest private spot would be best?"

He rubbed his arm stub and sighed. "I guess."

Approaching the boulder, her determination faltered, and she slowed her pace. Balavati had suggested romantic love might help her Crown, but if she kept this up, one of them would get hurt. As much as she feared losing them, she dreaded hurting them more.

Each step brought her closer to stating her choice. Being true to herself was necessary for Crowning, but Oneness, she didn't want to do this.

A moment later, they reached the boulder, which in her current exhaustion seemed to loom above her like a mountain. Too sleep-deprived to climb, she plopped down on the ground, her legs tucked under her. Of course, they chose to sit on opposite sides of her.

"So?" Eka looked from Kahali to her.

She took a deep breath. "I want to clarify things so that if you want to run, you can."

Kahali sagged back against the rock. "I'm pretty sure I can't move again, so I'm not running. What about you, Eka?"

Eka stared at him a moment, and then said to her, "When I suggested earlier that we should talk, I kind of assumed it would be only you and I."

She laughed nervously. "Right. Sorry. Look, I know you both like me, and I feel the same way."

Kahali leaned forward and snickered. "You're in love with yourself?"

She turned on him. "Kahali, I swear, if you don't cut the jokes, I'll—"

"Fiiiiiine." He thumped back against the rock and gave her a pained look.

"Look, I love you both. But my first priority is to Crown, and this"—she waved her hands in front of both of them—"is too distracting and isn't good for any of us." She took a deep breath. "I think..." The expectation on both their faces nearly killed her. "I think we should all just be friends."

For some reason, Kahali grinned like a fool, while Eka turned to look straight ahead at the horizon as if peacefully contemplating the shapes of clouds. Whatever she had expected, this was not it. She waited. Perhaps she had just lost them both.

Finally, Eka said, "You know you can't avoid this forever."

Kahali chuckled. "Oh, you're quite attractive, Eka, but I think she could."

Eka rolled his eyes.

"I know, Eka," she replied. "And Kahali, your only response is to flirt with him?"

Kahali leaned forward and turned to face them both. "Would that work?" He lowered his face and looked up at Eka through his long lashes. "Maybe I can scare him off?" He began batting his eyes in a ridiculous manner.

She ignored him. "So Eka, in case you're wondering, this"—she waved toward Kahali's absurd facial expressions—"means you're now officially his friend."

Kahali stopped batting his eyelashes. "How can I scare him off if you tell him my secrets?"

"Ugh. I'm done here. I promised the humans I'd get them real food. Join me or not." She stood to leave, and both of them jumped up as well. She had expected this to go worse. Far, far worse. Relief washed over her that they understood and weren't mad. But turning down their love broke her heart. If only she could be like her peers and trust that she would Crown without going to such extremes.

She sucked in a shaky breath. "So, we're good? All friends?"

Eka nodded. "I can be your friend, but you know how I really feel."

Kahali frowned. "Same for me."

She nodded. "Thanks, but the idea is that you can both move on, not wait. My parents never Crowned."

"You'll Crown," Eka stated.

"I'm fine with your current state," Kahali said, grinning.

She snorted. "I meant what I said. I'm not doing this to both of you, because it can't end well. I can't stand the idea of hurting any of us. I'm focusing on Crowning." She gave them her sternest look.

Eka looked unimpressed, and Kahali only smirked.

She groaned in frustration. "Fine. I have to go get them food."

Eka's gaze narrowed. "You just got back. Don't you need to rest?"

"After they're fed. They risked everything for me, and besides, those three have kind of grown on me."

"Feeding them will only make them stay longer," Kahali complained. "I've had enough humans for the day." He gave her a long look and then turned to leave. "Catch you both later."

"Okay." Rana gave him a quick hug goodbye and headed toward the guest hut with Eka, relieved that their friendships seemed to have survived her talk. She suspected she'd have to say it again—both for them and herself—but for now she could focus on Crowning.

# Chapter 67

*eleguin-Rookery-By-The-Lake: Atsushi Collins*

P    Despite the frigid cold, Atsushi had never been happier. He sat in the ice hut with the other humans, waiting for dinner. He counted them all as his friends—Ayanna, Neviah, and Girak. Even better, they seemed to think the same of him. He hoped that would continue now that they were no longer in life-threatening situations.

Beside him, Girak had removed his glove and stared at his wedding-inked palm. Ayanna dug through her pack, pulling random things out and asking Neviah to explain them. And near the exit sat the super-kind Daman, one of Rana's peers, who kept answering their endless questions.

"Girak?" Atsushi tapped his elbow to draw his attention from his tattoo.

"Hmm?" Girak blinked as if exiting a dream and turned to him. "What?"

"Do you think you can go back to Northern Haven?" This had been bothering him ever since Girak had led them out to the Surface. Already being a Deplorable, it seemed like a one-way trip for him.

"I think I might be stuck out here." Girak glanced over to Daman. "Not that here is bad, of course. I simply don't belong here."

A half-smile crept onto Daman's round face. Atsushi wasn't sure if he meant to reassure Girak, or if he was agreeing that he truly didn't belong here.

"Right." Atsushi turned to Ayanna, her cheeks aglow from the cold. "What about you? Are you going back?" He held his breath, waiting.

She grinned. "Never go backward, my friend."

*Friend.* He blushed. "I'm serious."

"I'm doing whatever Bleu does. I can't imagine they'll let him back after helping destroy the nuclear weapons." She glanced over at Daman. "Do you allow immigrants?"

Daman gave her a baffled look. After an awkward moment, he stood and left the hut.

Atsushi laughed. "I think you scared him off."

"Let's hope not." Girak shifted as if considering going after him. "We need some allies."

"I want to be wherever you guys are, including you, Neviah." Atsushi picked at his coat. "But what if they force me to go back? You know, genes and all?"

"Then we hide you," Ayanna said, grinning.

"It might not be that simple, Ayanna." Girak sighed. "First, we have no way to live up here. Second, I'm sure the star beings don't want the council any more annoyed than they already are. Usually, in diplomatic relations, both sides give in or relinquish something. We might become pawns caught in the middle. If it comes down to it and one of us has to go back, I'll go. I've lived my life."

Atsushi snorted. "Yeah, right. You're what? Thirty-five years old? I say we stick together."

Girak's face hardened. "I'm your educator, Atsushi. I'm responsible for your safety."

"Actually, you're not. You're no longer an official educator. Besides, we volunteered to join you. Right, Ayanna?" He playfully poked her side with his elbow.

"Exactly." She nodded, folding her arms across her chest as if challenging Girak to argue with her. Or she was cold.

Girak gave then a sad nod, looking defeated.

"I'm going back." Neviah gave them a questioning side glance. "My father would be lost without me, and I want my technology. Also, they need me as a pilot now that Stamf is…dead." She bit her lip and glanced at Atsushi apologetically. "You understand, right?"

"I get it," he said, making her smile with relief. "You have stuff to go back for."

Neviah frowned. "I didn't mean it that way. But I feel like who I am is back there. None of you feel that way?"

"I want adventure," Ayanna said, eyes full of passion, "and this place is awesomely dangerous. Plus, as much as I love my parents, I'd rather hang with Bleu."

"Bleu might go back," Neviah persisted.

"Are you kidding?" Ayanna grinned. "This is his dream."

"Oh." Her face fell, and she turned aside, repacking Ayanna's backpack.

Ayanna turned to Girak. "What about you? You could do all kinds of experiments up here."

He traced his palm spiral again. "That was Josefina's dream." At her name, his voice caught, and his eyes misted.

Atsushi and the others exchanged concerned glances.

Girak sighed. "I'll figure it out. I'm sure I'll be needed for something." He gave a mirthless laugh. "I can cook. Maybe I can help the star beings in the gathering hall."

Atsushi brightened. "Maybe you could teach their kids science? They don't seem to have any tech. How did aliens get here without tech?"

Girak shrugged. Lately, he was all sighs and shrugs. "Maybe that's why it's called star beaming? In any case, I suspect I'd learn from their kids," he said, grinning, "not the other way around."

"Maybe." Atsushi turned to Neviah. "If you go back to Northern Haven, could you build something so we can all stay in touch? You know, like the special comm you made me?"

She nodded. "Probably. But it will be hard to get the materials. If the Surface exploration opens up, they'll be scrounging for materials to outfit the expedition." She tucked back a strand of her black hair and regarded him with concern. "If you stay up here, you'll lose access to all the records on Japan."

"Oh." His heart fell. How could he choose between the last remaining links to his identity and his friends? "Right," he mumbled.

Girak stirred from his grief. "Atsushi, you don't have to choose, because they'll want you back. They *need* you back. You have something to negotiate with."

"Hmm." To negotiate for the records on Japan, *his* people, felt odd.

"Speaking of negotiating," Neviah added to Girak, "*you* can probably negotiate as well."

"No..." Girak sighed in resignation. "If I go back, one way or another, Savas will have me killed."

He was right, of course. Commander Savas had said as much to them the night they escaped. Could Atsushi negotiate with someone like that?

"Maybe it's time..." Atsushi sucked in a shaky breath. "Maybe it's time I decide for myself who I am. I mean, I've only been away from those records less than two days, and in that time, I've found all of you." He looked away. "I mean, I knew you all before, but now..." He gave them mischievous grin. "Now we've committed a jailbreak and fought off peleguins together. We've really bonded."

"Don't forget discovering aliens," Neviah added.

"I used to be a responsible educator to you three," Girak mumbled, but then shook his head, chuckling.

"Exactly, we're a team now." Ayanna said, putting an arm around Atsushi. "It seems you're stuck with me." She flashed him a consider-yourself-forewarned smirk.

Stuck with her? That was his dream.

"I can deal with that," he retorted, and his bring-it-on grin met hers.

# Chapter 68

Peleguin-Rookery-By-The-Lake: Bleu Reinier

Bleu trailed Bahujnana through the village along icy, sinuous paths to where he would meet up with his friends. The star beings they passed seemed to accept his presence, yet each time they acknowledged Bleu with their traditional bow, he flushed more deeply with guilt. How could they bear his presence when he had murdered some of them?

Despite his goggles, the glaring sunlight reflected off the ice huts and stung his eyes. The sheer size of the village reminded him of the number of bodies he'd created—star beings who'd never return to these homes, never hug their families again. What had he been thinking? He yearned for the safety of four enclosed walls, to be hidden below ground and not spotlighted by the high sun for all to see.

The healer asked, *What are you afraid of?*

"You must all hate me..." His voice broke. "Northern Haven hates me for bringing in Kalakanya and letting her destroy their weapons, and here..." A mother and young boy passed them, the child staring at Bleu. "Here, I've directly hurt or killed many. I don't even know how many." How? What had happened to him? "Why do you allow me to walk around like this?"

Bahujnana stopped walking and stared deeply into Bleu's eyes. *Are you still a danger?*

"No, of course not. I can't believe I did that." He grasped his forehead as if he could somehow expunge the deaths that ran through his mind.

*You were told we were the enemy, and believed your life was in danger if you did not kill us first. Correct?*

He looked down. "Yes."

"Mmmhmm." Bahujnana stoked his chin, deep in thought. *What would you propose we do with you?*

Bleu swallowed the lump in his throat. Did he really want to give them ideas? *Could* he give ideas to mind readers, or had they already read his thoughts? "Kill me? Lock me up? Punish me somehow?"

The healer grimaced. *That is not our way. It would neither bring back the dead nor heal the injured. I'm including you among the injured as it's not normal to kill for no reason.*

"I believed I had reasons," he stated in a monotone.

*You humans specialize in conjuring reasons for maiming and death. We must do something about that, or I shall be kept very busy.* He laughed. *I like things slow, Bleu.*

Bleu covered his face with his palm. "I'm sorry."

*You've been forgiven.* Bahujnana rested a hand on his back. *The affected families may wish to speak to you at some point, but your efforts to save Shams and then stop the missile have demonstrated your change of heart.*

"I don't understand that. If someone had killed Ayanna..." His hands fisted at his side.

*Ayanna is right in that hut.* Bahujnana pointed toward a larger hut with a woven door of striped orange, green, and blue. *Perhaps, if you'd like, we can teach you our ways?* His hand clasped Bleu's shoulder tighter. *If I may be so bold as to give you an assignment, you must start with forgiving yourself. When you're ready for some specific techniques, like tomorrow* –he grinned—*someone will direct you to my hut.*

With a warm nod, Bahujnana turned and headed off.

The healer's forgiveness blew his mind. How was it possible that he was angrier at himself than the star beings were at him? Maybe he *should* go learn from him, if only to never be mindlessly violent again. He paused before the striped door, then lifted the mat.

"Bleu!" Ayanna, Neviah, Atsushi, and Girak rushed him en masse and group-hugged him. Their crushing bodies created the enclosing safety he

478

so needed.

When they released him, Ayanna and Atsushi spoke over each other in their excitement to share their adventures. As they gabbed and laughed, he blinked at his new reality. He'd made it to an ice hut on the Surface, his sister had been healed, and things were as he had once dreamt. But an uneasy surreal feeling enveloped him.

He belonged nowhere. He feared never being good enough for the lofty star beings and felt out of place now amongst his fellow humans. And what had Kalakanya and Kahali meant by that prophecy?

The others chitchatted around him as he slouched back against a wall. Girak leaned over. "It's a lot, right?" He gave Bleu a sad smile. "We've changed everything without any time to process the repercussions, and now, we have to deal with those changes."

He nodded, glad Girak seemed to feel the same way. The other three thought the whole thing a grand adventure and themselves heroes. Oddly, he only wanted to talk with Kalakanya. She'd become his compass in this unknown land.

A lilting voice sang from outside, and they all exchanged confused glances.

*That translates as The One In All brings Love.* The mat swung up, and Rana grinned at them. *Who's hungry for some real food?*

She held the mat up for them to exit, and Bleu frowned at the tall, loose-haired star being behind her. He was dressed in the same leather tunics, pants, and furred coat that they all seemed to wear, but his were simple and form-fitting compared to Kahali's beaded ones. Was Kahali rich, or special?

Bleu glanced around for his angry friend. "Where's Kahali?"

*He needed to rest.* Rana gestured to the star being next to her. *This is my friend, Eka.*

The guy stood super close to her, and even Bleu could tell he was more than a friend. A moment ago, he and Bahujnana had given her privacy with Kahali. Perhaps *friend* meant something different to star beings?

"Hi," Bleu said noncommittally to him as they walked up the hill to the dining hall.

This Eka seemed friendly enough, though if he also liked Rana, then his friend, Kahali, had tough competition. Bleu knew nothing of star being beauty standards, but this guy seemed the type the girls at home would go gaga over.

As they entered the gathering hall, the sizzling of exotic meats and spices made his stomach growl. He'd expected tables and chairs, but trees were limited in this tundra. Instead, woven mats served as tables, and leather pillows lay about in ample supply.

Two teen star beings jumped up and waved them over to a corner mat.

"Daman." Ayanna grinned at the guy. "We thought we scared you off."

As usual, Ayanna knew everyone.

*No, I thought some food might make you feel more at home. This is Balavati.* Daman motioned to the girl with dark hair even curlier than Ayanna's. *At Rana's request, we cooked this for you.*

"Wow, it smells great." Bleu smiled, hoping they'd accept him as they had Ayanna. *First lesson: forgive yourself.* "Thank you for going to all this trouble."

*No problem,* Daman sent. *I like to cook.*

*Come on.* Rana motioned to them. *Grab a space on the mat. As I promised, here's some real food. Here.* Smiling, she grabbed clay bowls and passed them around. *First, smoked salmon and salted deer cheese.* She doled out portions, watching them for reactions.

It took a moment for Bleu find a comfortable sitting position, given his bullet-grazed thigh and gunshot wound to his chest. The star beings were great healers, but they weren't magicians.

As soon as he settled, Neviah sat beside him. "So, you want to live up here and eat this way forever?"

It seemed an odd question, like a trick. "Maybe?" he said, accepting a bowl from Rana.

Neviah's lip trembled. "You haven't even tried it yet," she retorted, turning to face Girak.

Bleu scowled, unsure what was up with her, but now that Ayanna was healed and he was on the Surface, nothing was going to ruin his day.

He laughed as, on his other side, Atsushi grabbed the fish and smelled it, his eyes lighting up. "Mmm." He nibbled. "Whoa. This is unbelievable." He handed his half-bitten fish chunk to Ayanna. "Try it."

She wrinkled her nose. "I've got some, thanks." She reached in and grabbed a piece from her bowl. She bit it and chewed luxuriously. "Well, if the offer still stands…" She playfully grabbed the half-eaten piece Atsushi still held and shoved it into her own mouth. "Ve-harry hood Ra-ha."

Bleu rolled his eyes. "Not making us look very good, sis. The star beings will think we're animals."

Ayanna swallowed. "We are animals," she retorted. "Did Mr. Fancy Pants Graduate forget all his schooling?"

"Be civilized," he admonished. Then, leaning toward Atsushi, he whispered, "You sure you want to date her?"

Atsushi grabbed a bite of fish from Bleu's bowl and grinned. "Absolutely."

Suddenly, yelps came from outside the hall, followed by a screech. "Rana!"

Rana sprang to her feet and flew out the door. Bleu rose to follow her and the others outside, his leg pulsing with pain from the bullet graze. He hobbled after them and then halted at the impossible sight. A section of the ground appeared to be churning, and star beings stood wide-eyed as a hole appeared in the path. A snout popped out.

"Digga!" Rana raced toward the animal head while he and the others stepped back, gasping.

A short squat animal with thick brown-and-white fur and black stripes crawled from the hole.

"Oh, Digga." Rana knelt and held her hand out to the creature.

"See, she waited until she was hungry and popped out right by the dining hall," Eka said.

"Awww, it's her baby cave digger," Ayanna explained. "She's been missing since Commander Savas took off after her."

The cave digger peered at Rana with her beady brown eyes and yawned, making a squeaky noise at her jaws' widest point before snapping them shut. She padded over to Rana and inserted her muzzle in her cupped palm and vibrated with soft, grumbling noises.

*Hungry, aren't you?* Rana turned around and beamed at them.

*What fun am I missing?*

Bleu would know that mind talk anywhere. He spun, grinning as Kalakanya hurried up the path with such grace that he had to momentarily look away to catch his breath.

*Rana, it's such a relief to have you back.* Kalakanya's gaze fell to the animal being plopped into a leather satchel on Rana's chest. *You found her?*

*She just popped out of that hole.* Rana laughed. *Guess I have some work to do, filling it in.*

*She came back? That's impressive.* Kalakanya turned the full brightness of her cheer on him. *Bleu, we need to get your mother in a few minutes. Did you get to eat anything?*

"A few bites. We were eating when Digga showed up."

He laughed as the pup's hiccup made Ayanna jump back. It was such a relief to see his sister well. But how long would it take for the star being healers to know if she was cured or required ongoing treatment from them?

Burdened by the weight of her illness and the sheer number of his mother's patients, he turned to Kalakanya. "May I ask you a question?"

*Of course.* She flashed him a warm grin.

"I know I already asked, but..." Flustered by her intense jade eyes, he had to clear his throat before continuing. "Are you sure you haven't seen any signs of other humans living around here?"

Kalakanya paused. *No. We or the other villages would have spotted them.* Her eyes twinkled with humor. *You're not exactly a subtle crowd.*

"Right." He nodded in agreement, unsure how to appropriately ask the rest. "I overheard some star beings speaking. They said there was a prophecy?"

His face reddened at the memory of her and Kahali speaking of him when they thought he was unconscious. "And that you star beings were supposed to help us? Is that true?"

Kalakanya glanced from Bleu to Rana and back to Bleu.

At her intense gaze, his neck tickled, and he rubbed it with his gloved hand. Despite his scratching, it continued to tingle.

*Yes, there was a prophecy that when the three blues met, both our civilizations would face extinction unless we helped you.*

"Three blues?" He frowned. "Am…" He looked about and tensed. "Am I one of them?"

She nodded. *You, your pendant, and the sky. Remember right after I found the pendant on you under the open sky that your people sent the poison sky weapon?*

"So." He grinned broadly. "I was destined to help you stop it?"

She shook her head and laughed. *Sorry, but no. The prophecy was a warning that you signified trouble, that your appearance meant things were about to get dangerous. However, I believe we've saved both communities from that threat.*

"Oh." *I'm the problem?* His heart sank and he looked away from her.

If he was the harbinger of doom, and Ayanna possibly needed ongoing treatment, would his doom-making mess things up so much that the star being healers wouldn't help her? He opened his mouth to ask Kalakanya, but she had switched her intense gaze from him to Rana.

Rana gasped and touched her own neck. *Why are you scanning me? I already helped find them. I'm done.*

"Scanning you?" Bleu asked.

Kalakanya explained how her transtemporal scan allowed her to see the past and future time threads of specific people around specific issues.

When she was done, his jaw dropped open. "You just saw my future?"

*Potential threads for you and Rana. Yes.*

He bit his lip at her power, considering how much she and the other star beings could help Ayanna and Northern Haven. He had to risk facing his shame about his role in the prophecy.

He could do this. For Ayanna, he'd do anything. He took a deep, steadying breath.

"Any chance my future involves you helping us with the Sickness and with finding the other humans?" He gave her a grin. With a start, he realized it was Stamf's winning grin, as if his friend were here, helping him. His smile grew even wider. "We originally ventured out here to find the other Havens of humanity."

*Ah, finding humanity. It seems you have found humanity in a different way. You're now a different, more humane being. As is Zach. And time will tell with Commander Savas. There are many ways of finding humanity.* Her eyes filled with mirth.

He scowled. She could be so cryptic. "Yes, but I mean *literally* finding other humans. We still need other humans to prevent genetic problems. I was hoping, if it's not too much to ask, that maybe you could help us search? Three other Havens were created underground centuries ago. They may have survived, but if they're still underground, like we were until recently, maybe you wouldn't have noticed?"

She frowned. *From what I've seen, your people need both—literally finding other humans, and remembering your humanity.*

He shook his head and sighed. "I'm afraid what you've seen is who we are. Our history is filled with war and violence."

Her hand clasped his arm with gentleness, but her steely expression teemed with a challenge. *Perhaps its time you left your past behind. There's more to being human than war and violence.*

Beside him, Rana grimaced as if she, too, doubted humanity's potential. *So, we're not done? Bleu and I...there's more?*

*My friends, we have just begun.*

Bleu snorted. Crowned Ones had amazing power, but Kalakanya was hopelessly high-minded if she believed humanity would ever become nonviolent like them.

# Chapter 69

Peleguin-Rookery-By-the-Lake: Bleu Reinier

Bleu stood on the path with the others, studying Kalakanya's face for a clue about what she'd seen in his and Rana's future. A flurry of shouts carried down a path toward them. "Bleu, is that you? Bleuuuuu!"

He spun toward his name but then froze as he recognized the voice as Savas'.

"Bleu, Atsushi," Savas yelled, this time with more panic and frustration in his voice.

What would it take to panic Commander Savas? That guy didn't care about anything but himself and protecting Northern Haven, both of which should be fine.

Something wasn't right. Bleu sprinted toward the yelling as best as his injured leg would allow. Ayanna kept pace beside him, and the Crowned Ones abandoned huts and activities to also rush toward the cacophony.

"I thought he was safely restrained?" Bleu grumbled to Kalakanya, who hurried beside him. She sped up.

They rushed around huts and past other Crowned Ones until Bleu slid to a stop, hands out, barely stopping himself before he skittered into the bubble of light surrounding Savas. Inside paced the furious commander. He lit up with relief as he spotted him. "Bleu, don't trust them. They're not who they pretend to be."

*Sorry.* Samasti sent to them all. *We were taking him back to his hut when he heard you and tried to escape.* She reached into the shield and grasped

Savas' arm as another Crowned One grabbed his other arm.

"Bleu, don't trust them," Commander Savas shouted.

"Are you okay?" Bleu strode around the shield that enclosed the furious but restrained man.

"They told me who they are, Bleu. They lied," Savas said quickly as if expecting them to smite him at any moment.

"Lied?" His heart rate spiked as he spun from Savas to Kalakanya. "What is he talking about?"

Kalakanya's face had again transformed into an unreadable mask, but she met his gaze and held it.

"Bleu, they're not aliens. They're the Undescended!"

"What?" Bleu's hand dropped to his dagger as he backed away from her, his breath coming in gasps.

She began doing her pink, calming glow thing.

His eyes narrowed. "Don't."

*I was only going to send you calming energy, like before. Savas' fear is infecting you all.*

"I can think without any outside influences," he said.

*Okay, but Savas' fear is still influencing you. I was only trying to bring you all back to your natural state.*

"Don't let her trick you," Savas shouted. "Atsushi."

*Savas, you are in no danger,* Samasti interrupted.

"Then let me go." He twisted in the Crowned Ones' grip to again face Bleu. "Tell Zach. He needs to know. Promise me that you'll find him." His icy eyes searched Bleu's. "Please!"

Bleu stepped backward, dagger in hand, torn between his duty to Northern Haven and his desire to trust his new friends.

"Who are you, really?" Girak asked Kalakanya, shoving Atsushi and Ayanna behind him as if he could singe-handedly protect them from a whole village.

*I never said we were aliens.* Kalakanya smiled. *How is being related to you worse?*

"You swore to destroy us," Bleu said, tightening his grip on his dagger.

"We've done everything to protect ourselves from your attacks since Descension Day.

Kalakanya glanced at the other Crowned Ones, who all shrugged. *I have no idea what you're talking about. We are descendants of those left to die, yes. But we have no oath against you.*

"So you're..." Bleu gasped, and his thoughts nearly hit light speed as he considered the ramifications of Savas' accusation. "You're human?"

She grimaced, then smiled as if in apology. Humans were that low to her?

*Not low. There's no ranking in the Web of Life. You're humans, and we're star beings, your descendants. While you were underground, we evolved.* Her eyes sparked with mischief. *Technically, you're the non-descendants.*

She thought this was a joke? "Are you here to destroy Northern Haven?"

*Of course not. We didn't even know you existed until the prophecy. I told you, we're here to help.*

He glared, wanting to believe her. She and her people had prevented a nuclear war, and Rana had healed Ayanna. Yet he was still reeling from the revelation. Nearly every terrifying story he knew involved the Undescended breaking in and murdering every last one of them. Now, he was standing in their village and being asked to trust them Even worse, he *wanted* to trust her. Was he the fool in the beginning of horror tales, who got everyone murdered?

She met his gaze. *Bleu, you know me. You can trust us.*

"You destroyed Northern Haven's weapons," he accused.

*To save all of this.* She motioned to the entire Surface. *Besides, you don't need those weapons. You have no true enemies outside yourselves.*

None of the monstrous Undescended in their dark tales ever wanted to preserve life. The creators of the horror stories that haunted Northern Haveners knew nothing about those left on the Surface. All contact with SHAST had been cut the week after Descension Day.

He narrowed his gaze at Commander Savas, then Samasti, and finally back to Kalakanya. "Right."

He glanced at Girak, who gave him a nod of agreement.

Bleu relaxed and slid his dagger back into its sheath.

"Bleu, don't trust them," Savas ordered.

He turned his back on the shielded commander. "How could you evolve from the humans left on the Surface? It hasn't been millions of years."

"Some theories include rapid evolution in times of severe planetary changes," Girak interrupted from behind him. "The sudden switch from global warming to an ice age *might* qualify as severe." He gave a dry chuckle.

*Why is this bad?* She frowned.

Bleu growled in frustration. "We've been replaced by a better model of humanity. How am I supposed to feel?"

Kalakanya shook her head. *As I said before, all life is equal to us.*

"We've been warned since our founding that the Undescended had only one goal—to destroy us." Bleu couldn't quite let go of it.

Grimacing, she glanced about, taking in all the humans. *Does fear invade every aspect of your lives? If the humans left behind had spent all their resources on revenge, they never would have survived. They forgot about you and chose to survive.*

"Bleu, don't listen to her," Savas commanded as Samasti and the other Crowned Ones led him away. "She's controlling you," He yelled back to them.

"Hmm…" Bleu's gaze went from the esteemed commander to the Crowned One. Savas had never seemed trustworthy, while Kalakanya had saved Bleu's life after Savas shot him.

In the years of SHAST, the Undescended had been like terrorists, swearing revenge on the Havens for not saving them all. By all reports, they'd been terrifying, but being left above to starve and freeze to death must have been horrid.

Bleu's shoulders slumped. "I'm sorry my ancestors did that to yours"—he gave her an apologetic frown—"and left them up there to die while they went below to be safe and warm."

She laughed as if he'd made a joke.

"I'm serious," he insisted.

She covered her grin and nodded. *I know, and someday, maybe I'll explain the irony of your apology. Don't worry, we don't hold grudges.*

He studied her for a sign of what had caused her laughter. Nothing. She was completely unreadable when she wanted to be. "Why not explain the irony now?"

*All shall be revealed when the time is right,* she sent to all of them.

"You have more secrets?" He and the others exchanged concerned glances. Was Savas right?

*She always has secrets,* Rana reassured them. *Even from us.*

"I'm not okay with that," he countered.

Too much was at stake. Where had they taken Savas? The guy freaked him out, but he always seemed to know more and be one step ahead of everyone else. As strategist to the council, that was literally his job. "What are you hiding?" he demanded of her.

Kalakanya's gaze met his, but she remained silent. After a long pause, she sent, *We will help you cure the Sickness, and we'll meet with your leaders about helping you find humans. But we expect no more violence to us or the planet. Otherwise, we will take action to protect All.* She smiled placidly. *I'm sure you can all learn to get along with the rest of the planet.*

He gaped at her. Hadn't she learned anything about humans? The odds against Northern Haven overcoming patterns of violence that had trapped humanity for millennia were odds he'd never risk. "I'm...I'm not sure that's possible..."

Ayanna wrapped her fingers around his. "Not normally, but these aren't normal times."

"Right." He took a deep breath and returned his sister's hand squeeze.

He wasn't alone, and since he was the prophesized problem, he probably couldn't fix things no matter how hard he tried.

But he *could* help Ayanna, Girak, and Atsushi find the other Havens and arrange treatment for the Sickness patients.

And, maybe Kalakanya, Rana, and Kahali would help as well if he dared trust these star beings...Undescended...or whatever the *shast* they were.

"Okay," he said. "Count me in. If you help cure the Sickness and help us find the other Havens, I'll commit to learning how to survive without violence." He feared he'd made an impossible bargain to keep, but this involved his little sister's survival.

After exchanging nervous glances, his friends uttered their agreement. Perhaps their small little group *could* shift humanity's future. There were less than three hundred people remaining alive to convince.

Besides, with the superior star beings claiming the Earth's Surface, humans no longer had a choice.

# Continue the adventure...

Can't wait until January of 2022? Sign up today for Branwen OShea's newletter and receive an exclusive free short story featuring the star beings in your inbox Spring 2021.

Newsletter signup: www.branwenoshea.com

*CONTINUE THE ADVENTURE...*

# Also by Branwen OShea:

## Silence of the Song Trees, a short story

When everyone he loved died,
he became the Ghost to save his planet.

Available on Amazon Kindle

# Acknowledgments

While writing is often a solitary act, the creation of a book involves many. The Calling was written over a ten-year period, so the number of people who helped me on this particular book journey is quite extensive. I hope I didn't forget anyone.

First and foremost, I thank my children who grew up discussing these characters with me. When I shared the dream that inspired this book over breakfast, my then seven-year-old son told me, "That's not a dream, that's a book." Over the past ten years, he has read every version, offered support with every decision, and even written a symphony inspired by the story. My daughter has given priceless feedback on character development, cracked me up with her theoretical 'shippings' of various characters, and drawn all my characters for me. While I wrote the words, this book has both of you in it, and it would be very different without your support and assistance.

Another special shout out to my first critique partner, Dawn. It was scary meeting a stranger and agreeing to share our books, but I'm so glad we both took that risk. Your feedback has been priceless, especially with Kahali.

I also want to thank my amazing editors Stephen, Trish, and Ioanna. You all taught me so much.

For her amazing cover, a hearty thanks to Rai, cover artist extraordinaire, character artist, and designer of the compass series logo. You went above and beyond what I hoped for, and I can't wait to see your cover for book two, The Chasm.

This book needed a lot of sensitivity readers. Though I'm not supposed to mention you by name, you know who you are and I thank you from the bottom of my heart for your wonderful feedback. I also want to thank my rock-climbing advisor, and Mike, who spent hours explaining helicopters to me for this series.

Two writing friends went above and beyond the call of friendship with this story, and I give a special thank you to Jean and Lisa. Like Dawn and my kids, you two have also lived nearly a decade with these characters and been incredibly helpful and supportive. Thank you!

I'm in several writing groups, and you have all been guiding presences along this path. A big thank you to Trish, Dawn, Storm, Nur, Rai, Samina, Judy, Michelle, and June.

I could never have finished this without the support of my early readers, publishing advisors, friends, and teachers: Alyse, Amir, Angelita, Annie, Barb, Beth, Brenda, Cindy, Carol Beth, Ellie, Emily, France, Gary, Great Bear, Hari, Jamie, Jen, Joan, Justin, Karianna, Karla, Kendall, Lynne, Megan, Melissa, Michael, Molly, Nicole, Rodney, Sandy, Satya, Tasha, and Victoria.

Much of this book was written pre-Covid while waiting around during my kid's activities—in parent waiting areas, various libraries, and coffee shops near their classes. A big thank you to the librarians who allowed me to quietly eat lunch while I wrote, and to all the baristas who tolerated me camping out at my favorite table. You all provided me comfy writing places, great coffee, and tolerated my weird expressions while I wrote scenes that made me squirm or grimace. Thanks!

Much gratitude to all my #WritingCommunity friends on Twitter. Your daily support, humor and wisdom is priceless.

And finally, a huge thanks to all you readers who take the time to get to know Bleu, Rana, Atsushi, Kahali, and Savas. Without you, writing wouldn't be as nearly much fun. I truly appreciate you and your emails and reviews. Thank you.

# About the Author

As a young girl, Branwen wanted to become an ambassador for aliens. Since the aliens never hired her, she now writes about them.

Branwen OShea has a Bachelors in Biology from Colgate University, a Bachelors in Psychology, and a Masters in Social Work. She lives in Connecticut with her family and a menagerie of pets, and enjoys hiking, meditating, and star-gazing. Her previously published works include contributing to a nonfiction yoga book, wellness magazines, and her published science fiction novella, Silence of the Song Trees.

Sign up for Branwen OShea's email updates and receive an exclusive free short story featuring the star beings in your inbox Spring 2021: www.branwenoshea.com

**You can connect with me on:**
- https://www.branwenoshea.com
- https://twitter.com/branwenoshea
- https://www.facebook.com/BranwenOShea
- https://www.instagram.com/branwenoshea

CPSIA information can be obtained
at www.ICGtesting.com
Printed in the USA
LVHW031422231220
674968LV00005B/49